CU00481800

Camillus – Dictator of Rome.

The Fall of Veii (Part 2)

The amazing cover is designed by Ruth Musson and the remainder of the book is self-published. The artwork is the copyright of the author of this book.

This book is the third in the series Camillus - Dictator of Rome

Prequel – The Ancilia Shield

Book 1 – Dawn of the Eagle

Book 2 – The Fall of Veii (part 1)

Book 3 – The Fall of Veii (part 2)

Book 4 – Vae Victis (Woe to the vanquished)

Book 5 – King of Rome

First Published in e-book 2014 – Copyright F.M.Mulhern

Published in paperback 2018

"It is the privilege of antiquity to mingle divine things with human; it adds dignity to the past and if any nation deserves the right to a divine origin, it is our own" Livy

Chapter 1

The evening skyline blazed with a golden hue as the sun sank below a deep bank of startling white clouds topped with a ridge of brilliant gold. Each ray of light seemed to stream into the heavens proclaiming the glory of the Feriae Latinae, the festival of the Latin Alliance, led by Rome. As the fires burned brighter in the rapidly dimming light and the athletic contests came to a close men began to mingle in the firelight, renewing old acquaintances and starting fresh ones anew. Proud boasts of deeds of valour and stories of local tribe successes in the previous season's campaigns turned to glorifying friends who had fallen in action against Veii or the Volsci or Aequians. Each story gained a new twist as memories flooded back to the drunken minds of the teller, some weeping at the loss of valiant kinsmen. The small gatherings grew larger as the men shuffled into their tribal groups attracted by the warmth of the large pit fires. Valsuida had had too much to drink, his head was beginning to feely fuggy as he blinked swayed from side to side listening to the sound of the pipes from the far side of the fire.

"Good music" he said to the younger man next to him as he raised his arm towards the location of the music.

"Mmm" came the noncommittal reply.

"Alasaric, you seem quiet my friend, what is the matter? Today is a celebration of the glory of our alliance, why do you look so glum? "

Alasaric sat with his elbows on his knees, his back bent forwards. His head nodded forlornly as he stared into the dancing flames of the fire. His mouth turned up at the corners but no mirth showed on his face as he turned his head towards his uncle. At twenty two summers Alasaric had seen two campaigning seasons, both hard-fought seasons away from his home and his young sons. He glanced at the long scar running along his right arm, a red streak along his forearm which reminded him how close he had come to death in the heat of battle.

He closed his eyes as he remembered the mad eyes of the attacker, his stinking breath coming to his nostrils as it had done on the day he had gained the scar. The spear thrust had been too quick for him, his shield arm had been slow and the thrust had run along his arm, digging into his flesh and burning as if he had thrust his arm into the fire in front of him. He let out a deep sigh as he opened his eyes and turned them to his uncle. Valsuida was a veteran of more than ten summer campaigns. His bright eyes sparkled with a love of life that made Alasaric recoil as he contemplated his own sorrow at the things he had seen in two summers, the death, the destruction, the hatred of men.

"I am not one for these wars, uncle" he replied forlornly. "I do not glorify the deaths of men or the raping of women and boys" he said as his head moved slowly from side to side, his long dark hair covering his face.

"Ha" laughed the older man, his eyes narrowing as he placed a soft hand on his nephews arm, squeezing slowly. "I've told you lad" he said, his drunken eyes seeming to grow sharper. "The gods have their plans and we men simply play our parts in their designs. It is wrong to ponder on such things as our own mortality. Glory and plunder is our way lad. You are a born killer. These arms of yours" he said as he squeezed Alasaric's thick bicep muscles, his fingers hardly able to reach around his bulky arms. "These will keep you alive, these and your prayers to the gods" he added with a yellow-toothed grin.

After a moments silence Alasaric shook his head. "The war with Veii has been eight years uncle. Eight years. How can men stand to be away from home for so long? I couldn't" he exclaimed. "My farm would be nothing but wasteland by now" he added as he looked into his uncle's face.

Valsuida nodded and placed his heavy wooden cup to the floor, glancing around at the noise of the men around the fire as they laughed, drank and played dice into the early part of the night. The festival of the Latin League was nearly over, the spring was coming and Valsuida knew that the time for the Ancilia Shield to be drawn around Rome by the dancing priests of the Salii was only days away. The festival marked the renewing of the vows of alliance between the tribes of the Latin delta and Rome, the greatest city of the alliance.

"Yes." His words were quietly spoken as he patted the strong muscles of his younger kinsman. "The war with Veii has been long, longer than anything any of these men have ever known." He smiled. "Some say it will last longer than the siege of Troy" he said as Alasaric nodded in response.

"I have heard that too."

A silence, filled with the music of the pipes and the noise of several drunken men dancing and singing around the fire, came over the two men. As the flames jumped in time with the dancing men Valsuida smiled.

"You should be glad you are not a Roman, Alasaric" he said, nudging his nephew with his arm.

Alasaric grinned, his first proper smile of the evening as he let out a sharp breath and sat up, stretching his back, which clicked noisily as he rubbed vigorously at a point above his left hip. "You are right uncle. To be a slave to the military and to be camped summer and winter in front of the highest walls man has ever built" he shook his head. "Troy was nothing compared to Veii" he said as he picked up Valsuida's drinking cup and drank a long draught.

"They are not slaves" Valsuida replied with a huff as he grabbed the cup and looked at the almost empty vessel and the grinning face of his kin.

"That's what the Romans say."

"Only the Plebeian politicians say that. The men get paid and also get a share of the plunder from the wars. *A year's pay for a year's work* is what they say."

"There is no share from Veii yet and the years roll by with no opportunity for the men to return home" replied Alasaric. "I heard that the soldiers at Veii petitioned their Senate to return home for the winter but were refused *again*." He added. "I also heard that every day the King of Veii calls for men from Rome to join them. The city is filled with food, water, women and is warm in the winter while the soldiers of Rome sleep in their thin blankets and freezing cold wooden huts."

"I heard that too" Valsuida said with a knowing look. "But such things happen in war. What if a few men creep away and desert to the enemy in the cold months? The might of Rome will overcome Veii" he said with a firm nod.

"A few?" exclaimed Alasaric. "I heard it is hundreds every day."

"Haha young Alasaric. Hundreds? Well surely there must be no men left at the walls of Veii if such numbers are running from the cold. Surely the soldiers of Rome are hardy men and will suffer such hardships for their city. I think you are listening to the grumblings of these plebeian politicians who are working to gain their own glory instead of the glory of the alliance." He finished with a grim look as he glanced around the fire quickly to check that nobody was listening to his words, chiding himself for allowing the drink to fuel his anger. He knew such words could mean a knife in the back if he said them too often or too loudly. Alasaric glanced around the fire too, placing a hand on his uncle's arm.

"Such stories will be the death of us all" Alasaric said quietly with a wink. After a short silence he continued.

"Which unit have you been voted to uncle?" he asked more brightly.

"The Eagles of Camillus" said the older man with a broad grin, his face showing how much he was looking forward to the deployment.

"Hmm" said Alasaric. "I hear he is chosen of the gods and a great leader" he said, his eyes scanning the nearest men for signs that they were listening.

"He got the soldiers pay. He follows the laws and rituals like no other and the gods love him for it" Valsuida said as he touched a bracelet on his left wrist, the bronze shining in the firelight as Alasaric's eyes glanced to his movement.

"He allows the politicians to argue their cases and he makes firm decisions."

"I hear he is firm with his men" Alasaric said with a look at the older man, his scar covered arms and tightly drawn face smiling into the fire as they talked.

"The men need a firm hand" he replied. "They should put him in charge of the camp at Veii, you know the stories" he whispered as his eyes widened.

"Yes I know the stories" replied Alasaric with a slight nod. "But no Roman patrician will ever be found guilty of supplying food and weapons to Veii."

"It happens though" came the quiet response before another short silence.

"They say that this Camillus was the man to get Calvus the role of Consular Tribune" Alasaric said with a quizzical look to his right.

"Yes" replied the older man "and didn't he and the plebeians do a great job in command that year. The word is that they were so good that the patricians of Rome connived to bring him and the rest of the Tribunes down."

"I heard that too."

"And" continued Valsuida "they say that Rufus and Calvus made such great changes to the laws in Rome that the public purse will be secure for many years."

"I heard that Camillus sanctioned their changes in the Senate. The people like him" replied Alasaric as he stretched his back again and looked around the fire as men started to stand and head back to their sleeping tents, the night had drawn in already.

"I hear he has many enemies now, uncle"

"Which man does not?" came the stout reply. "Indeed nephew, we should feel lucky that our job is to stand in line and thrust our spears, not to play two games, one of war and one of politics" he laughed at his own words.

Alasaric laughed too, genuinely agreeing with his uncle's summary of life. He looked into the face of his uncle, seeing the eyes of his long dead father staring back at him. "And these Eagles, I have heard they fight like demons who cluster around the spears and fight close to their enemies with short swords and thick shields?" he asked.

"I have heard this too" nodded Valsuida. "I hear that Camillus is a great leader who thinks his way through a battle rather than throws men at it. That can only be good" he said as he touched the bronze bracelet again. "I also hear that he is consulted by the other Tribunes on every decision" he said quietly as his eyes quickly scanned two men who were wondering past.

"I doubt that" came the reply. "These Roman high-borns don't take easily to being given orders by others, you know what they're like." He whispered the last words quietly with a roll of his eyes. "Glory, glory, glory" he mouthed with a shake of his head.

"I hear the patricians consulted their Sibylline books" Valsuida said, the look of awe coming to his face making his nephew smile at him and shake his head.

"Do you really think they have such a thing? I hear that was a trick used by their old Kings to keep power over the people" he said genuinely.

"Don't say such things" Valsuida said, looking to the sky and mumbling a few words of prayer and rubbing his bracelet. Alasaric didn't follow this goddess Fortuna or Mater Matuta as many of the men did. He kept his faith in his strong arm and sharp sword, though he glanced up at the sky for any sign of response to the old man's mumblings and found his heart beating more rapidly in his chest.

"You heard about the two-headed calf?" Valsuida said once he had finished his words of supplication to his gods.

"No!"

"In Retia a two-headed calf was born. They said it brayed from both mouths at birth and Augurs descended on the town to try to understand its portent."

Alasaric looked at his uncle, his mouth open at this news.

"When was this, I've not heard of it"

"Three weeks ago" came the reply. Valsuida leant forwards and whispered "It's an ill omen" he added.

Alasaric looked into the eyes of his uncle, a fear coming over him as the man stared at him with a grim expression. "But what does such a thing mean?" he asked.

"Nobody knows yet. But it cannot be good."

"I heard from Lassius that the plebeians are angry at having no Tribunes this season" Valsuida said with alarm in his voice.

"What does Lassius know, the man is a snake"

"He runs messages between Veii and Rome and knows more than you credit him" Valsuida said in defence of his friend.

Alasaric huffed, but his interest was piqued and he looked at his uncle again. "And what does he say?"

Valsuida shrugged. "He says that Rome is in disarray, the plebeian politicians are attacking the patricians and the patrician politicians use the law to hold the plebeians back from all the senior offices."

"But I heard the plebeians Tribunes did well!"

"So did I Alasaric, but you know how these Romans are power hungry. The patricians completed the Augurs and said that the pestilence that swept through Rome was caused because the gods were angry at the people. They say the gods sent messages to tell the patricians that they, and only they, should be the Consular Tribunes."

Alasaric laughed, everyone knew that only the patricians could divine the auguries and so used them to further their own cause. "I heard that too, and that Appius Claudius had stood in the assembly and called for peace between the political parties" he added.

"And they impeached that administrator for stealing the war taxes, what was his name?" Valsuida said with a frown which showed his mind was trying to remember the name.

"Lars Herminius Aquilinus" came the cold reply. "Thieving bastard."

"Poor lad more like" said Valsuida. "No doubt he fell foul of one of his masters schemes and paid the price of being sacrificed for the greater good of someone higher up the ladder" he said in reply.

Alasaric nodded and looked at another group of men heading for their tents. The two men sat in silence for a few moments before Alasaric spoke again.

"So you will join Camillus tomorrow?"

"Yes, with Ambasius, Fatius and Collinius from the town, and their men" came the slow reply.

"The word is that you will be journeying to Veii to support the attacks on the siege works" he stated.

"So I hear, and it's needed. The attacks from the Capenates and Faliscans as well as the raiding parties from the city are causing problems in the camp. I hear discipline is bad and that the men are in low spirits. This war will never be won at the walls of Veii" he said glumly with a look to his nephew.

"Cheer up uncle, maybe this great man Camillus will topple the walls and win us a great victory" laughed Alasaric with a shove at his uncle who grinned back at him.

"Maybe."

"They say he has never lost a battle. Is it true?" asked the younger man with a measure of respect in his voice. "If it is then surely the gods do favour the man" he added.

Valsuida leant forward, his eyes roving the ground around the fire where only small pockets of men now sat, all deep in quiet conversations. "Some of the soldiers say there is a prophecy that he will lead Rome to great glory" he whispered. "Him and his *Eagles*" the old man added.

"I haven't heard this" came the astonished reply.

"You have only two seasons Alasaric, what do you expect?" laughed the old man as he winked at the wide eyes of his kinsman.

"Tell me more of this uncle" Alasaric asked in hushed tones as he edged closer to his uncle and smiled, a sudden hope growing inside him that this war might finally come to an end.

*

*

Chapter 2

The scout held his breath, pulling lightly on the rope he'd tied to his waist to signal to the men behind him to stop. He strained his eyes and watched the lights away in front of him as they bobbed and weaved through the trees, the yellow glow faint but clear in his vision. The darkness was almost total, the rustle of the trees the only sound in the thickness of the night. Ahead he knew were the ravines which led almost directly to Veii, the deep gullies carved by the gods as a marker to signify its greatness. Behind him lay the great Alban Lake, the waters low as the spring rains had been light this year and the place where the Romans had set up their main camp. A movement caught his eye again, the lights were leaving as the guards headed back to their posts, as he expected. His business dealings with Comus of the Aequii had been good, but not as good as his latest dealings with the Roman Senator, the man was a genius and knew every trick to get his supplies into the besieged city. With his uncanny ability to see in the dark better than any man alive, the scout had been sought out and had agreed to organise the supply runs for the Senator. For the past seven years he had made more money than he could count and still the Senators information was beyond reproach, every detail of the troop's movements was almost exact, as if the man were moving them himself. The rope tugged and Servius turned to glance behind at the source of the sudden movement. Despite the darkness he could see three of the men attached to the rope so that they wouldn't get lost in the darkness as they stretched behind him into the trees. Beyond them he heard a splashing sound and shook his head, if the man needed a piss he should wait until he'd been given the all clear. These men were poor, he thought to himself shaking his head. Turning back to the darkness in front of him he nodded his head, counting to ten before tugging the rope three times to signal the men to walk again.

With a slow step he led the men to the edge of the clearing and took out his water pouch to take a few small sips as the six men appeared beside him, the first two muttering about the stupidity of their colleague. Servius made a mental note to leave the man's body in the woods. A man who ignored the rules and put the others in danger didn't deserve to make it home he thought as he scowled into the darkness.

"Men" he whispered. "Here" he said. The light in the small clearing through which he had seen the guards travelling allowed some visibility and he could just about make out the shapes of the men and the faces of those nearest to him. He noted that it was Felix who was the perpetrator of the sound and grinned; he didn't like the man and certainly didn't trust him. Losing him on the way back would be a pleasure, it was a shame he had lost two of his usual men to the plague that had hit Rome over the winter. The City certainly seemed to be having bad luck recently, with plagues and sudden spells of hot weather disturbed by thunderous rain for days before the oppressive heat came back. Maybe the patricians were right, he thought, and it was the gods telling men of their anger at the confusion over who led Rome.

The last man stepped closer and bent his ear towards Servius.

"The city is within a half mile. This ravine is narrow so you will have to hold your packs above your heads for some of the way as it is narrow at the bottom near your legs. We leave the packs at the end of the ravine as I explained to you and some of us will return to the mules to collect the rest. No stopping" he said with a glance to Felix. "We have two hours to get the sacks into the Cuniculi and get them to the foot of the wall, no longer. If you get lost I will leave you behind" at which his eyes moved to Felix. He waited a heartbeat before continuing. "Use the rope if you have a problem, two tugs to stop, three tugs to go." Without waiting he turned and looked at his surroundings. The low rocks were strewn with clefts, the largest of which showed the signs of a path which disappeared into the darkness. Saying a quick prayer to Fortuna, Servius picked up his sack and strung it across his back, the corn inside shifting as he stepped forwards. He knew from the Senators spy that there would be no guards but his heart still beat hard in his chest as he set off through the natural ravine, a great place for an ambush.

Within ten minutes he had brought the men to a stop again, the Cuniculi, the long thin water course, called rabbit holes by the locals, which led across the open fields to the walls of the city lay straight ahead of him. He marvelled at the work it must have taken to cleave these ditches from the land to water the fields as he looked across at the thirty feet high walls of Veii. Turning to the men behind him he whispered "Artius, I will take the three men back and start collecting more sacks, you know what to do" he stated coldly as he glanced at Felix, the man's stupid face grinning in the low moonlight. "Right, let's go" he said as some of the men untied their ropes and started to shift the sacks into a pile. "We'll be back within the half hour" he said to Artius, patting his trusted friend on the shoulder before heading back into the woods with the remaining men.

****

"Tribune" came the strong voice of the dark haired Centurion, his dark blue tunic under a thick brown leather chest guard as he tapped the thick vellum map on the table in front of him. "The plateau is some thousand paces long and four hundred wide" he said as he drew his finger along the crudely drawn picture of the surrounding area. "Here" he looked up at the other officers "the gorges connect to the western walls which are entrenched with a mound and ditch" he nodded, his expression grim. "The walls are made of *tuff*, hard and strong but only the height of three men and maybe an arm's length deep; easily scalable if we can get through that ditch" he nodded at Potitus. "There is no slope into the city and the only entrance is the main gate, here" he finished with a finger on the picture in front of him.

"A good report" Marcus replied placing a hand on Rufus's shoulder as the older man looked at him with a smile. "Do we think they will stand and fight or will they hide behind the walls?" he asked the gathering of the senior officers who were all looking at the map with pensive faces.

"They won't fight" Virginius replied with a cold look on his face. "My bet is that they'll hide behind their ditch and try to see the summer out."

"I agree" Fasculus said, his new Centurions helmet shining along with his bronze breastplate. Since coming across his old enemy in a skirmish a few years before Fasculus had become a good leader in Marcus's army, taking the initiative and working well with the first spear, Narcius. "We need a way to bring them out of their city and face them here" he tapped the map at a low point a thousand paces or so from the walls of the city. Every head nodded except Virginius.

"They won't come out" replied Virginius with certainty, his eyebrows raised as his lips tightened into a frustrated scowl.

Marcus looked at the officer, his brown eyes and hard face almost bitter as he looked at Fasculus. Virginius was a good soldier but he held longstanding grudges and was petulant, showing his emotions too often in Marcus's view, a sign that he was indecisive and weak. He shook his head slightly as he edged forwards towards the map. Virginius had been thrust upon his command for the third time in as many seasons and whilst he was capable his views with regard to the plebeian officers were already causing discomfort amongst the men who led his army. There was no place for the political issues of Rome in its army Marcus thought as he glanced at Virginius and wondered how he could remove the man from his officers without offending him or his rich patrons.

Marcus had been voted Military Tribune, a great honour and one which he hoped would lead his family name to greater glory. His first command had been commissioned to seek out the supporters of the Veientines who regularly attacked the Roman lines at the walls of the city. The Falerians and the Capenates were the two main culprits and so he had set off to the closest town of Faleria, from where the scouts had said many of the raiding parties had been led.

"Potitus, how many days to fill those ditches and scale the walls?" he asked with an appraising look at his old friend. Gaius Potitus was the opposite of Virginius, his bright eyes and clever mind endearing him to his contemporaries and his men. Marcus had seen the man grow into a leader, his 'engineers' creating new machines and developing ideas to support the attacks of the phalanx and the *Eagles* to ensure the lowest possible loss of life before the decisive attack. In the past five years Potitus had been assigned to Lucius, Marcus' brother, at Veii but as soon as Marcus had been appointed Military Tribune his first call was for his old friend to rejoin him. Scipio had been assigned to the siege works at Veii and had been stationed there for almost two years, his military bent endearing him to the rough lifestyle of the army and Marcus agreed to his wish to remain at the walls.

Potitus took a series of wooden covered wax tablets from a pouch and laid them on the table, rough sketches and words scrawled across each individual tablet. As he looked up at Marcus he smiled with a sparkle in his eyes "two days, maximum three, but I need to see them for myself rather than rely just on these reports" he said closing the tablets and placing them neatly back into the pouch. The bulk of Marcus's four thousand foot soldiers and five hundred horses were still a half a day's march from Faleria and were camped at the southern edge of a small hill overlooking the surrounding countryside as the sun started the slip lower in the sky.

Spurius Caelio, his eyes darting between the officers as he licked his lips before speaking, leant forwards and pointed to the low ground which Fasculus had pointed to moments earlier. "If we set up a forward camp here with a third of the army we might entice them into an attack" he suggested with a glance to Marcus.

"You assume they don't know that we have four thousand men heading their way" Marcus replied with a smile, his words warm as the new, young, officer nodded at the response, his eyes flicking to the others nervously. Caelio was a cousin of Senator Javenoli and as such had been presented to Marcus by his old mentor in the cold months of the winter when the patrician clans wined and dined their friends to succour votes for the coming tribuneship. Marcus had taken to the young man quickly, his eager enthusiasm was infectious and his intelligence and wit raised him above the humdrum of young men trying too hard to gain their first commission. His light brown hair and grey eyes were a throw-back to some ancestors beyond the walls of Rome but his lineage was good and his knowledge of warfare was better than most men for his age. Whilst eager he was not overly forceful in his demands, learning through his questioning rather than telling his peers as many of the more senior officers seemed to do.

Caelio grinned at Marcus' reply and stood, his grey eyes bright against the candlelight in the tent. "*I did*" he said loudly, a short laugh coming from his grinning mouth as Rufus chuckled next to him and slapped his shoulder. "I've seen no scouts" he said to all the men around the table, his wide eyes still smiling.

Virginius shook his head in exasperation, annoyed that the young fool commanded such attentions. "Tribune, can we return to the planning?" he said coldly as he turned back to the map, stepping forward to peer down at the pictures of the city and its surrounding hills and ravines. "These ravines could be used as a strategic advantage" he said as he traced his finger along a series of small black lines drawn in front of the tuff walls and looked up at Marcus. Nodding Marcus looked to Narcius "I agree with Virginius" he said as he looked to Caelio and then back to the handsome face of the taller man. "We should take a closer look at the defences before we decide the final plan." He tapped his finger on his bottom lip as his brows furrowed and he glanced around the men in front of him.

Since taking the role of Tribune Marcus had found himself judging his officers more sternly than he had done previously. He had wondered whether it was the pressure which came with the role or whether he just didn't trust all of the men under his command now that the ultimate decision over life and death was his. Virginius was certainly capable but his arrogance towards the other men and his lack of focus in battle were weak points which he knew could cause disaster if not checked with a good Centurion giving sound advice to the man. Rufus and Fuscus were good soldiers who had shown strength in command for many years. Narcius was beyond reproach; his loyalty to the Furii had been tested over and over in the years since he had first held the sword of the Eagles at the battle of the three crossroads. The candle flickered and Marcus noted that the men were shuffling as he looked around at their faces, each of the men showing traces of nervousness as their eyes flicked to Marcus and then back to the map.

"Potitus and Fasculus, take a hundred of the Eques and take the forward position. Virginius take five hundred men and follow at double speed and we will bring the remainder of the men behind." He looked at the map and then back at the silent men, each nodding to their comrades at the command from their Tribune. "We will set up a camp here as suggested and maybe allow Caelio to set up a camp here with his slaves to entice the enemy out" he said with a serious frown as a momentary silence filled the tent. Rufus let out a deep belly laugh at the face of Caelio as his usual bright face suddenly paled at the thought that this might be a real order, his head whipping from man to man, almost appealing to them, before Marcus and the rest of the officers slapped him hard on the back and continued to laugh off the tension which had grown in the small, humid, tent throughout the meeting. Caelio blustered his reply, sticking out his thin chest and wiping a bead of sweat from his brow as he grinned at Narcius. "Ha, I could take on a whole city with 3 *Eagles*" he said as he held his lips tight and put his face into a fierce scowl. "No problem" he said again as the men laughed at the little peacock strutting around the tent with his chest puffed out and hand held firmly on his thick sword. Marcus smiled. He had learned that a little humour was a good way to distract the tension of the men, but he also knew that being too soft on them would allow weakness to creep into his command. Caelio was a good distraction but he was also young and green and must be kept in check if he was to improve his skills as an officer. Virginius wasn't smiling and Marcus found himself looking at the man again and wondering what was going through his mind. Taking a short breath he rapped the table lightly with his hand, causing all the men to look to him.

"Fuscus, Narcius" he nodded "you will be in charge of setting up the camp. Any questions?" After a moments silence he nodded to the men "then let's get to it gentlemen, we have a city to capture."

As the men left the tent Marcus sat and touched the wooden eagle around his neck, his mind rushing over the words of the prophecy given to him all those years ago. He still didn't understand what the words meant and his eyes wandered to the votive candle to Mars that he had lit before the meeting of his officers. If he was truly chosen by the Goddesses Fortuna and Mater Matuta, Juno, then surely the words of his destiny would be fulfilled, but as he creased his brow at the thought of the words *'the eagle will be the greatest leader of Rome there has ever been'* and considered his career since the day of the prophecy he was still unsure what it meant. Each line of the prophecy was filled with riddles, words he couldn't fathom and which he tried to interpret and use as he considered each decision he needed to make. His brother Lucius had been Military Tribune four times and was already one of Rome's greatest generals, but he, Marcus Furius Camillus, had only now gained the highest order of military service below that of Dictator.

Dictator. The word hung in his mind as he considered the power the role commanded for the people of the Republic of Rome. He smiled inwardly at the conversations he had held with Calvus regarding the role, Calvus ridiculing the position as a way for the plebeians to be held under the foot of the patricians, another rule that the elite of Rome used to push through their own reforms in time of dire need. Marcus half laughed as he stood from the chair he had slumped into, his eyes suddenly becoming tired despite the fact that the sun had not long risen over the horizon. Outside he heard the unmistakable noise of tents being collapsed, horses snorting as they moved into position and officers shouting at their men to form into lines and prepare for the march. '*The Eagle will lead Rome five times*' the prophecy had said. Was this the first of the five he wondered? He shook his head and considered whether his command was truly *leading* Rome rather than just a section of its army. Sipping some lemon infused water he looked into the candle of Mars and nodded his acceptance of the will of the gods. Lucius had said that the prophecy would be fulfilled before he really understood the words and Marcus had agreed with his sentiment. The gods planned the future and men simply lived to make the future work in their favour, but eventually fate was all powerful and all men must fall to fates designs.

Taking a final look at the map and checking that his orders were correct he blew out the candle, thanking the gods for looking over his decisions and crossed to the tent flap and stepped into the dull light of the morning. Three tunic clad legionaries were standing five paces to his right waiting to pull the tent poles from the hard ground and load his personal belongings onto his private cart and they jumped to attention as he appeared. With a nod to the three men he glanced at the activity around him, thousands of men hurrying to positions, dust clouds creeping into the air as the horses were brought forwards and noise, a noise that Marcus loved, the noise of war. He breathed the noise in as he watched the men moving efficiently from task to task, the years of training making light of the hard work. He smiled at seeing Fuscus shouting to a troop of men to remove the final section of the marching camp, the thick poles being dragged from the earthen mound in which they had been placed. Taking a deep breath Marcus looked to the sky and smiled, today was as good as any for seeking out Rome's enemies.

*

*

Chapter 3

Aulus Manlius gestured to his brother with a confused look. "A two headed calf in Retia?" he asked.

"Hmm" came the reply from his brother as he filled his mouth with dates from the bowl in front of him.

"I don't understand its significance" he added to the fruit munching figure lying across a reclining couch in the cool air of Senator Javenoli's garden. A small bird flew into his vision, its quick movement taking it to some crumbs of bread on the floor and away with a beak full of sustenance within seconds. He smiled. The bird had had time to cock its head at him, almost as if asking for permission to take the crumbs before flying off.

"The augurs were clear" said the voice of Javenoli as Aulus looked at him. The man had grown around the middle since they had last met, surely he couldn't get any larger without exploding, he thought as he turned his attention to the Senator.

"The two heads are two great powers fighting for one body. The braying is the noise of war. The problem faced by the two heads is to gain control of the body. The gods have given us a clear sign that we must throw all our weight into the issue of Veii" Javenoli said in his quick, sharp voice.

Weight thought Aulus, his mind distracted by the word as he looked to the Senator.

"But it doesn't give us any clue as to which head will win" Aulus replied with a slow shrug and a look, again, to his brother.

Javenoli turned to the older man on his right. "Cicurinus, what say you?" he asked.

The older senator took a deep breath, letting it out slowly as he shook his head. "We have been unsuccessful in eight years of war with Veii" he said, shaking his head and looking to the floor. "Before long we will have a siege to rival Troy" he added. As he narrowed his eyes he seemed to be struggling to form his words before he spoke again.

"The two headed calf is a sign from the gods that we will win. It was in our lands and is a sign to us" he said firmly to some grunts of agreement from around him. "But it is also a concern. It also tells us that the gods are not happy" he glanced to the older Manlius brother, his thick Greek style beard curled elaborately and oiled to a point at which it was almost dripping. Cicurinus tried not to frown as he instinctively rubbed his clean-shaven, Roman, face and considered his next words carefully. "The gods are still confused about who has control in Rome" he added more loudly as Manlius huffed and shook his head in protestation of the words being spoken by the Senator. "It is correct Manlius" he said, turning his tired face to the older Manlius brother. "I know you are their champion and you fight their cause, but look at the signs and you will see the displeasure of the gods" he shook his head slowly as he glanced back to the nodding form of Javenoli. "Pestilence in the streets again" he said, raising a hand and counting by holding up a finger. "A wolf seen in the streets" he raised another. "The two-headed calf" another finger slowly moved upright. "A string of premature births amongst the patrician class" he added. "The winter was another divine message, the cold and snow deeper than any in living memory. All are signals from the gods" he said with a final finger and shake of his head.

"And the continued losses at Veii, don't forget them" Javenoli interjected.

"Yes Senator, I agree. Veii continues to be a thorn in our side. It all adds up to one thing Manlius. The gods are not happy with us" he finished with a slow stare at Manlius, who simply tightened his lips and shook his head in reply.

"With all respect" nodded Manlius "that is all supposition and rubbish." He edged forwards on his couch, "the plebeian tribunes did splendidly" he continued. "They re-filled the Republican purse, organised the building of new tenements" he raised a hand and smiled as he raised two fingers and then a third as he continued again. "They organised the festivals with such precision that the people proclaimed them the best in more than ten years" he smiled again. As he raised another finger to speak again Cicurinus spoke over him.

"They have rallied the people in the forum every day, complaining about taking away the liberties of the men who serve at Veii. They claim that the Patricians have sent them away so that we can hold back the reforms they wish to push through." He huffed before continuing, raising a hand to Manlius, who shook his head at the older man. "They claim that the

Patricians suffer less than they do because they can return home in the winter to their warm fires and warm beds. And" he added raising his hand again to the shifting form of Manlius. "They claim it is a form of *slavery*" he added with a final shake of his head.

"That is old news Senator" Manlius replied. "Appius Claudius resolved this issue with them a long time ago, as you know" he added with a little more venom in his tone than he had intended. "Apuleius doesn't speak for all the plebeians any more. The man is bent on his own power and Calvus and Longus and Philo have no time for his plots and schemes" he added as he looked at the other men around them, all patricians and all grimacing at his words.

"There is no resolution Manlius" Javenoli replied. "Each day in the forum these plebeians stand and call for more reforms, shouting that the enforced slavery of their young men has taken away their liberties and starved their families. There is no resolution as you would like to think. The Senate is out-voted every day by the plebeians and the gods see this and frown on us Manlius. They are unhappy that their chosen representatives are not leading the City as they ordain. The two-headed calf and all the auguries testify to this."

Manlius looked to his brother Aulus, who was nodding at the words spoken by Javenoli. He shook his head at how easily the younger man had been swayed by the invocation of the god's displeasure.

"Then what do you propose, gentlemen?" Manlius asked as he sat forward on his couch and took another deep breath, almost sighing in resignation as he spoke.

A short silence fell as Javenoli and Cicurinus locked eyes. Manlius watched the two men who seemed to be speaking to each other with eye movements and gestures as the larger man raised his right shoulder and glanced towards Aulus.

"We have thought through some ideas" Cicurinus finally said as he shifted his legs on the couch and turned to look directly at Manlius. "I understand you wish to run for Censor,

Aulus?" he asked as Manlius's mind raced through the comment, a sudden rush of blood making his heart beat more quickly. Aulus glanced to Manlius before replying.

"Indeed Senator" he said, his eyes narrowing at the game that was about to start.

"Hmm" said Cicurinus as his eyebrows rose and he nodded, his mouth dropping at the corners as if appraising the younger Manlius brother. "It would be a good appointment. You have proven yourself since that issue with Postumius" he said, seeing the anger suddenly rise in Manlius's face, though Aulus simply nodded his head and flinched his shoulders, clearly remembering the strikes of the whip across his back.

"The Senate believe that we need to send a clear message to the gods. The sibylline books have been read and they agree" he added with a firm nod to Javenoli, who nodded in reply.

"Tomorrow we will announce that a *lectisternium* will begin and last for eight days" he said as he noticed Manlius sit back in his seat, his clever mind already working through the process and rationale for the festival to the gods in which every Roman would open his doors to his friends and enemies alike and even prisoners would be removed from their shackles.

"The festival will support the easing of tensions between the classes and will bring a peace to the city in which no litigation and no angry voices will be heard in the forum." Cicurinus looked to Manlius. "We need your help in gaining the support of your plebeian friends, Manlius" he said with a determined look in his eyes. "In response to your assurances we will lend our *considerable* weight to the campaign for Aulus to be Censor" he smiled.

****

"What is it?" Mella asked, his eyes scanning the small cloud of dust appearing in front of the small scouting troop he led.

"I would say it is about a thousand men moving very quickly" came the reply from his left.

"Go, Viscus and come back with your answer. This could be bad" replied Mella as he sat back on his horse and glanced nervously at the five remaining men around him. Viscus kicked his mount into a gallop and rode into the long grass which was swaying left and right in the strong circling wind.

Mella had been sent east with his scouts early that morning before the sun had risen, his cold hands only just coming back to life after the early start. For over three hours they had seen nothing, but now a sudden dust cloud had appeared about a mile away, its size bringing a fear which Mella had not felt for some time.

"I want a circle at two hundred paces" he said to the anxious faces around him. "Eyes wide open soldiers, but we stay here until Viscus comes back with his report." The location was not perfect, it would be easy for archers to crawl within striking distance and launch their arrows at his men, but he needed to remain here until his scout returned. Setting a circle would mean any attackers would need to spread out in order to attack, but it would also thin out his men. A risk worth taking he thought as he nodded to the men as they spread out into the grass. The dust cloud hung in the air and he considered his next move, taking a wax tablet and scrawling a few words on it so that he was prepared in case they needed to make a quick exit. Marcus and his force were moving on Faleria and by now, he looked to the sun, still low in the sky, they would be within sight of the walls. Had the Falerians seen the attack and sent troops to attack Marcus's rear? As he thought through the issues his eye caught a movement high and to his right, a sudden panic coming to him as he caught his breath, an arrow? He flinched as he instinctively turned to the location. No, it was small bird darting along the top of the grass searching for food. A good sign, he told himself. Any archer in the grass would scare the birds away. He took a deep breath, feeling his quickened heart slowing in his chest as he glanced at the dust cloud once again.

Twenty minutes later the form of Viscus appeared riding low on the back of his horse, the animal beating a fast pace through the knee length grass. He raised his left hand to signal the 'all clear' but continued his face pace.

"Close in" Mella called as the horsemen around quickly responded to his order and gathered next to him.

Viscus reined in, his dirty face showing long wet streaks at the corner of his eyes from the hard ride into the wind. "Falerians" he said "as I thought, about a thousand in full marching column heading towards the forest there. I saw three scouts but they didn't see me, but we need to move from here as soon as we can, they can only be five minutes behind me" he said pointing towards the thick trees away to their left. "My guess is that they are looking to get behind our forces" he added as he licked his dry lips and took a water pouch offered to him by the man on his right.

Mella nodded as he looked at the dust cloud and then again to the trees. "Well done Viscus" he said as he scrawled on the wax tablet. Turning to the men he handed the tablet to Viscus and then placed his arm out dissecting the remaining men in half. "You go with Viscus back to the army and take this straight to Camillus" he said motioning to the men on one side of his arm. "You three will remain with me and keep an eye on this force."

With a firm nod Viscus saluted and turned to trot away. As the men set off into the distance Mella turned his remaining scouts towards the trees with a glance towards the grey-brown cloud thrown up by a thousand marching men.

*

*

Chapter 4

"Message from the scouts" chirped the voice of Rufus' Optio, a young man called Quintus Sulpicius, his hard weather-browned face belying his young years as he stood to attention in front of his senior officer. Marcus looked at the boy and smiled, he knew Sulpicius well from his days as Censor in Rome, the urchin was always in trouble for stealing fruit or chasing slave girls but had grown into a tall, athletic, youth who was just about shaving. The boy had been assigned to Rufus through his association with Manlius as he was cousins with the man whose brother Marcus had been forced to whip following the death of prisoners in Postumius's marching camp some years before.

Nodding to the Optio Marcus took the wax tablet held out by the scout, his face showing that he was eager to tell his commanding officer what was held within. "Viscus, isn't it?" Marcus asked as the man caught his eye for a moment and a beaming smile came to his face at the recognition before he snapped to attention and looked at a point over Marcus's shoulder. "Sir" came the reply.

"What does it say?" Marcus asked as he picked up a short dagger and sliced the ribbon to open the two pieces of wood.

"A thousand Falerians marching to the south towards the rear, sir. Spotted them myself" the man said as Marcus raised his eyes at the final comment but said nothing as he read through the scrawled writing of his former sword master. Mella had written more detail than the man, Viscus, had given and Marcus nodded at the words as he glanced back to Viscus with a smile. "Well done Viscus" he said, looking over the man's shoulder at the other men who were standing next to three sweating horses "and you men" he called to the nods of the dust covered scouts. "Viscus, I need you to return to Mella and take him a message" Marcus replied as he started to rub the wax to create space to write. After a moment he handed the tablet back to Viscus. "There is no time to tie a new ribbon" he said "this is an order for Mella to make himself visible to the scouts and to retrace our steps back here," The scout looked up quickly with a frown, his face showing he didn't understand why the men should make themselves visible.

"Don't worry Viscus" Marcus said, reading the man's expression. "There is a good reason why I want our enemy to know we are aware of their position."

Viscus saluted and set off back to his horse as some of the officers wandered across to see what the new message was.

Marcus looked across at the camp, half way through being built as the soldiers detailed to set up the camp dug the trenches and unloaded the carts. He glanced back at the direction in which the thousand men may be marching at his rear and pictures raced through his mind as he visualised the movements they would make, how they might attack and how he would defend this position. In his mind he saw the gates of Faleria opening and thousands more men streaming out from his front. As the officers approached him Marcus had already thought through several possibilities and started to plan his defensive lines. He half-laughed at the sudden change. Until this point he had been concerned with attacking the city, and now it seemed he would need to consider defence instead.

"Problem, Tribune" Virginius said, his lofty expression instantly annoying Marcus as the man looked at him.

Marcus smiled. "Gather the senior officers please Virginius, we have some new considerations to make. Send a runner to get Potitus as well, I need his thoughts" he added as he turned and walked towards his half erected command tent.

****

Scipio stood and watched as the water lapped against the shore, the clear blue almost inviting him to slip off his sandals and step into the cooling lake. He searched the banks with his eyes and frowned as he pursed his lips. The lake, which the locals called the Alban Lake, was about seventy yards across, its cold depths no doubt filled with fish he thought as he stared out into the bright daylight which glistened off the water.

"And where was it yesterday" he asked the legionary who was standing to his left at full attention.

The legionary stepped into the water and pulled out a wooden stake, a thick line carved into the wood. Returning to Scipio's side he held the stake out and pointed to an area about four inches below the current water line. "Here, sir" he said. "And the day before, here" he added as he pointed to another carved line which was three inches below the one he had just highlighted.

Scipio looked out at the lake and back to the stake. He turned to his left to see the rows of tents and huts which the men were living in, the smell and sounds of cooking coming from the Roman camp. Working through some calculations in his mind Scipio frowned and looked back at the stake, taking it from the legionary and turning it in his hands.

"Carve another line Marcus" he said as he passed it back. "We'll check it again tonight" he said as he patted the man's shoulder and headed back to the camp.

As he threaded his way through the tents and wooden huts built by the Romans as they camped close to the water which fed Veii his mathematical training suggested that in less than ten days the first of the tents would be under water. He wondered what had caused the water to rise and why. There were no reports of an earthquake and there had been no heavy rain reported for weeks, the spring turning quickly into hot days and cold nights as it had done for the past three years. A sudden gust of cold air made him shiver and he gripped the rue sprig he held on a string around his wrist and mumbled a quick prayer to Fortuna to avert any evil which had just passed through the camp. In his years at the walls of Veii Scipio had succumbed to all the fears that the men held. Fear of the evil eye picking you out for death. Fear that your thoughts would haunt you if they were bad and fear that his throat would be cut in the dead of night by a Veienteine assassin. He shook his head and sighed as these fears ran through his mind. He wondered what portent the men would see in the waters of the lake rising? As he stepped up to the command tent the guards eyed him and stood to attention, the taller man, his beard thick but well trimmed nodding that he could enter the tent without being challenged.

Inside the heat was stifling as the Tribune, Priscus, looked at a series of new drawings of the siege works at Veii. A great earth ramp had been built over the last twelve months, the back-breaking work taking longer than planned due to the fierce winter. He wondered whether the men's fears that this war was cursed might be true. It was true that whatever new tactic they employed seemed to fail. The earthworks were enormous and had proceeded at great speed, the men digging and building ferociously to create the ramp and fit it with stones to create a walkway upon which the army could march. But then the damned Capenates had attacked the siege works and slaughtered hundreds of men, the gates of the city opening and a force of Eques charging down the fleeing men before the enemy retreated back to the walls of Veii with shouts and jeers. He grunted and clenched his teeth. The winter had frozen everything, the snow as deep as a man's thigh. How many men had died in their tents? He had lost count. At least the spring had seemed good, the warm weather followed by light rain but now many months of warm weather had lifted the men's spirits, though only by a small measure. The mood was sombre and Priscus had decided that the earthworks and re-digging the trenches would keep the men busy – too busy to grumble anyway, he thought.

The appearance of Scipio brought a smile to his face as he looked up from the map.

"Ah, Scipio. Here have a seat and tell me how to defend the workers from more attacks from the gates of the City" he asked warmly, his brown eyes smiling in his thin face. Priscus liked the wise counsel of Scipio, his quick military mind and ability to think through the actions as if he were standing in the front line with the men making him a favourite of the Tribunes.

"Certainly Sir" relied Scipio. "But there is something else I wish to discuss with you first" he said as his tone made Priscus look at him more intently.

"A problem?"

"I'm not sure" replied the junior officer as he removed his helmet and wiped a bead of sweat from his forehead.

Priscus was older than Scipio and the fine lines around his eyes showed his jovial nature. He had a thick head of dark brown hair, cut short in the military style, as was Scipio's. His short forehead and low hair line made his eyes seem more prominent as they searched Scipio for information.

"For the past few days the soldiers have been complaining that the water in the lake seems to be getting closer to the tents" Scipio started as a frown appeared on his commander's face. "So I placed a stake in the water and marked the level each morning" he said as Priscus nodded, his face softening at the clever actions of his junior officer. "In three days the water has risen some eight inches. I've checked with the local tribesmen and there has been no earthquake or tremor which may have caused a problem. The lake is not connected to the sea so cannot be affected by the tides." He shrugged. "I calculate that within ten or twelve days the majority of the camp will be ankle deep in water. I am at a loss" he admitted as he stared into the eyes of Priscus.

Priscus looked at the map and drummed his fingers on the table for a moment as he took in the information and considered it. "The lake is what, seventy yards across and forty wide?" he asked without looking up.

"Yes, Sir"

"No rivers feed the lake that we know of according to this map"

"I've scouted the borders of the lake myself and there are no rivers or streams which feed the lake"

"Hmm" replied Priscus as he breathed deeply and rubbed his temples with his fingers. "An interesting puzzle Scipio" he said as his eyes narrowed and he looked up. "How many people know of this?"

"The majority of the soldiers know the lake has risen but I have not communicated anything yet with regard to reasons or actions" replied Scipio, his cool eyes and confidence pleasing Priscus.

"Good" he replied. "I take it your next consideration is to appease the men by pouring some libations to spirits of the water?" he half asked and half suggested.

"I had considered this" Scipio said "but the problem remains that if the water continues to rise it will affect the morale of the men. You know how jumpy they are at the moment. Bad winters; unseen attacks; food and supplies getting into the city which our scouts never detect. The men are convinced that this war is unjust and we have angered the gods" he finished, his eyes looking at the table as he had spoken so freely.

Priscus agreed with every word but knew that as commander he needed to remain stoic and show the men that the gods did favour them above the Veientines. He looked at the map again, his eyes roving the pictures of hills, trees and earthworks, looking for something which he could use to take the men's thoughts away from the issues of the rising water.

"Ideas?" he asked.

Scipio glanced at the map and shook his head as he chewed his bottom lip before sitting taller and speaking. "Libations will help but it will have to be a patrician officer who completes the ceremony" he said as Priscus nodded. "Keeping the men busy will also help. We could move the camp forward, closer to the city and further from the water, which will also help somewhat. We could build a barrier around the lake to keep the water back should it rise any further?"

After a moments silence Priscus sat back in his chair and pinched the bridge of his nose before looking to Scipio. "I agree with all of those ideas" he said with a smile. "Let's see if the water has risen any more in the next two days and then we will set some of them in motion. For now I want the men to re-double their efforts on the ramp. We must get over those walls."

Scipio nodded as he stood and saluted. As he left the tent and felt the cool breeze on his face he turned towards the gate of the camp and wandered across to the guards, who saluted smartly as he approached. Nodding to them he climbed to the walkway and scanned the scene around him.

Directly ahead lay the high bleached walls of Veii, their guards clearly visible as they wandered along the ramparts nonchalantly as if they were simply out for a morning walk. The fields around the city lay scorched and parched from the years of war, the Cuniculi, the long thin ditches which fed the fields, caked and dry after years of neglect. He smiled at the thought of the ditches, knowing that the longest was almost three and a half miles from start to finish, the Veientines engineering skills would please Potitus, he thought. As the lead City of the Etruscan Alliance he knew the City was well ordered, a central square around which the houses of the rich were clustered. He knew from the maps of the City that a series of roads radiated in a grid pattern from this central square, orderly and wide as the Etruscans liked, unlike the random building that had occurred in Rome in more recent years.

He looked to the left and right at the precipitous cliffs which bordered both sides of the City, making a frontal assault against the high walls the only feasible assault tactic and he took in the remains of the small scattered buildings which had been razed to the ground outside the walls when the Romans had first attacked the city, the broken walls almost completely demolished as the soldiers had scavenged everything they could carry to build their own huts and walls.

Away to the right and along the well made road into the city were the tombs, some of them as big as a small house in the Subura in Rome. The soldiers had avoided them, though some had written graffiti on the walls. The more richly decorated had seen a few of the terracotta statues stolen as the less concerned men had clearly taken them to sell when they returned home, which the majority had not done for several years. The city was magnificent, Scipio thought. Well supplied with water from the wells within and the lake behind him, miles of fertile land and these strange, but useful, Cuniculi to water the fields. He glanced to his right to see the area behind the wooden stakes and deep trenches of the camp where the soldiers had built their own farms, the thick foliage testament to the fertility of the soil. The river Tiber was somewhere further to his right, but with the cliffs and the trees he could not see it. He wondered if the river was unusually high and decided to go and see later that day, it might help with the lake problem.

The ramp was enormous and had reached some three quarters of the way to the city gates, stretching some four hundred paces from start to finish and nearly as high as three men. Potitus had started the works over two years ago before he had been called back to Rome at the sudden death of his wife. Scipio shook his head at the thought. Potitus had been one of the most energetic men he had ever known. The death of his Julia had caused a hole in the man's life which had taken some of his spirit from him. It had taken Marcus, his oldest friend, to get him out of his dark house and back into public life and Scipio smiled at the memory of the long arguments the men had held regarding the will of the gods, mortality of men and how fate dealt a bad blow to everyone at some time. Indeed Marcus and Livia had lost two children in infancy, one boy and one girl. Scipio gripped the small token to Juno he held on a chain with his wooden Eagle, a gift from Marcus, as he thought these words, his mind going to his own two boys, healthy and strong as he quickly thanked his patron goddess for their vitality.

Turning back to the camp he saw the miles of trenches stretching across the front of the city, the high palisades bleached by years of sun. Along the walls were several forts, each holding thirty men or more and each showing signs of fire or other attack. The Etruscan alliance had continued to harass the Roman siege during winter and summer and the forts were continually being re-built after short skirmishes. Some bore the marks of recent changes, the deep brown contrasting to the bleached, older, wooden supports.

The lake was another matter. Its fresh water and good defensive outlook made it a natural backdrop to the Roman camp. Scipio could see across the water to the far bank where large fir trees were interspersed with oak. The area around the banks of the lake had been cleared for fifty steps in each direction to provide the walls of the camp, the huts some of the men slept in and firewood, of which four large log stores were sited across the camp, each one piled high with the thick wood. Scipio wondered if the loss of trees would affect the level of water in the lake but shook away the thought as the loss was minimal compared to the depth of the forest. As he looked back into the camp he considered the war at Veii and its problems. He could see no action which would complete this war other than to get into the City by scaling the walls. The ramp was wide enough to march ten men and with the will of the gods it would be complete by the late summer. Maybe this was the year to defeat the old enemy he thought as he smiled at the high walls of Veii.

*

*

Chapter 5

Mella raced through the trees as another arrow struck the thick trunk of a broad pine, ducking his head under another low branch and feeling the leaves brush against his shoulder he gasped for breath. "There" he called to the remaining man of his scouting party, the other dead somewhere behind him in the thick forest. The Falerian archers had appeared from the thick undergrowth as his men sat eating from a small fire early in the afternoon, their arrows striking at the horses first and then at the men. Two horses had gone under a storm of arrows before the men had even seen the attackers, their skill evident in the heart piercing shots against the beasts. Mella had managed to release the reins from the last horse before it had bolted into the forest and he had to run for his life as the animal careered into an archer, knocking the man to the floor and no doubt saving Mella from an arrow in the back.

Vidus, the remaining scout, crashed through the undergrowth, his breath rasping as he ran as Mella tried to get his bearings and work out which way they should go. "The gap" he shouted as he saw a dark patch between two short trees and veered in that direction.

How the archers had crept up on him he'd never know, they were good, too good. They had appeared from the edge of the short cliff, an area he had thought was safe. How had they climbed those crumbling rocks without making a sound? He cursed as he thumped his hand against a branch as he ran past, the flare of pain coming in an instant as he winced and gritted his teeth, his eyes focused only on the dark patch between the trees ahead. Vidus was falling behind, the man labouring in the chase. He glanced back and caught his eyes, mad with terror. In that instant both men knew that their best hope was to split up and Vidus nodded to Mella as he turned and sprinted to his left, a shout coming from behind them at the movement.

Mella pounded into the dark space, his eyes adjusting quickly as the canopy overhead thickened and drew away the light. He heard a cry behind but he kept running, the thin path he fetched upon clearly some kind of animal track. His speed improved as he was unimpeded on the path, but he knew it would help the archer's too so he scanned the vicinity for somewhere with thicker undergrowth he could move into, but there was nothing. The trees seemed smaller, the trunks somehow thinner despite the thicker foliage, and his knowledge of woodland told him that this suggested he was closer to the edge of the forest, a bad sign; he knew being in the open would be his death. He edged to the right, a quick glance over his shoulder seeing no movement behind. A thick bush a hundred yards ahead became his next target and he forced his legs to pump despite their screaming for him to slow down. He clambered through the low branches of the bush, his eyes continually darting left and right as he strained his ears for any sounds except his own, instinctively slowing and catching his breath as the silence grew. He kept moving, but now more slowly, more aware of his surroundings than the past twenty minutes of hurtling through dense undergrowth and along animal tracks. His thoughts lurched to Vidus, had he escaped? Had he been caught? Mella had been clever enough to keep the details of the last report to himself in case any of the men were caught. He felt a pang of guilt at the thought, but he pressed on knowing it was the right thing to do, a good torturer would know that Vidus knew nothing and he would die quickly. Hearing no sound he came to a stop and crouched in a low bush, the leaves thick but the inner area near the knotted trunk clear of all but a few spindly branches. He scanned as much of the area as he could, hearing a cry of alarm from some distance to his right. Something told him to climb a tree and wait for darkness, but he knew that held risks of its own and indecision bit into him again as he gritted his teeth and sucked in the warm air of the forest. In a matter of heartbeats he resolved to get back to the main force and give his news to Camillus, but he still didn't know in which direction Faleria lay.

****

"Ready?" Marcus said to Potitus as he strode forward to the front line of his deep ranks of soldiers, their spear tops glinting in the late afternoon sun. The men in the line grinned at him as he passed, the skin of their faces nut-brown from hours of marching and drilling in the sun. "Ready, sir" Potitus winked as Marcus grinned back at his friend.

A short slave in his brown, knee length, tunic raced forwards and placed a wide wooden stool on the floor as Marcus, his blue cloak and long blue helmet feathers blowing in the breeze, stepped up onto the rostrum so that all the men could see him. He took a moment to gaze across the ground at the soldiers, their eager faces turned to him, some old and familiar, others young and eager. Rufus, his plebeian friend who had been a Military Tribune himself, one of six in the previous years - an enormous achievement for the plebeian movement, smiled back at him from the front line of spearmen. Narcius held a long thin line of Eagles, their new throwing javelins in their hands, behind the front two phalanxes and beyond that were the older Triarii with their heavier armour and larger shields, men like Quintus Fabius and Caelio standing with the richer patricians who made up this rank. He glanced to the left and right, the majority of his horse soldiers, the Eques, were on the right, their horses idly picking at the grass as if they were out for a morning ride back on their farms in the foothills of Rome. He had given Virginius a special role with the Eques, a high ranking position which he hoped might make the man feel more confident amongst his officers. He was an excellent horseman, but Marcus still held misgivings about his attitude towards the task and ability to act on his instincts.

Marcus smiled as he looked out over the men, his smile bringing grins to the faces of the soldiers closest to him. Potitus grinned back from his position at the front of the men. "Men of Rome" he called as the clink of metal showed that each man had stood taller at his first words. "The Falerians have killed our kin every year at Veii. They have taken arms against us on the roads and have boasted that they are *unbeatable*." As he said the word a series of calls and groans came from the ranks bringing a wider smile to Marcus's face. "Today we will see whether they are men of honour or cowards." He let the words sink in as silence fell in the ranks. "Today the wind of war blows on their city" he said as a few heads nodded at the words which were being relayed along the lines of men by their Centurions.

"They have refused to surrender and have taken arms against us" he said, waiting until the last Centurion finished before speaking again. "I, Marcus Furius Camillus have taken the auspices" he said raising his right hand to the sky. "Mars is with us, Jupiter agrees with our cause, Justitia and Juno will look after you men of Rome as our cause is just" he said as the cheering began, starting closer as the words were relayed and then growing into the distance as the men further away heard his words. He glanced to the woods away in the distance, and took a deep breath, a slight fear mingling with the excitement he felt at the start of the offensive against the town.

"The finger of Rome" by which he meant the phalanx, the Greek for finger, "will jab into the heart of the city." He waited a moment until the last call had been completed. "And we will win."

After a moment he bowed his head, noting that most of the men did the same. "Mars, war bringer, has ordained that all men bearing arms against us shall die today" he called as the noise of some of the horses whinnying came from far away to his right. "Men of Rome, show mercy to those who bear no arms, take them as slaves and take their possessions as they will rightly and justly be ours by custom and by the laws of the gods" he called as a great cheer started again.

Marcus waited until silence had fallen.

"You have your orders. Bring victory to your gods and to your families" he called as he held his sword aloft and a throaty cheer of 'victory' came from the ranks of men, their cheering lasting a full five minutes as Marcus looked out over their heads with occasional glances to the woods.

Nodding to Rufus and Potitus, who set off purposefully towards the rear of the army, he stepped from the wooden rostrum and watched as a number of men raced forwards, some with wicker screens and bows, some with wooden boards and planks which would be set across the ditches which the Romans had been attempting to fill since they had asked the Falerians to surrender some hours earlier.

Narcius stepped forwards to join Marcus in the front line of soldiers. "A good speech Camillus" he whispered as Marcus laughed at his friend, seeing the joy of war in his face. "Any news from Mella?" Marcus asked, already considering the plans he had set in place for the attack to his rear that had been spotted that morning.

"Nothing since the last report" Narcius said. Mella had reported that the Falerian force seemed to be heading to Veii rather than to attack Marcus as they had supposed but that a smaller force had been sent against them in an attempt to catch the Roman scouts. Mella also confirmed he had sent a man ahead to the defences at Veii to warn them that a force may be approaching them, but he was remaining to see if they turned back and attempted to make for the men at Faleria. Marcus remained convinced that the Falerians would attempt a double attack and had set plans in place to deal with this should it occur; he hoped Virginius would be equal to the tasks he had set him and glanced nervously in his direction once again at the thought.

Turning back he heard the first calls from the walls of Faleria, men were throwing their slings at the attacking bowmen and other men were rushing to the ditches to fill in the last few feet of their defensive trenches. The clatter of stones on wood and the thrum of archers going about their killing routines began and Marcus grinned. A great cheer came from the walls as two men fell under a hail of arrows and stones, their bodies jerking as they were hit simultaneously from all sides, their small cries of pain were instantly drowned by the crescendo of noise from, firstly, the walls and then cries of 'For Rome' from the deep phalanxes of men standing waiting to attack the city.

****

At last the defensive ditches were filled. It had taken nearly an hour and the Roman's had lost a number of men as they risked their lives under the hail of stones and arrows to fill them and lay as many planks or logs across the detritus inside for the soldiers to clamber across as they could.

Men ran forwards, shields raised above heads, hands holding long ladders for the attack on the walls as another hail of stones clattered onto the broad Roman wood. Marcus remained just out of slingshot and arrow range and watched the men as they danced over the ditches and slammed the ladders against the walls, moving like ants up the ladders, quickly and in single file, as they had been trained to do. Nine ladders lurched with men, each precariously balanced against the parapet and each one filled with shouting men, the Roman lines standing watching, urging them on as their blood started to heat at the chance to run into the city and begin the killing.

Something nagged in Marcus's mind. The number of defenders at the wall had seemed light, Rufus agreeing with his thoughts that morning, and for each man that fell it seemed no new defender sprang to his post. He stared intently at the walls, his eyes searching the attack and his mind considering the lengthy discussions with his officers and the interpretation of Mella's scouting message. Why were the walls not as heavily manned as the Romans expected? He glanced behind at his marching camp, seeing Potitus standing at the gates watching the action in front of him, his steely gaze watching dispassionately, as was his way. Looking back at the city, on the right wall men were falling into the crowd of attackers below, the ladders gaining no purchase as the defenders shot arrows into the melee below and dropped large boulders onto the heads of the climbing men. Marcus frowned. This was going to be a bloody battle, he thought, his mind running along the actions at the wall and looking for any advantage he could glean. But inside he had a nervous feeling. He gripped the wooden Eagle on the cord around his neck anxiously. On the left a Roman gained the walkway, a sudden cheer going up from the front rank as he hacked his sword into three Falerians whose helmeted heads appeared to block his path. Within seconds the man's dead body was ejected over the wall, the lifeless form crushing two men at the base of the ladder he had climbed up only minutes before. His death had bought time for his comrades though and two more were already on the parapet, the men on the ladder to the left of this also suddenly gaining ground as the defenders rushed to support the breach beside them.

"Attack" called Marcus, his sword swinging to the left and calling forward Narcius and his first century of Eagles.

As he ran forwards he was passed by the fitter legionaries, their eyes fixed on the ladder and the brighter men also watching the walls for arrows and stones. Narcius eased past his commander and screamed at the soldiers at the ladder to climb or be killed by his own sword, his angry voice causing a skirmish amongst those holding back from the climb as they forced themselves upwards. Grabbing the first rung Marcus hauled himself up, his shield slung across his left shoulder and his sword gripped tightly in his right hand. He felt the elation of battle overtake him as he pumped his legs to climb the short ladder, his eyes darting left and right as he came to the top of the climb and leapt over the low parapet to land in a pile of thick blood, the floor already slippery from the death that preceded him.

"Here" called the voice of Narcius as he stepped into a lunge and pushed his sword through the chest of a thin, grey haired, Falerian, his bow slung over his shoulders and his long blade hanging uselessly in his hands as his attempt to swing the blade in the small space on the walkway failed him.

Marcus looked behind him, they had the wall along the parapet, the Romans scurrying into the city like a nest of ant's intent on destroying anything in their path. He glanced into the orderly streets below him, empty of life, doors open and roads silent. As Narcius and his men sliced through the small knot of defenders Marcus turned and looked out across the open fields below the walls, the Roman phalanxes cheering the men who had gained access to the city, and behind them the marching camp. He grinned as he saw a flash of movement in the trees and waved to Potitus, his reply the wave of the red cloak they had agreed as the signal.

"Centurion" shouted Marcus as Narcius stood watching the men dart into the city as they had planned, groups of eight men heading into houses intent on searching for hidden soldiers.

"Sir" came the reply as Narcius stepped forwards. "It looks like you were right" he said with a grin, a speck of blood dripping from the side of his face. "These men were nothing but the suicide squad to draw us in. The attack was too easy."

Narcius nodded and returned to calling orders to the men around him.

Marcus turned, his heart calming in his chest after the energy of the climb. He had been unsure whether he was correct, but the dead defenders at the walls were not the choice troops of Faleria that he would have expected. Their old faces, thin arms and cheap armour showing that they were probably the old and sick as he had expected. The report from Mella had said a thousand men were marching towards their rear and Marcus had thought that this number would be more than half the people who lived in this city. The rest were mostly women, children and old men and must have fled when their scouts had warned of the approach of the Roman army.

The sudden clash of swords in the city pulled his attention below him. The last of the walls' defenders were throwing their swords to the floor and kneeling, begging for mercy as the attackers stood over them and looked up to the walls for orders.

"Keep them as prisoners" Marcus said as he waved to Rufus, standing below with his front three phalanxes of Romans. Rufus waved his sword back and turned to the men around him.

"Form up and move" he called as the Centurions saluted and began to re-organise the men, turning their long spears as the Triarii split and moved aside to create a gap in the middle of the Roman army.

Marcus watched the movement, drilled into the men over the past few hours as he had agreed the plan with Rufus in case his fears were correct. He glanced nervously into the city behind him, still silent, almost eerie in the late afternoon sun and sighed deeply. Narcius moved next to Marcus and saw his action and smiled. "Let's hope they attack as you planned" he said as he looked out over the scene below. Rufus's central phalanx had turned and started to march back towards the Roman camp, their spears standing tall as they moved quickly. The two flanking phalanxes were turning more slowly, waiting for the centre to give them space before they fell in behind. Narcius knew that his job was to flush the city and make sure no hidden force remained within its walls. His Eagles were ideally suited to this work, their shorter swords better suited to warfare in tight conditions and high-walled streets.

"There" he said pointing quickly to the tree line directly behind the marching camp as he leant forwards and squinted, his eyes narrow as he leant out over the wall.

"I see it" replied Marcus, his voice cold as he watched Potitus turn and move along the walkway of the fort towards its rear. He held his breath as he watched the trees, his mouth saying words that nobody could hear as he willed the Falerians to appear from the tree line and attack the fort.

****

"Now my lord, they are at the walls. Strike, take the victory and kill these Romans" spat the voice of Mintraxthus' adviser with his thick beard and greedy eyes.

Mintraxthus held his breath. His city had been taken, the Romans easily scaling the walls as he had expected. He cursed his judgement for sending more than half his forces to attack the

Romans at Veii only weeks before this force had been seen approaching the city. Yes he'd had the throat of his augur opened and his blood spilt on the altars across the city, the man had not seen this future and was clearly not beloved of the gods, but was this simply bad luck or was this *Camillus* truly as blessed as many men said? He clenched his teeth and breathed out slowly, his eyes darting across the scene playing out in front of him. One of the Roman scouts had gotten away from his men a day earlier, but they didn't think he had returned to the camp as his observers had seen no-one enter the camp from the trees.

He felt the hot breath of Vixurtus beside him, the adviser trying hard to hold his anger, or was it fear, as he continued to look into the plain before *his* city. The plan was simple, to strike a quick blow at the Roman Camp at the very moment they thought they had beaten Faleria and take all their goods before following the rest of the population to the larger city of Capena. He'd sent all but his three hundred best warriors on the road to their ally, and these men were standing silently in the trees along the roadside behind him. But something was nagging in his gut as the lord of Faleria watched the cursed Romans climb their ladders into his city. Wait. He shifted, lowering his neck as he narrowed his eyes and strained his vision into the distance. There, a flash of blue. He glanced to Vixurtus, his greedy grin showing that he, too, had seen the man climb into the city. Yes, this *Camillus* was not as gifted as they said, he had fallen for the trick, this would be an easy win for him and his chosen men.

"Start the count" he whispered as the man next to him let out a breath as he said "one, two" and continued. Turning to the officer behind him Mintraxthus raised a hand and pointed towards the camp. "On the order, be prepared and may the gods bless your sword arm and your men's bravery" he said as he nodded urgently to the eager face of the soldier. As the man left Mintraxthus heard his adviser reach "eleven" and he stared at the Roman camp. He could just make out the gates of the city from his location and he willed them to open, his heart starting to beat faster in his chest as the tension grew. "Fifteen."

The noise of the Roman advance hit his ears before the dust cloud appeared from the flat land between his city and the Roman camp. Both men glanced at the source of the noise and saw the cloud kicked up by the marching men and grinned, the adviser licking his lips as he turned to his Lord.

"Now my Lord, they march into the city?" asked Vixurtus.

"Now" came the reply.

****

Potitus walked to the rear wall, keeping his head low as he searched the trees behind the fort. The dark forest held only one navigable track upon which an army could march quickly, the smaller tracks through the trees were too narrow with dense undergrowth. The scouts and officers had combed the woods for vantage points, and all had agreed that the only way to attack the camp would be by a direct attack from the main road through the woods. Marcus had spent some time with Rufus and Narcius placing soldiers in small groups in front of the camp and returning to the trees to check the view any attackers would have of the Roman marching columns. Satisfied, he had laid his plans before the officers and all had unanimously agreed. It was risky, but further scouts had seen the Falerian troops marching slowly through the forest towards their rear. Potitus looked back over his shoulder, the men were moving, their preordained marching patterns kicking up the cloud of dust that Marcus said would be needed to fool the Falerians into thinking the march was into the city and not away from it. He grinned. Marcus was clever. At every step he had a plan and a counter movement, and each was discussed and drilled into the officers so that they could not fail but to follow the orders given. The front column of troops were reaching the gates of the city whilst the men in the rear were now turned and facing back towards the camp, their iron-topped spears clearly visible in the sunlight. Was it too early? He whipped his head back to the trees as he heard a sudden clattering noise and the drum of hoof beats as the leaders of the enemy appeared. The first Falerians burst from the trees, teeth clenched and heads low as they ran at the Roman camp, its low palisades seemingly undefended and its gates wide open. Potitus grinned, his eyes moving to the ten feet wide hole in the trees from where the bleached stone and dirt of the road gaped, as he watched he heard the deep-throated screams of men as they charged from the forest and raced the two hundred paces towards the camp. "To arms, close the gates" called Potitus from the walls, waving his arms theatrically as if he had been caught off guard as he looked along the walls of the camp and nodded to the fifty men sitting waiting, all eyes fixed on his.

The noise of archers standing and driving their arrows into the sky filled the air as the Roman defenders rose from their positions on the walls and, without picking targets, lofted their deadly missiles into the air. The arrows hung in the sky as the attackers instantly split apart and raised their shields.

A scream turned his head to the right as a heavily muscled Falerian crashed into one of the pits that Marcus had had the men dig in the dead of night, the sharp stake fixed into the bottom slicing through the man's shin and up out of his knee as his lower body crumpled into the trap. Potitus involuntarily winced as he watched the man, half in the pit and half out, scream as his fellow soldiers simply parted and left him in their wake as he thrashed around like some trapped burrowing animal. Arrows thumped into the ground around the thrashing man as others fell to their lethal tips and more Falerians crunched to the floor into the death pits dug by the Romans. Potitus smiled, maybe that first man was lucky, he thought as he watched him attempting to drag his mangled leg from the hole. A sudden sound turned his attention back to the battle.

Marcus had been clear on timings and as expected Rufus and his men were now only one hundred and fifty paces from the camps front walls, their double time march covering the ground so rapidly that the first Falerians to reach the outer walls saw them and were suddenly caught in two minds, some continued to run for the rear gates, thoughts of glory and plunder swaying their better judgement, others stopped and turned their heads looking urgently for their leaders to tell them what to do. The bulk of the Falerian force had cleared the road from the forest, their leaders, easily noticeable by their deeply coloured garments and high quality armour, were thirty paces from the trees, their horses stamping the ground in their desire to charge into the noise of battle ahead of them. As they stared over the heads of the running men their smiles turned to fear as men began to turn and look towards them, some even starting to run back towards the trees.

"Now" muttered Potitus as he stared away to his left and then to the right. "Come on Virginius" he whispered as the archer to his left glanced to him nervously at his commanders words. Noting the reaction Potitus stood taller and smiled at the man "We'll have them trapped like lambs at the slaughterhouse" he said jovially as the archers laughed, continuing to nock their shafts into their strings and fire into the mass of half standing, half running men below them. His voice betrayed no nerves, but he knew the moment that Virginius should have acted was past – it may be too late for the decisive action to play into the Romans hands he thought. He gritted his teeth and let out a slow breath as his knuckles whitened from his angry balled fists. He knew Marcus would be seething that Virginius had missed the key moment of the battle plan – again!

"Hurrah" came a shout along the walls as the flash of movement from the right tree line dragged his attention back to the dust covered scene in front of him. 'Lose any of my scorpions Virginius, and you will be paying for them yourself' thought Potitus as he watched fifty horses bursting from the trees, each horse carrying two men, one holding the precious three legged devices, the other steering the mount with the arrows held firmly across his lap in front of him. The scorpion holders leapt from the horses and flicked the legs open, planting the machines heavily into the ground, some pressing hard to get the machines fixed in position as their fellows hammered small stakes into the ground and tied the horses reins to them before running forwards and slicing the ropes from bundles of thick shafted arrows, each one four feet long and three inches thick. Within a few minutes the new arrivals had set up the weapons as the Falerians reached the camps rear gate. Twenty men stood shoulder to shoulder in the gateway, the Eagle motif on their shields as they grinned at the first men to arrive. Spears clunked onto the Roman shields as the Falerians, arriving in threes and fours and launched their weapons from ten yards, none doing any damage to the Roman defenders standing two men deep across the narrow doorway. Arrows rained into the front line of the Falerians, men falling as they screamed and launched themselves into the shield wall of the defenders.

Potitus leant over the parapet, his eyes expertly scanning the scene below the walls. The leading men of the Falerian attack started to bunch at the gates, the Eagles struggling to hold the weight of men back as the press of bodies grew behind them. He cursed, if Virginius had been on time the scorpions would have caused confusion and thinned down the attacking men. A sudden pang of fear hit him as he looked behind and out across towards the city, Rufus's heavily armoured men were at least two minutes away, maybe three. He looked at the Falerian leaders, their horses dancing in circles as the scorpions cleaved gaping holes in the men around them, the thudding sounds of their launch followed swiftly by deep red spray and guttural screams as men fell to the relentless hail of death. Falerians raced into the trees, others ran to their leaders and were pleading for instructions, the scene was one of terror and mayhem, and Potitus smiled, but he knew the men at the gates were unaware of any of the actions behind them and would soon overwhelm the soldiers bravely holding the gates. There was nothing for it, he had to commit more men to the gates and with a flourish of his own sword he called to the closest archers to follow him down the steep steps to the gate.

****

Marcus watched from the walls of Faleria as the movements below him played out. In the city captives were huddled together, bound by thick ropes and circled by a ring of spears as the Romans continued to scour the city. On the field the first movements had worked to perfection, the outer phalanxes circling as they created the dust cloud which would hide their movements before moving back to the camp, before the remaining men split, half towards the city, the other half to remain in a thin line across the battle field as a support should they be required. The movement, noise, smells and screams of the battle made Marcus feel truly alive. He mumbled a prayer to Mater Matuta and Fortuna, thanking the goddesses for guiding his plans and giving him strong leaders. As he spoke the men around him nodded and mumbled their own words. Marcus silently pledged three goats to the deities for their support and help, his mind going over the words as he considered what bargains he would have to use in the future. The Roman gods were fickle. They watched over their favourites but were as easily swayed to let them die as to raise them to glory, and each man bought greater and greater favours with the gods as his virtus rose in society. Each man had to bargain with the gods, not knowing if their offers and prayers would be listened to until the gods allowed their actions to be a success. Marcus touched the Eagle that hung around his neck as a reminder of the words he had heard all those years ago. He had bargained with his gods, he had given them great sacrifices and he had asked their favour, but he still felt the cold fear that one day they would turn their backs on him. His thoughts grew darker as he watched the camp, his heartbeat quickening as the Falerians appeared and rushed at the wooden palisades, Rufus and his men moving into a double time run to close the gap to the camp as quickly as they could. Dust and noise filled the air. Marcus glanced away to the right, where was Virginius? He felt himself gripping the tuff wall of Faleria, the white-grey stone brittle but strong as his nails scratched along the surface. Where was he? He cursed for giving the man his chance

and shook his head angrily. Wait. There, at last, the horses appeared. Rufus was closing the

gap, excellent. Falerians breached the trees as they scampered back into the woods but the

main body of the attack seemed close to the gates. Marcus suddenly felt worried for his friend

Potitus, had he made an error and left enough men to hold that gate? He rubbed his face,

pinching the bridge of his nose as he let out a deep, heavy, breath.

"Sir"

Marcus, startled by the sudden words, turned to see Narcius appear ten yards away, his face

stern but calm.

"Yes Centurion"

"The city is empty of everyone except a few stubborn old men and a few dogs. It seems the

Falerians have fled" he said with a shake of his head and a glum expression.

"Hmm" replied Marcus, his thoughts more concerned with Potitus' situation than the city,

which he had already guessed was empty. "Food, water, stores, and goods?" he asked as he

saw Potitus move from the walls and start to run back into the fort.

"Some, sir, but not much" came the reply as Narcius came and stood next to his Tribune.

"Problem?" he asked softly, noticing the concerned look on Marcus' face.

"I'm not sure" came the half whispered reply as Marcus was clearly thinking.

Narcius watched and waited for his commander to speak again. The noise from the camp was

growing as men screamed and cheered. From this position neither man could clearly make

out the activities at the walls and Narcius understood why Marcus seemed suddenly sullen.

He'd noticed a change in his commander since he had been made Military Tribune. He

seemed to weigh the burden of the leadership more heavily than he had done before when he

was an adviser and a leader of small attacks. Leading thousands of men and the elite of

Rome's patricians was no easy task. Men like Virginius, Rufus, Caelio and even Potitus could easily make mistakes despite Marcus' detailed and constantly drilled instructions, and every mistake would fall on Marcus' shoulders to burden. Any loss would blemish his military record, not those of his junior officers. He glanced at the face of the Tribune, his eyes continually scanning the field and his mind working through what would happen next. "Potitus is a good commander" Narcius replied slowly. "They will prevail" he said as he saluted and headed back into the city to continue to oversee the garrisoning of the gates. "I hope so" Marcus replied.

****

The line of men had been reduced to fifteen soldiers, the dead still being stood on by their comrades as there was no time to drag them out of the way. Spears were thrust through the lines, men darting left and right to avoid the deadly strikes. The rear line was now inside the gates, the front line slipping backwards under the press of Falerians.

"Engage" called Potitus as he slipped between two of the Eagles and hefted his short round shield into the face of a Falerian, who, seeing the sudden gap appear, had stepped forwards to press his advantage. Before Potitus could move his long sword to follow up on his lunge with his shield the soldier to his left thrust his shorter, stabbing, sword into the face of the shouting attacker. The sword crunched into the man's teeth, shattering the upper jaw as his shriek died in his throat and the man fell instantly, dragging the sword of the Roman towards the floor with the speed of his body's sudden fall. Expertly the soldier regained his feet and had closed next to Potitus before the officer had even had a chance to raise and blood his elaborate, highly polished, weapon. Without another word the soldier called "Step" and every man in the front line edged forwards.

"Get those bodies out of the way" yelled Potitus as he was barged from the front and his foot slipped on the slick of blood across a dead man's armour. The archers, not experts with their swords had filled in the gaps but two were already down, one clutching at his throat as a stream of red leaked from a slice across his neck his bulging eyes telling the words his voice could not. Expertly the Eagle to his left thumped his chest with his right elbow and the man fell backwards, out of the way of his sword arm as the archers' elbows were restricting his movements. Potitus had never fought like this, parrying, clawing, gripping his sword and stabbing forwards, not able to swing and bring the weight of the blade into action against the enemy in front of him. His arm tired almost instantly, the muscles tensing and tightening as his movements were constrained. His breathing became rapid and short as he lunged into an attack, his shoulder smashing into the shield of the man to his right who swore indignantly as a spear shaved his helmet, the rasping sound followed by a grunt as the Roman thrust his sword into the armpit of the Falerian, shrieks of pain echoing from the square roofed doorway.

As Potitus edged forward at the command from the soldier to his left there was a palpable easing of the force of pressure in front of him, a sudden lessening of the weight of men shoving against them and then brightness appeared as gaps in the press of soldiers became spaces as the Falerians turned to run. Elated Potitus roared at the fleeing enemy and raised his sword, slipping on the corpse of a brown clad soldier as he tried to take a running step forwards before being yanked back by the scruff of his neck by the soldier to his right. Twisting angrily to stare into the eyes of the man, he growled "What...?" before the soldier shook his head with a grin and simply said "Sir, your orders were to stay here at the gate and not to give chase. That is someone else's job." He finished with a wink to his officer before returning his stare out to the front and a letting out a deep breath from his grinning mouth.

*

*

Chapter 6

"How many dead" Marcus asked, his face cold as his senior officers stood around the room he had made his head quarters within the city. It had only been an hour since the Falerians had turned and fled, leaving over half of their number dead or captured in the field. The men had laughed and joked as they arrived at the briefing and soon came to telling tales of their own valour in the attacks, but Marcus had remained silent.

His voice stopped the quiet conversations in their tracks as heads turned to him and men stiffened. He was sat behind a thick oak table, a platter of meat and figs laid out in front of him, with several cups and an ornate black vase, probably Greek by the look of the mythical beasts on the glaze, next to them. The men edged towards seats, some of the more politically astute already grabbing the seats directly opposite Marcus so that they fell into his eye line. Marcus turned his head to Narcius as he was handed a series of tablets depicting the dead or injured from each century.

"No more than sixty, sir" came the Centurions reply.

Marcus nodded, his appreciation clear in his eyes. "A good result" he commented as he glanced around the faces in the room. "Has anyone found Quintus yet?" he asked sombrely with a shake of his head. Quintus Fabius had last been seen chasing Falerians into the woods, his sword swinging into the back of several as he screamed in rage at the fleeing enemy soldiers.

"Not yet" came the reply.

Marcus smiled as he looked up. "I am sure he is well" he said "though he may run a few miles before he realises nobody is with him" he added with a small shake of his head. Fabius was a favourite with many of the men, his friendly demeanour and rich *old* family making him easy to get along with as well as being a man to be close to if you wanted a good political career. A short rumble of laughter went around the room.

"A job well done men" Marcus said as the heads of his officers nodded to him. "I will read your reports and recommendations for promotions and phalera before the night is out" he added as he patted several wax tablets to his left. "But, as some of you will know" he glanced to Rufus "we are not done yet" he said as a few of the officers cocked their heads in interest at his words. "Our task is to stop Faleria and Capena from being the needle that pricks our side at Veii" he said. "Tomorrow at sunlight we march for Capena."

Some of the officers glanced to one another, others grinned and nodded their heads, Marcus committed each action to memory as he watched the men, the cleverer, more stoically trained, simply looking at him with an expressionless look on their faces.

"Narcius will hold the rear" he handed a wax tablet from a pile on his right to the Centurion. "Caelio" he said, looking up at the small faced man "you have the watch tonight and will follow with Narcius in the morning." Caelio nodded.

"Fuscus, Fasculus" you will lead the main body out at dawn" he handed two more tablets across. Glancing at the decreasing pile of tablets he looked to Potitus with a warm smile "you have the camp and the scouts, my friend" he added to a few nods from the men. "I want the reports from the scouts following the Falerian leaders relayed to me as soon as they arrive" he said with a nod.

"Virginius" he looked up for the handsome face of the officer, whose features remained a picture of calm. "Eques" he stated, the patrician beaming as he saw this as a vindication of his actions in the battle and took the orders from the outstretched hand of his Tribune with a curt nod. Marcus noted the smile and inflation in the man's chest and smiled inwardly. Giving the man a promotion might make it easier to palm him off on another Tribune later in the season. This had actually been Potitus' idea and Marcus reminded himself that he must pay more attention to asking advice from his junior officers. Marcus was all for giving the man a dressing down and blaming him for the loss of several of his soldiers, something about which Narcius was livid. Virginius had been lucky that the Falerians had concentrated their efforts on the gates and not wheeled to attack and overwhelm the scorpions, which Marcus knew *he* would have done. He nodded to the officer, who nodded a warm response. How he wished he had Scipio running his Eques, Marcus thought as he smiled to Virginius as the man snapped his order shut and saluted theatrically.

After handing out the orders he spoke again. "Have we collected all we can from the city?" asked Marcus with a half turn to Narcius.

"Yes sir. The Falerians have stripped the city, It seems they took everything of value before they left." He sighed before continuing. "The prisoners said that half their army is at Veii and the rest of the population has moved to Capena where they have been granted safety by the National Council of Etruria. They left the city in three groups over the past week with escorts from the Capenates."

Marcus took a moment to answer, his eyes narrowing as his thoughts ran through his head, counter thoughts fighting rational ones as he grappled with his next move. Looking up he caught the eyes of his senior soldiers, each one raising eyebrows as his eyes caught theirs and he grinned. "Then Capena will be doubly laden" he stated with a smile as a few of the men caught his meaning and grinned back before the slower officers caught up and started to mumble agreement with their laughter.

****

"I cannot sanction any more" said the urgent voice, his eyes wide and fearful. "If the Senate find out I will be hung from the walls" he added as he stared at the greasy hands of his *guest*. A silence fell into the room as the Senator lay back on his couch and took a deep breath, ruing the day he had agreed to this scheme. Yes it had been successful and he had pocketed a great deal of silver, but it was starting to get dangerous as the Senate clamoured for an end to the war, some even calling for peace terms to be agreed with Veii.

Wiping his hands to remove the chicken fat the guest nodded his head, his dark eyes and deeply ridged forehead frowning as he did so. The Senator knew he was working through ideas and options and decided to play the stoic, keeping his face and body movements to the absolute minimum as he sat and drank from a beautifully crafted wooden cup, the grapes and leaves standing proud from the surface as he raised it to his lips.

"The King" the man said as he cocked his head to one side and turned his eyes to the Senator "has ordered me to offer you three pounds of bronze for a thousand arrows and two pounds of bronze for each thousand weighted stones" he said with his eyes narrowing.

The Senator caught the movement in his eyes and tightened his jaw as he considered the increased rate for the weapons which he had been smuggling into the city. The stones were easy, he had his gangs of slaves scouring the fields to pick the best missiles. The arrows were more difficult as their production had already caused him to silence two local officials and the net around him seemed to be closing as his political enemies continued to spy on his every move. The wood alone was costing him almost his entire fee, but three pounds of bronze per thousand was a good rate and he licked his lips at the thought before he twisted his body back towards the *guest*. He contemplated the man, knowing that he was skimming off a decent profit himself and wondering where his gambit should be.

"Agreed on the stones" he said, putting his hand up as the *guest* raised his eyebrows and was about to speak. Shaking his head and dropping his chin, whilst staring back at the Etruscan, he added, "the arrows are too difficult. It has cost me a lot of money to silence local officials." He looked up and nodded "Four" he stated with a set jaw and a determined look.

"Four?" spluttered the man, his dark pupils suddenly alone in a sea of white as his stare widened at the Senator and his mouth gaped. "Four?" he said again, shaking his head. "No, no Senator, I cannot agree four. The King" he continued shaking his head "he cannot afford such costs."

"The Alliance can" replied the Senator with no emotion in his voice. "Each day they sit back and watch the Veientines in their city. They send raiders to attack the Roman lines, but they avoid any major losses. As you know Camillus has been sent to attack Faleria and for all we know he has sacked the town" he said as a scowl came across the guests face. "If he has, then the alliance will want Veii to win and they will pay for supplies."

The guest swallowed loudly as the Senator watched his eyes narrow and his face grow stern as he considered the counter offer.

"Camillus is indeed lucky"

"Camillus is one of those fellows upon whom the gods smile with military intelligence and luck in equal measure" replied the Senator, knowing that he had his man as his features screwed into a grimace.

"Four then!" he said with a look of anger as he held out his hand. Gripping it the Senator smiled.

"In seven days I will have ten thousand arrows delivered to the usual place." The guest marvelled at the words as he calculated the profit he would make from this transaction and a broad grin slowly crept across his face.

****

"The winter comes and once again our men will freeze in their huts, deprived of their liberty and starved of the love of their families" called the plebeian councillor, his wide eyes protruding from his face. "Each year their land goes un-worked and their women are left to be raped by bandits and thieves" he added as he shook his head, a series of calls of agreement coming from the hundred or so men standing listening to him in the forum.

"What can we do Apuleius?" called a voice, a deep scar across the man's left arm as he raised a fist in the air. "The Senate have decided, the Tribunes have agreed with them" he called, his face a mask of anger.

"Vote for me as Tribune, Virgillus. Vote for me and I will champion your cause, taking the true word of the plebeians to the Senate, not the soft over-fed words of the Tribunes this year. What have they given you? What have they done for you?" he called as the noise grew around him and the crowd cheered his name.

As he waved his arms for silence two men wandered away from the back of the crowd, the taller man taking the hood from his head as he stepped around a beggar who was pleading for alms, his blind eyes staring pitifully into the distance as people avoided his stench.

"What do you think?" Manlius asked quietly as the two men walked slowly through the crowds, the market stalls crammed with colourful vegetables, flowers and exotic herbs, the smell sweet in the air.

"Apuleius is whipping up a storm" came the cold response from his right as Gatto tightened his lips and stared ahead. "Like as not he will come to a sticky end if he pushes too hard" he added in a matter-of-fact tone which brought a short laugh to Manlius' lips.

"Maybe" came the reply. "I wander if the Senate are truly concerned about his words" he added slowly as he looked to Gatto with wide eyes.

"Javenoli has not mentioned him."

"Maybe they think his cause is too weak?"

Gatto's face creased as he considered the thought. "No. I think they have bigger things to deal with than a few men in the forum going over old ground."

Manlius thought about this for a few moments as they walked past the old stone lion, Gatto instinctively rubbing its paw as he passed by. "I think it is time I met with Apuleius, my friend" he said with a wicked smile which raised Gatto's eyebrows. "Yes, I think we might have some common ground to explore" he added as he winked at Gatto, who shook his head as the two men carried on into the dim streets of Rome.

****

"Scipio" said Priscus, his eyes roving the tent as he looked up into the faces of his senior officers. Finding him he smiled. "How is the lake today?" he asked.

"No change, sir. Seems like the water has stopped rising" he smiled in response.

"Good, good" came the reply as Priscus gripped a report and stretched his neck to see if all of his officers had arrived.

"As you know" he started, standing and looking at the report in his hand "Camillus has taken Faleria and has marched on Capena. A job well done" he stated as men nodded and agreed with him. "I suspect that the Veientines will soon know about this and try to send an envoy back to support the city." He looked at the tired faces of the men. "I know it's difficult and the men are in sour moods, but we must double the guard each night and block any attempt the enemy make to escape the city." He continued, ignoring the grumbles that came from the plebeian officers in his ranks; "The success of our siege includes neutralising support attacks from Faleria and Capena. With Camillus's force stopping that flow the men will have an easier winter. Think on it gentlemen as you detail your sentries." He looked at the tired faces of two of his more senior officers, their hollow eyes showing the hardships they had endured in three years of constant watch over Veii. "Remind your men that the gods favour the people of Rome and that we will destroy Veii" he said, the belief not quite ringing in his words as he wished them to do. "To your duties gentlemen" he said as he sat back in his chair and a series of salutes went around the tent before the men shuffled out.

As the silence fell Priscus looked up to see Scipio standing in front of the table, his hands behind his back and his stare fixed somewhere above his commander's position.

Laughing Priscus sat back and looked at his junior officer. "What is it Cornelius?" he said warmly as Scipio motioned to the chair and moved to sit on it at Priscus' nod.

"I've never seen the men so disillusioned" he started. "Yes they do their drills, dig ditches and mend the defences, but..." he shook his head and looking warily at Priscus "there is danger in them" he said guardedly. Priscus looked up at these words, a question forming on his face as Scipio nodded and took a deep breath.

"There is talk of another ill omen" he added with a heavy sigh. "It seems that the men have seen a wolf entering the camp at night, some say it's a large black beast, others pure white, so I hold no heed to the story. But it's gone around the camp like wildfire and everyone is convinced of some impending disaster to come" he finished shaking his head.

"Idle hands and idle minds" came the reply as Priscus gritted his teeth. "Gods I wish this war was over" he said, stooping to pick up a jar from a small table behind him and grasping two of the small cups in front of him.

"We need a good fight to sort this scaremongering" he said as he filled the cups.

"Maybe we will get one now if the Capenates try and leave the city to return to Capena?" replied Scipio, taking a cup and nodding his thanks.

"I hope so" replied the drinking Priscus. As he gulped down the last drops from his cup he smiled back at Scipio. "If you were them what would you do?" he asked.

Taking a moment to think Scipio narrowed his eyes. "Probably attack the rampart with horse and then sneak the men out via the fort at the river" he said as a smile came to his face. Priscus took a small pouch from under the table and opened up the vellum map inside. Searching the map he traced the river and said "here?"

"Yes, there, but" Scipio's eyes roved the drawn scene. "I'd feint here first" he added as his finger lingered over a point much closer to the Roman camp. Priscus nodded and glanced along the etched line of defences on the vellum.

"I would too" he said as he handed a small wax tablet to Scipio. "I've drawn the order for you to have a thousand men and dig pits in that area and cover any escape, are you up for it soldier?" he asked grinning.

"Yes, sir" replied Scipio as he grinned back and nodded his approval.

*

*

Chapter 7

It had taken two days of forced marching to travel to the foothills surrounding Capena. Marcus had ordered the baggage and carts to follow behind and had left Virginius in charge with his Eques and a hundred foot soldiers. In this way he hoped he could gain ground on the Capenates before they had much time to secure their city, expecting him to take four or five days to travel the distance from Faleria. As the dust cloud became visible to the city envoys had been seen by his scouts as they dashed in each direction to call for reinforcements or to call local tribes and clansmen into the city to bolster its defence. Marcus had sent men ahead to scout the land and create the maps which would help him in his battle plans, though he fully expected to assault the walls as soon as he could, and had already agreed this with his senior officers.

The last few miles had seen an increase in scouts and small groups of Capenates on the road watching as the Romans moved into position, the dust cloud rising hundreds of feet into the air in great grey plumes.

Another messenger appeared bringing the news that the baggage carts were within a day's ride and unhampered by any enemy. Marcus nodded his thanks as he sat back on his horse and looked over the heads of the marching men, their faces grey and dust-covered as they marched purposefully along the old road, the brown cart tracks interspersed with shots of green grass just visible under the feet of the soldiers. Salutes were called as the men passed, and Marcus made a point of saluting each man and calling to those he knew by name to tell them that riches lay just ahead, the cheers that greeted these words making the men seem to step faster into the distance.

"You should have stayed with the carts" Marcus said as he glanced to his left at the hollow cheeks of his old sword master.

"And miss this?" Mella replied as he waved a hand at the men striding past.

Marcus laughed before looking at the determined face of his old friend. "I had a bet with Rufus that you would be back" he said as Mella started and looked aghast at his commander.

"No!" he exclaimed. "You never take a bet" he said with a grin.

"It was my hope that you were alive my friend" he said, his voice sounding weary as Mella closed his mouth and looked into the face of the man he had known since he was a boy.

"It will take more than a few scouts to kill me off" he laughed, noting the tired eyes of his officer.

"The next few days will be even more dangerous. We *must* take Capena, our war with Veii depends on it" Marcus said, his voice intense and strong as a sudden determination came into it.

Mella nodded. "You're right" he replied. "As you have said, the Capenates weakness is the number of people they have taken into their city. With so many civilians they will struggle to defend in an organised manner. Attacking the walls quickly will throw them off their guard and panic the people." Mella remembered the words Marcus had used the previous night as he had laid his plans before the officers, the strength of conviction, the cold-hearted call for all men bearing arms to be slaughtered and women and children to be taken as slaves. In all of this Mella saw a new strength in his old friend, a strength which leant itself to the war machine that was under his command. Yet here was also a frailty, a measure of the younger man who had been inspired by the writings of the Greeks and the stories of great battles. Here was the boy he had known. He smiled to himself as he watched Marcus call to a legionary who had saluted him as he strode past.

"Is Quintus Fabius truly the right man to lead the first attack?" Mella asked hesitantly.

Marcus considered for a moment, his decision had not been questioned the previous night and as such he had not offered any reason. Nodding, he turned to Mella. "In every short skirmish and in each fight we have had Fabius is the first man into battle and the last out. He has a brute force about him which I am hoping will encourage the men as they follow *us* to the walls" he said, his eyes suddenly gleaming as he looked away into the distance.

Us Mella caught the words and whirled to Marcus. "No, Marcus, you cannot storm the walls, your role is in the rear with the older families and patricians" he blurted, his voice quiet as his eyes glanced to his officer and then back to the smiling rows of men passing by them. "You cannot place yourself in such danger" he whispered.

Marcus seemed to ignore the words as the exasperated Mella wriggled on his horse, his confusion causing the beast to stamp its feet and skitter to the side.

"Sit still man" Marcus said, his eyes remaining on the marching column. "It is my destiny to destroy the enemies of Rome." He glanced to Mella and his eyes softened at the incredulous look on his face. "Think, Mella, how the words of the prophecy were spoken. In battle I will take the Eagle and conquer all our foes. If this is true" he glanced to the skies as he said the words "then my place is amongst the soldiers, not sitting on a horse with the Triarii watching as men gain glory." His eyes became distant as he spoke and Mella saw the determination return to his face once more. "The time has come for me to fulfil the words of Mater Matuta, Fortuna and Mars the war bringer. In this way will I create the Rome that will be the master of all we see before us and strengthen the rights of the men who fight for her. It is time for the

Republic to take control its own destiny and for me to act my part in her glory, as the words of the prophecy say" he said.

Mella sat dumbstruck at the words. It was the first time he had heard Marcus talk of the prophecy for some years and the first time he had seen the glint in the eye of his friend which seemed to light when he fought in battles. His heart beat faster in his chest as he glanced at Marcus and saw the face of a man who truly believed that the gods were watching over his destiny.

"But to lead the men against the walls? It is suicide" he stated.

"Rather it is a chance for the men to see that patricians are prepared to stand alongside them in the front line, Mella. To show that patrician and plebeian alike stand for Rome, not standing in separate lines with leaders shouting at the men to die while the rich stand behind and wait for the battle to run its course before acting. How many times have you said this to me, my friend" he asked with a smile.

"That's different" Mella replied haughtily.

Marcus laughed and reeled his horse around to come alongside Mella. He placed a hand on Mella's arm and grinned. "We will know if I am right within a day" he said as he set off at a trot back to the front of the army.

****

A spear thudded into the ground as Marcus finished offering the surrender terms to the leaders of the city, their highly coloured robes staring down at him from the battlements of the city.

"I take that as their answer then" Quintus Fabius said with a grin.

"It would seem so" Marcus replied, his eyes wandering along the walls at the faces of the men standing staring down at him.

"Tell me what you see there, Quintus?" Marcus asked.

"Where, Camillus?" Fabius answered as he moved his head along the walls. "What have I missed?" he asked as he shook his head and looked to his commander.

"Fear" came the cold reply

Fabius looked at his commander and then back to the men on the walls, some spitting and some cursing the Romans, other throwing stones which would never reach where they stood. Yes, he thought, there it was, a fear was clouded along the walls. He could see it in the eyes of the leaders, surprised by the speed of the Roman march on their city and by the confidence of Rome's commander. He grinned back at Marcus."Pallor" he mumbled. *Terror* was etched in every one of the noble's faces.

"Fetch the Augur and my set of robes" Marcus suddenly said as he turned to his Optio and waved to him "and make it quick" he snapped as the man raced away.

Fabius smiled, he knew exactly what Marcus was thinking and he approved. Fear was a great weapon.

****

A half an hour later Marcus finished the invocation to the gods in front of his men, arrayed in three great lines directly facing the gates of Capena. The city sat on the plateau of a hill called locally, La Cavitucola, and Marcus had invoked the spirits of the hill to join Rome in its fight against the Capenates who had, he said, turned against them by raiding Roman lands. The Capenates had wailed as he spoke, the cries of women coming over the walls as many of the townsfolk had flocked to the walls at the bells and calls to the gods from the attacking Romans. Marcus has guessed that this would happen as the town was bursting to the seams with common folk, probably outnumbering the soldiers in the town. He had played on the words he had used with his own soldiers; that those who bore no arms would not be slaughtered, but would be taken as slaves. He had also invoked Juno as the mother of all lands, and the chosen deity of Veii, to support his actions, actions he clearly claimed were right and just as the Etruscan alliance had broken its treaty with Rome, its neighbour.

As he turned and smiled to his officers he nodded at the noise from the city, cries of women were being shouted down by deep throated Centurions and the fear in the eyes of the Nobles on the wall had turned to anger. Marcus had gambled that they would not launch an attack on his small group during the ceremony, but he had also prepared for just such an eventuality, though he didn't call on his reserves.

Throwing his white priests robe to his Optio he grinned at Fabius. "Ready?" he asked.

"Oh yes" came the reply as Fabius hefted his long sword, the metal shining from the oil he had loving prepared it with over the last hour.

Turning to the officers Marcus raised his voice. "For Rome we will take this city" he called. "For Rome and its Republic we will smite the enemy" his head turned to the walls of Capena. "For Rome, for Mater Matuta, For Mars and Fortuna we will make these dogs pay for the death of our brothers, our fathers and our friends" he called more loudly as a great cheer went up from the deep ranks of the Roman army.

"You have your orders" he stated as he turned, hearing the words of the officers as they also turned and jogged to their positions, Rufus taking the lead role in the Triarii that Marcus should have taken. He had prepared the leaders of the attack with his proposals, counter strike thoughts and suggestions for retreat should the need come, but now he turned and took a deep breath, his heart starting to hammer in his chest as he nodded to Fabius and stepped forwards. Fabius, unable to contain himself, screamed "Forward" as several details of wicker screens and ladders charged at the walls, arrows flying in both directions as the men ran into a hail of stones and iron-tipped death that suddenly sprang from the defending walls.

It took moments for Marcus to see that the forces at the wall were still struggling to remove the townsfolk who had come to stand and watch. As he stood he looked across to Narcius, who was waiting with a few hundred of the best trained Eagles, and pointed. "Look" he said. "There, they haven't cleared the walls. They aren't ready for us. Press the advantage" he said as he looked to the gleaming eyes of Fabius whose face turned to one of anger as he turned and screamed "attack!" and charged, alone for a few steps before the men could react to his call, at the walls.

The vantage point was a rear gate, small but wide enough for three men to pass through it if it was taken. Marcus remembered the map of the city. The gate led to a long roadway to the city square but, from memory, there was only one other alleyway beyond the gate, a good back entrance, he thought, though he also remembered that the walls of the store houses inside were high at this point and may prove troublesome.

Narcius clapped Marcus on the shoulder and screamed "For Rome" as he and his men ran forward, in a more measured fashion, towards the twenty feet of grey stones that kept the population of Capena safe. Marcus fell into the second line and trotted along, his lungs instantly gasping as he suddenly felt the weight of his armour as he ran. An arrow thumped into his shield, the dull thud of others hitting Roman wood also came to his ears as his eyes stared at the walls. Ahead the first details were scurrying up the ladders, men falling as others shoved past the dying men who were fighting above them. At fifty yards Marcus was aware of cheering to his left, and incredulously he watched as Quintus Fabius stormed onto the parapet, his sword whirling in a blur of red as several defenders attempted to hack him down. Narcius had already sent several Eagles racing to the ladder before Marcus could give the order and he smiled at the soldier's efficiency before cheering for Fabius as the men did. The ladder came before he realised, the soldiers pushing and shoving to get into a line, shields held above their heads, although the crash of stones or arrows was suddenly quiet. More cheering came from the left, and then from the right as Marcus gripped the rung and forced himself upward, two places behind Narcius, men calling to him to speed up as he climbed. Landing on the wooden boards over the walls Marcus was immediately pelted with stones from the defenders, one cracking into his shoulder, the thick leather no defence against the power of the throw. His shoulder went numb momentarily as his fingers suddenly struggled to hold his sword. He swore as he gripped the leather of the handle and gritted his teeth.

"Here" called Narcius, his men lining up a wall of shields with their backs to the walls. Marcus peered over his shield to get his bearings as more soldiers rushed over the wall. It had only been a matter of ten minutes at the most and the Romans had already gained the wall, the people inside the city were screaming and running manically, soldiers battering women who were gripping them and calling for them to save their lives as Roman archers now appeared on the walls and started to rain arrows into the city.

"Now" cried Marcus as he sensed the opportunity to strike had come. Narcius led the charge as the floorboards creaked and groaned under their feet, the men at the front tripping and being dragged to their feet by the men behind.

"Steady" called Narcius as he butted a defender with his shield boss, the man falling back into the stairway below him before landing on the thick grass bank inside the city. Some of the Romans had leapt from the parapet in their urgency to get into the city, one or two falling immediately to the quick thinking defenders, others landing heavily and screaming as their legs bent or buckled under them. One or two lucky ones jumped to their feet and ran at the defenders holding the base of the stairs.

A trumpet called Marcus' attention to the road which led to the town square, immediately in front of the gates, and the noise of hundreds of feet came clattering along the wide roadway towards the Roman attack. Jumping the last few steps Marcus realised that Narcius and his hundred or so Eagles would soon be overwhelmed by the defenders unless they got to the gate first and opened it.

"Narcius, the gate" he called urgently as his officer snapped his head around and searched out the location.

"I will take the roadway, we can hold it for a few minutes but you must get the gates open" screamed Marcus above the noise of fighting.

"First cohort, with me" called Narcius as he screamed at three approaching Capenates and launched himself into a run, followed by a blur of blue clad soldiers.

"On me" called Marcus as he stepped forwards and launched himself into the remaining defenders who were backing away from the walls. "We must hold that road" he called to the men around him as he slashed at a spear that was thrust into his face by a dark skinned defender, his eyes blazing with hatred and his muscled arms bulging from years of working the soil. The spear slipped past his head as Marcus ducked and rammed his sword up into the man's ribs with a crunch, pushing his shoulder into his face as the man screamed and fell as Marcus rushed past him towards the roadway.

The defenders were running, their leaders calling them into defensive positions as the noise of the main army came from the road ahead of Marcus and his rushing men. A young defender, his face not yet shaving, ran at the Romans and launched an overhead slice with a long iron sword, his scream high-pitched yet strong. Marcus didn't change his stride as he moved his body to the right and smashed his shield edge into the boy's thigh before the sword edge had even begun its downward swing. The bone snapped with a thick crack as the youth crashed forwards under the weight of his body movement. Marcus didn't have time to consider the age of the youth as he snapped his sword into the throat of the boy, his scream dying as his eyes suddenly filled with tears and he collapsed into the dust as Marcus ran on.

The road was eight or nine men wide and already several defenders were lined up, their nervous faces glancing to each other and then behind at the approaching mass of spears from the town square. "Kill them" Marcus called as he slashed into the shield of the closest man, his back pushed against the wall of a house as he stepped backwards to avoid the attack. The thump of an arrow caught Marcus unaware as he felt the man next to him twist and fall. Glancing upwards he saw three men knocking arrows from the roof of one of the buildings. "Bastards" he spat as he flung his sword up to counter the attack of the grinning Capenate who used the wall as a lever and threw his whole body behind the heavy sword he carried. The sword smashed into the metal boss of Marcus' shield as a quick thinking legionary to his right stepped inside the attack and punched his sword with lightning speed into the chest of the olive skinned defender, the metal heartsaver buckling under the ferocity of the strike. The man fell to his knees as the Roman pulled at his sword as it grated on the heartsaver and stuck as his body buckled forwards. Marcus skipped sideways to push the legionary under his shield as a defender struck with his spear, the length of the shaft being the only thing that saved the legionary as it was slow to move in the cramped space. Kneeling the legionary retrieved his sword and stood to nod thanks to his Tribune as he slid back into the line. A flash by his side made Marcus twitch involuntarily as an arrow sliced past his ear embedding itself in the shield behind him. A quick look showed that one of the men on the roof had been taken by Roman arrows and the others were firing indiscriminately into the Roman soldiers. Knowing that there was nothing he could do Marcus turned his attention to the mass of spear men coming towards him.

"Is the gate open" he called behind him.

A few seconds later the reply came. "Nearly."

"Then we have no time to lose men, get this road set for defence" he called, stepping into a lunge as a tall defender, his eyes wide with fear jumped back from his attack and knocked into the two men beside him. At the sudden movement all three men momentarily turned to look at each other before they threw their spears and shields at the Romans and turned to flee back down the road.

Ignoring the cheering of the Romans Marcus looked left and right. The road was wide enough to defend with no obvious weakness or steps which could give the Capenates an advantage. "Felix" he said to the man away to the right, the soldier nodding at his name. "That house" Marcus pointed "check the doors, I don't want a way through to our rear" he called as the soldier tapped two men and raced forwards to bash into the door ahead of them. The trumpet call came again as Marcus heard the first of the Capenate spearmen start to yell from thirty yards ahead of him. A sudden blur crossed his vision as a man fell from the roof, an arrow through his throat as he clutched at it as he wriggled in the air before crashing into the stone. *Good* thought Marcus, glancing up at the roof and smiling.

Felix came thundering out of the house, his sword slick with blood and a handful of jewellery being stuffed into his tunic as he grinned at his men as they came rushing out behind him, one chewing a thick leg of pork as the other simply shook his head and laughed before they returned to the line.

"No other way out, Camillus, sir" Felix grinned.

"Good. Take the right edge Felix and hold that line." Marcus looked back over his shoulder. He had no more than thirty five maybe forty men to hold this road. "Four lines" he called, the men instantly moving into order as a crash and some swearing came from behind them.

"What the..." Marcus said as he turned to see the short, stocky, form of Quintus Fabius grinning at him as he shoved his way through the line.

"Reporting for duty" smiled the manic eyes of the officer, the men around him grinning as the blood covered man stepped to the front line.

Marcus shook his head. "Second line Fabius. That's an order" he said as Fabius glowered at him. "There's no place for that long sword here" he said as a way of explanation as a soldier with an Eagle burnt into the leather of his chest guard smiled but roughly pushed the patrician back into the second line, the soldiers there welcoming him with words of encouragement which took away any anger he may have been feeling.

"We hold this line" Marcus called "until the rest of the men arrive" he added as the throaty screams from the defenders came from the spear wall ahead of them.

The spears clattered into the Roman shields, the jabbing and thrusting incessant as the Romans struggled to deal with the weight of the pushing Capenates. Marcus was sure that the weight of the lines of soldiers would be a disadvantage in the narrow roads of the city, but the Capenate leader was clearly an able soldier as he held the lines back and reset the attacks in short waves, allowing room for the soldiers at the front to do their work effectively. The grunting of men became louder as the razor sharp spear tips slashed through the air, catching arms, thighs and shoulders as they came in pairs or threes, the men drilled well in their attacks.

Marcus ducked an attack, blocking with his shield and thrusting the short sword into the underarm of the attacker, the tip of his sword slicing into the soft flesh before the man jumped back, wounded but not killed. Another spear slashed across his vision, the tip screeching as it scraped along his helmet as he twisted his head. He stepped back and took a deep breath, not daring to glance over his shoulder. His arm was tiring from the constant dodging and thrusting at the attacks of the Capenates. To his right two men had fallen, one dragged back by his comrades as he screamed in agony, the other simply trampled by the men as they closed the gap over his dead body, a frantic pulling and kicking removing the obstacle before it became too hazardous.

Darting forwards again as an opportunity presented itself Marcus felt the warm gush of blood cover his hand as he thrust the sword deep into the belly of the attacker and twisted it before returning it to his side with a sucking noise as it left the belly of the man. Gasping for breath he saw that the other men were also struggling to hold the line, the men behind stepping forwards and slashing into the gaps as the Romans became ragged in the front line. Thinking quickly Marcus realised the line must change, he needed fresh hands to face the Capenates. A scream to his right made his mind up as Felix fell to a spear in his shoulder, his cursing disappearing as he was dragged backwards and the Capenates pushed forwards again.

"Second row" called Marcus, taking another deep mouthful of air "On my mark take the front line" he screamed. "Front row" he yelled "move back."

A sudden movement confused the Capenates as the front rank momentarily pulled their spears back expecting an attack. This gave the Romans the vital seconds to switch places, only one man getting a spear to the forearm during the movement. Gasping, Marcus stepped back, stretching his back as he moved into the rear line, several happy blood-spattered faces staring breathlessly at him as he did so.

"What's happening at the main gate?" he called as he turned to see a line of soldiers still holding the narrow archway to the small gate behind him despite the press of Romans against them. It was almost the opposite of the scene in which Marcus had been fighting, a smaller number of men holding out against a larger number. More Romans were coming over the wall, but not yet enough to make an immediate difference. Archers stood idly on the wall, their arrows knocked but no targets easily available. Striding backwards Marcus glanced up to the roof, and saw that no defenders remained above him. Relieved he stretched his back again and marched to within earshot of the walls.

"You" he called to a group of archers who were studying the city from the walls and sending the occasional arrow into the city. "What is happening at the main gate?" he called.

"Still fighting at the walls. Same here" he added as he pointed along the walkway where a knot of soldiers was busy hacking at defenders.

"Right, then fetch a ladder and as many archers as you can" he shouted. "Now" he yelled as the man looked at him as if he was speaking a foreign language before suddenly moving into action. A sudden cheer came from the gate as the Romans stepped forwards as a deep groan came just as quickly from the defenders as they fell to the Roman onslaught.

Searching the roads Marcus noted that only one other narrow alleyway led from the gate to the centre of the city, as he had remembered, but this had been blocked by a mound of stone and rubble by the defenders. As it turned out this was now hampering their own defence and Marcus noted spear tips appearing behind the stones as he watched. The main road was holding well considering the overwhelming numbers, but the gate needed to be cleared. As he was thinking this he heard a crash to his right and saw several ladders being flung down from the ramparts, their thick wood clattering onto the stones. A flurry of men appeared before him all dressed in the uniform of archers and all eager for instructions.

"Which of you is in charge?" he asked, as the men looked to each other momentarily and no-one spoke.

"Me sir" chanced a youth, tall but clearly no older than his eighteenth birthday. Marcus smiled as two indignant veterans cuffed his ear and he ducked as one of them stepped forwards with a salute.

"Officer was killed, sir" he said "and we are from three different clans" he said with a shrug.

"Name soldier" he said as the bearded man looked at him with a measure of interest but clearly unsure who this blood covered officer was.

"Amaelius, sir" he saluted.

"Right Amaelius, as Tribune of Rome I make you a Centurion and you are in charge and *he*" he pointed to the tall youth who was staring angrily at the veteran "is your second. I want that roof swarming with men and I want every Capenate in that alleyway" he turned and pointed "and that one, dead. Understand?" The man saluted, his words stumbling as he tried to reply. Before the man could mumble his words Marcus had turned and pointed to the roof. "Get those ladders and get up there. *Now*" he called before marching back towards the gates. Turning he saw the youth, his face now flushed with pride, grip a ladder and call to several men to help him get it to the wall. With a smile Marcus watched as they did as they were told, their training taking over their pride at this strange turn of events.

As he stepped into the back of the line of men at the gate a sudden surge at the front finished with a cheer, the men beside him seeming to relax at the sudden cacophony of cheering from their colleagues. Seeing their commander, several muttered his name and moved aside, Marcus was happy to step into the gap. At the front Narcius was calling for the heavy wooden blocks from the gate to be removed, his left arm hanging uselessly by his side as he winced and gritted his teeth.

"Narcius?" Marcus asked as he looked at his First Spear.

"Bastard got me with a cut" he said, trying to hold his arm up but gripping it quickly as blood ran down his arm.

"Come on, sir" said a soldier, wrapping a thick red bandage across the arm and tying a quick knot before shaking his head to Marcus to indicate that Narcius would be out of any more action that day.

"Well done men, especially you Narcius" Marcus called as the men grinned and cheered. The gate swung open with a loud squeal, as if in protest at the Romans taking the city. The iron hinges moaned at the weight of the small, but sturdy, gate and Marcus smiled at the scene outside.

A great cheer came from outside the city as the Roman legion started to march forwards, the officers trotting ahead to see what was required before the men arrived. Marcus gripped a soldier who was cheering loudly, his face a sudden mask of fear as his commanding officer turned to address him directly.

"Run to the Centurion there" he pointed "and tell him that they should hold the line at the front gate, send no more than three hundred men in this gate. Run" he called as the man threw his weapons to the floor and dashed out towards the trotting officers, their faces now visible as Marcus waved to them. Potitus' face grew into a questioning scowl as he saw Marcus's hand raised towards him.

****

Mascullus yawned and then stopped mid-way through the action as his feet felt wet, a sudden sloshing noise making his tired eyes stare towards the floor of his tent. Having completed the night shift at the walls he had slept until late in the afternoon and had awoken bleary eyed just as the sun had begun to drop into the early afternoon.

"What?" he said s he took a deep breath and blinked his eyes.

"Attus" he said loudly to the man to his right, his deep sleep untouched by the noise of the call. "*Attus*" he called again, jumping from the cot, raised above the ground so he didn't have to worry about snakes or rats.

Attus jumped, his arm reaching for his dagger as he instantly thought they were under attack, the other three soldiers in the tent also jumping at the noise, two yelling as they jumped from their cots into the ankle deep water before jumping back and blinking their eyes.

"Is this a joke?" a large man, his bald head but thick beard making his face look all the more terrifying , called. He stepped up and down before walking to Mascullus and frowning. Both men pulled aside the tent flap to see several men standing outside their tents, ankle deep in water. Attus appeared, his bleary eyes gazing at the water and out into the lake.

"It's a sign" he said, a tone of fear in his voice. "The gods don't want us here" he said, gripping the talisman around his neck as other men looked to him, their mouths open. There was a sudden movement, almost a wave, as a small rise occurred in the water, as it rose another inch. The men looked to each other and froze, their worst fears running through their minds.

"Get your kit and get to dry land" came the voice of their Centurion, his groggy eyes showing that he too had only just been woken from his slumber after their night shift.

Scipio arrived moments later as tents were dropping and men sloshing through shin deep water with armfuls of sopping wet gear, their armour and swords clearly the first things they had rescued from the water.

Scipio sloshed through until the water nearly reached his knees, standing and searching the horizon for something as the confused men stared at him. "Get on with it" he called to the laggards who were standing and watching him, the shout causing an instant increase in activity.

Scipio gave orders for the tents to be cleared and the huts closest to the water to be emptied. Men rushed to and fro as muttering and cursing began across the rear of the camp.

Priscus arrived as Scipio cleared the last edge of the water, his tunic soaked up to his waist from his splashing through the water.

"What is it?" Priscus asked, his eyes wide.

"I have no idea" replied Scipio. "The water had receded for the past few days. There is no reason for this to happen" he looked back to his commander with a shake of his head.

"Fetch the augur to my tent and bring the officers. We need to work out what to do" he said. As he turned he saw several legionaries staring at them, all wondering what was happening.

"Get that gear shifted" Priscus yelled "or you'll all be on a charge" he added venomously.

*

Chapter 8

The thump of arrows was loud as Marcus gripped the top of the wall and pulled himself onto the roof, his arms still stiff from fighting in the street below. Ahead of him several archers were firing into the road below without bothering to aim. To his right the wall stretched towards the main gate and another group of archers were aiming more cautiously at the knot of soldiers fighting to gain access to the main gate. It seemed that the covering archery was making a difference as the Capenates were visibly falling back, more Romans joining the attackers as Marcus watched.

"Excellent" he said, clapping his hands and rubbing them, as much to try and bring some life back to his tired hands as show his appreciation.

"Here, sir" said Amaelius , his creased brow showing the urgency with which he had called his Tribune to the roof. Potitus appeared beside Marcus, his face fresh and smiling as he perused the work of the soldiers around him.

Amaelius squatted and edged forwards to the front of the long flat roof on which they stood and beckoned his officer's forwards. At the end of the roof he lay flat and nudged his body slowly to the lip.

"See, sir. As I said. The main army is standing in reserve in the town square and they have blocked every entrance. A last stand" he said knowledgably as Marcus and Potitus lay beside him and looked out across the many roofs of the city to see the spears and some of the bodies of men amassed in deep phalanxes across the town square behind the central road to the main gate.

Marcus grinned, patting the archer as he moved backwards and grinned to Potitus.

"How quickly could you get twenty Scorpions across those roofs?" Marcus asked, clearly surprising Potitus who had not even considered this action.

Stunned for a moment he took a few seconds to think through the idea. "Fifteen minutes" he blustered, his mind still wheeling at the thought.

"You need to do it in ten" he said, his face earnest. Potitus stared at his command for a moment before turning and rushing across to the ladder and disappearing from the roof.

The noise of fighting below them continued as Marcus stretched his neck to look over into the narrow gap. Men continued to parry and thrust, red spots of blood appearing as men screamed, but the impasse remained, neither side as winning.

"Amaelius" Marcus beckoned the archer over. Get all the archers over here and hit this lot hard. Find the leaders and kill them first" he said with a calculating look at the newly promoted man. I want them in panic within ten minutes.

"Sir" said the archer as he saluted and ran away calling to his men.

Climbing down the ladder Marcus called a messenger across and quickly wrote on the wax tablet, his instructions short and precise.

"Take this to Rufus" he said "he must do precisely what it says" he added. "Repeat the order" he said, a trick he had been taught by Lucius many years before when he had first joined the army. Messengers were prone to fear as they were often the poor soldiers who had the least armour and could not afford the cost of the spears and shields which added them to the ranks of the Roman legions. As such many were prone to fear and often got messages mixed up or even lost. The order was repeated and Marcus nodded before the messenger sprinted away through the open gate, some of the soldiers jeering the man as he ran.

Despite continuously changing the front row of the attackers and raining arrows into the mass of men progress up the roadway was still stuck. Additional men were of no use and Marcus had considered removing the rubble in the alleyway to attack the defenders from the rear. They had held this location for several minutes now but so far no additional support had come from the Capenates, clearly satisfied that the Romans at this gate posed no danger. So far they were right, despite Marcus' best efforts he needed his next attack to work.

A deep cry and a series of groans came from the road as more arrows rained into the narrow street, the thumping of iron on wood intermittently mixed with the screams of a successful shot.

Horses clattered into the doorway as men jumped from their backs carrying the four feet high wooden scorpions, other men arrived on foot carrying wrapped packages of heavy iron-tipped bolts, sweat dripping from their faces as they gasped for breath from the run.

"Up there" called Marcus as the men looked around at the narrow, high-walled, alleyway in which they found themselves. The first men struggled to climb the ladders with the heavy scorpions, soon resorting to three men on the ladders passing the implements up to their colleagues. Marcus was pleased with their efficiency as they quickly adapted to the circumstances in which they found themselves.

A sudden cheer went up from the Romans at the roadway and a body was pulled back through the mass of soldiers crammed across the mouth of the road. The blood soaked body jumped to its feet, as if rising from the dead, the man's chest heaving as his eyes roved the scene and he pulled a water pouch from a legionary and poured it over his face to clean the gore from his face.

"Fabius" Marcus said as he wondered over to the man, his eyes bright and face now washed mostly clean of blood.

"By the gods Camillus this is what life is for" he said as he hefted his sword and breathed out a long slow breath. "The men had to drag me from the front" he said with a manic smile as Marcus grinned back at him and shook his head.

"You are a talisman to the troops, Quintus. But I need you to recover your sword arm. I need you to take Narcius's place as he has been injured."

The slight smile was quickly followed by "Not badly?"

"No, a flesh wound but he is out of action" came Marcus's reply. "Take command of the men by the gate and await my instructions" he added as he grinned at the younger man's enthusiasm for bloodshed, hoping that he never angered him as he was surely a force of nature whom some god watched over.

The men by the gate gave a low cheer as Fabius wandered over and started to tell them of his exploits. Marcus made a mental note that he must talk to Fabius about his fraternising with the men. It was a double edged sword and his privilege as a patrician would soon mean he may have to make life and death decisions for the very men to whom he was now boasting about his skills. It would be a hard discussion, but it needed to happen.

Potitus called from the roof top "Ready" he called.

Marcus nodded and moved to the gate, stepping into the sunlight to see more men racing towards the main gates as arrows and stones arced onto them, the half-hearted attack failing as Marcus had ordered. His plan seemed to be working, the attack at the main gate was stalling and so was the one in the rear. As far as the defenders were concerned the Romans had made no major in-roads into their city. Marcus grinned, the screw was about to be turned.

****

"This war is cursed" the men shouted, more calls coming from the back of the ranks of men who were standing watching the augur as he took the chicken from its cage.

Sallus, his white flecked beard trimmed to a long point, breathed slowly as he closed his eyes and invoked the gods to guide his divination. The candle spluttered in the light wind as he held the bird over the silver dish and quickly split its throat, removing the head and gripping the legs before they kicked too strongly. Expertly he removed the breast meat and sliced open the guts, adding the entrails to the larger silver bowl and then slicing the heart and liver from the bird and placing them in the smaller dish. As he wiped some of the blood from his hands on a white, embroidered, cloth he peered at the entrails, picking through them as he used the point of his iron tipped knife to nudge aside the thicker entrails from the thinner. He grimaced at something, some of the closer soldiers falling silent as others muttered words about curses and war as Sallus tried to block out their words. Priscus had been clear in his instructions, whatever the reading the troops should know that it was good, any bad omens would be delivered to the Tribune alone.

Smiling he raised the entrails and grinned at the officers standing closest to him. "The signs are clear." He spoke quickly placing the knife under the entrails and slicing a chunk from them, which he added to a wooden bowl carved with a dancing nymph along the outside. These entrails would be burnt as an offering to the gods when the reading was finished. Turning to the liver he sliced it in three places and nodded as if happy with what he saw, taking one slice and placing it in the wooden bowl, the rest he left on the silver dish. The heart he sliced and inspected for a few minutes before declaring it strong, a good sign from the gods.

As he finished he turned to the Tribune and said "the augury is finished. There is no curse on this land and no bad omen on our just and righteous war with Veii. The rising of the water is simply the water spirits angry that we are fouling the water. The gods ask us to move the men away from the water and make daily supplication to the spirits and all will be well."

Masterful, thought Priscus, even better than he had hoped for.

Silence fell amongst the men as Priscus stepped forwards. "You have heard the Augur. Officers" he turned to the ranks to his right. "Make it as the Augur has commanded on behalf of the gods and the spirits of the water. Move the camp to the west and have daily supplication rites each day by the lake." He smiled as the officers saluted and began to clear the men.

Returning to the command tent Priscus sat and poured two large cups of un-watered wine. As the Augur crept into the tent Priscus smiled at the old man and waved towards the seat. "Well, brother?" he asked as the man sat and let out a deep breath, his eyes smiling at his younger brother.

"Not good at all" he said gripping the cup and taking a long draught of the cool wine. "You will need to send to Rome to get the Pontifex to check the reading but I saw two distinct problems facing us before the war will be won. Firstly" he drank again. "The intestines give the timelines of one year or two for resolution. But they also show great loss before great success." He screwed his eyes tight, as if in pain. "And then the liver was stained with a circle. I need to consult my books before I confirm this, but" he looked at his brother and shook his head "it suggests that a blot will fall on the victor of Veii, something bad will occur. It might be death or something as close to death as I can fathom. I will consult my books."

Priscus frowned. "And the heart?"

"The heart was strong, we will win." He added with a shrug.

Priscus looked into the eyes of his brother, seeing those of his long dead mother looking back at him. He smiled at the thought. "So, I should not be the one to defeat the city of Veii" Priscus said out loud, his brother nodding. "Something bad will happen to whoever has that joy" he smiled. "But it will be soon" he added, his thoughts already wondering which of his enemies he could place in charge of the attacks in the coming year.

"There was one other thing though, brother" added Sallus. "The liver and heart contained water. Something I have never seen before, but it is a clear mark from the gods. Whoever wins at Veii will have to overcome a challenge involving water."

****

Potitus crept over the rooftops keeping his head low. A call came from the wall to his right as a man saw the troops creeping along behind him. More men turned and Potitus cursed the fact that he hadn't brought any covering shields for the scorpions. As the men at the wall turned one fell instantly to an arrow through the neck, his mouth spewing a long slow trickle of blood as he toppled into the city. The men on the wall ducked to avoid further attacks from outside the city, but the damage was done, he had been seen.

"Quickly" he called to the soldiers, waving to the watching Marcus and pointing to the walls. As if he could read his thoughts Potitus saw his friend sending a troop of archers towards him, their arrows would provide covering support whilst the scorpions did their work. Moving swiftly he jumped across the small gap between two building, each stone-built and sturdy, and raced to the far edge. At this point he gained a better view of the city square, thousands of men lined up ready to buffer any attack from the Romans. Eyes searched the rooftops where he was crouched, searching for the danger that the men on the walls alluded to, though none seemed, yet, to have seen him. Scanning the surrounding buildings he decided that this would be as good a place as any and waved the men forwards to set up their deadly machines.

A snap to his right announced the fall of arrows as one of the missiles clapped into the building across from him, the implement falling into the street below. Men from the square were now racing to the building on which he stood. The archers arrived and began to pelt the defenders on the wall, their range too far to do any permanent damage.

"Quickly" Potitus chided, pacing up and down as more arrows fell short of their position. "Ready" came the first call as Potitus licked his lips. Another call came quickly after that, then another.

"Get the sights lined up boys" he smiled as he spoke, his eyes moving from left to right to judge the wind and distance. "Hardly any wind, the gods are with us" he added in a low voice as he knelt to one knee and looked through the sighting mechanism of the first of the scorpions. Turning he pulled the red cloth and waved it to Marcus, who waved back and turned to bark orders at a handful of men who were lying prone on the roof top with several long ladders. The plan was audacious but it would drive fear into the enemy and cause panic, and as Potitus knew panic could win you the battle.

****

Marcus waved to Potitus, his grin growing as he yelled to the men lying along the roof top above the Capenates in the road. Hundreds were dead below him, but so far the men had remained strong and the junction was secure.

"Now" he yelled as more men appeared on the roof beside him, climbing up in small groups as he could not trust the roof to hold the weight of many men. This initial attack had to ferocious and Fabius bared his teeth as he clambered over the roof and fell behind three men who were already dropping down the ladder to appear behind the defenders in the street. Speed was vital and Marcus fell in behind the men, his eyes racing around the scene. Thos defenders closest to him and behind the front line were mostly their shields above their heads to stop the deadly arrows and had not yet seen the ladders fall behind them, but as he thought this the cries of anguish came and the Capenates at the rear began to turn. As one a thrum of arrows took the first men to step from under their shields, one running forward three full steps before he buckled with four arrows in this chest.

As Marcus jumped the last two rungs of the ladder he called to Fabius to get the line closed up, more men rushed down the ladders, the more ambitious jumping the last five or six rungs in an effort to get to the ground quickly. Fabius was engaged with a defender, his long sword battering the wooden shield in overhead cuts as the man dodged and attempted to parry the strikes.

"Fabius" yelled Marcus, looking to his right. "Close the line. *Shields*" he called, his eyes peering over the top of the wood. More men dropped into the road, others rained arrows onto the defenders. The leader of the Capenates seethed with anger as he barked new orders to his men, the rearmost turning and preparing to attack as the Roman line was not at full strength. A sudden snap took the man's head backwards as his eyes rolled in his head momentarily and he sank below the line of men in front of him, a great groan going up from the soldiers around him before the second in command took the lead and called his men to keep their heads.

Thump. There it was, the first scorpion bolt had been sent flying and Marcus knew that now was the time to press the advantage. "Advance" he called as the line of Romans roared and stepped forwards. At best it was three to one in the defenders favour but Marcus knew that the shorter sword and powerful shields of the Eagles were capable of easily destroying the men in front of him in this confined space, even with such odds.

A Capenate launched his spear in a long thrust, his grunting exploding from his lungs before the spear tip smashed into the wooden shield. Marcus waited, rocking on the balls of his feet, watching the men to right and left for a movement which would give him an opportunity to strike. Fabius clattered his blade against the shield of another man as spears started to press upwards and shields came together in the melee of the road. *Perfect* thought Marcus as his grin unnerved the man who was staring at him from only a few inches away, his spear now stuck in the press of men behind him. Marcus took only a second to note the sudden fear in the man's eyes as his shoulder twitched at the jammed weapon, his head half turning to call to the men behind to back up. With a short step forward Marcus punched his shield into the enemy, darting his sword through a small gap and landing a cutting blow in the man's guts, twisting quickly and ramming his shield forwards again. The man yelled but didn't fall, a gush of blood hitting the stones below Marcus's feet. To his left and right the same happened, Capenates falling to short stabbing movements before the familiar sound of Roman shields closing into a thick wall of wood rang across the alleyway.

"Reverse step" came the slow call as Marcus prepared. "Go." At once several Romans stepped back, the movement causing the front line of Capenates to almost fall forwards into the small space. Instantly the Romans stepped forwards and stabbed again, the man facing Marcus too focused on his blood-red mid-section to notice the thrusting action which hit his throat and nearly severed his head in one movement. As his body and that of five other Capenates fell Marcus heard the cheers of the Romans at the road entrance as they hacked into the defenders more vigorously.

Within moments frenzied fighting broke out, the Capenates suddenly realising that they were hemmed in began to break ranks and throw their spears to the floor in favour of their long blades, usually only used when chasing their enemies after the phalanx had broken. Marcus remembered his training with Mella and the many long sessions he had undertaken with Narcius and his men to perfect his technique. Parry, thrust and step back, keeping low, don't hack to left or right, remain calm. He went about his bloody routine, smashing his shield boss into the angry face of a desperate soldier who was trying to climb over the shields in an attempt to escape the death trap that this road had become. The road was slick with blood, slippery, with the tang of iron in the air. Marcus stepped back and took a moment to look around at the scene, noticing the thump of the scorpions again for the first time since he had heard that initial attack. Looking for Fabius he saw him being supported by a legionary, his head bloody where his helmet had been removed. At least he was still alive, Marcus thought as he heard the first cry for mercy from the remaining Capenate soldiers, the cry suddenly rising as the remaining fifty or sixty men threw away their swords and the eyes of the Romans looked to their officers before they accepted the surrender.

"Hold" commanded Marcus, stepping forward, his breathing ragged and deep. Searching the men he found a face he knew. "Centurion Bassus, take these prisoners. Injured move to the walls, the rest follow me" he called as he turned and waved to the legionary with Fabius, jerking his thumb towards the gate as the man nodded and leant Fabius against the wall to allow the soldiers to pass.

Behind him he heard the trumpet call he had ordered as a signal to launch the full scale attack on the front gate of the city once they had secured the road, and he took a long deep breath before calming his nerves and focusing on marching the men, eight abreast, towards the main square.

****

Potitus heard the trumpet. *He's done it again* he thought as he gritted his teeth in a long smile and watched another bolt race into the enemy ranks, still standing in the square despite the death that was raining at them from their own roofs. He'd lost two men to arrows but so far none of the defenders had been able to get close to the scorpions, though each weapon now had only two or three more bolts left to throw. The enemy were unsure how to cope with the attacks, some men had run off into the streets, their officers calling them but to no avail. Others stood nervously, jumping left and right as bolts slammed into the twelve men deep squares in an attempt to avoid the bolts. Arrows and stones slammed into the roof but very few hit their mark. *Lucky again* he thought as he looked back along the road and saw the men streaming into the rear gate as, finally, the Capenates wheeled one of the phalanxes to the right and trotted towards the main road. He counted maybe another thousand men in the square as he considered Marcus's plan and nudged the soldier ahead of him.

"Slowly" he called to the men, some eyes flicking to his as the men slowed their pace. "Pick out the leaders with the last shots" he said slowly as the sights were edged up and down to pick out the men heading for roadway.

"When you are done leave the weapons and retreat" he called, moving to the edge of the roof and peering back along the road. Civilians raced to and fro, most heading towards the main square with arms full of possessions, others dragging children and wailing for the help of their gods as the noise of the marching army grew from within and outside the walls. The archers were almost spent of arrows too as Potitus turned to them and jerked his head towards the rear, the closest men nodding and calling to their colleagues to finish their last shots.

A great cheer came from Potitus' right as a Roman breached the wall above the main gate and instantly the archers ran forwards and rained their final arrows into the backs of the defenders as more men streamed over the parapet.

The last bolt flew with a wicked thump and Potitus saw it stop the whole of the phalanx as it scythed through the first four men and knocked several others to the floor, the remaining men staring with horror at the roof top as well as back at the mangled remains of their dead friends. "Go" he called to the soldiers as they took a last look at their bloody work and turned to sprint back along the roof. Potitus smiled and turned to walk back along the roof, a tall young archer falling in behind him, his final arrow knocked as he walked backwards behind his senior officer and the two men headed for the rear gate, their tasks finished for now.

****

Rufus watched as the left hand attack breached the wall after the second major attack, the first faltering to a steady hail of missiles and some fierce defending on the walls. He smirked, a new thought coming to his mind as the first man over the wall held his ground, the cheering of the ranks of men in front of him causing the noise of fighting at the wall to disappear. If

Camillus was right the defenders were now splitting their forces, exactly as he wished them to. Some would be heading for the rear gate, others would be preparing to repulse the attack at the front. All in all this looked like the time for him to get as close to the gate with the main attack force as he could, within minutes it could be opened. Horses to his left caught his eye and he turned, a sudden well of fear coming as his mind immediately thought of a counter attack by the enemy, his hands rising to call for new orders before he realised it was Roman cavalry, not enemy.

"Who is that?" Mella asked, sat to Rufus' right. "Is it Virginius?" he said with a note of incredulity in his voice.

Rufus ignored the question and leant forward to wave to the trumpeter to call the first five rows forward into a steady jog to reach their pre-designed positions. Almost instantly the call came and the men moved, the dust cloud growing and loud clanking of armour rising into the air. Turning back to Mella with a shake of his head he replied "I don't care as long as it's not the enemy. Go and see what he wants Mella, and tell him to keep those men back, they will only get in the way" he said with a shake of his head. "Oh, but be more polite about how you say it" he added with a smirk.

The wall was bristling with Romans now, surely Marcus and his men had found the way to the gate and were preparing to open the door to the city. Rufus smiled as he stretched his back and rasped his sword from its scabbard. "Not long now boys" he said loudly as a number of eyes turned to watch him at the sound.

****

The road was longer than Marcus expected, the alleyways to left and right held only the occasional defender, most young boys who hoped to sneak at quick attack before running back to tell their tales of valour. All were dispatched. Marcus ran through his prayers to

Fortuna and Juno in his head, his bargain with them was simple and he would keep to his words. It was the Roman way to set a bargain with your gods and then to honour it when they favoured you with victory. He remembered how his bargaining had grown in recent years as he felt that he needed to offer more supplication and more sacrifices as his battles grew in stature. So far this battle had gone as well as all the rest, as he hoped the prophecy foretold. Ahead he could hear the stomping of the phalanx of Capenate defenders coming from the city square and he said a quick prayer of thanks to Fortuna in the hope that the scorpions had thinned their ranks sufficiently.

"Hold here, men" he called as he looked left and right at the intersection of the roads he had seen on the map. "Go, and may Fortuna be with you" he called as several men split off and headed into each narrow road, their task to find a way to the gate or at least to draw more soldiers away from it.

The sound of soldiers catching their breath came from around him as Marcus glanced up and down the street, houses boarded up, shutters closed and the only noise that of his men and the stomp of the approaching soldiers.

"We must keep the momentum up, men" called Marcus. "Are the archers there?" he called as a reply came from the back of the men and he nodded to himself. "Right. Form line, and do your duty as soldiers of Rome. The spoils will be large and you will be rich men after today" he called as the soldiers cheered his name and began to shuffle into their small groups across the road.

Within a minute they had set off in a steady walk towards the square, the light dim in the tall sided road as the houses blocked the late afternoon sun. Ahead the wall of enemy soldiers appeared, instantly greeted by jeering and cursing from both sets of soldiers. Marcus grinned, moving into the second line as he had agreed with the Centurions and from where he could direct activity. He wondered how the attack at the gates was going, and assumed that the appearance of this phalanx of men was testament to the success of his plan to lure the Capenates to split their force.

"Archers" called Marcus as the Capenates got within thirty paces, their bristling wall of spears long and deadly. Immediately the rank of soldiers eased sideways leaving enough space for a line of archers to squeeze to the front. As soon as they had room the archers fired indiscriminately into the phalanx, the front line safely behind their shields but the rear ranks unaware that death was coming until it was too late. After firing four arrows each the archers turned and fled back into the ranks of foot soldiers and Marcus screamed "charge" as the Romans launched into the leading edge of the defenders, the front line of whom had continued to march as the rear ranks faltered to move their shields above their heads. The momentary halt had given the Romans a chance to slice into the heart of the phalanx and Marcus and his men took it with glee, charging straight through the long spears and slamming into the shields of the defending soldiers. Romans fell to the spears, but others clambered over their dead and rained short thrusts into the bodies of the men who were struggling to remove their shields from above their heads, the confusion giving the Eagles the time they needed to ram their advantage home.

"Press on" Marcus called as he thrust his sword into the shoulder of a thick bearded Capenate, his deep scream obliterated as the legionary to his right slammed his sword through his eye socket and the man disappeared under the feet on the rushing Romans. The speed of the attack took the front four rows by surprise, the fifth row recovering sufficiently to block the retreat of their colleagues as they struggled to manoeuvre in the confined space of the road. Capenates fought Capenates as the Romans marched relentlessly through the front of the phalanx, men tried desperately to claw their way back to safety but were butchered from both sides as they screamed their death cries.

"Hold" Marcus called as he realised the defenders were now getting into position. "Archers" he called as the first two rows of Romans closed the shield wall and lowered their bodies to peer out at the yelling defenders, who, thinking they had stalled the Romans, took a step forward. Stepping up from the back the archers grinned as two rows of legionaries knelt and placed their shields across the road, the archers stepping onto them as they had trained to do in the camp only the night before as the legionaries lifted the shields and the men rose above their heads.

As the Capenates stepped forward toward the Roman wall some of them stopped in their tracks as men rose from the ranks of the Romans in front of them. *Giants* one man thought before his rational thought came back and he realised they were holding bows and pointing their deadly arrows directly at his face. Throwing his shield up to cover his body he forced himself not to whimper, but it was too late an arrow had crashed into his arm, knocking his spear from his grip as he screamed curses at the Romans.

Three shots each was what Marcus had ordered, the archers dealing the blow within twenty seconds. Instantly the front rank of Romans were moving forwards before the archers had dropped out of sight, the same confusion now causing the rear ranks to step backwards at this tactic that they had never faced before. *"Hold"* came the call from deep within the Capenate ranks as Marcus grinned and pushed his shield into the face of a man with an arrow through his right arm, the blood hardly visible but the pain etched on his face showing just how badly it stung. The rear ranks began to buckle and Marcus knew now was the time to attack with all the might of the men he had around him.

"Attack" he screamed as he stepped forwards and smashed his sword into the breastplate of a short man, his cheap spear cracking against the stone of the house beside him as he wheeled his shield across to try and stop the lightning fast strike. He had fallen before Marcus had had the time to make a second strike and he kicked at the body, making sure he was flat so that he

could move over the body safely. More men fell, a few Romans succumbed to spears or swords as the defenders started to peel away from the back of the phalanx.

"Maniples get ready" Marcus called. "Archers to the roofs" he shouted as he heard men start to climb the houses to find vantage points from which they could strike.

"A horse to the first man to get the gate open" he called as men cheered around him. A horse was extremely valuable and could raise a man from his current status to a higher level much more than silver or bronze could, and Marcus knew this as he grinned to the man next to him, his eyes suddenly lit up at the thought of owning his own steed.

An arrow sliced into the cheek of a defender as Marcus parried his spear thrust, the moment of agony allowing Marcus the time to step under his spear point and thrust his sword up into his ribs, the leather body protector jarring the strike but not stopping it. The end of the road was now in sight, the brighter light of the square opening out as the Romans marched through the ranks of Capenates. Marcus knew that his next move was the most dangerous yet, but his men had trained for it and even though Narcius was not there to see the fruits of his work he knew they would win.

The last three rows of spearmen turned and ran as soon as they reached the square, some edging backwards with their spears in an orderly formation, others simply throwing their weapons and running.

"Maniples" Marcus called as his men split and ran pell-mell in different directions in groups of eight soldiers. This was a tactic Marcus had seen used many years before by the long haired giants from Gaul who had faced his brother in a skirmish with the Romans. It had been so effective he had gone through various forms of attack with Lucius, Scipio, Potitus and Mella since that day. Now he would find out if his theories would work. Maniples, *handfuls,* were men trained to fight in small groups, using quick combat techniques to drag the enemy out of their rigid formations and then dash in for the kill. Each group set off across the square in different directions, the movement allowing Marcus to stand on a protruding block of stone which stood proud from the building where he was standing.

Scanning the square he could see that the enemy were less than he had imagined, maybe a thousand men at most, all crammed into the one central square but also hampered by its size. Immediately he knew that if they could open the gate they would be victorious. Gripping the man next to him he looked back along the road from which they had come, seeing more Romans racing along the narrow, steep sided, walkway.

"Maximus, get to Rufus and tell him to march at the gates now" he yelled above the noise of combat around them before he swept his sword away to his right; "to the gates" he shouted as he set his jaw and moved away into the melee in front of him.

*

*

Chapter 9

"Has the messenger left for Rome" Priscus asked as he sat with his elbows resting across the desk, piles of reports stacked on either side of his resting arms.

"Yes sir" said the duty legionary who had just entered the tent, his clean uniform showing he had not been party to the moving of the soaking wet equipment down by the lake.

"Good" mumbled Priscus, rubbing at his tired eyes before yawning and leaning back in his chair. He eyed the legionary. "Rustulus, isn't it?" he asked as the legionary suddenly bolted to attention expecting a dressing down, his mind running through a series of excuses before nodding and saluting vigorously.

"Here Rustulus, have a seat. Let's talk, man to man."

Rustulus looked at his commanding officer warily, his chin pulled tight into his neck as he considered what the officer might want from him. "Sir" he replied as he pulled up a seat and sat.

"Wine?"

"Not on duty, sir"

"Then you are excused duty from now until dawn, Rustulus" came the reply, though the look from Priscus was more mischievous than stern. Rustulus nodded and his shoulders relaxed as he gripped the wooden cup offered to him.

Taking a sip of the wine his eyes widened, his appreciation of the thick white liquid showing in his face as he licked his lips and took another draught.

"Ha" laughed Priscus. "I forgot the piss that you have to drink in the legions. Years ago I swore blind that if I ever rose to the rank where I could bring my own wine on campaign I would do it" he added with a genuine smile as he looked into his own cup before drinking.

"It's the best wine I've ever tasted" Rustulus said with a nod of his head.

"Here." Priscus leant forwards and filled the cup to the brim. "No, go on man" he said. Rustulus took another slow sip and savoured the taste before looking at his officer.

"Tell me Rustulus, what do you think of all this talk of bad omens and bad luck, especially the lake water rising so suddenly?" Priscus asked as he looked over his cup at the legionary, noting the sudden unease in the man's face. "Be honest" he added as he leant forward with the wine jug and motioned to fill the half empty cup again. "My officers tell me the men pay no heed to such tales and such thoughts of disaster" he added with a wave of his free hand and a shrug.

Rustulus took a moment to answer, leaning forwards and looking around the tent conspiratorially before speaking. "To be honest, Sir, the lads think that the whole campaign is cursed" he said, watching Priscus' face intently. Priscus for his part nodded as if he agreed with him and motioned with the wine jug again, Rustulus grinning before downing his third cup in as many minutes. "They say that the two-headed calf, the constant attacks and the fact that we can't get into the city just shows that the gods aren't with us" he said with a slight slur. "The water is a sign, well that's what they say, that the gods don't want us here." He nodded before drinking half the cup in one go and looking over at Priscus.

"What about the Augur though? He said it was just about fouling the water" he replied.

"Well, sir" Rustulus said. "The trouble is that the lads said they saw a black wolf come out of the lake and walk through the camp on the night the water rose. It sniffed at the tents, sir, honestly. I didn't believe them, but, well, look at it now, water everywhere and" he drank quickly "no-one knows why" he finished.

Priscus looked surprised as he listened, his face remaining as neutral as he could keep it. "So what do you think the men will do now that the omens are so bad?" he asked, his voice low as his eyes seemed to scan the tent in case anyone was listening.

"Do?" Rustulus looked incredulously at Priscus. "Do" he said again, the wine really starting to catch up with his wits now. "They'll do what you tell them, sir. You're in charge" he said with a deep frown as if the question was one which he just couldn't comprehend.

Priscus smiled, his fears suddenly relaxing as he leant across and grinned at the legionary. "Here" he said. "You finish this and I'll get some more" he said. "I think we should have a night of drinking and telling old war tales. I'll get some food. You're a good man Rustulus" he added as he strode from the tent and nodded to himself.

****

Darting into the shadow of a tall, wooden topped, building Marcus gripped the shoulder of the man in front of him. Behind him and to his left the maniples were causing mayhem, three hundred soldiers fighting a thousand spearmen who were moving forwards and backwards like waves crashing onto the shores, their spears thrusting but missing everything as the men dashed backwards and forwards in their small groups. The man peered over his shoulder at his leader and nodded as Marcus pointed towards the gate where a fierce battle was ensuing, the defenders holding their ground against an increasing number of Roman soldiers as they appeared from the upper walkway. Glancing upwards he could see that the right hand wall was being held by his soldiers, the left was still under Capenate ownership. The gate was crucial, he thought as he gritted his teeth and charged into the right edge of the defenders, six men deep at the gate. His mind calculated the rate of loss of his own men, knowing that maybe five minutes was the maximum they could hold out and hoping that Caelio was coming to his rear through the streets with support, as he had ordered.

Taking the sword thrust of a heavily built soldier on his shield he snapped his left arm up and across his body, catching the man's wrist with the speed of his movement. Stepping forward at the same time as his action with his shield he had already looked beyond the fear in the face of the defender to spot his next victim as his sword came up and slid effortlessly into the armpit before he dragged his body backwards, using his momentum to pull the body to the floor. Stamping hard on the man's head he felt him judder as the legionary at his back sliced the man's white neck, turning the sun burned brown face and milky white neck into a spray of red.

"Left" he called as a sudden movement caught his attention. The defenders had given ground as a well dressed man with a thick leather breastplate stumbled under the attack of three of the Romans, the first catching his sword arm as his life bled from a wound in his belly; the well dressed soldier letting out an ear-piercing scream as he struggled to remove the heavy weight of the Roman clinging to him. As the scream rose in intensity all eyes of the defenders had moved to their talisman, his decorations covering his thick chest, as he took sword thrusts to the arms and thighs before one sliced into his cheek as he thrashed from side to side.

The movement had given Marcus the opportunity he needed and he tensed his jaw as he took a half-running stride into the melee and smashed his shield into the Capenate defenders left shoulder taking him off his feet. A sword strike clattered along his shoulder guard but missed his exposed neck as Marcus felt a sudden fear at his impetuous movement, his mouth mumbling supplication to Fortuna as he back-handed his hilt into the face of the large man and then used his body weight to press down on his sword as it slid into the chest of the Capenate leader, the thick leather holding his sword point for a second before it jerked into his chest. Marcus felt the point smack into the floor under the prone man and stared into his eyes as he swore before the light went from his face and he choked a few droplets of blood before his head fell to the side, lifeless. Two shields had covered Marcus as he had moved forwards, the wood clattering with attacks as he tried to regain his feet, but the damage was palpable, the Capenates groaning loudly as their hero died.

Several men edged backwards, then more as they began to give way and a call of 'mercy' came from within the defenders thinning ranks. Marcus righted his feet and gripped his sword, double checking that the form below him was dead before stepping back and peering ahead at the gate. Behind he heard the clatter of spears and swords and without pausing he screamed "advance" as the eyes of the defenders grew wide with fear.

The Romans were brutal, slicing through every living man at the gate and viciously hacking at their dead bodies as they marched over them. Glancing behind Marcus saw that Caelio had appeared with more men and set up a line of men across the square as the phalanx of Capenates attempted to march to the gates.

"Quickly. Get it open" he screamed, his voice taking on a higher pitch than he expected, but non-the-less his command was obeyed instantly by the men. The heavy wooden beams were removed and thrown to the side as another great groan came from the defenders. Marcus dived to the side, his arms suddenly weary and his eyes blinking from the blood that dripped from his helmet. The Roman attackers charged into the space, the lead men screaming hatred as their eyes searched prey and they darted off to attack the phalanx as it started to buckle from the relentless attack of the Romans. Within a minute Marcus was leaning against the stone wall of the city, his breathing ragged as his chest rose and fell as he watched the Romans continue to stream into the Capenate stronghold, the screaming of women now mingling with the cries of men as the doors to the cities houses were kicked in by the attacking force.

"Sir" came a voice as Marcus turned to see Fuscus, his pale face seeming clear amongst the blood spattered men standing at the gate.

"Fuscus" Marcus replied with a smile.

"Any orders?" he asked as he gripped his shield tightly in his left hand.

"You have your orders. Kill all men who bear arms, make prisoners of the rest" he said before the soldier turned and trotted into the square to disappear along a side street with thirty or more men at his heel. The square was almost empty, the Capenates had fled into the roads and alleyways. Only the dead remained, great clumps of bodies, some lay in clusters, others alone. A legionary handed him a water pouch, which he gripped tightly as it was covered in a red film of blood.

Standing tall he took three great gulps and then splashed a little across his face, using his shield hand to wipe away the excess. He nodded to the man with a smile, noting a hungry and determined look in his eyes as he returned the look before glancing away quickly.

"Well done you men" he called to the six men still standing around him, the remaining men of Narcius's own maniple. "I will tell your Centurion how well you fought" he said as he clapped one man on the shoulder and nodded appreciatively to him. As another series of Romans charged into the city from the gateway Marcus knew the look he was getting from the six men, a mix of loyalty and desire to secure spoils from the city. He glanced around and then out of the gate, above the heads of the on-rushing soldiers. Rufus was within fifty paces, the Triarii walking at a steady pace towards the gate.

"Go on" he said with a smile to the eager eyes of the six men. "But remember to get something for your Centurion" he called as the men gripped their swords more tightly and darted into the nearest roadway yelling their curses at the unseen Capenates hiding their treasures within the city.

****

"The news is indeed mixed, but I believe we have covered everything for today" said Cicurinus from his seat at the front of the Senate meeting, his long nose pale in the mid-morning sunlight that streamed through the low windows of the temple.

"The waters at the lake may be a bad omen" he conceded as he remembered the argument from the right. "But the glorious victories of our esteemed Marcus Furius Camillus must surely outweigh this bad news?" he half questioned as silence remained in the room around him.

Priscus had sent his news three days earlier, followed soon after by the news that Camillus had gained both Faleria and Capena in short succession, the news bringing a cheer to the Senate meeting where it was announced.

Cicurinus had sent a delegation to the Oracle at Delphi to try to understand the omen and meaning of the water of Lake Alba rising, news which had caused a series of mini riots in the streets as the plebeians came out in droves and claimed the gods were showing their displeasure at the patricians retaining an all year round siege at Veii and depriving Rome of its healthy farming men. The delegation was the only way in which he could placate the plebeian tribunes and bring calm to the city.

He continued to sweep his eyes across the heads of the Senators, his cold stare forcing some to drop their eyes as he caught them with his fierce gaze.

"It is late in the season gentlemen and our next decision will secure our actions for the winter months. Your votes will be counted and agreed within two cycles of the moon" at this he pointed to the candle lit on the table in front of the senate which denoted the power of the gods overlooking their decisions with regard to the next years Military Tribunes. The names of the men put forward were scrawled on tablets around the thick white candle. "I will call the council again at this time and we will discuss the decision and, we hope" he turned to his left as a row of elderly, toga clad, gentlemen nodded "we will have news from Delphi. Until then Priscus remains in charge at Veii and all orders stand. Genucius and Titinius will control the armies in the field under his command" he said.

As the leaders of the Republic stood and, noisily, left their seats Cicurinus watched the small groups of political allies as they quickly huddled together, some of their words drifting across to him as they discussed their family members or favourites and how to elevate them in the military ranks. He shook his head as he sat and took a deep breath, a weariness coming over him as he contemplated his future. Maybe it was time to retire to the country, he thought, a short smile starting to spread across his age lined face.

"Ah Senator" came a reedy voice which pulled him from his thoughts.

"Yes." He forced himself to smile as he spoke.

"Surely you will support the agreement to have Virginius appointed Military Tribune during the next vote" Ahala pronounced rather than asked, which took the older Senator somewhat by surprise.

*

*

Chapter 10

It had been a cold winter, the snow coming deep and fast once again, as it had for the past three years, and the news at Veii continued to be disastrous. Raiding parties continued to harass the Romans at the walls of the city, with losses reported every day. Priscus had been taken ill, having to be removed to his home as he caught a deep fever and was at deaths door, the bleeding of his physicians not making him any better. He had been replaced by an inept patrician called Honorius who had simply thrown men in small skirmishing groups at the enemy in a vain attempt to keep the Roman line secure. As it stood the soldiers at Veii were at their lowest point, more than a hundred had been known to have run away from the siege within the last month. The plebeian council had once again called for the return of the army, but this had been vetoed by the Senate. Constant arguing filled every political meeting, arguments for and against continuing the war turning into angry shouting matches as propaganda and graffiti covered the walls of Rome accusing patricians of enslaving the people of Rome. The plebeian's spoke of half of Rome being crippled by war tax and the other half being crippled by military service, tensions were at an all time high. And now there was even more bad news as the early part of Martius approached and Rome was awakening its population for another year of warring campaigns in the Latin Delta.

In the frozen lands beyond the Alban Lake a war band had been seen approaching the siege works to the East of the city of Veii. Honorius had sent Genucius and Titinius out to meet them, Titinius circling the attackers in an attempt to get behind them and catch them unawares. The Etrurian commander had been clever and had laid a trap for the Romans, which Genucius had paid for with his, and his men's lives, by attacking without the support of Titinius. The attack had been caught on rocky ground and the phalanx of soldiers succumbed to the worst of fates as they were butchered by the Etrurians, a shock of cavalry appearing from Veii and riding into their rear before Titinius could come to his aide. Titinius had recovered to higher ground and defended his position for two days before the enemy had retreated in glory, music and dancing coming from within the city for days after the attack as they celebrated their success.

The news had just broken, and Marcus left the Senate house deep in conversation with Lucius, his older brother, as men scurried away to inform their masters and allies of the disaster at the hands of Veientines.

"I don't believe it. Could it get any worse, brother?"

"Yes" replied Lucius as he scowled and his eyes darted around them to check who was close. "Virginius and Sergius are to be appointed Military Tribunes this year" he said quietly as Marcus stopped suddenly a look of absolute shock on his face.

"What?" he said loudly as two Senators turned to him with quizzical looks.

Lucius gripped his sleeve and smiled to the two men as he moved Marcus away from the temple into the empty street which ran up the hill towards Marcus' house in the richer part of Rome's Equestrian district.

"I heard it from Ahala" he said once they had gained some distance from the prying ears behind them. "You and I will also be called, plus Sulpicius and Servillius" he said, naming the six men who would be voted at the next meeting of the tribes.

Marcus groaned at the thought. He had promoted Virginius to Ahala in an attempt to remove him from his own line of command, but he had not expected the man to be made Military Tribune. He closed his eyes momentarily as he took a deep breath and let it out with a huff. Lucius smiled back at his exasperated face. "Wasn't it you who said he was an excellent commander of the horse and had saved your baggage train?" he asked.

Marcus glowered as he remembered the report he had written, knowing that the truth was that less than fifty men had attacked the baggage and had been over-run by the hangers-on and traders before Virginius had done anything about the sudden raid which had happened just before the attack on Capena.

"I know" was all he could say in reply. "But *Tribune*" he shook his head slowly as they climbed the steep slope.

"I hope they give me Veii" Lucius said with a frown. "Or you" he added with a sideways look to Marcus. Lucius had had a sparkling military career, being Tribune on four occasions and having many successes in the field. Yet he knew that Marcus had already outshone him with his tactics and the sheer amount of booty he had won for Rome. The attack on Capena had yielded so much treasure that for months the plebeians had been quiet as the war seemed to have taken a new turn, one which included success at last.

Marcus didn't look to his brother but caught the look in his face and the tone of his words as he spoke to him.

"I would be honoured to serve under you again, brother" Marcus replied warily. Lucius placed a hand on his shoulder and stopped them both, peering around to check the road was quiet.

"Since Uncle died we have had no-one to discuss your prophecy with" Lucius started to say as Marcus shook his head. It was always the prophecy with Lucius, always testing if he had thought through what it meant and how he could fulfil it, always asking what new links he had found that he could exploit using the words he had written in a small capsule around his neck. Their Uncle had been Pontifex Maximus but had died shortly after their grandmother in the summer whilst both brothers were campaigning. It had been a sad loss and Marcus had spent many days in mourning. *Uncle* had no children and his wife had been given his house and country estate and Marcus had spent some time visiting them all in the winter months to ensure that everything was as it should be.

Lucius caught the shake of the head and looked deeply into his brother's eyes, the intensity causing Marcus to flush slightly as he did so. "This is important Marcus, you know that this could raise the family to new heights and secure a future for your children" he said, almost scolding him. "You must make every effort to maximise the love the gods have shown you" he added as Marcus simply looked back at him blankly.

Marcus lowered his chin towards his chest. He knew what he was saying held a grain of truth but he still didn't truly understand how the words of the prophecy would come to pass. His future was as grey to him as the clouds in the skies and he looked at the floor as his mind stretched through the words he had contemplated time and time again.

"Surely you have thought about the link between these waters at Veii and your prophecy?" Lucius questioned, his raised eyebrows searching Marcus' face. "What does it say? *The waters will shrink before him*" he said urgently as he nudged him into a walk as another group of men appeared in the road below them. Marcus frowned as he looked to his brother, a sudden realisation coming to his mind.

"Surely you listened and connected these thoughts? Tell me you did brother?" Lucius was looking with disbelief to his younger sibling, his dark eyes a mask of confusion. Marcus hadn't even given it a moment's thought, his mind had been consumed with the idea of supporting the soldiers, of creating his Eagles to be the servants of Rome. He looked again at his brother but no words came to his lips as his mind started to connect thoughts and words. Lucius shook his head, more in exasperation than anger.

"On our Uncles shade I could kick you. Marcus" he chided with a smile as Marcus simply shook his head in reply. Taking a moment to consider he turned to Marcus and laughed. "Maybe, brother, this is the thing with the prophecy. That you cannot see it and others must help you to see what the words can mean and how to act upon them" he said with his eyes narrowed. "It must be so" he said, more to himself than to Marcus, and with these words ringing in his ears Lucius set off again, with Marcus one step behind him thinking about the waters of Veii and what the prophecy could mean.

****

"We must support his rear" came the high-pitched squeal from the Centurion as Virginius stared absently into the distance, his face bored despite the deafening noise only three hundred paces away.

"He has not signalled for support and therefore he does not require it Centurion. If you see a signal, do please make me aware of it. Until that time please do not repeat your comment." The Centurion saluted, his face an angry mask of confusion as he turned and strode to his position at the front of the troops.

Veii had sent another raiding party out in the first light of dawn and had been surprised by the waiting Romans, a trap laid by Servilius as the overall leader of the Roman troops, with Sergius and Virginius supporting each other as leaders of the attack parties. The two tribunes had argued like spoilt children as to who would lead the main attack and after a petulant outburst by Sergius, Servilius had given in to his claim for the senior role. The animosity between the two men had grown steadily over the preceding days and as the attack began to take shape Virginius had announced loudly to the departing Sergius that should he require his support he would be awaiting his signal. Sergius had gotten his meaning instantly and resolved that there was no way that he would request the help of his enemy.

The Centurion stood and watched the scene in front of him. The Veientines had attacked the siege works at a fort along the edge of the forest where the cunicula were widest, the deep holes making the ground uneven and the defences weak. Sergius had rallied his men and taken the initiative, moving his troops into two deep lines and spreading them across the long ditch of the defences. The Veientines had jumped the ditch and come around behind the

Roman line, but the rear group of spearmen had already turned and taken arms against them. The fighting was fierce, with men falling from both sides and the cacophony of noise echoing off the wooden walls of the defences. The Centurion had seen the danger, a new troop of soldiers had appeared from one of the deep trenches along the wooden wall. They must have crawled for hundreds of yards to get to this position, but now that they had pounced they were in amongst the Romans before Sergius could react. His men were hacked from three sides, almost boxed in and falling in their droves. The Centurion hopped from one foot to the other, gripping and re-gripping his sword and staring at the Tribune to see if he would send a signal, but nothing came. He watched the head of an old friend, his scream dying in his open mouth as it fell into the mud and bounced once before disappearing into the ditch. His anger nearly spilled over, but he held his breath and gritted his teeth. More Romans fell, more than half the original force already dead. Sergius was fighting like a bull, charging into the enemy and being dragged back by his men, their curses and screams ringing into the air.

Sergius pulled back and peered around, his eyes falling on Virginius who sat with four hundred men to his left and stared blankly at him, the corners of his mouth curling. The men from the ditch were scything through Sergius' remaining men and he turned and called retreat to his soldiers, struggling to find his feet as he edged backwards towards the safety of the fort. The Centurion glanced to his officer but saw no trace of any emotion on the man's face. The Veientines cheered as the last few Romans were hacked, Sergius taking a sword to the helmet which knocked him senseless for a moment before his second in command picked him up and dragged him out of danger.

"Ha" laughed Virginius as he watched Sergius lifted bodily from the scene. "Carried off like a child" he mumbled to a few sniggers from the closest soldiers to him. "Back to the camp" called Virginius as he watched the last Roman disappear behind the defences and the

Veientines cheer wildly before diving onto the dead bodies and stripping them of as much armour or coins as they could find.

****

The camp had fallen into the kind of silence where everyone was busily doing as little as they could and were surrounding the Senior Tribunes tent to listen to the rebukes that carried into the still air. The angry shouting and cursing had lasted for a full twenty minutes as Honorius berated the two Tribunes, each berating the other as the reason for the death of nearly three hundred Romans. Men looked to each other and shook their heads as they wandered past on delivery runs which were hundreds of yards out of their usual passage and they strained their ears as they slowed their pace to hear the commanding officer calling his Tribunes *inept* and *useless*. Many men smiled at the dressing down the useless officers got. Others smiled at the thought that there may be some payment for the death of their friends, brothers or cousins.

"You cannot be serious" yelled Honorius, the veins standing out in his neck as he stared at the two men standing in front of him. He rose from his chair. "What sort of fool does not support a fellow Roman who is clearly losing to a greater number of enemy soldiers?" he called, the spit rolling off his bottom lip as his eyes bulged in anger. Honorius was tall and thin, his long face clean shaven and his blue-green eyes pale in his olive skinned face. He held up his hand as Virginius stepped forward aggressively to speak.

"And what sort of fool doesn't call for support when heavily outnumbered?" he added to Sergius, his head covered in a thick bandage which was already red with his blood from the wound he had taken to his head.

Both men stared at each other with a level of loathing which made the tent almost crackle with the hatred they held towards each other.

"You are both the worst soldiers I have ever seen. Do you understand what damage you have done to the soldiers out there? How can they line up behind you after this... this.." he pointed at Virginius who stared angrily back at him. "Farce" he finished, rounding on Sergius with a deep glare of anger.

"I am returning to Rome for medical support" Sergius said, a glance at Virginius with a curl to his lip.

"No, he cannot leave, Sir" Virginius added. "A knock to the head is all he has, there is nothing wrong with him." Virginius felt a pang of fear as he knew that the first man to Rome would spread the word about the attack and garner favour with the Senate and the plebeians, spreading rumours that could ruin the others career. He had to stop this or at least get to Rome first. His mind wheeled as he sought an excuse. "He" he pointed at Sergius. "Requested that I did not support him until he gave the signal, Sir. As I have stated and I will swear it in the Senate house, he gave no signal despite the fact that on several occasions I rallied the men to support him."

"Rubbish" cried Sergius. "We've been over this you jumped up..."

"Gentlemen" yelled Honorius, his voice booming. He took a breath. "I would send both of you back to Rome if I didn't need you, however pathetic you are, here. Sergius, get to your tent and report back in one hour. If your wound is still bleeding I will send you to Rome myself." He turned to Virginius, whose face was a mask of anger and fear, his position suddenly weakened by the Senior Tribune. "You and your men are on wall duty tonight. No I will not answer any more of your questions" he said loudly as Virginius motioned to speak. He shook his head angrily, his eyes red-rimmed from shouting. "Get out, both of you." He called as he stomped back to his chair and sat heavily in it.

"Orderly" he called as a man rushed in, his face solemn as he stared at the back of the tent. "Fetch a messenger at once and prepare two horses, I need to get a message to the Senate immediately."

****

The news of the death of hundreds of Romans at Veii and the behaviour of two of its Military Tribunes reached the City within a day. The Senate had called an emergency meeting and as leader of the Senate Servilius Ahala had given no reason for the meeting, simply calling it as urgent. Within an hour of sending the message to the Senators there was a knock on the door of his house on the Capitoline Hill, a great booming sound which echoed through his atrium and caused his wife to grip her weaving in fear.

"Open up Ahala" came the cry as the Senate leader stood from his seat at his desk in the study and walked, with some trepidation, to the doorway. His door slave had just slammed the portal closed after peeking out to see who was at the door at this early hour.

"Well?"

"Many men, Sir. With Apuleius and that other plebeian tribune" the slave replied with a look of fear.

Two burly bodyguards appeared from the kitchen area, cudgels and daggers in hand. Ahala smiled to them. "I'm sure I am not to be murdered in my own house" he said as he moved to the door.

"Open the door slowly" he said as he took a deep breath and raised his chin to stare haughtily at the crowd as their faces appeared in the gap as the doorway opened and the light fell into the atrium.

"There he is" called a deep voice as a chorus of booing rang around the road outside his house. Fifty or sixty men and women stood in the road, the women starting to wail and pull at their hair as the Senator appeared in his doorway.

"What is this Apuleius? Why do you bring these people to my door?" he called above the noise of the crowd, two of the men spitting at him as they drew closer and were pushed back by the bodyguards who had slipped into the space in front of their master.

Apuleius looked at Ahala with a serene face, his eyes not moving from those of the man at whom he stared. "Tell these women that it is not true?" he asked theatrically. "That their children are not killed by the incompetence of the patrician Tribunes, men not fit to carry the title and not fit to lead even babes in arms into battle."

Ahala cursed inside but kept his face straight as he looked beyond the plebeian tribune into the crowd. Men stared at him with hatred in their eyes. He made a mental note to have the messenger whipped and tortured.

"A report has been received Apuleius" he replied in a level tone "and will be read at the meeting of the Senate this morning."

"And can the plebeians attend this meeting? These people whose sons have died at the hands of poorly led armies *must* have recompense for their deaths" he added with a sweep of his arm. "If the reports I hear are true" he looked at Ahala with a smirk "then the Tribunes owe these people compensation for the deaths of their sons. Deaths which could have been avoided. Deaths which add to the slavery of our people at Veii. Slavery which is causing pain, suffering and hardship to the citizens of our great city. You, *Senator*, must allow the plebeian tribunes to come to your meeting and to hear what words are in your report. It is our right as citizens of the Republic to have a say in the outcome of this latest *disaster*." He finished with a cold stare at the Senator as loud agreement came from the men at his back whilst the women continued to lament, some falling to their knees and raising their arms to the skies.

Ahala stared at Apuleius and took a moment to think. The plebeians were growing in power and this *incident* could cause a major riot if not handled properly. He glanced again at the women, noting that one he had seen acting in a performance in the forum only days before. Paid, he thought, not the real mothers, but he knew that the real mothers would be far more vocal and would call upon all the gods to curse the leaders of this ill-gotten campaign against

Veii. Why was this city so blessed? What was it about Veii that made it so difficult to break? He looked back to the plebeian tribune, noting his impatient look.

"The plebeian tribunes can attend the meeting. I will have the order sent" he barked as he turned and walked back into his house.

Apuleius grinned as he turned to the men around him, each one cheering as they clapped him on the back and raised his arm, cheering his name.

Across the road Manlius stood in the shadows and smiled. Apuleius was gaining power and he must do something about it. He considered, for a moment, removing the man, but decided that he needed to keep his potential enemies close and widen his net of spies. With that thought in his head he fell in behind the cheering crowd as they headed back towards the forum.

*

*

Chapter 11

It had taken three days to call the two Tribunes to Rome, Sergius arriving early as his head had continued to cause problems. On arrival both men had vehemently berated the other, calling each other cowards and fools and telling different stories of the loss at Veii.

The trial had lasted a further two days, each man standing proudly before the Senate and the plebeian tribunes and denying all counts against them, blaming the other for incompetence and inability to lead men. The Senate was at a loss and Ahala had called a final sitting to finish the matter, his anger rising as he had listened to the arguments each man had put forwards.

The meeting was being held in the high ceilings of the Temple of Jupiter Capitolinus, high on the prow of the hill above the city with a view of the snaking Tiber below. The temple was sacred to Jupiter, Juno and Minerva and highly coloured statues adorned the terraces along the front of the building, flowers and baskets of fruit laid along its frontage in devotion to the gods.

Jupiter's statue sat in the middle of Juno and Minerva, his eyes staring down as the people gathered around the temple to await news of the decision against the two Tribunes, both of whom remained steadfast in their refusal to accept any blame. The roof of the building contained Jupiter driving a quadriga, a chariot drawn by four horses, said to have been created by the finest sculptor in Veii a generation ago before the current crisis.

Outside thousands thronged in the streets, the noise growing as sellers of meats and breads mingled with the common people of Rome. Bodyguards had cleared spaces for the rich patricians to enter the Temple and then sat on the steps waiting for them to return.

Inside Marcus and Lucius sat along the front row of the left hand side of the temple, its two hundred paces frontage one of the only buildings that could hold all the Senators and the plebeian Tribunes for this meeting.

So far the discussions had not changed, each man denying any guilt and calling the gods to punish them if they saw any error in what they said. Ahala and the two leading Senators stood, the crowd coming to silence at the movement. Looking around at the faces before him, he spoke.

"We have listened to many days of argument and counter argument and come to our decision" he said with a look to his left and right as the other Senators nodded. "The Senate has agreed that both Tribunes were culpable for their actions and loss of men at Rome" he glanced at both men who remained stoic as they stared at him. "And because of their inability to support each other they will be removed from office immediately" he said as men stood, some waving their fists and other s cheering and berating the two soldiers.

Ahala called loudly for silence, the Temple reverberating with noise as he tried to calm the Senate. On his right Apuleius and Decius, the two plebeians looked to each other and smiled, their faces showing how they believed this was a great success for their continued arguments against the patrician leaders.

As Ahala continued to call for silence Sergius raised a hand and turned to face the rows of men behind and to his side, his jaw set firm as his eyes scanned those who were cheering and noted who they were.

"Senators" he said, his voice loud but not shouting. He glanced to Virginius who frowned at his theatrics and turned his head away. The noise level began to drop as he stood with one arm raised and a deep frown on his face. "Senators" he said in a lower tone as he turned back to Ahala with a short smile on his face. Marcus nudged Lucius and nodded towards Javenoli who was scribbling in a wax tablet, his usual method of recording everything so that he could relive the events and plot schemes against those who differed from his views. He smiled at the thought of how he had once acted as the man's scribe before returning his attention to the Tribune standing in front of him.

"As Tribune of the Republic I understand our laws and I know the feelings of the people. I understand that this *situation*" he sneered at Virginius "is deplorable" he said with feeling in his voice.

"But" he said more loudly, suddenly capturing the attention of the assembled nobles of the Republic. "By law as Tribune I still retain the right of veto." A shout of indignation came from the back of the room, several heads turning to see who had called out in disgust. Another voice called back that this was right and proper as Sergius raised his arm again and turned back to Ahala. "I veto this resolution" he said. Roman law was such that as long as one of the Tribunes disagreed with the decision made by the Republican leaders they could not enact such a decision. Virginius smiled but inside he cursed. Why had *he* not thought of this action.

"You cannot be serious" Ahala called as men began to rant at the two Tribunes, calling them cowards and murderers as Ahala waved for silence.

Marcus shook his head and whispered to Lucius "Dictator?" at which his brother raised his eyebrows and nodded thoughtfully. At times of dispute the Republic had one final act it could use to resolve such issues, the appointment of a Dictator. The Republic only chose such a role in times of dire need as it gave all encompassing power to one man for up to six months, a power which was as close to that of a King that Rome would ever allow. Other voices were mouthing the same thought as Sergius continued to stare around the room, his hand in the air. "Gentlemen" Ahala called, his voice starting to crack as he yelled into the temple. "You do yourselves no favour with such..." he looked exasperated as he stared at two of the more vocal Senators, each red-faced from shouting. "Noise" he added with a shake of his head and a deep exhalation of air.

"You have that right" called Ahala to Sergius. "If you take that path you will leave the Senate no option but to call a Dictator" a loud cheer came from the back row again "to resolve this issue." He stared hard at Sergius, his eyes glancing to Virginius, and then across to Apuleius, before continuing.

"I warn you both as Tribunes that a Dictator will have the power to enforce rules stronger than those of the Senate. Found guilty you could be banished or imprisoned" he added, his face cold. "You men must decide your own actions. But I warn you gentlemen I will call a Dictator to review the case against you. Decide. Veto the decision to re-elect new Tribunes for the year or agree to it. I *will* call the Senate to elect a Dictator if you veto the motion, the Republic will not allow incompetence in its soldiers. You have one hour to decide" he said dispassionately as he shook his head and frowned at both men, the meaning of his words not lost on either of them.

****

An hour later the Senate had reconvened and Virginius stood forward, his head bowed. The Senators sat in silence as both Tribunes stood in front of them.

"Senators and Tribunes" said Virginius as he looked coldly at Ahala. "The Republic is stronger than any one man or his actions. The Republic and our laws must be followed under the eyes of the gods and we as humble men must accept these laws." He spoke quietly and without emotion, his words firm yet not angry or aggressive.

"Our actions at Veii" at which Sergius stood tall and his chest rose under his toga, though his eyes betrayed the emotion he was feeling. "Were not those of incompetent generals" at this a number of dissenting voices called out, but he ignored them all. "They were those of seasoned campaigners who believed their actions were correct" he said more loudly over the noise. "The outcome" he nearly shouted as the noise grew steadily "was the will of the gods, we are but men and we play our part." His voice was drowned by a chorus of booing and name calling from the seats around him, the Temple once again almost shaking at the cacophony that erupted at his words.

"Let the gods" he called. "Let the gods judge us" he shouted as Sergius nodded in defiance. "But" he called raising his hand for silence and turning to scan the room as waited for the Senators to fall quiet. "But" he called again.

"We" and he nodded to Sergius, who had the grace to nod in reply before dropping his chin on his chest as if in defeat, "will not veto the motion" he said as he sat and a great cheer went around the room.

It took five minutes for the leaders of the Senate to call the men in the Temple to order. Ahala stood, a measure of relief on his face.

"Gentlemen of the Republic it falls on me at this sad time to make null the roles of Military Tribune for this season and to call for re-elections. Voting will open at the close of this meeting and we will decide within the next day whom shall be the new Tribunes." He looked to the two men sat in front of the Senate and took a deep breath. "Neither of these two men will be allowed to stand for the roles." He looked back up at the silent men.

"Unless there is any other business I propose we adjourn to begin the voting" he asked with wide eyes to the room at large, fully expecting the men to agree and rush out to their lunches.

"Senator" came a voice to the right near the Temple doors. He scanned the rows before he saw Apuleius stand and take a step forward.

"The plebeian tribunes are wondering what punishment there will be for the incompetence of these men?" he asked quizzically, his face a deep frown.

"Punishment" replied Ahala. "In times of war there is no punishment" he added, returning the frown.

"But these men and their incompetence has caused the death of the beloved sons of men of Rome. Men who would be tilling the land and growing the crops to feed the City. Men who would stand proudly under a new commander, their sword arms true and strong against our enemies if *these men* had not been so foolish and rash in their hatred of each other that they had not left them to be slaughtered by their ineptitude." A series of gasps came from the room.

"There will be no punishment, the loss of their roles and potential future political careers is enough." Came the quick reply, Ahala almost ruing his words before he spoke them as Apuleius smiled his predatory grin.

"Then" he called more loudly as Decius stood and stared at Ahala, ice in his eyes. "As is our right, we the plebeian tribunes call a law-suit against these two men for their incompetence as leaders. By their poor actions they have caused the death of fellow Romans. By their" the indignation of the act brought most of the room to their feet, angry shouts cursing the plebeians as both Virginius and Sergius gaped at the face of Apuleius. "By their acts men have died that need not have died. You called for the gods to judge you?" he shouted above the noise, an angry finger jabbing in the direction of the two men. "I call on our laws to judge you under the eyes of Justitia and under the laws of the Republic. We the plebeians *DEMAND* it" he screamed as the veins in his throat bulged and Decius moved to his shoulder with a face of stone.

****

Servius frowned into the semi-darkness of the trees, his eyes growing more accustomed to the light as he sat still on the horse, his head low. It had taken four days to traverse to the meeting point avoiding the main roadways and villages so that his cargo would not be spotted. Behind him were thirty donkeys loaded high with the next load of weapons for the defenders at Veii. This will be the last drop I do, he said to himself as he took a deep slow breath and watched the movement deep in the trees ahead of him. It had been by chance he had noticed the sudden movement ahead, a branch swinging and then another. Hopefully it was no more than a deer or a boar, but he felt a sudden fear and clutched at the lucky talisman he held around his neck. Muttering a prayer for luck he continued to scan the trees. No new movement came. He was a full day early for the meeting and expected no-one to be near the waterfall which lay another hour away from where he sat, especially in this thick part of the woods. Behind were seven of his best men, each clutching swords or other weapons as he leant forwards and listened for any sounds. Nothing again, but he remained still as a precaution. One error and they could be dead.

After another few moments he sat up and waved to Artius. The man crept forwards.

"I am going to scout ahead. Keep these men quiet and do not move. If you hear any sounds of running, stay still, pass the word. I can escape any man in this darkness" he added with a grin. Artius nodded and turned, creeping back to the waiting men behind.

Slipping from the horse Servius slid the long blade from its scabbard, removing the belt and placing it over the horses back before stepping quietly into the darkening woods.

The undergrowth was thick and clawed at his legs but he continued to step forwards slowly, speed was not important, a misplaced step could announce him to any number of men or beasts. After only a hundred steps the darkness had grown, the low light from above the trees giving only the minimum of vision at floor level, an advantage only he could use. For years his ability to see so much better than any man he had ever met in the dark had been his route to his fortune, today was no different. He stood next to a thick tree, his breathing slow as he continued to scan the area. Nothing.

With a frown he decided it must have been a deer moving through the forest and went to turn. A sudden blinding flash behind his eyes announced the pain he felt before he fell to the floor and disappeared into unconsciousness. As he slipped into the darkness his only thought was *betrayed*.

*

*

Chapter 12

The voting had been completed and the new Military Tribunes were Marcus Furius Camillus, Titinius Saccus, Philo Maelius, Genucius Augurinus, Manlius Vulso and Atillus Priscus, all patricians and all of the older families of Rome. The men had been sworn in and accepted their roles in the traditional manner, each setting off to the camp to which he had been assigned.

Marcus had, after a request from his brother, been assigned the siege at Veii and had set off with a heavy heart. Veii was one war he felt he could not win, surely the city held the love of some great god more powerful than those who watched over Rome. He had considered his approach with the siege at Veii for some time and had sent riders forwards to receive reports of the strength of the standing army and its most recent actions. Ahala had *suggested* to Marcus that he defer to Honorius a great feast at the siege works to thank him for his year in charge. Reading the reports he found it hard to find anything to celebrate. Continued skirmishes battered the Roman defences around the raised walkway which had moved no more than five paces forward during the whole year. Men continued to defect to the city of Veii, reports showing that troop morale was low and the waters of the lake continued to rise, indeed the water had recently caused a long section of the siege works to fall as it had risen another foot in the last cycle of the moon. Marcus frowned at this news, considering the words Lucius had said to him regarding the lake and the waters receding in his hour of need. What did it mean?

His tent was dark as he pondered the latest report by candlelight. He heard the voice of Mella outside and sat up, his eyes squinting as a knock on the central tent pole announced his arrival.

"Sir" came the words as the smiling face of his old friend entered the tent, two Centurions close behind.

"You asked for an update" he said, scanning the area for a seat before Marcus pointed away into a dark corner. Stepping across and gripping the chair he passed it across to one of the men and then returned to fetch another. "We are less than a day's ride to the defences." He said, passing across another chair and returning to fetch the last. "And you have the latest report. Word is though" he said as he sat and looked up "that the water has stopped rising, no increase for a few days now" he smiled.

Marcus nodded but didn't reply.

"Caelio" Mella said as he looked to the officer to his right "has a brother at the defences and has suggested he ride ahead tonight and get the latest update from him before we arrive."

Marcus glanced to Caelio with a nod and returned his eyes to the report before handing it across to Caelio, who took it and leant forwards to catch the light.

"Good idea" Marcus replied. "Caelio" he said as he took a small tablet and stylus and began to scribble, looking up as his mind went through his thoughts. "This is what I need to know" he said as he continued writing. "Morale. Weapons. Defences. Centurions who are liked and those who are not." Mella looked up at this odd request, but Marcus was still scribbling and talking. "Food supplies. Duty lists"

"I'm not sure my brother will have all of that" Caelio said with a smirk.

Marcus nodded. "Agreed but you can stay and find out the information and we can discuss tomorrow evening when we have arrived and completed all the necessary hand-overs with Honorius." He spoke quickly and decisively. Caelio nodded, handing the latest report to Mella.

"It's a shame Scipio isn't still at the camp" Marcus said without looking up from his writing. "He would know all of this" he said. Scipio had returned to his family at the end of the previous summer following the death of his mother from the plagues which continued to eat into Rome's population each year. Mella nodded, thinking of the withdrawn man he had met at his house only days earlier. Scipio had declined the offer to join Marcus as his wife was due a new child in the coming days, promising he would join once the child had been accepted into the family and all the correct rites completed.

"There" Marcus said as he handed the tablet to Caelio and sat back. He looked to the three men and relaxed. "Narcius how is the arm" he asked, knowing that the leader of the Eagles had spent weeks working harder than any of his men to regain his full usage of the arm hurt in the recent battle at Capena.

"Better than I could have expected" he grinned, a weary look in his eyes which Marcus caught.

"You should take a day or two's rest when we reach Veii" he said as his eyes narrowed. "I need you to get around the other Centurions and officers and see what they think of the defences, which are the weak points and which are the strongest. The men will know" he said as he clicked his fingers and a slave, his brown tunic tight on his lean frame, stepped into the tent from the rear quarters. "Wine" Marcus said without looking at him. Bowing, the man disappeared.

"Veii is a thorn in the foot of Rome" Marcus said. "A thorn I want to pull out" he added, his voice suddenly determined. "I asked you here as I need your advice and I need your support" he said as the men looked to each other.

"I've sent Fasculus on a little *trip*" he added as he noted the surprise in the faces of all three men, each flicker of their faces telling him that they had not known of the *task* the new man to their inner group had been assigned. Before he spoke again the slave arrived and dutifully poured out a measure of water and wine for each man, the three across from Marcus waiting for him to drink first.

"Gods Mella, don't stand on ceremony, you'll unnerve me, man" he said with a smile as he raised his silver cup and said "For Rome and the Republic" at which Mella grinned and replied "Fortuna and Mars." The men drank their cups dry and placed them on the table, Mella reaching across and filled them with the jar before holding it out to the slave who disappeared into the back to refill the jug.

"What's Fasculus doing then?" asked Narcius.

Marcus leant forward slightly and spoke in a quiet half whisper. "I had intelligence that Veii was receiving weapons from a source outside the City. My informant gave me some details of a new meeting and I sent Fasculus to" he paused "intercept it" he finished.

The men creased their brows. "Who" said Caelio.

"I don't know yet who has been supplying the weapons but needless to say it is from within Rome" he said with eyebrows raised as the three men shook their heads and sucked air in through gritted teeth, Mella looking angrier than the rest.

"Bastards" he spat.

"That's as maybe, Mella" Marcus continued. "If he has intercepted the drop he will gain the information we need to tighten the screw on whoever it is" he smiled. "But I need your help on another matter" he said, looking to Caelio more than the other men whom he had known longer and trusted more explicitly. Marcus considered the three soldiers, men who fought for the glory and honour of Rome, but he also knew that they fought for wealth and social standing. He felt nervous as he began to speak.

"We must conquer Veii" he said sternly. "Rome demands it and so do the gods." The men looked grave as he saw their faces become serious. "I believe" he sat forwards again "that there are too many families who are too close to those in Veii and that they support them wherever they can. Supplies, weapons, even poor tactical decisions" he said as the men raised their eyebrows, Caelio looking as if he was about to speak but holding back his words.

"Speak openly Caelio" Marcus said, noting the sudden reluctance on the man's face.

Caelio, his lips suddenly dry glanced to Narcius and then back to Marcus. "Sir" he said, his voice low "such words are treasonous. The Senate would not allow such a thing, they would find and kill any man found guilty of such a crime."

"*Find* is the key word, Caelio" replied Marcus. "Rome has defeated every enemy for miles around, yet we have struggled for nearly ten years to defeat Veii. Why? There has to be a reason beyond the high walls and defences of the city." The men sat in silence. "How can any city under siege hold out for so long, surely there is not enough food for ten years held within its walls? So there must be other reasons."

"The gods favour them" Caelio said with a twitch as he glanced to the rue sprig, a talisman to Fortuna that he wore on his left wrist.

"I thought so too" Marcus replied "until Potitus overheard a discussion in the baths between two men who I shall not name yet." Marcus gulped back some of the wine, the three men doing the same as his action prompted the same response in all of them. "That is why I sent Fasculus on his trip. Potitus heard a father complaining that his son had gone on a trip to deliver goods to Veii but that he had not returned. As you can imagine the words were hushed quickly but Potitus followed them to their home. It took some time but a few well placed spies and a few coins" the men smiled, money always bought information "gave us our first clues."

Mella looked to Marcus, his face firm. "Why did I not know of this?" he half demanded as he looked to Marcus.

"My friend" Marcus replied "I could not involve any of you" he started to say.

"But Fasculus" Mella replied a little louder "can you trust the man?" he asked indignantly. Marcus took a moment to take in the meaning in his words. Fasculus had, indeed, been Javenoli's spy from many years ago, but he had proven himself in battles and had been as loyal as any man in the army, but he was especially good at finding information that other men could not. Marcus contemplated Mella's words before speaking. Mella had been his friend as a boy, his sword tutor and bodyguard as well as his drinking partner. But things had changed. Marcus had risen in status to command a Roman Legion, thousands of men would live or die on his words. He looked to Mella, who flushed slightly under his gaze. "Fasculus was the right man for this job, you know his skills Mella, and the fewer people who knew about it the better. In fact" he said as he sat straight in his chair "now only you three, my brother Lucius, Potitus and Fasculus know this" he said as Mella's bottom lip protruded slightly and he nodded.

"I must find the ways in which Veii is being helped, and *that* my trusted friends is where I need your help. I've been thinking about the fortifications and the camp at Veii" he said as he leant back on his chair and reached for a heavily laden leather sack. Pulling out a series of closed wooden tablets and a vellum map he laid them on the table as all the men moved closer. "I wish Scipio was here" Marcus said as he looked at the vellum and began to unroll it, a picture of the siege works and the city behind them appearing before the men.

A short silence ensued as the four men perused the document. "From the reports I have read and the stories I hear" he started "the siege works are attacked every night, but the defences are also attacked by skirmishers from either within the city or from outside, somewhere in these woods, maybe" he pointed to an area on the map.

"The ramp being built to assault the walls is over three hundred paces long and seventy paces wide at the front but has, in five years, moved no more than ten paces forwards. Something cannot be right" he stated as he looked up at the men, their nods agreeing with him. "I too thought that the omens were bad and the gods favoured Veii, but I began to think it through" he spoke mainly to Caelio. "How many men have left the siege works, hundreds?"

"More" came Mella's glum response.

"And this water" he shook his head "is that a divine message?" he looked at the men who glanced to each other without speaking, their silence testament to their belief that it was indeed a divine message. Looking back at the map in front of him he pointed to the lake.

"The Alban Lake is here" he tapped the lightly coloured area which marked the water. "Here are the fields of Veii, stretching for many many miles" he added. "How long would it take for the water to build up if it was not being used on the land, I assume that these Cuniculi are used for that" he added with a frown.

Mella looked at the map and then back to Narcius his face confused before he spoke. "Surely it is not that simple" he said as Caelio stared open-mouthed at him.

"I don't know Mella" Marcus replied honestly. "But I need you men to find out everything about the lake, the water and the reasons the men may think it has risen. It has been a strange summer and winter, with drought in Rome, heavy snow, long rainfall and then dry months. This could all add to the mystery of Veii. Maybe the gods are posing us a puzzle which we must solve before we over-run Veii. A test, if you like" he said pleased at the instant effect his words had on the three men.

"A test" Caelio said, a smile starting to spread across his face.

Marcus smiled a reply. "We must work to understand the issues at Veii because I am certain they lie in the mortal world more than the divine. If we have been set a test by Juno, mother goddess, then we must rise to it. Juno resides in Veii and it is my wish to complete the work of Servius Tullius and raise a Temple to her in Rome upon defeat of the city."

All three soldiers sat in silence at these words. Tullius had dedicated a temple to Mater Matuta many years before following considerable successes in the field, but at each turn his political enemies had stalled the funding of the building. Marcus had known this from his years as a Camillus and, following lengthy discussions with his brother, had alighted on the scheme to raise the hopes of the men at the camp. They needed a talisman, something to work for, Lucius had said. Marcus had used the words of his prophecy to suggest the removal of the statue of Juno, whom many also called Mater Matuta, the earth goddess, from Veii. A powerful symbol Marcus had said as Lucius beamed at the idea. But, of course, they needed to get into the city first, and that was the tricky part. Marcus was working through his thoughts as Narcius, usually quiet at such meetings, spoke.

"Sir" he said quietly. He glanced to Caelio and then back to Marcus. "The prophecy" he said as Mella turned urgently to him and then looked at Caelio. "Does it say anything about this?"

"Prophecy?" Caelio said with a deep frown.

Marcus looked to Caelio. Narcius and Mella had known of the words spoken by the augur Antonicus years before and had, as sworn by oath, not spoken of it to anyone. "It is a long story Centurion" he replied "though many seem to know of it in these troubled times." He pulled a small tube from a string around his neck and handed it to Caelio. "Here, read the words for yourself and then we will begin to plan how we will change the siege works at Veii and conquer the city" he said.

****

Four days later Marcus was sat in the wooden hut which was used as the command centre for the siege. Around the square building a marching camp had grown into a fully fortified fort, deep ditches and spike traps set out around the high wooden walls. Extending to the left and right were the long wooden lines of fortifications which hemmed in the great walls of the city. Marcus had ridden the entire length of the defences, noting weak points and attempting to match the reports he had read to the locations and people he visited. The men cheered as their new commander appeared, his presence had created a lift in the spirits along the thin lines of defence.

As required by the Senate he had held a feast for Honorius before setting the man on his way back to Rome with a bodyguard of heavily armed Eques.

A knot of officers and Centurions sat or stood in the room and Marcus had not, yet, looked up to greet any of them. The door opened and two more men entered, their helmets and feathers denoting their rank. They saluted and joined a group by the low window on Marcus' right. More men entered and Marcus looked up momentarily at each footstep.

"All present, Sir" came the words from the Optio stood to Marcus' side as he tapped the wax tablet with his stylus and closed the wooden panel.

Marcus stood, his eyes looking out over the men.

"Today is the first day of my command at Veii" he said as he watched nervous flickers in the eyes of the leaders of the siege camp. He looked to the Optio who produced another wax tablet, larger than the last and handed it to Marcus as some of the men shuffled more nervously. Narcius watched the men, a slight grin appearing on his face before he wiped it clean and stared at his commander.

"The candle is lit" Marcus said "and the devotion has been poured" he motioned to the small silver dish and white cowl, the mark of a Camillus, which he had used to prepare for the meeting.

"This" he held up the tablet "is a list of the changes I will make at this camp. Changes that are necessary if you men are to help Rome to a successful victory here." He looked at the men, seeing anger in some faces and nods of agreement in others. Narcius, Mella and Caelio had given him the names of the officers the men liked or disliked and the reasons why. He knew which men were slacking in their duties and he knew those who were trying hard to keep the morale despite the long siege. He also knew which men were running the gambling tents and the prostitute tents, his anger at finding that many of the prostitutes actually lived in the city of Veii and came to the camp at night having to be calmed by Mella who stated that if Marcus acted too quickly the leaders would not be found. Agreeing, but not happy, he had simply fallen back into the quiet role of watcher, allowing the leaders of the camp to carry on with their activities unabated, hoping they would find him to be a soft fool like Honorius. Some of the Centurions moved closer together, a few whispers coming from across by the window where Marcus now glanced before speaking again.

"These changes" he said "include a series of measures which will make this camp fit for the purpose in which it was created, to defeat Veii." His eyes grew dark as he motioned to the Optio, who stepped forwards.

"Officers, please move into line East to West as the forts of the defence are aligned one to ten" he said as a few frowns greeted his words but men started to shuffle into a line. The defences were split into ten forts ranging across the front elevation of the city, the furthest bordered by rocky cliffs or deep woods which fell into a deep ravine. As the men started to line up in the order in which they commanded each fort several men stood to the side, the baggage command, the medical Centurion and so on. The Optio urged them away to the right of the room, handing them a red ribbon which they looked at in confusion before the Optio said that the colours would relate to the new orders. Narcius stood with them and happily took a red ribbon of cloth, his smile making some of the men around him seem to relax as they knew he was close to the new commander.

After a minute or two the movements all stopped and the men returned their gazes to Marcus. Moving in front of the table Marcus looked at the men. On his left was the officer and leaders of fort one, their leader a Centurion the size of a bull, his stretched stomach hard under his thick tunic. "Spurius" he said as the man stood taller and responded with a salute and the words "Sir." Marcus noted the glances from other officers who were waiting to see what would happen next.

Marcus opened the wax tablet the Optio gave him and looked at the words, then back to the man, a drip of sweat falling along his temples as his eyes stared into the distance over Marcus's shoulder.

"An excellent record of achievements in the service of Rome, five years here at the walls" he said with a nod as the man simply stared at the wooden wall as if he found it fascinating. Marcus smiled at him. "You have lost no men to desertion in that time" he said, noting a sudden nervous shuffle from the centre of the room, "How is that?"

"Discipline, Sir. Just good solid soldiering and discipline" came the deep voiced reply.

Marcus fell into silence as he perused the tablet he held in his hands and walked along the line of men, stopping to look at one or two officers before smiling weakly and moving on. As he approached the far right the men holding the ribbons stood taller, each man glancing around the room before setting their gazes into the corner of the wooden building.

"Discipline" Marcus said as he motioned to the Optio, who moved quickly to the door and opened it to a sudden flurry of sword wielding Eagles, each man hand-picked by Narcius. As they entered Narcius drew his blade and stepped in front of Marcus, who remained calm as he watched the Centurions and officers start to draw their swords and stare around the room.

"Drop your weapons" Narcius called to the officers who were standing in the room, repeating the order as some failed to move, their angry calls coming quickly as they stared with indignation at their new commander.

Moving quickly to pick up and remove all the weapons the men of the Eagles withdrew to stand behind the officers, swords still drawn.

"Men of Rome" Marcus said, his eyes moving to Spurius' furious face and smiling, a confused frown coming to the man's face. "This is a necessary evil I must do to you at this time." As he spoke he moved to the men with the red ribbons, some of whom had thrown their cloth to the floor angrily. "You men have nothing to fear" he said "but you will remain to listen to what I have to say" he added coldly.

"This camp is lax" Marcus said as he moved across to his left "and I intend to change that." Shuffles came from the centre of the room, at which Narcius turned and levelled his sword.

"You have no right" a Centurion with a thick beard and deep brown eyes said, his tongue flicking out to lick his lips as he spoke.

Marcus looked at the man with an icy stare. "I have every right, soldier" Marcus said, not using the man's name deliberately. "As Tribune and commander of this camp I hold the power of life and death over every one of you and every man under your command. As

Tribune of Rome my word is sacrosanct here" he said slowly and deliberately as his eyes roved the room.

"Basus" he said, turning to the officer standing next to the vocal Centurion. "I believe you run the prostitutes tents" he said as the man nervously looked to his friend and stepped back slightly.

"It's a lie" he said quickly, his eyes darting to the sword of Narcius. "I have sworn statements here that you have entered the city of Veii on several occasions in the past few months to pick the women who work for you" Marcus said coldly as the men nearest Basus parted from him as if he had the plague, the man floundering as his head twitched from side to side.

"Is that the act of a true Roman? We will find out what information you were giving to the Veientine leaders whilst you were in city. Take him" he said as the man launched himself at Marcus, a snap of Narcius' wrist sending him sprawling back as his sword hilt smashed his left eye into a bloody pulp and three soldiers grabbed him and pummelled him before dragging him into the corner and tying him with ropes.

The action caused mayhem in the room, men started to move around and some shouts came, but the Eagles closed ranks and shouted their officers back into a line as Basus was dragged away.

"Lokitius" Marcus said as a thin man, his clean shaven face and short hair making his eyes appear to dominate his facial features, almost whimpered at the change of atmosphere in the room. Lokitius had a short scar along his forehead which seemed to dance as his eyes bulged and his eyebrows creased.

"Gambling" he said as Lokitius' mouth opened and closed without speaking. "Not a bad crime" he added as a moment of hope came to the man's face. "Yet fort three has had over sixty defectors. I hear that you have a list of men that owe you more than a years pay and you administer punishment as if you were the paterfamilias of your villa" he said as the man started to cringe, his hands wringing together. Again a parting of the ways occurred as men shifted from his side, his eyes glancing to the man who had spoken up at the start of the meetings sudden change in direction. A sword pushed into the small of his back and he turned, his hands swinging out as another soldier stepped forwards and gripped him around the chest before two more shuffled him backwards as the man let out a yell "Amelius" he called as if calling for his mother.

"Amelius" Marcus said slowly, turning to the thick bearded man. "Centurion of the fifth fort, the very one in which we stand" he smiled. The man looked back at him levelly and his fists balled as if he was going to strike at his officer. Marcus smiled at the man, bringing a look of hatred to his eyes. "Camitius" Marcus said, looking to the right and cocking his head as another man stepped back, one the officers beside him shoving him with a grin on his face, as he stared malevolently into his face.

"Hold, Maximus" Marcus said loudly as the man looked at him in surprise. "I know what he has done to you and your men, you will get a chance to repay the hurt he has given you" he said calmly as the surprised man turned and saluted smartly. "Yes, Sir" he said as another two Eagles gripped Camitus' arms.

"You patrician bastard" Amelius called as he leapt forwards, Narcius and Marcus both reacting instantly and catching the man in the stomach and face before he was dragged backwards by a mix of the Eagles and those men closest to him, some raining kicks into his prone body as he fell to the floor, Marcus allowing it to last a few seconds before he called the officers back from the Centurion.

"Take them out" Marcus said as the Eagles dutifully trussed up Amelius and then dragged him outside.

All eyes returned to Marcus.

"As I speak the junior officers of these men who are culpable along with them have been arrested and imprisoned." He stared at the men, seeing some flinch and others grin, before he returned to his desk and sat in the chair, a sudden relaxation coming to the group of men standing in front of him.

"Amelius and his men are like a plague. I know, I have served in a camp where the leading officers condone such actions. I know how hard it is to stand up to them when the Tribune turns a blind eye" Marcus said, his memory of Postumius flashing through his mind.

"However, gentlemen" he looked at the officers. "I am sure I have not wheedled out all the bad fruit and I will not allow anything to stop Rome defeating Veii. Spurius" he said looking to the heavily set man. "You are promoted to camp prefect" he held out a tablet from a pile on the table to the astonished man. "I want your discipline to rain on these men like the gods have opened the heavens" he nodded to the grinning face of the man. "Your orders are there. Don't thank me" Marcus replied as the man's face seemed to move into one of great joy. "The job is the hardest and most difficult you will ever face, this camp is a mess and you and the other officers will face my wrath if it is not sorted out within a month." The man saluted and stepped back, nervous glances coming from along the line of officers.

"Manucius" Marcus said. "I knew your brother" he added with a smile "a fine officer and I believe doing well as a magistrate" he added to the nodding head of the junior patrician who had stood with his mouth open at all the happenings in the room. "I hear you are good with numbers and logistics, so you will support Spurius as his deputy" he stated as the man looked across at his new boss and nodded, his mind already working through how pleased his father would be at this promotion. "I need everything listed and bolted down and I do not want any more deserters" Marcus added with a cold look at the newly appointed camp deputy.

As a silence fell into the room, Marcus moved a few of the tablets around the table before picking up a darkly coloured one, his eyes flicking into the remaining men in front of him.

"Within the hour I will call a full camp meeting and address the men" he said "no doubt the news of the arrests has caused a commotion among them" he added with a look to Narcius. "I will tell them that I am removing four of the forts, we do not need so many men spread so thinly along the defences. I will also be setting off to the woods at the Eastern end of fort nine to root out the skirmishers who constantly harry our defences for food and water. As I understand it these men are actually most of our deserters who have set up a camp there" he looked to Spurius who nodded his agreement. "I will drag them all back here and pin them to the walls" Marcus added with his jaw set firm. "The men must see that desertion is punishable by a slow and painful death. If the men are not afraid of their own officers how can they be afraid of the enemy" he added as he looked into the faces of the assembled group of men.

"I want the ditches dug to three men deep and the walls raised to twelve. We will have no more dealings with the city and we will certainly have no prostitutes in the camp" he turned to Spurius. "The civilian camp must be dismantled and removed" he said as a number of the men shuffled nervously at the words. "I know how it will be to the men, but the camp has over two thousand people living there, a hotbed of spies, thieves and sickness, and another reason why the men are slack in their work. The civilians can go home or remove themselves to two miles, too far for an evening's journey for the men to see their sweethearts or bastard children" Marcus added as he looked to Spurius. "Within the week" he commanded as the bull of a man glanced to Manucius and nodded, the patrician, already looking as if he had thought through some of the logistics, nodded in return.

"Every man here has to earn my trust" Marcus said coldly. "I will not accept failure and I will not accept defeat. Veii must fall." The soldiers stiffened at his words.

Handing the pile of tablets to the Optio Marcus stood. "Every soldier will renew his vows to Rome under the flames of the gods and the standard of Rome. I want every man to know that we are here for one purpose, to defeat Veii" he finished as the men saluted and said, as one,

"For Rome."

*

*

Chapter 13

Mella slumped into the chair and grabbed the wine jug in a mud covered hand. "I won the bet" he smiled to Caelio. "Ditch dug in two days" he grinned despite the weary look on his face. "Those pricks in the third are too fat and lazy" he added as he slurped the drink, spilling some on his dirty tunic.

"What news from Fasculus?" Caelio asked, his clean hand waving for the wine jug.

Mella sat forward and raised his eyebrows. "Camillus has a name but he hasn't said who yet. Seems that it's a go-between so he's sent someone to check it out."

"Good" came the reply. After a moments silence Caelio continued. "How are your lads? Any better?" Caelio was referring to the sombre mood that remained over the soldiers in the camp. The hard work of dismantling forts and reinforcing the defences had added to their miserable conditions they already had to endure. Constant sneak attacks from Veii continued to harass the men as they worked, but Marcus had forbidden any skirmishes as they led to the loss of too many un-prepared Romans, he had simply told the soldiers to retreat to safety and await the Veientines return to their city. To him the priority was to shore up the defences, not to waste time and energy on repeat attacks against small groups of raiders.

"Same" Mella replied glumly. "Nothing much pleases them, especially since the civilians and prostitutes left" he laughed dryly at the thought. "Every day I get some jumped up plebeian who wants to make it as a politician telling me how I should do things and exclaiming that the gods are still against us" he shook his head with a sigh.

Caelio added that his were the same before asking "do you think we will win?"

Mella shrugged and returned to the jug of wine. "Marcus Furius Camillus is the greatest general I have ever seen or heard of. The things he can do in battle and the way he plans assaults" he shook his head admiringly "well, if he can't do it, no-one can" he said. "When is he back?"

"He arrived in the dark, more prisoners are to be tied to the walls this afternoon when the sun reaches its high point" Mella replied, his eyes downcast at the thought of more runaways screaming into the long nights as they died tied and nailed to the walls. Marcus had now cleared every camp that the soldiers knew existed, hundreds of bodies lining the walls to be pecked at by crows and other birds. On the first day the first man had been nailed to the wall a large brown eagle had soared over the camp and dived at his jerking body as he screamed for mercy. The Eagles had called forth their standard and prayed to the gods in justification of the act, the sign clear for all the men to see.

****

"Centurion" came the call as Narcius turned to look along the line of soldier's furiously packing earth into the front of the great walkway which would be used to attack the city. Wicker screens were covering their work, but in reality a stalemate had grown in which the Romans worked hard all day to built the walkway and the Veientines came out at night to knock down as much of the earthwork as they could. As the walkway had approached the city it had been too dangerous to leave more than a few guards at the head of the great ramp for fear of a full scale attack killing all the defending troops, as had happened in the early days of the siege.

Narcius wandered across, the boredom showing in his face as he nodded to the man. "What is it?" he asked.

"Look there" he said, pointing to the walls where a group of men had appeared, the oldest wearing the long brown and blue robes of an Etruscan Augur. He seemed to be chanting some words, which Narcius couldn't make out. The Roman looked fearfully at his Centurion as both men turned their attention to the old sage.

"Is he cursing us?" the man asked, his face draining of colour as he gripped a circular talisman depicting an eye which was held around his neck.

Narcius ignored the comment and stepped closer to the wall, stopping at thirty to forty paces to call up to the man.

"You" he shouted. "What magic are you calling for. It will not work. We will take your city and grind it into the dust" he yelled.

The men above looked down on him as one took a bow and knocked an arrow onto the string, Narcius raised his shield in reply before the sage placed an arm across the bow-wielder. They spoke words that Narcius couldn't hear as he strained his eyes to see what was happening. The sage smiled down on the Romans as two men came to stand next to Narcius.

"What is it, sir" asked one of the men, shorter but wider in the shoulders than his officer. Narcius shrugged and returned his gaze to the walls.

"You Romans will never defeat Veii" the sage laughed back at him, his arms rising to the sky as he spoke. "The gods have willed it so" he added as a brown-toothed grin split the age old beard on his face.

"What does he mean?" the legionary, Vestus, asked as Narcius looked to him and his face grew angry.

"How do I know. Get back to work you little.." he started as the legionaries face turned to one of fear. His words were cut off by the shout from above.

"The water has risen to show the will of the gods. You have no idea how much the gods favour this great city" the man shouted as his arm swept back behind him, several more soldiers appearing on the wall all laughing and pointing to the Romans below.

"What do you mean? Tell us if the gods have spoken to you" called Narcius, a number of thoughts running through his mind. "Tell us, old man, if there are words which we can take back to Rome" he added as he looked to the shorter soldier and whispered "Fetch Centurion Mella at once, go" he commanded with a slight shove to the man's shoulder.

"Look how fearful we are of your gods" called Narcius as the legionary raced away. This brought a fevered discussion high on the wall as Narcius remained wary in case any missiles came towards him. He also became aware that the men behind him had stopped their work to watch the discussion, no doubt listening to the banter so they could relay information back to their tent mates and friends.

After a few minutes the old sage turned back to Narcius and called down "You cannot take this great city. Its walls are protected by the mother goddess Juno and by Jupiter himself. The prophecy of Minios has spoken and you cannot take her walls, the lake has spoken to us." He shouted.

Narcius didn't understand a word of what the old man had meant and he stood, staring at the walls with his mouth open. The men on the walls laughed again, some calling him stupid, others simply laughing at his open-mouthed gaze.

A noise to his rear announced that Mella was approaching, bucking his sword belt as he ran, his face a picture of urgency. Within a moment he arrived. "What?" he said as he stared up at the walls.

"I'm not sure" said Narcius. "It seems that the Veientines have a prophecy too. Something to do with the walls and the lake, but I'm not sure" he added with a puzzled look.

"I've called for the Tribune to be woken, he got back late this morning" he added as Narcius looked to him.

"Is that your leader?" called the sage, his eyes searching the two men.

"Who wants to know?" Mella shouted, his face looking to Narcius as he raised his eyebrows quickly and smiled.

A silence fell as the men at the wall seemed to fall into a long discussion, arms waving and faces turning to scowl at the two Romans. After a moment a tall man, his thin face covered by a neat beard, turned to look down at them. "There is no more to say" he called "we have nothing to speak of. Carry on with your digging, it serves you well to dig like rats in the garden" he finished to a burst of laughter from the men around him.

Mella noticed that the sage looked angrily at the tall noble and turned angrily away as the Veientines continued to laugh at their leaders comment.

****

"So Apuleius, there you have it my friend" Manlius said as a broad smile stretched across his face.

Apuleius, his eyes constricted as he thought, simply sat and looked at the information he had been handed. He turned to his left and shrugged to a large man, his ruddy face showing the deep tan of a man who spent a long time in the sun. The man took the vellum, its pink and yellow cover showing it had only been created a matter of days earlier, and read along the rows of information, his eyes rising at some points and his brow furrowing at others.

"Ten thousand Ases" the man suddenly said, his eyes growing wide as he almost fell backwards from his chair.

"Each" Apuleius smiled happily.

"Each?" the man said. "They will be bankrupt" he added, his face dropping and his chest rising more rapidly.

"That is the decision of the court" Manlius said in solid, cold, tones.

"It is good enough" Apuleius said as he stood and turned to the lawyer next to his, his eyes still bulging at the enormity of the sum. "The families of the dead will receive a percentage, the rest will go to the treasury?" he asked, returning his gaze to Manlius, who nodded his reply. "Good" he said.

It had taken weeks of continuous harassment of the patricians for the plebeians to bring the case against Sergius and Virginius, the Senate stalling the action as long as they could. Eventually they had appointed Manlius as the lead in the case and he had ruthlessly questioned both men and had set the delivery of his decision within a week. Unknown to the Senate he was brokering an agreement with Apuleius and was, today, finalising the words before delivering his final verdict.

"You see Apuleius I remain loyal to the plebeian cause. You have no need to doubt me" Manlius smiled as the plebeian tribune cocked his head to one side.

"Doubt?"

"Oh I have my sources. They say you have stated that I cannot be trusted to deliver *real* justice against a patrician"

A momentary grimace came to Apuleius' face before he smiled back at Manlius, his annoyance at the words dissolving as he looked to the large man and nodded. The man stood and thanked both gentlemen before disappearing through the door behind the men in Apuleius' study.

"It seems I had you wrong, Manlius" he said with a look of concentration on his face, clearly choosing his words carefully. "Though I do not understand what it is that drives you, a wealthy land owner to support the people" he said.

Manlius took a few seconds to answer, his eyes fixed on Apuleius as if appraising him.

"Rome is my concern Apuleius" he said levelly. "It matters not to me what status a man is or what wealth he holds. This city is the greatest there is and will grow more with strong leadership. Leadership which can come from any quarter as long as it is strong and guided by the principles of our fathers" he said.

"Fathers of patricians?" Apuleius asked.

"Fathers of Romans" came the reply.

A short moment of silence came as the two men sat and smiled to each other, neither willing to break the stillness that had fallen between them.

"You truly believe that there will be a day when it doesn't matter what the background of the man is for him to be a member of the Senate of Rome and speak on behalf of all of her citizens?" asked Apuleius.

"I believe that the people of Rome want someone to stop the criminal acts of the patricians, but they also want to trust their own leaders" he added, the mixed words causing a frown to come to Apuleius' face. "They see injustice and debt as their want in life. Why? Because they are born into inferior families. Ha" he laughed. "I am sure the gods do not care whether a man is a patrician, a plebeian or a member of the headcount. The gods wish to see Rome become the greatest city in the world, what they want is a strong man, a new Hercules, to lead Rome by supporting the people. We happily conquer every land we feel should bend its knee to us, yet we desire more. Or do we Apuleius? Do the patricians desire power and the plebeians not? Tell me, if the people wish to continue to be the sheep that provide the food for patrician greed I will renounce my position as champion of the plebeians. I will Apuleius. But I think they do not know what they want because they have been subservient for too many generations. I will change that, Apuleius" Manlius said slapping his hand slowly on the table as he leant forward with a mad glint in his eye which unnerved the plebeian tribune.

"I will be the strong voice of the men of Rome, not the patrician, not the plebeian, but the *Roman*." Manlius finished by sitting back in his chair, his breathing slow and steady as a calm manner came over him after the sudden intensity of his words.

Apuleius sat and stared at the older man, his arms now folded across his chest and did not know what to say. He took a moment to think through the words he had heard and then nodded "strong words indeed, Manlius" he said, his eyes looking around the room as he spoke. In his mind he was grasping for straws, the words had certainly been strong, but he did not understand what was driving the man sat across from him. It sounded like a desire to be the leader of Rome, maybe even the King. But such thoughts and words would bring death and he doubted he had understood them clearly, he needed time to understand what Manlius really meant.

"You speak well, Manlius, and I will discuss your thoughts another day in more detail" he smiled as he stood. "But now I must leave as I have an appointment with the council" he lied, his head nodding as he replaced the chair and ushered the patrician from the room.

****

Narcius had spent some time talking through the words of the sage with Marcus, both men unsure what they actually meant but sure that there was something in them which they needed to understand. Marcus had sat alone for an hour and couldn't shake the words of Lucius from his mind; that he needed someone else to help to fathom the words of the prophecy. He looked at the table in the centre of the command room in which he sat, the wooden fort given to him by Javenoli sat off-centre, wooden blocks showing the forts and soldiers placed where his men were strongest. He walked across and stared at the scene, trying, in his mind's eye, to picture the lake, away to his right as he looked at the scene. How did it relate to the city and what part did it have in its capture? What had Narcius said? 'The prophecy of Minios' whatever that was, had said that the walls could not be taken because of the lake. He wondered what it meant, thinking of ways in which the water could be used to attack the walls. He remembered that the Senate had sent a deputation to the oracle at Delphi when the water had first risen and he decided he needed to know what the answer was before he decided what to do next. He had to defeat Veii. Each day that the men toiled at the earthworks was another day in which he felt ineffective, useless. He shook his head angrily as he looked at the wooden fort, imagining how he could batter the walls. Smirking he almost lashed out at the table but decided that was petty.

As he started to go through the same ideas again his Optio entered the room, another report in his hand, which he passed across after saluting smartly and stepping backwards. Scanning the words Marcus clenched his teeth and took a long breath, another man found hiding in the damned Cuniculi. The rabbit holes were everywhere and it had been days before his scouts had realised that many of the deserters were simply hiding in them, some as deep as a man and as wide as two sitting side to side. What had they been used for? To water the fields? He shook his head again and wished Scipio was here with him, he had a clear head for thinking things through and would spark off his own imagination.

"Optio" he said, a sudden thought hitting his brain. "Ask Potitus if he would join me here please." The man saluted and left.

Within fifteen minutes Potitus and Mella had appeared, the former asking if the latter could join them as they had been eating together.

"I have a quandary" Marcus said as he stood with his hands gripping the table. "The prophecy of Minios says the walls cannot be taken for some reason to do with the lake." He licked his lips as he looked into the two puzzled faces of the men. "My prophecy" he said with a glance back to the table "says the waters will shrink in my hour of need" he said as Potitus moved closer, his interest suddenly alerted. "How do they relate?" Marcus asked with a puzzled look.

Potitus tapped the table. "Can we speak to this sage?" he asked.

"They wouldn't let him" Mella replied.

"How will the water shrink?" Marcus asked, sitting.

"The gods will drain it?" Potitus replied with a questioning look.

"We could get the men to drain it?" Mella said with a grin spreading across his face. Marcus looked up at this.

"Good idea, but we don't know how it will help us defeat Veii"

"Maybe we will when we drain it?" Mella said with bright eyes.

"I'm not sure that is what the gods have planned" Marcus replied as he returned his gaze to the table. He watched Potitus trace his finger along the sand on the table, then again leaving two faint lines.

"These are the two largest Cuniculi" he said, a thought coming to his mind. "There must be fifty" he looked to Mella and then to Marcus "no eighty of the channels out there." He walked around the table again.

"What are you thinking?" Marcus asked.

Mella stepped forwards and looked interested.

"I don't know what the prophecy says, but let's suggest it says the walls will not fall as long as the lake is there and the spirits of the water protect the city." He shrugged, as good a guess as any without any further knowledge of the prophecy.

"Agreed" Marcus said, his eyes starting to twinkle as the conversation continued.

"We could invoke the spirits to join our cause?" Potitus said. "We could drain the lake, but that would take a very long time" he looked to Mella. "We could fill these Cuniculi with water and see if that makes any difference?" he added with a look to Marcus.

"Or" Mella said, a sudden strength coming to his voice as he stared as if a great light had suddenly been shown to him. "We could dig under the walls" he said. "I bet these things go right under the city. Look" he said as Marcus felt as if a door had suddenly been opened and he saw the future rolling out in front of him.

He stood. '*Under the walls*' his mind said as Mella started to talk but he didn't hear the words, visions flashing through his mind of tunnels, men in armour crashing into the city of Veii. Mella was speaking but Marcus wasn't listening, the silence causing him to look, blankly, at his old friend before shaking his head slightly and staring at him before saying "sorry, repeat that."

Mella grinned, his teeth showing through the trimmed beard.

"I think these things feed the city its water supply. From memory each of these trenches goes right up to the walls, disappearing maybe ten feet from the stone. Who's to say that they don't disappear to an underground water system or some other tunnels which go right into the city."

All three men stood in silence as Marcus started to grin, the corners of his mouth splitting his face and his dark eyes growing in intensity as he looked to Mella and said "Genius."

"Hold your horse" Potitus said before the conversation went any further, the other two looking to him with surprise.

"Camillus" Potitus said. "We must test this before we do anything else." He looked to Mella. "Give me five of your best men and I will check the Cuniculi" he said before turning to Marcus. "I suggest we keep this to ourselves for a while. I still don't trust half of the officers, the other half are liars and thieves" he added the old saying with a smirk as Mella laughed at the words.

"Agreed" nodded Marcus as he stared at the walls of the fort. "Under the walls" he said with a smile "why did no-one think of that before?"

*

*

Chapter 14

The drill had taken longer than Narcius had expected, a sudden, warm, shower of rain turning the topsoil of the field into a sticky quagmire as the troops struggled to hold their footing during the move from phalanx to maniple and back, their full kit causing them to sink heavily into the soft ground. His drill master, Silus, had berated everybody and called them a number of choice names but the shouting didn't improve their footwork.

"Halt" cried the Centurion, his face red with anger. "Rest" he ordered, knowing that taking out his displeasure on the men wasn't fair, until the rain had come they had completed the manoeuvres adequately.

"Silus" he called as the man trotted across. "What's that?" he asked, pointing to a movement by the city gates.

"School children" said the clean shaven legionary with his slight lisp, his nose twisted to the side and a deep scar on his left cheek.

Narcius looked across at the group as it left the gate and started to walk slowly along the front of the city. "I've never seen that before" he stated as he watched a group of ten or more children, each carrying a wax tablet, walk along as if they were out for a stroll in the forum to catch the mid-day sun.

"Do they do that every day?" he asked.

"Most" came the un-interested reply.

At the distance Narcius couldn't be sure but there was something familiar about the teacher, his beard overly long for any sensible man. He strained his eyes. "Silus, is that man with them every time they come out?" he asked.

The drill master shrugged, looking back over his shoulder. "No idea, Sir. Can't say I've taken much interest to be honest" he said. "Problem?" he asked after a second or two of watching his Centurion stare at the man and the children.

"That man is familiar" Narcius replied, "but I don't know why."

"It's the old sage from the walls" said the short legionary who had been with Narcius the previous day. "He must make his money from teaching, like a lot of them do" he shrugged. Narcius looked at the face of the man, who suddenly stood straight and looked apologetic for speaking to his officer without being spoken to first.

Narcius saw his stare had sent a shiver up the legionary's spine and smiled. "I've got a job for you" he said with a deep grin as he winked to Silus, the older man grinning back.

****

Marcus was alerted to the commotion in the Comitia outside the command centre by the cheering and shouting of the men, a momentary fear of attack suppressed by the lack of trumpets which would have announced such an occurrence. Rushing to the door he watched as Narcius and two soldiers appeared thronged by a troop of soldiers all cheering and clapping. He looked to the left and right, but it was clear that none of the men around him knew what this was about. Whatever it was it seemed to be creating great joy amongst the men. Stepping forward Marcus checked he had his sword in the correct position and readjusted his tunic.

Narcius beamed, his drill master, Silus, at his side and a smaller man carrying what looked like a sack over his shoulder, although the sack had legs and was thrashing about making a great deal of noise.

Marcus half-laughed as the comic scene approached him.

Coming to a standstill in the Comitia Narcius saluted briskly and turned to the two men.

"Legionary, release the prisoner" he said with a smirk as the short man let the legs fall to the floor and pulled a brown sack cloth off the head of a long-bearded, dark skinned man, his Etruscan features plain for all to see as he cursed everyone who was staring at him, his legs wobbling as he tried to find his feet and caught his breath.

"What is this? Who is this?" asked Marcus, unsure what the commotion was about.

Narcius gripped the right arm of the fugitive and marched him across to his Tribune. "Marcus Furius Camillus" he said loudly "this is the sage of Veii, the man who holds the answer to the mystery of the lake."

Marcus caught his breath as he stared at the old man, his legs thin and wiry and his white hair and beard tangled from being within the sack. The man's eyes locked on his and he spat on the floor, a glob of phlegm landing with a splat in the dirt.

"I know you Marcus Furius Camillus" he said, his voice gravelly and deep. As he spoke he pushed the hair back from his face with an angry swipe as he swirled his head around the watching soldiers, some grinning and leering, others avoiding his gaze as if he held the evil eye. "They say the gods favour you" he called, his eyes roving the scene around him before adding "as they do me." His meaning was clear, do not harm me or the gods will punish you. Marcus smiled at his theatrical words and pose but didn't speak, his mind running through how to maximise this opportunity.

"What is your name soothsayer?" he asked loudly.

The man stood tall, his chest out as he answered "Gerittix."

"Then Gerittix I have some questions for you. Answer them truthfully under the eyes of the gods and I will release you unharmed."

Gerittix lowered his head and his eyes squinted slightly as if he was trying to focus on Marcus' face before he spoke. "I trust you Marcus Furius because they tell me that you follow the rituals of the gods and are dear to their hearts. Ask" he demanded.

"Inside there is food and wine. You will be treated as a guest until you leave the camp" Marcus replied, stepping aside and waving his arm towards the wooden building behind him. "The Centurion and his men will join us" he added as an after-thought "to ensure that the gods are satisfied that all those involved in this discussion are content" he added to Narcius' confused face. Marcus was already thinking ahead. Having two of the common soldiers in the room to tell everyone in the camp what had been discussed would be as good as having the conversation out in the open. He smiled at Gerittix and waved again as the man scoffed at the soldiers, dusting his arm as he walked forwards and nodded as he passed Marcus.

"Optio, fetch Mella, Potitus and Caelio please" Marcus asked as he saluted to the soldiers and turned to enter the room.

Inside the room was stuffy but tolerable and Marcus moved to the right corner where two eating couches and a series of low tables were sited. Gerittix had already lay upon one seat, clearly used to being treated well in any household, Marcus smiled; this was something he could use to his advantage. He nodded to the two soldiers and waved to the wooden chairs around the campaign table, at which the two men began moving the chairs into the area around the couches, the legionary looking hungrily at the wine jug which sat just beyond on Marcus's desk.

"Gerittix" Marcus started. "Would you do me the honour of lighting the candles to the gods so that they may oversee our discussions and ensure that we speak with honesty, integrity and truthfulness?" Marcus nodded to his right, where a small wooden chest sat on a low-legged table, the candles and ointments set out perfectly, as he always liked them to be.

"Hmmm" said the old man, his finger twisting his beard as he looked at the votive candles and back to Marcus. Marcus noted his nervous eyes and slight twitch at the question and wondered how long the man had been a soothsayer or whether he had been trained at all.

He sat forward and bowed his head, a long smile stretching his bearded face. "This is your camp, Camillus. Please, you light the candles and say your Roman words. As you will know from my name I am a Gaul, we have Etruscan training, but our gods are somewhat different to yours" he replied, his eyes narrowing slightly as he spoke.

A knock at the door made the man jump slightly, the young legionary also almost jumping from his chair, at which the drill master stifled a laugh and Narcius coughed, staring the man down angrily.

Marcus laughed to himself at the tension in the room, knowing that the stories the legionary would tell would be better than anything he could try and create on his own. As he turned to the door he saw the Optio wave in a number of slaves with plates of meat, stuffed olives and bread, the two soldiers licking their lips at the arrival and smiling to each other. Marcus winked at Narcius and raised his eyebrows with a smile, the man suddenly relaxing at the gesture and nodding his understanding.

As Marcus took his white hooded robe from the desk and started to light the candles and intone the words of the prayers Narcius whispered to the two men loudly enough for all to hear "you've done well today lads, eat and drink your fill and you're both excused duties tomorrow." At this Marcus noted great grins splitting both men's faces and an equally quizzical look from Gerittix. By the time the prayers were completed the remaining officers had arrived and were seated next to the couches, the soldiers moving behind the officers but closer to the food and wine.

The food lay untouched and Marcus noted the hungry looks on the faces of the men, two slaves standing at the rear looking to the floor. "Pour some wine for the guests" Marcus ordered "and fetch more food, there is hardly enough here for my own tastes and I eat like a dormouse" he added with a curt shake of the head. One of the slaves instantly rushed out of the room as the other took to pouring the watered wine, both the soldiers faces were now split from ear to ear in great wide grins, Narcius shaking his head at Marcus' mischievousness. "Gerittix, please do me the honour of taking some of this poor soldiers food. I am sure that in your city you have not had such a feast for some time as you struggle under the siege."

Gerittix composed himself, licking his lips as his stomach rumbled and he looked slightly ashamed for a few moments before adding a small mountain of food to the simple dish he had taken from the pile. "Narcius, your men next as they deserve to help themselves for bringing the very man I wished to see to me, almost as if you heard the gods calling you, Gerittix" he smiled as the two men looked to Narcius before stepping forward and adding a few crumbs to the plates.

"Lads" said Marcus "you will do me dishonour if you are not stuffed to the last belt of your tunics within the half hour" he said "take as much as you want" he added with a friendly smile, the two men stopping to check he wasn't joking before adding handfuls to their plates and disappearing back to their seats.

"Please Centurion" Marcus said as he stifled a laugh at the two soldiers and the confused look on Mella's face, "explain how Gerittix has come to be here" he asked.

Narcius cleared his throat and saluted, a little overdone, Marcus thought.

"Sir. Whilst drilling with the men along the front of the defences at fort three, I saw" he looked at the soothsayer "Gerittix, here" he said "with a group of children taking a stroll around the city as part of their lessons. It was legionary Vestus who saw that he was the sage from the walls who called to us about the lake." At the words Vestus had tried to sit taller in his chair and a large drop of oil had dripped off his chin onto his tunic, Marcus looking away before he started to laugh at the fury in Narcius' face. "And so I decided that we should capture him and bring him here for questioning, Sir, as I knew you wanted to know the prophecy of Minios" he finished.

Gerittix continued to scoff food noisily, almost as if he wasn't listening to any of the words the men around him were speaking. The slaves refilled the soldier's cups, Narcius staring angrily at them and Marcus trying to use his eyes to tell him to relax.

"I hope they didn't harm you in any way, Gerittix?" he asked, breaking the man's focus on his food as he looked up at the use of his name.

Gerittix looked back at the soldiers and sneered. "They couldn't hurt me if they tried, I am chosen as a messenger of the gods and am beyond human pain" he said as he returned his gaze to the plate of food. Marcus waited until he had taken another mouthful of fish cooked in lemon before he spoke again.

"We welcome you Gerittix and under the candles of the gods I offer you the hand of friendship. I will ensure no harm comes to you whilst you are the Roman camp and will give you escort to the city when we are finished" he added as he scrutinised the man's face for any reaction to the words. As expected the words created a twitch in the man's left eye which suggested he didn't want to return to the city. "Alternatively" he asked slowly "if you do not wish to return to the city I can make arrangements for you to spend some time in Rome, maybe at the Temple of the Salii where I have some friends?" he asked as he saw the man's eyes narrow as he watched him.

After a moment Gerittix took a long, deep gulp of wine, almost emptying the cup in one go. As the slave moved forwards to fill the cup Marcus noted the speed at which the two soldiers upped their cups and drank them dry, their eyes looking to catch the slave as he stepped back from the old sage. Marcus looked to their pleading faces and turned to the slave, his voice angry but his face soft as he said "why have these men got empty cups? Polythenes, keep up man" at which the slave bowed several times and re-filled the cups of the nodding and grinning men, Narcius still glowering at Marcus and Mella positively holding his sides to stop himself laughing out loud.

"I have never been to Rome." Gerittix said.

"Then I will arrange it" smiled Marcus. "But pray, my friend" he asked as he leant forwards, almost as if talking just to the old man himself "what is this prophecy of Minios you speak of? We poor Romans have not heard the great words of the sage."

Gerittix slurped more wine, a small drop falling to the floor before he spoke. "Camillus, you are beloved of the gods. They say you follow the rituals and that the gods love you for your devotion. The men of Veii guard this secret with their lives, it is forbidden to talk of it to anyone who is not a true Veienteine."

Marcus looked long and hard at the face of the man sat across from him, his eyes not catching his own as he had started the bargaining. Marcus caught his eye for a moment, seeing that he was trying to be clever, but also admiring him as he knew that with so many men around the table he must be careful not to give away Veii's secrets too easily.

"I understand, Gerittix, for it is the same in Rome" he added as all eyes watched him. "Yet we have a dilemma that you are here as a guest under the candle of truth and so must answer truthfully." He paused as if a thought had suddenly come to him. "You are a Gaul" he said "so as a Gaul the men of the City could not tell you their secret, you are not a Veienteine" he said quietly as the man's eyes widened at the thought. "So you cannot give away a secret if this secret was given freely to you. In fact it cannot be a secret at all" he added.

The Gaul smiled as he glanced to the two soldiers, both nodding at their Tribunes logic. "Indeed" said Gerittix "exactly as I was thinking. And surely the fact that I was placed in front of the city at just such a time as these fine men were training is a sign from the gods that I am to act as their messenger" he said as he looked at Marcus.

"And this Salii Temple, will I be fed there?" he asked as Marcus' heart beat quickly in his chest, he had netted his fish and he was almost bursting to shout at the man and ask what the prophecy was.

Marcus sat back in his chair and steepled his fingers under his chin. "I am sure I can arrange for lodging and the opportunity to learn a little of the Roman *disciplina*" he said "I am sure that it will help with your future *career*" he added. The Gaul smiled, taking more wine and holding his cup to the slave, who turned to the soldiers as soon as he had filled it, both empty cups coming out as soon as he turned in their direction. Narcius shook his head and Mella held his cup out for a re-fill too with a wink to the soldiers which was returned with beaming smiles.

Gerittix sat straight in his chair and looked serious, the move causing everyone in the room to lean forwards towards him.

"Camillus" he said. "Many years ago a soothsayer named Minios travelled through these lands and the gods spoke to him. They told him that Veii would be a great city if they built walls that no other city could conquer. They also told him that Veii's walls would never be conquered as long as the Alban Lake remained; *until the waters of the Lake run dry so will the walls of Veii remain unconquered*" he intoned. "The waters rose sharply, as you know, in the last month and the King of Veii sees this as a sign that the gods are with them" added Gerittix as he cocked his head to one side at the deep look of concentration on Marcus' face. Silence engulfed the room, all eyes looking to the tribune as he simply nodded his head slowly at the news.

"This is great news" Marcus replied, the soldiers suddenly looking confused as Marcus stood and held out his hand to the old sage. "You have been a great help to me and to Rome Gerittix. I will honour my part of the discussion and write introductory letters for you in Rome" he said. "Stay here and eat your fill, you too" he added to the soldiers as he placed a hand on the drill masters shoulder and nodded to him." The officers and I will discuss this military matter in another room to give you time to enjoy your feast" he smiled at all the men before walking to the door. "Oh Polythenes" he said as the slave stepped forwards and bowed. "Bring the tent mates of Silus and Vestus, they deserve to enjoy the same privileges as their fellows, isn't that right Centurion" he added as Mella let out a guffaw which he tried to hide as a coughing fit and slipped quickly through the door.

"Yes, *Sir*" Narcius said through gritted teeth.

*

*

Chapter 15

"Rubbish" spat Magnamus as he gazed at the five men around the table, the drinking vessels still half full despite the long hours of discussions. "The Romans are no better equipped than our own soldiers and have no divine right to success. They have been lucky, especially this Camillus" he added with a look of distaste coming to his face. "The King of Veii has confirmed that the waters have arisen to save his people, taking much of the Roman camp with it and calling a halt to their useless rampart" he sneered. "*Now* is the time to attack their defences, they are weak, tired from years of hiding behind their screens and bored of waiting at the walls and dying in the winter. I tell you my spies have told me it is so" he said with anger in his voice.

"They captured your city easily enough" said a heavily scarred man on his left, the flicker of angry eyes betraying a momentary desire in Magnamus to shout back, until he noted who had spoken.

"Tricks, deceit, the city was left full of weak men and women, no more." Magnamus said with a dismissive look which hid the anger he felt inside.

"Whatever the cause, my friend, I agree with your sentiment. We must attack them now or the alliance we hold so strongly in our blood will die on the vine." As his spoke the thin scar along the man's lower jaw made his lip jump as he set his teeth and looked hard into the faces of the other leaders of the Etrurian Council. Each man stared back defiantly, none willing to back down at his posturing.

"We have discussed it over and over Sentillius" came the reply from a Volscan, his blue and red clothing marking him as a leader of one of the Delta's largest trading cities. "The Romans fight too well at their walls. Unless you can guarantee that the soldiers from Veii will attack simultaneously" he said as Sentillius waved a hand at him, saying "bah" as if he was wasting his time listening to him. "Unless they attack" Amillus said more vigorously, his blue tunic wet on the sleeve where it had sat in a puddle next to his goblet "we will not have enough men to over-run the defence. I agree" he said to the shaking head of the brute of a man at his side "that now is a good time, but we cannot defeat them on our own" he finished with a long shrug, his arms coming out to the side in a placating gesture.

The Faliscan leader Vitulus shook his head. "We cannot attack, the plague has killed more than half of our able men, dying in the streets" he said with an anguished look on his face. "How will we draw the harvest?" he asked with wide, tear-brimmed eyes.

The comments brought a moments silence to the room as Sentillius looked at the Faliscan and couldn't find the words to say to the man who had lost his father, his wife and three children to the sweating fever in the past month.

"We must decide on what action we will take to support Veii" Magnamus said in a steady tone, his eyes moving around the men. "I vote to attack the Roman line" he said as he picked up the dagger that lay before him and stabbed its point into the table, keeping his hand on the grip as he stared at the other men.

"I will attack" Sentillius added, his dagger stabbing with a thud into the table.

"I will free the men to support you if they can, but I cannot commit my forces" Amillus said as he lay his dagger flat and pushed it into the middle of the table, a nod and a placatory hand to his shoulder coming from Magnamus.

"Soticus?" asked Sentillius with a dark look.

The shorter, wide shouldered, Volscan looked to his fellow leader Amillus and frowned. "My tribes can manage three thousand fit soldiers, maybe two hundred horse" he shrugged as he nodded and slammed his silver handled dagger into the table with a grin. "I want the Romans dead as much as you do" he added.

"Then we march in five days" Sentillius added. We meet at Napete and we arrange the details there" he grinned. "The Romans will never know what hit them" he smiled.

****

The darkness brought a kind of fear which Marcus had never experienced before, an almost empty feeling as if some creature was standing just in front of his face but he couldn't see the hideous beast as it leered at him. He bent and moved his had along the floor, ready to draw it back should it touch something feral. His fingers touched the wooden handle and he gripped it quickly as he turned and whispered back along the tunnel behind him "hurry up with that torch." For five minutes he had been stumbling along in the tunnel that Potitus had found leading from one of the Cuniculi which bordered the walls of the city, the right angled turn suggesting that it didn't actually go under the city, just along its frontage. As he had stumbled into a small water hole, his foot disappearing to his knee he had dropped the torch, the light flicking off instantly and leaving him with the sudden cold feeling of dread that remained as he heard echoing footsteps coming around the corner behind him, the yellow light flashing as the soldier moved along behind him. Marcus cursed himself for his eager pace and whispered and apology to Mella and two legionaries who were standing behind him, their breathing the only thing Marcus could definitely make out in the silence.

The torch aproached, Marcus squinting at the intense light. As it was passed forwards he thanked the man and held it out in front of him, the deep, dark, hole he had stood in shone back at him and beyond the tunnel seemed to stretch into infinity.

"What do you think Mella?" he asked

"I'm really not sure, Sir" came the unsteady reply, Marcus smiling at the apparent fear in his close friend's voice. "I suggest we let Potitus' men map out the tunnels and tell us where they go" he added more cheerfully.

"A good plan" Marcus said quickly "Let's get back to the camp and set it in motion." Stumbling into the light a few minutes later and dragging himself up over the lip of the low Cuniculi Marcus stood back and nodded at the hole below him where two soldiers stood with torches still ablaze.

Striding away from the hole Marcus took a moment to look back at the tall walls of the city and considered the words of the prophecy of Minios *until the waters of the Lake run dry so will the walls of Veii remain unconquered.* Smiling he clutched the Eagle amulet and a thought came to his mind, a sudden clarity which made him stop, Mella almost stumbling into him as he looked to the sky, yes there it was high in the air, circling slowly around the city, the wings hanging in the air as they caught the warm updrafts and allowed the heavy bird to circle for hours. *A signal*, he thought as he caught Mella and the other soldiers following his eye. The men needed a divine signal, one which would counter the movement of the waters of the lake and make them believe that the city would fall. Thoughts ran through his mind as he started to walk back to the tall walls of the camp, the sun-dried wood bleached in sections and dark where new structures had been added in the recent changes to the fortifications. By the time he reached the main gate a plan was forming in his mind.

"Mella" he said, urgently. "Fetch the officers, we need to discuss a plan" he added quickly.

****

Javenoli scowled, his eyes puffy as he had hardly slept. The news had been bad, the latest venture lost though he didn't know why. His men had been out for days scratching for information but so far no news had come back to him. He fidgeted with the large ruby ring on his index finger, the blood red stone almost the same colour as his red-rimmed eyes.

A knock at the door made him jump and his heart quicken. He took a long breath to steady himself before calling for the slave to enter.

Bowing low the slave announced "Quartius Volscius Gamnius is in your study, Master."

"What? Here? The fool" Javenoli exclaimed as he stood and waddled across the floor towards the door, the slave leaping back quickly to hold the door open as the large bulk of the Senator squeezed through.

Gamnius was covered in dust and dirt, his travelling cloak torn in patches and his hands dark and calloused.

"What are you doing here?" Javenoli croaked, the look of the man, usually so trim and neat, startling him.

The man's face turned to anguish and he fell to his knees, his hand reaching for Javenoli's clothes as he did so. "Master" he called, his eyes started to leak streaks of water down his dirt encrusted face as Javenoli stepped back as if his hands were poisonous. "They are all dead, all of them" he wailed, the volume startling Javenoli even more as his eyes grew wide.

"All?"

"Yes master. The Camillus, he caught them" he said as he gripped his air. "I don't know how he knew, we were found out" he beseeched. "Master, hide me, they will torture them and I will be found."

As the man babbled Javenoli had only one thought; how to distance himself from this mess. This fool had made a grave error of judgement coming to his house, and no doubt his enemies were watching as the idiot came crawling to his door, bringing with him the guilt that was written all over his useless face.

"Stay there" Javenoli said as the tearful man stopped moaning and started to thank the Senator. "Catmos" he called as the slave appeared "fetch water and food for this man" he said, then suddenly turning back to the slave and calling "wait, take that dusty cloak and clean it as well" he said as a thought came to him. The man continued to thank the Senator, his words angering Javenoli more and more as he kept thinking who had found out about his dealing with the Veientines. Someone had betrayed him and now he must find a way to clear every path that led to him. "Stay here, I will be back with some money and a letter of introduction for you" he said as he stepped out of the room and headed to the kitchen. As he stepped into the room the slaves looked up in surprise, the master never came here.

"Catmos" Javenoli whispered, gripping the fearful slave by the arm. "Get that cloak on and go out the front door, make a lot of noise about being mistaken and how sorry you are. Then make your way as quickly as you can along to the Tiber and disappear into the suburbs. I am sure you will be followed, make sure they see you leave, but lose them in the crowds, return only at nightfall when you are certain no-one has seen you." The slave nodded his understanding, he knew his Masters ways too well to be confused by what this meant. He went to the fire and used some of the ash to darken his face as Javenoli grinned and patted his shoulder and handed him a few bronze coins before turning back to the door and following another slave back to the study, where Gamnius was wiping his face with a dirty sleeve, his eyes alighting on the tray of food and smiling.

"Sit here Gamnius and tell me everything" Javenoli said as he moved a chair next to the desk, the chair making a low screech along the floor. With a nod the slave left and closed the door to leave the two men alone.

Gamnius took a long drink of the lemon scented water and turned his face to Javenoli who was stood beside him. "Eat first" Javenoli said with a smile as Gamnius nodded his thanks and turned his head to the tray of food. As he reached for the warm bread, the steam still rising from the fresh loaf Javenoli pulled a long thin dagger from his sleeve and sliced the blade straight into the neck of the man, pulling it back fiercely and twisting his body to rip a seven inch hole in the man's neck, blood bursting out from the orifice as soon as the knife was clear. Gamnius jumped at the first prick of the iron but his twisting body could do no more than fall to the floor at the speed and ferocity of the movement by the larger man, the chair clattering away as he did so. Javenoli stepped back, but not quickly enough for the blood to miss his robes as deep red spots lathered his lower legs. Gamnius lurched and died with a last arch of his back and a gurgle of defiance.

"I'm sorry my old friend, but I could not let you bring disaster to my door" Javenoli said as he looked down at the body of the man with distain.

****

The light of the day was coming to a close as Marcus finished the meeting, laying his thoughts out to twenty of his officers, all those that were not on duty. He nodded to Fasculus, who had been leading the raiding parties into the local area and seemed browner in the face than most of the other officers. Fasculus smiled in return.

Marcus had outlined a simple plan. The Veientines must expect them to carry on building the ramparts as their main attack focus, but in reality the men would dig the tunnels under the city using the existing tunnels which were part of the Cuniculi. The men would be divided into six groups and work on the tunnels around the clock, the digging, Marcus said, must not stop. He had also informed the men that the water of the lake would be drained, announcing that he would speak to the men in the morning and explain why and how, his eyes flicking to the old soothsayer who was sat, his face glowing with the healthy sheen of a man who was suddenly eating well again, in the corner. The men had taken to the old man, his affable humour and ability to gain coins for fortune telling making him popular with the more foolish men. Marcus had turned a blind eye as the morale of the men had increased at his presence.

Now was the time to explain the details to his men and so Marcus held out his hand to the votive candles and turned his eyes to the officers.

"Men. Leaders of Rome" he said confidently, his voice strong in the silent room. "As you know the prophecy of Minios says that the walls of Veii will not be taken until the lake runs dry. Well I believe that Juno and Mars have spoken to us and given us a sign which we can use to destroy Veii. The men will say that the lake can never be drained, it's impossible, and I don't doubt that for a moment. But think. The leaders of Veii will see the waters start to recede and they will grow fearful that the water spirits they rely on so heavily will start to leave as the waters do. We will ferry the water to the fields and distribute it into the Cuniculi, but we will leave these clear" he pointed to the table on which the scene around Veii was depicted by the wooden fort and blocks of soldiers he had used to explain the plans earlier. "I will call for Juno and Mater Matuta to leave the city" he said as a few short gasps came from the men in the room, their faces turning to each other at this news "and ask her to return with us to Rome. I will dedicate the Temple that our fore-fathers offered for their glory and was never built." He looked around at the faces who watched him apprehensively. "We will fight the Veientines by taking their gods and then taking their city" he said, a few men looking nervous at his words.

"And" he spoke with a softer face and a smile "remember the words of the prophecy of Minios. The walls will remain unconquered" he said with a broad grin as many of the officers coked their heads and looked to each other confused. "Because we will dig under them and attack their city from within. Narcius" he said as he stood and the men, realisation starting to dawn on their faces, grinned back at him. Narcius stepped forwards. "You must train the men, all of them to wield the short sword, we cannot carry shields and spears through that tunnel. We will need to get into the city and attack quickly. Caelio, you will have the reserves ready for the gates to be opened. You will train your men for fighting in the streets and close combat, we will not have time to set out the phalanx. Veii will fall gentlemen, and we will use every trick we can to make them fearful of the power of Rome before we appear beneath their feet"

The officers stood in silence, unsure whether to cheer or to clap as Marcus finished and started to hand out rotas and orders to each of them in turn. As each man looked to the tablets with short instructions etched in the wax Marcus raised his voice one last time. "Tomorrow I will tell the men that we are to drain the lake to fulfil the prophecy of Minios. But I will also tell them that in two days we will hold a festival to placate the water spirits and ask them to join us in Rome along with Mater Matuta and Juno. We will hold the festival in front of the walls so that people of Veii can hear our calls and see the water start to retreat. Fear, gentlemen, will become our friend. Tonight we start the tunnels and the training. Tomorrow we start to win the war against Veii."

At this the officers did cheer, long and hard, the men outside stopping to see what the noise was and some nodding vigorously at the sudden emotion coming from the command centre as hundreds gravitated over to the scene to try and be the first to find out what good news had caused the officers reactions.

*

*

Chapter 16

The city of Napete was small, too small for the thousands of men sited around the walls. The stench of rotting vegetables in the drainage ditches and over-filled urine pits permeated the air. Testosterone fuelled men, ready for war, strutted along the narrow roads and kept the local prostitutes busy. Whichever way you looked at it if the army didn't leave soon the men would turn on themselves and annihilate each other.

"Has Soticus arrived yet?" asked Sentillius, his beard dripping with goose fat as he picked his teeth clean with a fragment of bone.

"Not yet, Sir" came the reply. "The scouts said he will arrive by nightfall."

Sentillius nodded. So they would discuss the plan and march by the morning. Three days to Veii with so many men and then glory. He grinned.

****

In the darkness Marcus had watched as the men brought sack after sack of dirt from the tunnel, the rows of men carrying it to the lake and depositing it around the edge of the water. All day long other men toiled to lift the water and spread it onto the fields, the ground bursting into fresh growth at the sudden appearance of such a deluge. The Veientines continued to attack the ramparts, which Marcus' men also half-heartedly replaced during the day and retreated from attacks during the nights. As far as he knew Veii still did not know of their plans. Tomorrow would be the festival and he would call for the gods to leave Veii, offering them new homes within the walls of all-conquering Rome. His mind had worked through the words he would use and the details of the offerings to the gods, especially those that the Veientines would know and understand. Planning was everything, he thought as he walked back towards the wooden palisade. The words of the prophecy given to him coursed through his mind; *The water will shrink before him in his hour of need*, that seemed to be the case, though he was intervening with manpower not divine will. He considered how he would use the words to Fortuna, Mater Matuta and finally Juno, the patron goddess of Veii, to call down the goddess's wrath on the city and finally end this ten year war. *The city must be purged and killed, killed, all of them* he thought, the words clear in his mind. *Never to be a city again*. A sadness fell over him at the thought. How many thousands were hiding in the city, behind its high walls? He snapped out of the morose thought, his mind turning to the treatment he would receive if he were unlucky enough to be captured by the King of Veii.

The gods had spoken to him and it was as it must be, the city would fall and everyone who bore arms against them would be killed. Everyone.

He turned at a noise and Potitus, his face muddy, appeared at a trot, his eyes showing an urgent intent.

"What?" Marcus asked, a sudden fear coming to his voice.

"We've broken into a drainage ditch. It seems to run right into the city" he said, his white teeth gleaming from his mud covered face.

"Really? That's impossible. Already?" he beamed.

"Already."

"Come, tell me about it"

As the two men strode away Potitus described how the digging had hit a long stretch of soft ground, so soft he had added wooden poles to the sides of the tunnel as the silver miners did near his home town. After a while the soft ground had hit hard bedrock, which turned into a wide tunnel in which flowed a strong, steady stream of water, the man-made walls making it clear that it was the remnants of an old water course now used as a drainage ditch by the city and no doubt ending up in the lake. Marcus was delighted with the news.

"It gets better" Potitus said as Marcus stopped walking and turned to his friend, his face dark in the flickering light of the torches at the walls.

"How?" he asked.

"I've been in the drain myself and followed it to the end. It's as wide as two men and you can walk with a low stoop, it's this high" he held up a hand to just level with Marcus' ear. As Marcus was tall for a Roman this meant that most men could easily move along the drain if they walked with a stoop. Marcus looked into the beaming eyes of his friend.

"What's at the end?" he asked, almost not wanting to hear the news.

"The drain passes many channels which must be coming from the houses in the city, most too small for a man to clamber through. But it continues to rise and ends at a steep climb up a short well." Marcus held his breath as he saw the white teeth splitting his friends face. "The well is within the central Temple of Veii" he announced as Marcus' jaw fell. His mind went over the plans of the city that they had. The temple where the statue of Juno was held. What could be more fitting? Surely the gods were smiling on him now, he thought, his mind racing through possibilities. Potitus clapped him on the shoulder "Come on, let's get that drink before I take you to see for yourself" he called as he moved past Marcus and headed for the dark buildings of the camp.

****

The following day had broken with a low wind and a warm sun, the few clouds that hung in the sky breaking into thin wisps as the early morning brought a clamour of activity at the Roman camp. Wicker screens had been erected in the space between the city and the siege wall, men standing, spears aloft, as the defenders atop the battlements peered down at the Roman movement. The camp followers had been invited, some setting up colourful stalls in the space, though everyone kept a wary eye on the gates of the city as the smell of meat and sounds of music began to spring into the air. The soldiers that were on duty in the tunnel had been granted two hours leave to attend the festival and the Augurs and soothsayers were hawking their trade in drab coloured tents as the men and women milled about, all soldiers fully armed and prepared just in case the Veinetines should march out at them.

As ordered the trumpets announced the march of the religious symbols and the Eagle and other standards of the legions, each brightly adorned and covered in garlands picked by the men the previous day.

Marcus donned his helmet and stepped out into the sunlight, his officers lined up in front of him. He nodded to Narcius who set the marching cohorts into action under the loud trumpets and the dancing of a group of women he had commandeered the previous night. The music had a startling affect on the men, all the frivolity suddenly becoming sombre as thousands of men fell into lines and watched as the effigies of Juno, Mater Matuta and a shrine with a spear point and an arrow head filled with flowers and herbs for Fortuna were marched past. Marcus had walked the route and placed bowls at set distances from which he could stand and sprinkle the effigies with water from the lake as he called the spirits to attend the festival with the Roman gods and to leave Veii behind. As he called the words at the first bowl more men appeared on the walls, some jeering, others calling for quiet to listen to the words being spoken. Marcus spoke even louder to make sure that they could hear. Finally he approached the closest point to Veii, the men holding the wicker screens turning outwards to watch the walls more intently in case a hopeful arrow was sent at their Tribune.

Turning so that his voice would carry to the walls Marcus removed his helmet and covered his head in his robe, taking out the iron knife that he carried, a gift from his departed Uncle many years before and placing it down on a low wooden table that a slave had raced across and placed in front of him.

As he lifted his arms the enormous crowd, over four thousand Roman soldiers and another thousand or more camp followers hushed themselves into silence. Marcus felt a power start to reach into his body as all eyes looked to him, including the eyes on the wall.

"Romans, we celebrate the festival of the goddesses and the spirits of the lake, as we have been asked to do" he said, already noting the confused looks on the Veienteine leaders who were now straining to see what was happening below them. "I call on the gods to honour us with their presence as we dedicate this day to them." He called the name of each god and goddess, the cheers of the men rising as their Centurions orchestrated the noise, as Marcus has asked them to do. As he dedicated the sacrifices, sprinkling the animals with water from the lake, burning the offerings in the correct order and spending time to douse each of the entrails in the correct amount of oil he finally turned his body to fully face the walls of Veii. His heart rose in his chest as he felt it skip into a heavier rhythm, the beat almost like a marching tune as it skipped steadily along. The walls were full of jeering people, his prayers and rituals had been so consuming he hadn't had a thought to check the walls. But now, as he turned to look at them the people of Veii threw stones, rotten vegetables and pots of faeces at him, all of them falling well short as he stood and looked at their angry faces, biding his time before he spoke the words he had pored over for hours.

Marcus thought through the words, were they good enough for his protectors? Would Juno, Mater Matuta and Fortuna really support him in his hour of need as the prophecy seemed to say or would he stand here today and call on them and they turn their heads from him. A nervousness came over him as he felt his heart beat quicken and a cold wind blow along the front of the city. His senses became heightened as he heard the noise begin to calm, a few final jeers and curses coming out from the assembled lines of featureless faces along his enemies wall. He knew that Juno was also known as Uni Teran by the Veientines and that the shrine in the citadel in the South of the city held an archaic wooden statue said to have been carved by Hercules himself, though he doubted such myths. He felt the weight of the wooden eagle and the scroll he held around his neck as he swallowed slowly and licked his lips as he prepared to speak.

"Once great city of Veii" he called, a few jeers coming back to him from men in one of the lower sections of the wall ramparts. "The prophecy of Minios says that your walls will never be breached until the lake is drained." He raised his arm and turned theatrically to point behind him. "See how the waters shrink." Some moans came from the walls, the reaction settling his nerves a little as he let his eyes rove along the wall, every face turned towards him. Calling to the gods brought his fears to his mind, if the gods were with him then his cause was just, but he remembered the words of Calvus which said that great men fell from the grace of the gods because they did not pay due homage to them. It was as easy to be cast from the grace of the gods as it was to be struck with a spear, and he knew it. Yet, he thought, the prophecy was a sure sign of divine support and what he had to say next would surely prove that to him and all those who knew of its existence. He smiled broadly, his oiled beard moving as he swept his gaze along the walls.

"Great goddess Uni Teran" he called as gasps went up from the walls "Juno" he shouted. "The spirits of the water follow your great city, Rome. They flee this place, which they know will fall, its walls breached and its people slaughtered" he held his head low, his chin rising and falling in line with his breathing. He counted to thirty, knowing that this was the required length of time for supplication to the gods before he looked up again. Behind him some cheers began as women appeared on the walls, their high pitched wailing brining joy to the thousands of Roman standing listening behind him.

"Uni Teran" he shouted again. "Juno" he looked at the knot of men above the gate, the King staring back at him with his deep eyes in shadow. "Leave this town where you now dwell and follow our victorious army into our city of Rome, your future home" he called more loudly to cheers from the Romans. "which will receive you in a temple worthy of your greatness. A temple I dedicate to you now Juno. I say again, as the spirits of the water have joined with Rome and will be worshipped in our great city, your temple will shine as a star in the night amongst the gods of Rome."

Theatrically he slipped the final entrails into the small fire in front of him, the flames jumping as a sizzling sound was followed swiftly by a great black cloud, at which the people on the wall of Veii cried in alarm. The meaning was clear, and Marcus smiled at his words, keeping his eyes low as chants of 'Camillus, Camillus' came from the Roman camp.

****

The noise from the city had nearly been as loud as the sounds of joy and laughter that had come from the festival at the Roman camp, the majority of the people moving behind the walls soon after Marcus had finished speaking. Rations of wine were also reduced to keep the men sober in case the turn of events drew the Veientines into a rash attack. The festival continued unabated into the early evening as Marcus called all his senior officers to the planning room.

"How is the digging going, do we have enough space for three men at a time?" he asked Potitus without looking up from a report. This had been his latest order, knowing that they needed to get into the city with as much speed as possible. Since seeing the entry point himself he had been fascinated by how wide the final approach was and how quiet and dark the temple was beyond the walls, its shutters closed as if the building were hardly used at all. The men had taken to working slowly but steadily to remove the final elements of stone and mud which would give them the easiest entrance to the well and the work was almost completely finished.

"There is no more than two days work remaining" his friend beamed, his eyes twinkling at the answer.

"Excellent" Marcus replied his gaze returning to the plan of the city spread out on the table on a thick vellum map in front of the officers. The map showed the layout of the city, its walls on the right bank of the Tiber with the old salt road crossing along its northern edge. Marcus remembered how the Roman Fabii clan had built their estates along the river Cremera just off the map as he looked at it. The salt trade had led to many wars and the clan had been wiped out by the Veientines nearly a hundred years before, sparking hostilities between the two cities. Scanning the map he noted the well engineered roads, remembering his brother saying they were wide and straight with good solid flagstones and cobbles for floors. The soothsayer Gerittix had added a few new square *huts* where the soldiers camped at night by the walls, his local knowledge had been invaluable before Marcus had sent him to Rome with a purse of money and a full belly. These sentry bases would have to be attacked first before the gates could be opened. His eye was caught by the drainage tunnels, the Cuniculi, which were also used to water the extensive fields around the city. He smiled to himself at the skill of Potitus and his engineering men, knowing that without them he would still be sat on his hands back here in the camp with no opportunity to fulfil his destiny.

The city held a central square, similar to most Etruscan designs but much larger than that of Capena. The roads and houses were laid out in a grid pattern radiating from the central square with the only building that stood out as different in the whole city being the irregularly shaped temple in the south corner, that of Juno. Temple may have been the wrong word, it was a sanctuary, thick walls with high windows and sleeping quarters running along the side. He knew from his studies that the west side of the sanctuary held a wonderful terracotta statue of Apollo, though he couldn't remember which pose the god held and for a moment he considered visiting it after they had defeated the city before a sudden cold feeling made him shudder and he tapped the hilt of his sword involuntarily before looking up to the curious gazes of the men, most of whom had seen the movement.

"Thinking bad thoughts, Sir?" Mella asked as Fasculus smiled next to him.

Marcus smiled warily but said nothing, his eyes returning to the map. He sat back in his chair with a deep sigh, some of the officers raising their eyebrows at the motion. He narrowed his eyes as he looked around the room.

"I need to know more about what's in the city" he said without looking at anyone in particular. "I need to know how easy it will be to get to the gates. I need to know where their horses are kept." He pursed his lips in concentration. "I need to know what the morale of their men is like after today's festival and religious ceremony" he said, looking up for the first time to see several officers instantly flick their eyes away so as not to catch his stare. "I need someone to go into the city and scout around to find the answer to these questions" he said finally as he sat forwards and put his palms on the map, his eyes roving the room. "Caelio?" he asked.

"I'd be spotted within a minute, sir" came the quick reply. "Look at me" he said, raising his hands and shrugging his very Roman face at the men, some laughing quietly, others saying nothing. "I am honoured by being in your thoughts though, Tribune" he said genuinely.

"Then I need someone who looks Etruscan or at least maybe Greek, like a trader" he said as his eyes fell on Fasculus, who was shaking his head and sighing deeply as his eyes came to rest on him.

"A trader" he said in jest. "Do I look like a trader? Me with *my noble birth*" he said with a long smile across his face as several of the officers laughed with him.

"I will go with you" Potitus said as Marcus turned to look at him.

"You look nothing like a trader" Mella said quickly to another guffaw from the soldiers around the table.

Marcus smiled back at him. "It'll be dangerous" he said.

"I know, but who better to get to the gate and see the quickest way to get it open?" he replied. Marcus looked to the men's faces, set firm in their determination.

"I agree" he said as the two men nodded to each other. "But" he said you need to take another man with you, or a woman so you don't stand out" he added, Mella nodding at the idea.

"We can't trust a woman" Mella said "she might cry out and attract attention from the soldiers. Take Fabius" he said as he looked to Marcus. "He is short, wiry and has the look of an Etruscan, a noble one I grant you but an Etruscan."

Fabius was sat looking glum in the corner. He had been off-duty since the injury he had sustained at the attack on Capena and his eyes suddenly looked bright at the chance to see more active service.

Marcus contemplated him for a second. "You speak good Etruscan don't you Quintus" he asked, using the man's first name in an attempt to cheer him up. Fabius had been broody and drunk most days since he was off-duty and was often seen stomping sullenly around the camp shouting at men who were simply looking at him rather than do their chores. It appeared to Marcus that this may be a good way to get the man back into active duty.

"Indeed, Sir, as if I were a native. And I look more like a fisherman than a trader" he added jovially as the men laughed along with him, Marcus smiling at the happy face of Fabius, the most alert he had seen him in days. "Agreed" he said. "But I need you to go now and return tonight within two hours" he said drawing the eyes of all the officers to him.

"I need to know if we have enough soldiers here at Veii to destroy the city" he said coldly, his jaw set firm.

****

Gallus was a heavily set man but he could move quickly when he needed to. He skipped past the old spring in the forum and hid in the long shadows by the tall buildings which belonged to the potter Arthinetines, the low music of another house party coming from within. Ignoring the music he switched across the road and headed for the tavern, the picture of the overflowing jug creaking on its hinge above the door. Since leaving the army he had been kept busy doing errands for Fasculus and been a little more than surprised to be asked to do this job, but the money was good and he owed the old bastard no loyalty, especially since the whipping he'd received under his Tribuneship years before. He touched the lead sheet he held under his tunic, his notes scratched into the soft metal before he looked round the busy street and stepped into the tavern.

Manlius' slave sat in the corner, his clean shaven face staring back at him as he closed the door behind him.

"You're late" the slave whispered as he glanced around the room.

"My line of work doesn't always allow punctuality" he smiled back at the man, instantly taking a dislike to the slave telling *him* what to do. The slave glowered as Gallus took the jug and drank a long gulping series of mouthfuls of the liquid from within it. "I needed that" he said as he replaced the jug and waved to a scantily clad serving girl, her tatty ill-fitting clothes showing that she was as often out of them as in them. Her eyes caught his large frame and she smiled as she came across. "More water" he said handing her the jug with a grin as she pouted at him and turned away.

"I need to take the" the slaves eyes scanned the room suspiciously as he leant forward and mouthed "information" before sitting back and continuing "to my master."

Gallus shook his head at the stupidity of the man, his posturing making him appear more suspicious than if he simply asked for the lead sheet and left. He held out his hand for his payment, at which the slave surreptitiously slid a small bag across the table, Gallus grinning at the man's frightened look as he did it. Exchanging the lead sheet he sat back and watched as the slave bowed and disappeared, his frightened eyes scouring the room as he left. As the scantily clad serving girl appeared with the jug Gallus opened the pouch of coins and took out two of the largest, maybe now was as good a time as any to spend it, he thought, as he winked to the girl and held up the money to her grinning face.

****

Getting out of the temple had been harder than getting into it and Fabius winced as the pain in his arm caused him to stifle a moan as he replaced the heavy wooden shutter through which the three men had climbed after scouring the inside of the enormous room in which they had alighted from the well for several minutes.

"Camillus was right" Mella said. "If we hadn't come through ourselves we wouldn't be ready for the attack, imagine if we had a few hundred men stuck in that temple and couldn't find a way out" he grinned.

Potitus, being more serious in his nature than Mella simply looked back with a stern face and didn't reply. Outside the light was heading quickly towards darkness and the street quiet, his confidence that they could move around in the crowds of people within the city suddenly disappearing as he looked left and right. At least it appeared nobody had seen them. Fabius took out the two jugs and handed them across to his comrades as he slipped the heavy Etruscan sword he had brought with him to make him fit in more readily to his side.

"The gates are this way" Potitus said as Mella lifted his eyes to Fabius and followed like an obedient dog. A noise behind them alerted them all as a householder opened his door and threw the contents of a piss pot into the wide gutter, his eyes catching Fabius who quickly replied in his best deep Etruscan tongue with his jug swishing in the air as he turned "scared the shit out me, man. Gods be praised" he laughed as the old man laughed back at him and offered him the pot, to which Mella laughed and dragged Fabius back with a shake of his head, the old man closing his door swiftly with a grin at the '*drunken*' men wandering along the road outside his door.

"Didn't suspect a thing. And I could have filled that pot" Fabius said as he slipped from Mella's grasp and stepped into the shadow of a building, the tell tale splash of him relieving himself making even Potitus laugh.

"No point rushing" Mella said in his perfect Greek, the language they had decided to use within the city as it was widely spoken alongside the native Etruscan.

"Agreed" Potitus replied, leaning against the wall with his back. Let's go towards the square and then down to the gate" he added as Mella nodded.

The three men set off through a series of wide roads, the streets becoming busier as they neared the centre of the city. Most of the houses were built with a mix of stone and timber and each dwelling was meticulously tidy, the stone cleaned of any grime and the timber painted or in some cases oiled to preserve the wood. Potitus marvelled at the cleanliness contrasting it to the filthy streets in the suburbs of Rome. The roofs were two or three stories high with shuttered windows, all neatly painted, some with well painted pictures of flowers. The streets were fairly wide with a good gutter system which no doubt led into the tunnels they had found and excavated below their feet. He smiled at the thought.

Potitus breathed more easily as they mingled with the crowd, no-one seeming to take any notice of them. The square was over a hundred paces across but was crammed with soldiers, some in makeshift sleeping areas, others simply sitting in groups rolling dice or eating. Potitus took a few moments to scan the area, taking in the clothes, the faces, the weapons and the noise of the soldiers. The three men wandered through the crowd, hearing soldiers laughing and joking, some children screaming and chasing each other across the square as their mothers called to them and two men arguing about the food handouts, which had, apparently, been reduced in the last two weeks. Potitus noted everything. He listened to snatches of conversations which made him smile, others which foretold of the food shortages and how the soldiers were short of weapons and finally a conversation which suggested that the gods had finally decided to forsake Veii. The man who was speaking was rounded on by two of his fellows, their voices rising as the three Romans sidled past to avoid the confrontation.

"Did you hear that" Potitus whispered to his colleagues, who both nodded quickly. "It seems the draining of the lake and calling for Juno to leave the city has started to spread concern amongst the people" he grinned.

"Good" Fabius spat, his voice deep but quiet.

"There's the gate" Mella whispered before turning abruptly and gripping Potitus across the arm. "Quick, over here" he said urgently as he stepped back across a group of soldiers playing dice with sheep bones, the cheering suggesting someone had just own a large amount of money.

"What?" Fabius and Potitus said together as they rounded a steep sided corner and Mella looked around nervously.

"Deserters by the gate" he breathed heavily "I recognise three or four of them, so if I can recognise them" his eyes rose.

"They can recognise you" Potitus finished his words with a slow nod of the head. He narrowed his eyes in thought. "Will they know any of us?" he asked.

"I would guess" Mella said looking at both men "that they would know you, Sir. And Fabius" he shook his head "I guess most of the troops know you" he finished as both men nodded agreement.

"Then we had better look from afar and then get out of here" Potitus finished with a resigned look.

*****

An hour later the three men entered their commander's office, their faces flushed from the walk through the tunnel.

"Gentlemen" Marcus said as he smiled at their faces, his eyes moving from the wooden fort and soldiers he had placed on the table in front of him to each man. "Food" he called over his shoulder to a rush of noise from the Optio and slaves who were seated in another room just behind the central office. "Here, have a seat and then tell me everything. Wait I will get the map" he added fumbling with the heavy leather cover in which the map was encased.

After a moment, in which watered wine and a few plates of dates, grapes and smoked fish were brought to the hungry men, Marcus asked "So, what did you learn?"

The men looked to Potitus who was busily eating mouthfuls of fish, his eyes opening wide as his jaws worked furiously to catch up with the conversation, his hand raised as his head nodded along with the chewing action.

"What a city, Camillus" he started "the streets are wide enough for several men to pass along, even with shields" he said with a look to Mella, who nodded at his words. "The outer roads are quiet, with doors and windows closed to the road. The city is surprisingly clean, water is plentiful in many fountains around the streets and we reached the town square and these" he pointed to the small gatehouses which were sited along the inner walls of the city "you would be forgiven for thinking it was like any other day in Veii except for one or two things. There are several slaves nailed to doors or posts in the small squares around the city, probably those who tried to runaway or stole food" he shrugged as Marcus frowned at the words. "The people are frightened, hiding from their own soldiers as well as the threat from Rome."

"But, Tribune" Potitus smiled. "The army is spread out in several locations. The main bulk of men are here" he tapped the main town square. "Cavalry here and here" he tapped two locations beyond the square where they had seen a few hundred horses tethered together, their frames thin and malnourished and the beasts clearly unfit from lack of use. "The south side of the city" he tapped the temple through which they had entered the city "is unguarded" he shrugged. "The guards patrol each hour and move around the walls, they do not fear any internal threat and stay to the walls" he added as he saw Marcus' eyes narrow and flash around the map. "The main gate" he added as he looked up at his commander "is guarded by a mix of deserters and triarii, many with good spears and solid shields. The square holds maybe three thousand men, the outposts" again he drew his finger along the outside walls "maybe another three hundred, maybe four, here, here and here with smaller groups of fifty men in the remaining forts. The horses are poorly kept but the soldiers seem well fed and mostly jovial" he finished with a look to Mella and Fabius.

"So four maybe five thousand men?" Marcus said as he looked up.

"About that, yes"

"We have roughly the same number here if we launch everyone we have into the city" he said quietly as he rubbed his forehead with his hand, deep in thought. "And the people, how is their mood? Will they come to arms?" he asked as he looked up.

"There is an air of fear in the city" Mella replied quickly. "People are worried about the water of the lake being drained and we heard stories of Juno giving up on the city" he smiled as Fabius grinned and nodded. "They keep themselves locked in their houses and they give up food for the soldiers" he added.

Marcus took a moment to reply. "Good" he said "so the plan is working" he added as he looked to Potitus and then back to the map. Marcus thought about the words he had heard and his mind raced, thoughts of how to attack, when to attack and where to hit first. He glanced to the three men who were watching him closely, though no-one spoke.

"Opinions gentlemen" he said as he seemed to relax and sat up from his stooping position as he stared at the map. "My guess is that if we attack through the tunnels we will have the element of surprise, but we will also only have a few men inside the city, we cannot take three thousand men through those rabbit holes" he grinned. "So we must create a diversion which will force the Veientines to man the walls, or at least remove some of the guards from these outlying bases" he added. "The temple will hold maybe a hundred men" he looked to Potitus who nodded "before we have to launch ourselves into the city. Such a small force will quickly be overwhelmed in such wide streets. We won't get the same luck we did at Capena" he added, his thoughts instantly going to his patron goddess and the words of the prophecy. His calling for Juno to leave the city had been a masterstroke, evoking fear in the city but it had also given vent to his own fears. Did the gods truly support him? Were the words of the prophecy about to come true, and if so how? He paused long enough for his breathing to steady and his mind to refocus before continuing.

"The main street could easily be blocked by people coming out of their houses, all armed with knives and spears. They will fight to the death to protect what is theirs. I would" he added with a stern expression. "The walls remain our problem. The people of the city believe that they are impenetrable, and they are probably right" he said as his eyes flashed at Potitus. "Your towers would be too small and ineffective against these" he added glumly as he fell into a silence. "If we commit every man to the tunnels we leave our flank open to counter attack" he added after a moment. "But we have a way into the city and we must take our chance. We must launch a feint at the walls which commands their attention, something which seems to be an all-out effort against their strongest defence. Then we launch a force into the city and get them to open the gates" he added fiercely.

Potitus leant forwards. "I agree, Camillus. Yet we know we cannot damage the walls, any attack is as likely to stall as every other one has. We need more men" Potitus said as Marcus looked to him, a thought running through his mind.

"How many?"

Potitus looked to him and then back to the table, moving the map of the city and looking at the layout of the wooden blocks. Across the table the square fort which portrayed the city was surrounded by a number of squares of soldiers. He took a moment to think before saying "we would need four thousand here, another two here and then another thousand men to launch into the tunnels. Once inside the city the men spread out and head for the square and block these roads, then head to the gate."

As he spoke images flashed through Marcus' mind, his mind seeing the attacks, counter attacks and movement of troops. How would the king and his men react, which way would the leaders of Veii play their hands and how would the final act of the attack play out? Having missed the final words from Potitus and the first few from Mella Marcus looked up and apologised to Mella, asking him to repeat what he had said.

"Six thousand men is not enough" Mella repeated. "We would need to have ten thousand at the walls to provoke a reaction from them which would see them rush to man the walls. We would then need three thousand in the city and block off these roads, hit them here" he lifted the map and tapped the locations "and here as well as here" he added. "The tunnel would need to constantly flood men into the city and these men would have to fight with no shields." He looked up before speaking again "and only your Eagles can do that and we do not have enough of them."

Marcus nodded to Mella, but said nothing, his eyes moving to Fabius whose young face looked back at him before he shook his head to indicate that he had nothing to add.

"I agree with you both" Marcus said as he reached for his wine cup, the tension in the room suddenly relaxing. "We need more men and we need a force to storm the city whilst we attack through the tunnel" he said. "If the gods are with us we will win" he grinned "but I need to speak to the Senate and ask for more men" he added as his eyes narrowed and his mind starting thinking again.

****

Sentillius stalked around the camp, his anger growing at each scene of drunkenness he saw. He gripped the handle of his dagger as he set his jaw into a clench and took a deep breath. "Look at them" he snarled to his brother, Antithius "drunks, layabouts, no use to me as soldiers."

"They need a purpose, brother. To fight" he said. "We should leave for Veii today and attack the Roman lines. We have enough men now, surely" he half asked as he looked at the men gambling outside their tents.

"We must wait for that fool Soticus" Sentillius answered, his eyes scanning the scene again and shaking his head. "He will be back tomorrow and then we will decide" he added with finality. "I should have been left in charge of this lot" he added angrily "I would have had them training and preparing for war, not sat on their backsides singing, drinking and sleeping." He turned abruptly and headed back to the village of Napete, his feet kicking up a small cloud of dust as he walked.

Antithius shook his head. His brother was right. Since the tribes had met and agreed to support Veii they had dawdled, sitting on their hands and enjoying the fruits of the city and listening to the likes of Amillus who didn't want to lead his men to Veii. News had reached the camp that the waters of the Alban Lake had started to recede, he clutched his lucky talisman, a stone he had found on the battlefield which had the shape of an eye in its centre, and wondered what this meant. Surely the old prophecy of the lake was not coming true now? He considered the story the men were discussing of the two-headed calf and the old woman that they had heard wailing in the night but nobody could find. It was all pointing to bad luck and he didn't like it. Better to get to Veii and deal with the Romans before the stories gained more credence with the men, he thought.

He turned and smiled at his brothers back as he was walking away. There was good leader that men would follow, he thought to himself as he nodded. If only there were more like him. This army was two thousand men or more now, a force which was nearly as strong as the Romans at Veii. If they could get a messenger into the city and launch a double strike they could destroy the whole army. He grinned at the thought as he set off towards the gate where his brother was standing shaking his fist at a guard who had leant his shield against the wall and was sitting on the floor dozing.

*

*

Chapter 17

Javenoli placed the message on the table and nodded to his slave to pay the dusty messenger, adding that he would like two hours before the man delivered the message to its proper recipient. He smiled as he contemplated how he could use this to his advantage, nodding to the man as he took the message and replaced it in his pouch before disappearing through the doorway with the slave, the silver jingling as he placed that in his pouch as well.

So, Veii was to come back to haunt Rome again. Rome would win, he thought to himself as he stood and wandered towards the garden at the centre of his villa, but how could he gain favour with the Senate. He decided he would intercept Marcus Furius Camillus on the road, if he left now he would be a few miles from the city before they met. He had spent time and money getting close to Camillus and his family and if the men delivering the goods to Veii had been tortured he might need his standing to hold back any future trouble that might come his way. If Camillus needed more men then he must surely think he was going to defeat Veii and Javenoli knew that he needed his own men in the city to kill anyone who knew of his involvement in supplying weapons and food to the city.

It was time to change his plans and he smiled at the statue of Juno he had placed in the centre of his garden, the words he had read of Camillus' future changing his allegiance to the mother goddess and making her the centre of his household. He moved across and poured a large measure of his best wine into the bowl at the foot of the statue and closed his eyes as he thought through how he would honour the goddess should Camillus win at Veii.

****

Narcius and Fasculus had started the training for the close combat fighting, removing the men's shields as they were too bulky to get through the tunnel. The training had started at first light but within an hour it was clear that the men needed additional support as many were falling to heavy bruises from the wooden training swords they used which they were finding difficult to wield without a shield.

Mella had helped by fashioning a leather shoulder guard which could be tied to the chest guards of the men, but this too was restricting movement and the men were grumbling. After further tests and much adjusting the shoulder guards had been reduced in size and were holding up to the repeated knocks that were raining into them during the fighting.

"Do you think we can win in there?" Mella nodded his head in the direction of the city.

Fasculus and Narcius looked to each other, both men shrugging in reply.

With a frown he asked the question again, his gaze caught by one soldier whose footwork was particularly good.

"We have a good chance if the defence is at the walls, but we will need the luck of the gods to get the gates open and to hold them with three thousand men at our backs" Narcius replied coldly.

"And the people will come out of their houses and attack us with pots and pans" laughed Fasculus.

Mella grinned at the thought, knowing that thousands of civilians would cause just as much trouble to the Romans as the defending soldiers.

"Will the Senate send more men?"

"They must" came the quick reply.

After a moment Mella called a halt to the training, both Centurions jumping as he yelled the command.

"What? Why?" Fasculus asked indignantly as the junior officers trotted across to their seniors to see what the next set of orders would be and both men looked quizzically at Mella.

"You" Mella called to the soldier whose footwork he had admired, "over here" he shouted.

The soldier jumped to attention and trotted across, his face red from the exertion of training.

When the junior officers arrived and Mella was satisfied that everyone was there he turned to Narcius with a nod as he waited for permission to speak which came quickly with a confused frown.

"Name soldier" he asked as he took a wooden sword from a pile on the floor.

"Visculus"

"Right soldier, attack me" he said as he moved into his stance and stood back a pace from the man. The soldier looked to his own junior officer to await the nod which would allow him to proceed. The soldier moved into his stance, his right arm narrow to his side and left slightly out to counterbalance any move he made. Mella twitched his shoulder, at which the man stepped back and moved his body around to the right. With lightning speed Mella darted an attack to the man's shoulder, but with three short steps and a slight duck he had moved out of range. Mella pressed the advantage and stepped in closer watching the man's feet as they edged to the left then back to the right quickly. Visculus caught the attack with his sword and attempted a sweeping cut at Mella's arm, missing by an inch as he moved further around, turning Mella to his right. The man's eyes never left Mella's and the two men moved quickly in a circle before Mella stepped forward with a feint which drew Visculus into a movement of his sword arm which Mella easily parried and thrust his hand into the chest of the soldier before stepping back with a smile on his face. Visculus was angry but held his stance, not allowing the strike to do anything more than anger him. Mella watched his feet again, the same three step movement which kept his balance strong. One, two, three he counted as the feet moved and he tried to catch the man's sword arm, missing every time as Visculus was acting more defensively than he had seen him during the training.

"Attack me man, like you did over there" he snarled as Visculus' eyes widened.

"Give it to him Visc" came a shout from a group of men who were standing watching with grins across their faces. Mella wished he had been quick enough to place a few bets before he'd started, but there had been no time.

The words caused the legionary to move in a blur, the sword clashing into Mella's with swift strokes, followed by easy footwork. One, two, three Mella counted as he admired the simplicity of the steps before saying "four" and stepping into the attack, knocking the sword arm back and striking the man heavily on the shoulder with his own, to a groan from the men behind him. Visculus stepped back and winced as the movement caught him, his eyes darting to his shoulder before looking again to Mella. The footwork was good and Mella had seen something he liked, but he needed to test it again, he held up his hand and Visculus relaxed, a little crestfallen but unhurt.

"Excellent Visculus, but now I will demonstrate how you will beat me" he turned quickly to the group of men around him. "You three" he pointed his sword to three legionaries who quickly tried to disappear into the group behind them. "Here" he commanded.

"You" he said as the men arrived and shuffled forwards. "Watch" he said as he stepped into a crouch and moved with the same three step movement, almost dancing as he counted aloud the three steps, then repeated it as he stepped around the men, his stance wide but strong. He then called "four – five" as he stepped forwards with a slash and thrust, counterbalancing his sword arm with a swing of his left, before starting his count of one, two, three again. Visculus' eyes opened wide at the sudden movement, a light dawning in his mind at the sudden change to the stance and attack he had been used to taking. He grinned.

"Teach them, quickly" Mella said as he stepped to his equipment and picked up the water pouch, gulping down a long drink as he nodded to Fasculus. He turned to the men around him. "In the streets you need to fight close and dirty, to find an edge on your opponent, to kill or be killed" he called as men moved closer. "Visculus has a natural movement which will work in the streets, you must all learn it" he called, "it will save your life" he added.

Within a moment Visculus and the men had stepped forwards, each man with a glint in his eye at the chance to better an officer. "Imagine I am a soldier in the streets of Veii" Mella called "and you four men see me coming at you" he said with a smile. "You will work from left to right, one at a time. Step into the movement, hit and step back" and then he raised his voice "the next man moves forwards, then the next, you take the same three step movement, then *four-five*" he moved his sword to the action and stepped back. "In this way you will move quickly along the street, you will not stop, you will kill everything that comes at you and you will only strike once before the soldier next to you steps forward. *Understand*?" he called.

"Yes, Sir" came the chant from Visculus and the three men.

"Right. You men" Mella called to the men standing watching "get behind me" he said as they shuffled into place. "You men" he said to another group. "Get those shields and create an alleyway seven men wide so we can get used to fighting in a confined space" he added as the men threw their swords to the floor and stepped across to the shields which were stacked neatly to the right. Mella nodded to Fasculus, who shook his head but smiled back at him. As soon as the *alleyway* was formed Mella nodded to the man behind him and stepped back "go on then" he said with a broad smile at the confused face of the soldier. "What? You didn't think I was going to get my head cracked open did you?" he laughed as he pushed the man forwards and watched as his sword was parried and he was knocked across the helmet as Visculus said "four-five" and quickly stepped back for the next man to step forwards. It took seconds for the four men to slice through the defenders, taking each man quickly as they struggled to deal with the sudden movement; one or two did manage to put up a stern fight, but the fresh attack of the four men moving quickly forwards placed a new threat in front of the man defending as soon as he had covered the thrust of the previous attack.

"Good" said Narcius as he looked to Mella approvingly. "Remind me to ask for your opinion before my men spend an hour battering each other next time" he grinned.

****

"Is that?" Marcus looked confused as he saw the horses walking towards him. He had set out for Rome with a handful of sturdy cavalrymen, each riding a strong horse with a spare in case they were needed. They were no more than two hours from Rome and ahead on the old salt road was a column of thirty of forty men, many in high quality armour and at their head a figure he knew well, Javenoli. A rider was cantering across towards them, his spear in the air to show he was carrying a message.

Within minutes the rider had announced that Senator Javenoli and his men wished to know whom these riders heading for Rome were and what their business was. Marcus smiled at the words of his old friend and sent the rider back to say that it was a friend and they should stand to for Tribune Marcus Furius Camillus.

"Marcus" called Javenoli, his heavy horse clearly struggling to carry the man's weight and Javenoli clearly struggling to stay seated on the beast, as Marcus approached the thirty man column.

"Senator" he replied jovially, stepping from his horse and walking across to the Senator. He looked up at the old man, the lines on his face much deeper than when he had last seen him and his forehead creased into an almost permanent frown. He clasped hands with Javenoli, who was struggling to get from his horse.

"Stay seated my friend" Marcus added as he stretched his back, his face betraying the tightness he felt from hours of plodding on his mount. "We will be returning to Rome, and you must come with us" he said as Javenoli looked to him with a confused frown.

"But" Javenoli said with a look of incredulity "Why? Has something happened? I was coming to Veii to lend my support" he said with a confused expression.

"No, no Senator, nothing bad has happened. I will explain on the way. Come, let us turn and head back to the city. There is so much to tell you" he added as Javenoli smiled warmly at him.

****

The crowds thronged the Temple as the leaders of Rome met to discuss the return of the Tribune to the city. People jostled and pushed to get closer to the steps of the temple but the mood was jovial apart from when a pickpocket was caught and soundly thrashed by three burly brothers whom he had tried to rob. In the noise and clamour of the crowd nobody took much notice of the brown-clad, dirty, soldier who had left his horse at the gates and run the last few hundred steps to the forum, his breathing laboured after hours in the saddle and the long run to the location of the meeting. He pushed his way through singing crowds, men discussing politics and women adorned with their best silver and gold jewellery who were idling along the ring of stalls in the forum.

"Make way" he called, his voice only a creak above a hoarse whisper as he struggled to make headway through the crowd. "Make way for a messenger of Rome." A few heads turned to him, some wrinkling their noses at the smell of ingrained sweat and horse that permeated the air around him. He almost fell as he stumbled into a thick set man, his brown and white clothing showing he was a baker, his face a mix of Greek and Roman with a white beard, neatly trimmed. The baker turned to the messenger and eyed him curiously before he gripped his shoulder and looked into the man's eyes. "What news?" he asked urgently as a few other faces turned to the scene. The messenger, his own eyes tired and his breathing ragged replied "I have news for the Senate, a great army of the Etruscans" he said, his eyes wide with fear which was matched by the baker who simply gripped the man harder and turned to drag him forwards. "Clear the way" he screamed, his voice booming so loudly that people turned in fright at the sudden sound. "A messenger with terrible news" he called "make way." People flocked to the sound, a cacophony of noise turning to silence momentarily before the crowd began to ask questions, some urgent and others mocking the messenger, but every voice asking what this terrible news was.

"A great army is coming" called the baker "we must get to the Senate" he called as the crowd started to shift in front of him. "Clear the way. Make room" he shouted as he barged through the crowd, the exhausted messenger being dragged along behind him. At the steps to the temple the guards looked at the parting crowd in confusion as the noise grew to a crescendo of wails and calls for information, the crowd starting to get agitated at the sudden change in circumstances.

"Hold there" called the guard raising his spear to block the approaching men's path. "By what right do you wish to enter this building" he called, his trimmed beard showing yellowed teeth as he set his jaw firm and stared at the two men. The baker pulled the messenger forwards and placed him between himself and the guard, the messenger taking a moment to compose himself and look up into the confused face of the soldier.

"I am Decimus Matrius, messenger from Napete" he said with a few glances around at the crowd. "I have news for the senate that I must convey to them urgently" he said more forcefully as the soldier narrowed his eyes at the small man in front of him.

"Let him through" he said through gritted teeth, adding quickly "you can tell me the message away from this lot" he added with a stare at the baker who managed to hold his eyes for a second before shaking his head and crossing his arms in anger.

The messenger was taken to the massive wooden doors to the temple, the thick wood carved with crude flowers and grapes, and the soldiers spent a few minutes listening to his tale before ushering him into the building. As they entered a number of heads turned to them questioningly before the guard took him across to the small table at the back of the room where two patricians sat with a series of wax tablets and vellum scrolls. After a moment one of the men began to write furiously onto the tablet, his eyes growing wide as the messenger relayed his information. Turning to a slave, his lithe, pale, frame almost invisible in the shadows beyond the sitting men he handed over the tablet and pointed to the dais where the three leaders of the Senate were listening to the discussion regarding Veii.

"The fact of the matter is clear" said Cicurinus, his eyes darting around the room. "If Camillus is correct, and I have no reason to disbelieve him, then the city will fall to us within a few days. For that I am sure we are all grateful" he added with a broad, if not convincing, smile. "I agree with my friends" he motioned to his right to the men who had been discussing the need to send more troops to support Veii "and agree that we need to send more of our stout Romans to finish off this threat from Veii. The sooner we send them, the better" he said as he sat down with a firm nod as a few cheers rang around the high ceiling of the temple. As the noise died down a few men stood, their heads circling the room as they wished to speak and tried to catch the eye of the leader of the meeting, whose face remained stern in the low light of the room.

Before he could speak the slave edged forwards and handed the tablet across. Mugillanus took it with a frown and opened it to read the words within, his eyes growing wide as he took a moment to read the full details. A slow silence fell around the room as the Senators and leaders of the plebeian council alike turned to look at him, a few murmurs and frowning faces starting to look alarmed as the leader of the Senate looked to the dusty messenger and back to the writing on the tablet. He handed the tablet to Ahala, who was sitting next to him, his light brown eyes and lean face turning urgently to the words, his mouth opening as he read them. Mugillanus stood, his eyes glancing to Ahala and then to Marcus before he spoke. "We have a message from a *friend* at Napete" he called loudly as he waved an arm at the messenger. Everyone knew that Napete was an Etruscan town not far from Rome and a staunch ally of Veii. There had been rumours for months that the Etruscan council were gathering to send a force to Veii to annihilate the Roman camp, but so far no news had come and the Romans had largely ignored the possibility, believing that the Etruscans would be unable to attack if their largest city state, Veii, could not support them. Spies had been lodged in every city and now one of those men had appeared with this news. The audience fell into a stony silence. "The Etruscan council has met at Voltumna" Mugillanus said slowly as his eyes wandered around the crowd of men. "They have amassed an army at Napete" he said as a few gasps came from the assembled men "and according to this messenger they will attack the camp at Veii with *ten thousand* men" the noise level grew as startled men looked to each other. "And then" Mugillanus raised his voice "it is said they will march on Rome."

****

Three hours later the leaders of Rome began to step into the sunlight of the forum as they left the temple, many blurry-eyed from the long debate. At their head strode Marcus Furius Camillus, a thick red cloak thrown across his shoulders as the crowd stared in disbelief at what they saw – the red cloak, the mark of a Dictator. At the sight screams came from some of the women in the crowd as they realised the appointment of a Dictator was a portent of some great peril to Rome. Men stood and shuffled forwards, pushing and jostling to get closer as Marcus stepped up to the steps outside the temple and raised his hand for silence. The past few hours had been draining. Marcus had argued that an attack on Napete was the best way forwards whilst continuing to hold the line at Veii to stop any troops coming from the city. The element of surprise would help the Romans to victory he had argued.

He had been lambasted by the plebeian leaders, who argued that the best solution was to recall the troops at Veii and give up the *disastrous* ten year siege which had all been in vain and seen many of their sons die needlessly and bring all resources back to defend Rome itself. The arguing had gone backwards and forwards, with Apuleius continuing to disagree with any solution that the patricians suggested. In the end Ahala had called for order and called for a Dictator to make the final decision, without it, he had stated, Rome would do nothing and lose on all fronts. He held the floor for a full fifteen minutes and challenged anyone to disagree as he stated the outcomes of years of fighting against the Veientines and other Etruscan cities, stating that Rome must endure and that Veii was finally ready to be taken, Rome must act, he called, and by appointing a Dictator they would have one firm voice and one leader. Silence had followed and agreement reached that voting must take place. The voting had been called, several men putting themselves forwards. Javenoli had called for Marcus to be Dictator, citing his excellent record and skilful tactical victories. Others had championed their own family members. As the votes were counted Marcus had been taken aback by the flurry of votes for him, his mind reeling as men he thought were enemies turned and raised their hands at his name. In his mind he glowed with satisfaction, a sense of pride and belonging rose within him which he quickly held back putting on his stoic face and nodding to the men as they called his name, but his heart beat faster as his thoughts ran through the words '*the Eagle will lead Rome*' which had been spoken to him all those years ago.

After the correct sacrifices and tributes had been completed, the red cloak brought and draped around his shoulders and the votive candles had been blown out the Senate had discussed what action was needed, Marcus taking the lead in the debate as the new Dictator of Rome. He had felt uncertain of the position at first, his fears that he wasn't ready for the position coming to his mind. Yet as the debate continued he grew more confident in his decisions, the words of his father coming into this mind '*it is every patricians duty to serve Rome, and for the Dictator to be the most selfless yet most ruthless man of us all.*' The words had been spoken some twenty years earlier, but they came to his mind as if he had spoken to him that very minute.

Now it was time to tell the people of Rome and Marcus looked out across the forum, tens of thousands of men, women and children thronging the main square, every eye staring towards him as he stood tall, his chest out and his face stern. As he held his right arm in the air the crowd began to fall silent, some men looking with fear at him and others looking at him blankly.

"People of Rome" he called, his voice strong as he took a slow deep breath, the words forming in his mind. "I, Marcus Furius Camillus, come to you today not as Tribune, but as

Dictator." The silence was broken by some cheers among the crowd as his friends called his name loudly. "But I bring good news and bad" he said as he looked back at Ahala, noticing the angry look on his old friend Marcus Manlius' face. Manlius had argued strongly that he be Dictator, calling his military record into account and stating that Marcus had done little to warrant the role. In fact it had been the vociferous nature of Manlius' call, supported by Apuleius, that he thought had turned many of the patricians to his cause. Either way he knew Manlius was not happy. Yet he knew, as Dictator, what he must do. He also knew that this was the calling of his prophecy, to lead Rome and that Veii must be smashed *never to be a city again*. Juno was with him and his words must be chosen carefully.

As the crowd fell silent he continued. "I come with good news. By the labours of the men at Veii we have at last a way into the city." He paused as people cheered, faces turning to each other, some hugging, others unsure what the words meant. "Upon my return we will lay waste to the city, taking from it the great treasures of the Etruscan alliance that it houses, for Veii is bursting with gold, silver, spices, cloth and grain." A great cheer went up as he raised his arm again. He needed to get the people on his side and to want to go to Veii, the offer of great riches was always a good motivator and today was no different as people shouted his name and shouted that they would follow him. He waved his arm slowly, turning his face from side to side to ask the crowd to quieten. The mention of riches had stirred up a cauldron of noise and it took a few moments to silence enough of the noise for him to be heard.

"Veii will fall, but Rome needs more good men at her walls for the final assault. Good men with strong spears, sharp swords and a will of iron. The gods are with us. You know of the prophecy that protects the city" he took a moment as some heads cheered and some yelled '*tell us.*' He smiled before continuing. "There was a prophecy spoken many years ago that Veii would not fall until the waters of the Alban Lake disappeared. I tell you, people of Rome, that this had come true. The water has gone, the spirits of the water have chosen to return with our conquering armies to Rome." Cheering started at the front of the crowd, the words, and noise, spreading backwards across the forum like the rumbling of thunder. "People" he called, his voice hardly audible even to his own ears as the people in front of him cheered and shouted. "People. The gods are with us. I, your Dictator" he bowed his head as the noise level began to fall before looking up again. "have called on Juno, mother goddess, to give up the city of Veii and return to Rome. I have dedicated her a temple here in our great city when Rome is victorious." The crowd played just as he expected, the women folk screaming more loudly than the men as they cheered for Juno, goddess of the Earth and of women. "Mothers of Rome" called Marcus, his energy rising as he spoke, his eyes looking around the crowd to seek out all the women. "Mothers" he shouted as the crowd began to turn its head towards the women in the forum. "Pray to Juno that your sons will bring great glory to Rome and return in safety, for Juno is my protector and will return with me to Rome" he said as some of the people in the crowd stared open-mouthed at these words whilst others went mad with delight. Marcus felt a great weight lift from his shoulders as the words were spoken. He noted Manlius shift uneasily behind him as Ahala and Atratinus looked to each other, Calvus smiled and Javenoli simply narrowed his eyes and stared at him. It was a gamble to claim patronage of the gods, but he was certain that this was what the prophecy had meant, that his time was now and that Juno must return to Rome with him. He watched the crowd as it seemed to ebb and flow like the sea, faces turning to him then looking away, some with arms raised to the heavens and others simply standing open mouthed at his words. He took out the white garment he always kept close to him and held it up, placing the hood over his head as the people fell into silence almost immediately, many falling to their knees at the movement, arms raised to the skies.

He held his arms high. "Pythian Apollo" he called, his eyes closed. "Guided by your will and the love of Juno, Mater Matuta, I will go forth with your people to destroy the city of Veii. A tenth part of the spoils I devote to thee. Thee too queen Juno who dwells now in Veii, I beseech that you should follow us, after our victory, to the city which is ours and will soon be thine, where a temple worthy of your majesty will receive thee." As he spoke a chant went up from the mothers in the forum, a high pitched chant of joy, of motherhood and birth. The men stood silently as the women waved their arms in unison and Marcus looked out over the crowd, the fear of the gods palpable in the faces of the crowd as much as the love of the same deities. Inside his chest his heart thudded against his ribs, the blood racing through his veins as his eyes almost came to tears but he blinked them back.

Removing the hood he turned to Mugillanus and nodded, the man nodding in return. "Men of Rome" he called, gaining the attention of the entire crowd once again. The sound of the chanting slowly died away, the singing sounding shrill from the back of the forum as the last group of women finished. "Men of Rome. As Dictator it falls on me to tell you the bad news as well as the good, for the gods give and they take in equal measures" he said as the faces of the men closest to him grew fearful. "The Etruscan league amasses an army as we speak." At these words a great proportion of the crowd raised fists and called for death to the Etruscans, their calls echoed by the wailing of the women, some of whom started to sing the song to Juno once gain. Marcus waved his arms slowly once again and the silence started to fall onto the crowd.

"Men of Rome. This army is marching on Veii and will then march on Rome" a sudden gasp came from thousands of mouths as Marcus waved again for silence, the men at the front of the crowd turning to those behind and calling them to order as they waited for more details. "We, Romans, cannot let these enemies take advantage of us. I call for all men who can bear arms. ALL men" he called loudly as men realised what he meant. It was customary for men over 40 years of age to retire from active duty in the legions, yet many men remained fit and healthy from years of fighting in campaigns and maintained their armour and weapons. "Yes"

Marcus called "ALL men. I call you to bear arms, march with me to Napete and destroy this army of Etruscans in the name of Apollo, Mars and Juno and then to march to Veii and take the city. The spoils will be great. Those who march with me will be rich beyond their dreams and Rome will be glorious in her victory."

The roar of the crowd deafened him as the front rows surged forwards, cheering and waving, faces beaming as men strode forward asking when they were to march and how much food to bring with them. The cheering continued as Marcus moved back to the temple, catching Manlius' eye as he passed, a look of animosity clear on his face, which Marcus did not understand. Javenoli appeared at his side and slapped him across the shoulder. "A great speech. A great speech. We must leave and prepare the journey. I have sent a scout to see what army is at Napete and more to Veii to give them news of the potential attack, and for your soldiers to attend you, just as you asked" he finished, smiling. Marcus nodded his reply as two more men appeared, one suddenly asking for his son to join Marcus' service and the other pushing through to offer his own service. Javenoli brushed both men aside with a stern look saying reproachfully "you must follow the rules gentlemen, you know what to do."

As Marcus walked into the silence of the temple the words of the prophecy went through his mind and he closed his eyes to pray to Juno that what he believed was true, was so.

*

*

Chapter 18

Scipio grinned back at his friend in the resplendent red cloak, his eyes staring at the enormous trail of dust which followed them into the foothills.

"Can you believe it?" he asked.

"Not really" came the quietly spoken reply.

After a moment Scipio spoke again. "Dictator" he said quietly as Marcus glanced to him, the corner of his mouth tightening at the words.

"Why did I ask you to join me?" he smiled in reply as Scipio laughed at his jest.

"Because without me as your Master of the Horse you know that a bunch of old women with baskets of rotten fruit would wipe your army off the field" he grinned in reply.

Marcus huffed, his face staying serious as his eyes twinkled. One of his first actions had been to visit Scipio and retain his services as his second in command, one that his friend could hardly turn down. They had chatted through ideas for the attack on the army at Napete, scouring over maps and discussing formations. In reality none of them knew exactly what they were facing as no scouts had yet returned, but it felt good to be talking tactics with his old friend.

"How many men?" he asked.

"Just over twelve thousand with a further three thousand heading directly to Veii under Calvus" came the response, to which Marcus nodded. The call to arms, with the help of the suggestion that Veii was filled with great riches, had been too successful, Marcus having to turn down men who were clearly unfit for duty, including Javenoli, who seemed disappointed but was, Marcus felt, also relieved. The army was a mix of older men who would stand firm and younger men who had been too young for the last call to arms, the need for soldiers outweighing the short age gap. Marcus was concerned that the men would struggle with training and so had set a ratio of two older to one younger man to speed along the process, but also to keep the younger in check and stop anyone either deserting or rushing headlong to their death. He gripped the wooden eagle around his neck as Scipio looked to him and smiled. "When will Narcius meet us?" he asked.

Marcus looked to the sun overhead and then to the shadows on the floor. "Within half a day" he said as he turned to Scipio. "We need the scout reports or there might be nothing we can do" he added as Scipio motioned for them both to walk their horses forward and join the middle of the long trail of men snaking across the countryside.

Scipio looked nonplussed. "Well they should be back soon as well. If we can intercept the army at Napete before they leave we will have a better chance than if they reach Veii" he said. Marcus grimaced at the thought that the army had left for Veii and the Roman army would have to wheel around and turn back to the north, another two days march with this many men. As they continued to speak a call went up and both men strained their necks to see two riders coming across from the woods ahead and to their right.

"Scouts?"

"I would say so" smiled Scipio. "Come on" he said, kicking his horse into a trot as several Eques followed their officers across the open ground.

"Fasculus" called Marcus as they approached and the two riders saluted. "I didn't expect to see you here."

"Potitus sent me to scout the area and report back" he smiled, nodding to Scipio.

"What news?"

Fasculus looked to the rider and nodded, the youthful face of the scout swinging back to the Dictator in his red cloak. He gulped as if his tongue was suddenly too large for his mouth and swallowed hard.

"Here" said Fasculus thrusting a water pouch into the chest of the rider and shaking his head. Marcus and Scipio smiled at the man who had turned into a firm disciplinarian and who was clearly disappointed at the young man's inability to speak. The scout drank a quick mouthful of the liquid before turning and saluting to the officers.

"Sir. I have drawn a map of the city and the camp. I would say seven thousand men, less than five hundred horse and" he glanced to Fasculus who frowned at him and nodded for him to continue. "Well, sir, they seem to be having a festival" he said as he stiffened.

"Festival?" Scipio replied as both officers looked to Fasculus.

"A festival" he replied with a firm nod of the head. "Brantilus is correct, Sir. The enemy have been partying for two days at least. It seems that Napete has a good store of wine and the men have decided to empty it before they march on Veii."

"Do they know we are coming?" Marcus asked as thoughts started to run through his mind.

"Not that I know of, sir" came the reply. Scipio and Marcus looked to each other and then to Fasculus, who was already holding out a fresh tablet for Marcus' orders. "I can be with Narcius within two hours" he smiled, knowing that that was his destination. Marcus grinned and started to scribble in the soft wax.

****

Within an hour Marcus had turned the baggage train and sent it to Veii with a small escort and had gathered the officers to inform them of his plan to speed to Napete as quickly as they could travel. The officers grinned when they heard of the enemy, drunk on a feast and ready to be attacked and slaughtered. Marcus had warned that it could be a trick and that the men must stay alert and stick to the training that he had been drilling into the men as they had marched, but the word had spread quickly that the Etruscans were drunk and at the Romans mercy. The news had acted as a boost to the men who had marched at great speed towards their destination and covered the miles quickly and efficiently whilst being drilled in their new warfare at every water stop along the way. Even those who had been grumbling that the activity was too strenuous for their tired bodies seemed to work harder now that they heard the Etruscans were in disarray.

The sun was descending quickly in the sky as the men of Rome set up their marching fort and Marcus and a handful of his closest officers set off to see the camp at Napete, only four miles from their own camp. Arriving on a low hill which overlooked the valley in which the city lay Marcus stopped his horse under the shade of a clump of trees and leant forwards, patting the beast as it dropped its head and munched on the grass at its feet.

"They know we are here then" stated Fasculus" his face still grimy from the long rides he had taken during the day. Below them lay a long plain with two roads visible across it, both heading into the low wood and turf walls of the city of Napete. Sprawled around the city was an enormous mass of tents and fires, some already blazing with wood for the night and others just dots of red light which were only just being stoked. But a flurry of activity was happening as officers beat men into a frenzy of digging and fixing entrenchments.

"Good" said Marcus as a few faces turned to him. "They will be tired tomorrow from digging all night" he smiled. "Who has the map?" he asked as he turned to the men beside him, a long nosed man with a thin, clean-shaven, face handed him a vellum scroll which he opened and stared at the scene below taking a moment or two to peruse the full scene.

The map was accurate, showing the two roads and the city walls surrounded by the tents of the encamped army. He looked up at the terrain, seeing a small rocky outcrop to the left, some four hundred paces from the city and west of the road. He looked back at the map and up again as a cry came from the Etruscans, men pointing at the Romans and some falling back towards the city in fear.

"They've seen us, Sir" came the voice from behind Marcus, who simply frowned at the obvious statement and continued to scour both the map and the scene below him.

Scipio leant across and pointed to the map. "There is the dip" he said as his eyebrows rose. "Look here though" Marcus added calmly as a trumpet sounded at the camp and several men on horses started to gallop towards them. He pointed towards the dip in the ground and then drew his finger along to a thick line of trees further out from the picture on the map and nodded to Scipio.

"We need to leave, Sir" came the deep voice of the leader of the guard as he drew his spear and stepped in front of Marcus and Scipio. Both men nodded and with a last look at the terrain Marcus smiled and turned his horse, kicking it into a gallop and way from the charging Etruscans.

****

Manlius scowled at Apuleius, The man loved the sound of his own voice and could argue with himself and still not come to a conclusion. He also never seemed to agree with anything anyone said and his point was often lost in a flurry of diatribes on the evils of the Roman Senate and its patricians regardless of the subject matter at hand. His patience had worn thin and he raised a hand to the man as he was in full flow discussing the effect that losing more men to Napete was having on the strength of the plebeian party in Rome. Manlius had tired of the same old argument being raised again and, he suspected, so had most of the people sitting listening to his annoyingly monotone drawl.

"My dear Apuleius" he said with a fake smile. Apuleius saw him but continued with his speech disregarding the hand that was held up as a request to interject. Manlius considered simply getting up and leaving the meeting, but decided that may be a little too rude so he simply sat with his fake smile on his face and his hand raised and waited.

A number of small coughs and head nods to Apuleius eventually made him come to a stop and he turned to Manlius with a frown, which then turned into an equally fake smile as he asked "Ah, Marcus Manlius, what point would you like to make?" and stepped back from the rostra at which he had been standing.

Manlius smiled back and stood to look at the men sat around the room. This meeting of the inner council of the plebeian party had been called soon after the army had left for Napete, the discussion at hand was to arrange support for the city should the worst happen and the Roman army be defeated at both Napete and Veii. As it turned out Apuleius had seen it as an opportunity to lecture the plebeian leaders on the evils of the patricians and how he would change the balance of power in Rome for the better of the common man. Manlius nodded to Apuleius and stood for a moment looking at the faces of the men around him, most looking tired and bored.

"As you know my friends I have been a friend to the plebeians for many years" he started as a few men smiled back at him. "Talk of changes to Rome is welcomed, brother" he said with a turn to Apuleius "yet it does not help us to solve our problems today. We must continue to discuss the issue of what we will do should our glorious troops be defeated under the hands of the newcomer Marcus Furius" he said with scorn. "As I stated at the start of the meeting over an hour ago" he glanced to Apuleius, as did a few others in the room "it is my belief that we can hold the Capitoline Hill if we barricade it tightly. It has a water supply and we can easily store several or more months of grain in the larger temples on the hill. It would be my choice" he started to say as Apuleius stood and held up his hand. Manlius shrugged and motioned for Apuleius to return to the rostra.

"Thank you" said the drawl of the plebeian. "The Capitoline is where your house is, am I right?"

"You know it is."

Apuleius let a short silence fall in which a few men took the meaning and looked, almost angrily, at Manlius. "Yes it may be defensible, but I don't see how that will help us. We need to strengthen the walls. Create a wall as strong and as large as Veii so that our enemies cannot enter as we cannot enter that city. It would make sense to put our considerable efforts and money into that option than to build defences on the Capitoline where the *richer* houses of the patricians are based" he almost sneered as he finished the last words.

Manlius stood to reply but Apuleius continued in a louder voice "I am unsure where your loyalties lie Manlius. First you tell us that you are a friend of the plebeians and then you ask us to defend your home. I don't understand your thoughts and I am certain that many of the council don't either" he said as Manlius took a moment to steady his nerves and looked at Apuleius with a stony face, his anger held inside as he motioned for the opportunity to speak. "You misinterpret my meaning" he said, his voice cold but level. "In suggesting that the Capitoline would be a good place to defend should Rome's wall, gods forbid, be breached by attackers, I mean only to say that the topography allows it to be easily defensible, not to defend particular houses or dwellings. In fact, my dear friend" he said bowing as he spoke "I ask if you have any better suggestions as, from where I stand, we would not have the manpower or time to build walls as large or as strong as those of Veii and we certainly won't have the building material available in such a short period of time. In fact" he said, raising his own hand as Apuleius started to rise and his hand came up "I think Decius has a point" he said, motioning for one of the other men to take the stand.

As Decius took the rostra and began to extol the virtues of fortifying the walls of the city *and* the Capitoline Manlius groaned inwardly. It was no wonder that the plebeians and patricians could never agree on anything, the plebeians could never agree with each other. He took a slow breath and looked at Apuleius. The man was starting to annoy him, his actions and words were devious and divisive and his sudden turnaround in this meeting showed he couldn't be trusted.

Manlius sat and thought, ignoring the words being spoken around him. After a while he decided that it was time he started to re-develop his military career. Why couldn't he prove himself as Marcus Furius had done? Why was it that the Senate had chosen Furius over himself and what more could he do to promote his own claim for Dictator should such a need arise? He scowled, the facial turn making the man to his left look quizzically at him, to which Manlius smiled broadly and threw back his head with a silent laugh. Yes, that was what he should have done, played to his own strengths. On the battlefield glory was won easily for men like himself. He had won many skirmishes and fought many battles. If he was to fulfil his destiny, then now was the time to fight for Rome and show the people who he really was, their greatest leader. He nodded to himself and set his jaw firm at the thought.

"Manlius?" came the question from the rostra which pulled him back to the meeting.

"My apologies" Manlius said as he stood "could you repeat that please, I was considering the question but I have lost my thoughts for a moment" he smiled, noting Apuleius narrow his eyes at his words.

"Do you agree that we should consider both the walls and the Capitoline?"

"I do" said Manlius as he smiled broadly at the men around him. "Indeed it is an excellent idea." He looked around the room and turned to Apuleius. "Now that agreement has been reached I must leave for another appointment, please do forgive me" he said as he stepped quickly across and gripped Apuleius' hand and then moved across to the other men, smiling broadly as his mind went through what he needed and how quickly he could reach Veii.

****

Dawn was slow in coming and the men of Rome had already lined up in their ranks, marching quickly in the darkness to be ready for the light to appear. The officers had risen even earlier than the men and had attended the briefing in which Marcus had laid out his final plans for the impending attack, expecting that the Etruscans would line up in their phalanx at dawn in the traditional fashion.

As the men trudged through the calf length grass their feet became wet as the morning dew soaked into the leather of their sandals, some men finding it slippery as well as wet and being berated by angry Centurions. Other men grumbled at the early hour and marching in the dark, their grumbling causing others to shout at them to *shut up*. All in all it was a slow start. Marcus had ridden forward with Fasculus and approached the higher ground from which he has watched the Etruscan camp the night before. In the darkness he could just about make out the features of the Etruscan fire pits around the walls where many of the men had slept but it was too dark to make out any other features. He had used his velites to skirmish their lines all night, shooting fire arrows randomly into the tented area at irregular intervals to keep them awake. Their commander had been clever and sent pickets out into the open ground in twos and threes to keep an eye out for the attackers, catching one man before his colleagues raced in and butchered the pickets before fleeing. Marcus had rewarded each of the rescuers for their bravery and rebuked the man who had been caught. Scipio had called his decision harsh, but Marcus knew that, just like at the camp at Veii, success must be rewarded and failure frowned upon.

Below him he could make out the movement of a phalanx of soldiers heading slowly and silently into the open ground in front of the city, the noise of marching was dull in the heavy pre-dawn morning. Squinting he made out the lines of men as they headed across the open road and into the plain beyond, exactly where he had hoped that they would go. More men moved across the lines of fires, the black shapes lit up momentarily by the red glow of the dying embers.

"There" Fasculus pointed into the darkness as a movement caught Marcus' eye. Yes it was a series of wagons moving in the opposite direction, back towards the city but not into it, the light reflecting off the walls and the noise of the oxen braying as they pulled their heavy loads suddenly giving away their position. "They have set up their camp outside the city. He clearly thinks he will beat us easily and has not even bothered to place his spoils from raiding the local tribes into the safety of the town" Fasculus said, his voice betraying his surprise.

"An advantage we can use" Marcus spoke quietly but confidently as he tapped Fasculus on the shoulder and motioned that they return to the army.

Within ten minutes the men were back with the forward phalanx of soldiers, their shields still swathed in their leather covers as they marched with ten and twelve feet long spears towards the plain outside Napete.

"Fetch the officers Fasculus, we have to use every advantage. Also bring a messenger I need to get a new message to Narcius."

****

Narcius and his men had broken camp as many of the arrivals from Rome were just settling down to sleep. He knew his troop of a thousand men were critical to the battle to come, but so was stealth. Arriving too early or too late could lead to death for all of his men, timing was everything. The night march had been difficult, the leading officer losing his bearings twice and holding the men still as a long series of clouds swept across the sky and he couldn't discern the direction in which they needed to travel. Narcius had held his tongue as the man had blustered about the weather, cursing his ill luck and calling on his gods to avert the evil eye from him. It had taken a swift discussion with the man out of the earshot of the soldiers to get him back on track, the threat of leaving the man tied to a tree for the wolves to pick over his half dead body clearing his mind of any ill omen other than the wrath of his First Spear. Within four hours they had reached the dip in the ground that Marcus had described to him and the men dug their pits and settled down to catch a few hours of sleep, Narcius taking minutes to fall into a deep and untroubled slumber as the night was clear and cool.

Waking to find a slight dew on the ground he had shaken himself awake and woken his officers, quickly setting them duties which would need to be finished before dawn. Parties of men slipped over the ridge and headed into the darkness, their packs heavy as they disappeared silently into the gloom, the tools to dig pits protruding from them. Narcius marvelled at Marcus' tactics, knowing that he should really expect no less from the man as he had already shown his brilliance in several conflicts. This would be different though, a set-piece battle on a plain with two armies of several thousand men in deep phalanxes. The plan he had set out was, as usual, risky, but offered every chance of a sweeping success – if the Etruscans did what he hoped they would.

****

Vitulus and Sentillius stood in the dark and looked across to the low hills, the tree line visible in front of a lightening blue hue which was rising slowly into the sky. "Dawn" said Vitulus, his hand on his sword hilt as he blinked sleep from his eyes despite being awake for many hours. The two men had set up their forward lines in the appointed position. They knew the Romans would march at dawn and so they had set their lines out early to be prepared, and possibly to catch them unaware if they arrived in smaller groups.

Vitulus looked to his right at the sound of his fellow chieftain relieving himself, the warm smell of urine hitting his nostrils as he winced and turned his face away.

"Good, I might be able to see whose leg I am pissing against" laughed Sentillius as the men closest to them laughed back at his joke. Vitulus smirked, but kept his eye on the trees away to their left where the sunlight was beginning to show below the canopy of dark leaves, the trunks appearing like thin men standing in rows as he smiled at the thought, an old childhood nightmare of trees turning to men coming back to his mind, no doubt some story his mother had told him one night to keep him from running into the woods and being eaten by wolves. He strode along the line, not quite able to make out the faces of the men in the darkness, but certainly able to smell them and hear their whispered conversations. "Keep it down" he chided to one group who were laughing too loudly, the silence instantly showing that they knew who was calling to them.

Moving back to the front where Sentillius was standing he noticed that he could now make out more of the men than when he had marched in the opposite direction, dawn was moving quickly and the day was breaking.

"What's that?" came a fearful shout from one of the ranks of soldiers as Vitulus span around and sought the location of the noise.

"Who said that? What do you mean?" he growled in a low voice.

"There, Sir. Look" called another voice different from the first as Vitulus turned to look into the plain ahead of him. At first he saw nothing, his eyes squinting into the darkness as the light above the hills kept the plain dark. Then he caught a glimpse of a slow movement, then another and his heart skipped a beat. What could it be? He wandered across to Sentillius.

"What is it?" he asked. The other officer shook his head, the sound of the brass fitting moving on his helmet being the only reason he knew his head was shaking as he could not yet make out his features.

"I don't know. Feritas" he said quickly "run ahead and see what it is, come back as soon as you know."

A shaky voice replied "Sir" and jogged off into the distance, his feet padding on the grass the only sound that suggested he was still there. Then there was a sudden noise, unmistakable as arrow fall and a scream split the air as the front rank of Etruscans all flinched and stepped backwards, Vitulus and Sentillius looking to each other before Vitulus called "shields" and the men raised their shields above their heads, some kneeling and others simply remaining standing, but no arrows came and Feritas did not return.

"Bastards" snarled Sentillius as he squinted into the dark. To his left the tree line was starting to take more shape and the light began to suddenly grow. Behind him he could hear the unmistakable sound of numerous men marching into battle order. He grinned. As soon as it was light he would set the horses on the archers who were still standing out there on the plain, it would be like killing goats in a pen. Magnamus was on his right and Soticus on his left, both good leaders. They had discussed their plan and they were all set to march into the Roman line and smash them apart. What fools they had been to send old men and boys against true soldiers, were the Romans that arrogant? His spies had been slow in arriving with the news, but once he had known that the enemy was little more than old soldiers and young boys he had shouted it from every camp fire, telling his men that the Roman grandfathers and babies were coming to gnaw them with their rotten teeth and numbed hands. They had laughed and cheered him all night long and he had lapped up their praise. If this Camillus was such a good general then he would have to be truly divine to beat his experienced soldiers in their prime. He snorted at the thought, bringing a look from Vitulus which he ignored as he looked into the space ahead of him and decided it was time to march forwards to their battle positions.

"Trumpets" he called as another voice simultaneously shouted "Romans" then another and another. Sentillius flicked his head from side to side, suddenly thinking they were under attack, but it was Vitulus who brought him back to face the front.

"There" he pointed as the light began to spread across the plain. As his eyes caught the first rays of light to hit the plain in front of him he inhaled sharply through his gritted teeth. Standing in five deep phalanxes were several thousand Roman soldiers stood in absolute silence, their armour just catching the morning sun as it split the sky. To make him even angrier they were standing in exactly the position Sentillius had decided to take to gain the initiative for the coming battle.

****

Marcus rode down from the tree line as soon as the light spread across the plain enough for him to easily gallop across the few hundred yards, his heavy guard following at his heel. The manoeuvre had been perfect, the Etruscans now caught in the no man's land between the favoured position on the plain and the rocky outcrops to their right beyond which lay Marcus' Eagles with Narcius at their head. He had spent hours discussing the positions and counter movements that the Etruscans might take and now it was up to their leaders to decide the next steps, his officers were drilled for every eventuality – he hoped.

He heard an angry roar from the Etruscans as the sun gave them their first glimpse of the Roman lines of men, a cheer and a number of rude shouts coming back from the Romans as the curses of their enemy leader's anger split the air. Marcus grinned, knowing that this was a small victory, but a victory nonetheless.

Reaching the centre of the battle line he reined in and searched in the half light for Fasculus. Spotting him he called him over.

"Have you got the spear?" he asked as Fasculus nodded and produced a four foot long spear which he handed to Marcus and smiled.

"Are you sure this is a good idea?" he asked.

"We know the gods are with us Fasculus" came the steady but confident reply "but *they* don't, so I'd better tell them" he added with a broad grin.

The two armies stood in, mostly, silence as the sun continued its slow rise above the hill. As the plain became visible to each army it was clear that the Romans had stolen the better ground, forcing the Etruscans into the land which bordered the two roads to the town. The land was flat and green in many places, but also rocky with small outcrops and boulders which would hamper a marching phalanx. The Romans, on the other hand, held the better ground, flat plains of mostly grass with hardly any boulders and plenty of room to wheel a thousand men in formation. Sentillius snarled as Marcus smiled at the, unpopular but necessary, decision to march the men in the pre-dawn darkness.

As soon as the rays of light lit the plain enough for him to gallop forwards Marcus and two men, both draped in the robes of priests, set off into the gap between the soldiers, the enemy sending a number of skirmishing velites forward. Marcus held up the short spear, which would be known by the Etruscans as a religious instrument for proclaiming war. The velites stood, turning back to their leaders for a decision as Marcus continued forwards, his red robe billowing behind him. As he approached the first Etruscan he called in their deep throated language "I am Marcus Furius Camillus and this land is declared Roman by the rights of warfare set out by Mars, war-bringer, Jupiter greatest and most powerful and Juno, the queen of the earth who has made her decision known to come to Rome with her glorious soldiers when we take the city of Veii." At this he threw the spear into the ground and stared at the face of the two leaders in the centre of the Etruscan line, each staring back at him open-mouthed before he wheeled his horse and galloped back to the Roman line, happy that the correct procedure had been delivered as a prelude to the coming battle. Another small victory, and one that the Etruscan soldiers would understand.

Marcus fell in behind the leading phalanx of soldiers, their cheering at his return causing him to wave and smile to them all. As he turned he called the officers to him but remained on his mount as he craned his neck to see what actions the Etruscans might take. They too, it seemed by the horses racing across to the centre where the two leaders he had seen moments before were standing, were discussing their next actions. Directly ahead lay the Etruscans, four or five thick phalanxes of men bristling with long twelve foot spears, their number spread out across the two roads which led to the city of Napete. On his left, away beyond the edge of the road lay the river, its water wide and deep and a natural boundary which edged closer to the Etruscans line than it did the Romans as it meandered away from the city. To the right and moving towards the low hills were long stretches of deeper grass and clusters of boulders, the land not much use for any kind of military manoeuvre, yet the four hundred yards between the enemy right, as he looked at it, and the features could still hold options for both armies. Directly behind the Etruscans was the city, maybe a quarter of a mile, enough for them to beat a retreat and march to the city without being caught. Marcus believed the Etruscans would think their soldiers superior to his own and so would stand and fight so had ignored the consideration to march closer to the city to be able to chase any retreat, his preferred option of the better ground being more persuasive in his own mind. He clutched the wooden eagle and small tube holding the words of the prophecy which hung around his neck and closed his eyes to pray to Juno that her words were true and he would bring Rome glory. As he opened his eyes he caught the first of the officers arriving at a trot, seeing the others closing in fast. Nodding to the arrivals he stretched his back and blinked his eyes several times. His sleep had been fitful and the early hour at which he had risen had left him tired, though the sudden activity of the last few moments had wakened him quickly. He watched the Etruscans as their officers huddled together in the central line, no doubt watching him doing the same. He smiled at the thought, though he watched the rear of the Etruscan line to check that no scouts were heading out towards the river and the dip to his left.

"All present" came the chirpy voice of Fasculus as Marcus brought his attention back to the row of men standing, or sat on horses, around him.

"Good" he answered as he smiled briefly at the faces looking towards him, eyes peering from under thick rimmed helmets and brightly coloured feathers standing proudly into the sky, each face urgent and eager to hear his words. He considered the enemy for a heartbeat longer before he spoke. "You have your orders" he said as heads nodded sharply. "Whatever plan the enemy brings we will beat them. We will beat them because they think we are incapable of moving quickly and efficiently. We will beat them because Jupiter, Mars and the goddess Juno are with us" he said as the shadowy eyes of the men below him looked up at him more intently, some grinning, others tight lipped. "The attack plan starts as soon as you return to your units, we must take the initiative to allow Narcius the space to come to their rear. Scipio" he said as he looked to his friend on his right "are the Eques ready?"

"Yes Sir" came the stout reply. Marcus wished he had asked Narcius to bring the scorpions, but he knew that travelling with them would have slowed the men down and possibly left him without the quick and deadly Eagles that he needed.

"Then be brave and may the gods favour us" he said as he nodded to each face in turn before waving the officers away. He looked up quickly and saw that the Etruscan leaders were still deep in conversation, their heads bobbing up and down and arms waving left and right. *Perfect* he thought, they are not yet ready, they did not expect us to be here and had not planned for such an eventuality. As his personal fears rose up and his mind started to rush through things that might go wrong with his attack plans he heard the first trumpet from his left as the first Roman phalanx stepped forwards, its march leading to a second trumpet from directly in front of him and the second phalanx moving. Classic warfare, he thought as he scanned the leaders of the Etruscans, their faces turning at the movement and arms waving more wildly. The third trumpet set the third phalanx, on his right, into motion, a group of three hundred Eques stepping out beyond them to hold the right edge of his attack as he noted the Etruscans split their horses into two units, one heading left, the other right. As he expected, and hoped, none of the Etruscans were heading for the river, thinking that the natural boundary was just that, a limit to the edge of the battlefield.

Marcus knew that the drilling of the men in how to form the lines he wanted had been problematic and that to carry the extra, lightweight, spears had also been difficult, indeed some of the older soldiers had injured themselves in their attempts to wheel and move away from the man to their right, but it had to be done, and done quickly. He wondered if he had been too hasty as he watched the three phalanxes walk forwards slowly, he needed the enemy to close the gaps more quickly and tire themselves so that the Romans could make their changes to the lines before they hit the Etruscans. Velites raced ahead, stones and smaller javelins flying at the enemy as the men raced in and out across the plain, the Etruscan velites doing the same. Marcus looked to his right and left and saw the Eques holding their horses back at the edges of his lines, the beasts stomping at the ground waiting to be let loose. He smiled at the calm look on Scipio's face, his eyes meeting Marcus and smiling as he turned back to the men around him and yelled something that Marcus could not hear, the cheer being echoed by his men.

The rear phalanxes began to move and Marcus edged forwards with his horse, which angrily flicked its tail and pulled its head high as he nudged its flanks. Ahead over the city he caught a movement which made his heart leap, a speck, no two, which appeared and then disappeared under the dust that had started to rise in front of him. There there were again, their unmistakable wings spread into the soaring action of Eagles.

"There" he called, his words causing momentary confusion as the men around him, the older, richer men of the Triarii looked to him before following his eyes and outstretched arm.

"The Eagle" called one man, his greying beard trimmed close to his face and sharp brown eyes looking to Marcus with a broad grin. "The gods are with us, look" he yelled as more men called and pointed, the cry starting to rumble forwards as the men in front heard the shout. Within moments a loud cheer had started from the Roman lines as the men crashed their spears and sword onto their shields screaming "For Rome" as they marched forwards. Marcus swallowed hard, pride welling up inside him as he nodded to the faces around him and screamed "For Rome" thrusting his sword into the sky and thanking Juno silently for the sign.

****

"They are marching straight at us" Sentillius said with a snarl "set the lines and march straight back, we will push those dogs into the river, outflank their left and wheel them to the water's edge. Old men and boys" he sneered as the second trumpet came from the Roman lines and the middle of the three front phalanxes started to march directly at them.

"See" he waved wildly at the Romans. "They have no plan other than to walk at us with their old men and boys, *pah*" he added dismissively.

Magnamus grinned and slapped his shoulder. "I agree" he said with a look to Vitulus "look, they march straight at us with no thought other than to overwhelm us with their numbers." The leaders all turned to see the third phalanx start to march towards them, the lines of the reserve also moving forwards behind the main attack.

"Then we agree" Sentillius said. "Send the horse to both edges and set the men at the Romans, we wheel them to the right and outflank their left. Push the scum into the river and let the water spirits drown them" he said as the men all shouted and nodded agreement.

Instantly the men disappeared to their tribes and soldiers, Sentillius taking a few moments to check that the Romans were truly just walking straight at his sturdier and battle trained men. He shook his head at the arrogance and let out a deep sigh, today would be a great victory and he, Sentillius, would take all the land to the River Tiber as his spoils once the Romans were dead. He smiled at the thought.

As he thought the words the Romans let out a blood curdling yell and started to bash their shields, the sound bursting across the plain in a rising crescendo. What a noise, he thought as he looked to the men around him and started to shout back at the Romans, the men taking his lead and screaming curses into the air as they set off in their deep rows of men, shields and spears towards their enemy.

****

A high pitched trumpet called from the rear of the Roman lines, three long phalanxes spread across hundreds of yards all moving in unison as soon as the note came. At the sound the velites fell back from the leading Etruscans and turned to sprint back towards the twelve men deep ranks of Romans as the Etruscans raised a louder scream, their voices cajoling the running men as cowards and old women. The Roman velites smiled to themselves as they ran, the gap between the two armies now no more than sixty or seventy paces as each phalanx marched straight towards the other. As the velites approached their own lines the rear six rows of men were called to a standstill by their Centurions, those too eager stepping forwards two or three steps before being called back. The front rows split, every other man moving to their right so that to the oncoming Etruscans the Roman line seemed to double in length within a matter of seconds, the velites disappearing into the gaps between the men. The rear lines stopped marching and the reserve force also came to a standstill as soon as the front lines split. Marcus watched the movements anxiously.

The movement caused a momentary confusion in the front rows of the Etruscan phalanx, the front men slowing and being pushed from the rear causing laughter amongst the Romans. The front rank of Romans then threw their long spears to the floor and turned sideways, their arms stretching back behind them as they took a long look into the faces of the Etruscans. Sentillius frowned but saw only an opportunity, gaps in a phalanx, the Romans were turning to run, surely this would be an easy victory he thought as he turned his head to his men and screamed "Kill them all, forwards" and turned to see the sky turn dark above him, a sudden fear gripping his heart as he struggled momentarily to understand what was happening.

****

Marcus edged his horse forwards and lifted himself off its back so that he could see the movement he had drilled the men into over the past two days. It hadn't been long, but at every stop during their march the Centurions and officers had explained the movement and drilled the men in what to do. He realised he was holding his breath as the back rows of two thousand soldiers came to a sudden stop, the calls from their Centurions almost instant as the trumpet blew its high pitched note across the battlefield, the signal they had been trained to listen for had come.

Marcus marvelled at the sudden movement, men stepping forward three paces and to their right and throwing their long spears to the ground so that they could gain the space they needed to stretch back their arms and let fly the thin, deadly, javelins he had brought by the thousand. The javelins lifted into the sky, the noise of men grunting as they threw the weapons in one long line causing every other noise to suddenly fall still. The sky grew dark with the weapons as they arched into the sky and then began to fall, the Etruscans in their deep ranks starting to buckle as the sharp spears crashed into their rear lines.

Marcus watched, his military mind going through what he expected to happen and what the effect really was. He had expected the Etruscans to lift their shields but continue to march, but the effect was far more pronounced. The front five rows of Etruscans came to a standstill as they struggled to lift their shields in the confined space of the phalanx, the javelins slicing into the wood with a loud thud which was immediately followed by screams as men fell under the hail of iron tipped missiles. The rows behind the falling men jostled and pushed, their momentum causing a buckling of the line as the Etruscans at the front fell to the unexpected javelins, but the men in the rear continued to march forwards and pushed their comrades from behind.

'Now' Marcus thought as a series of yells came to his ears above the screams of the dying, the Centurions calling 'release' as the sky grew dark again and the phalanx edged backwards, the right edge moving more quickly backwards than the middle. He turned his head quickly to see the Eques darting into the right edge of the Etruscan phalanx, the first row cowering as the second series of javelins hit home followed by the immediate charge of the Roman horses. The Etruscan cavalry moved forwards just as he hoped, their action meant as a counter move to that of Scipio who began to wheel his men away from the flank as if in retreat. Marcus watched as one of the Etruscan leaders fell, a javelin straight through his left arm as he had lifted his shield. He smiled. Juno was guiding the Romans today.

The thinner Roman line was now vulnerable to Etruscan attack and Marcus breathed quickly, his heart thumping as he watched the men pick up their spears before the second series of javelins landed and stepped neatly back into their formation.

The Roman phalanxes stepped forwards more rapidly, closing the gap with a huge roar as they crashed into the Etruscans, metal scraping against metal and wooden shields thudding together as the melee began. The effect was instant, the Etruscans losing ground and the first lines of their defence obliterated by the hail of javelins and instant response from the Romans leading forces.

Marcus turned his horse to the left, towards the river, and galloped away to the edge of the Roman line where he hoped he would get a better view of the battlefield as the men on the plain began to thrust their spears into the deep lines of enemy soldiers. The Triarii remained behind, closing formation and starting to yell at the soldiers ahead of them who were now slicing into the Etruscans who were falling in their hundreds to the sudden onslaught of the men from Rome.

Marcus watched as Scipio began to retreat from the Etruscan horse on the far left. He had circled wide, almost reaching the river as they had planned as if trying to get behind the Etruscan line, but now the Etruscans had seen him and sent their own flanking manoeuvre to counter the attack. As he watched Marcus saw Scipio call his men back in a frantic escape as the Etruscan horses followed in a mad chase to cut off their retreat, their leaders throwing spears at the back of the withdrawing Romans. He narrowed his eyes as the final three rows of Romans in the phalanx on the left suddenly split and ran across towards the cavalry, no shields, just men with two or three javelins in each hand and raced through the dust towards the cavalrymen, who seeing what seemed like velites in front of them whooped and wheeled on them, easy prey to a good horseman in open ground.

The front edge of two hundred Etruscan nobles in bright colours on the back of their horses snarled and screamed as they raced in for the kill closing to fifty or sixty yards as they raised their swords and smelt victory. A sudden explosion of dirt and the nasal scream of a dying horse was followed by another, then another, as several of the front row of Etruscans collapsed into pits dug by the Romans the night before, the confusion giving the Romans who had split from the line the time to stop, stretch back their arms and let fly a volley of iron-tipped death at the remaining horsemen. A second volley and then a third arched into the sky within a few heartbeats before the screaming Roman horsemen of Scipio crashed into the side of the Etruscans who had almost come to a standstill as the pits and javelins took their toll. Marcus grinned, his eyes almost bursting from his head as he stared at the death on the flanks before turning his attention back to the field in front of him. The sun had barely risen above the tree tops and the plains were bathed in a brown and blue dust which seemed to swirl into momentary opaque screens which then dissolved into brilliant clarity as spears thrust and swords whirled in the melee of men before disappearing again behind the wind-fed dust cloud.

"Optio" he called, as the man saluted from below him. "Send the signal" he said as the man turned and waved quickly to the trumpeters who were standing watching the scenes in front of them. Three long blasts on the trumpets caused a great roar to come from the Romans as they re-doubled their efforts and the battlefield moved inexorably forward a few paces under their renewed efforts. Marcus grinned at the sudden movement, like a wave crashing along a shore and pushing back the pebbles. The noise grew louder as the cloud of dust obscured his view and he gritted his teeth. He knew that it was the training and drilling of the men that would win this battle now, not him sitting on his horse behind the line, but he also knew that it would soon be time for Narcius to bring his men into the battle. Timing was key, he thought, it must be done at exactly the right moment and Narcius would know what the three trumpet blasts meant and would, he hoped, be acting immediately. He prayed to Juno, his mind fearful that the men hadn't had time to prepare enough and offering her a new statue made of white marble if the men of Rome overcame their enemies this time.

****

Narcius heard the trumpets, three blasts, just as they had agreed. So the left flank was free, the horses cleared and the area vulnerable. He lifted his head from the ground where he lay, his body covered by his shield which was covered in dust and dirt to hide his armour from the sunlight. As he crawled the two or three yards to the edge of the dip in the ground he blinked back the dust that was in his eyes and squinted with a furrowed brow towards the noise which was ahead of him and to the right. Ahead and to his left was the city, its walls covered in people standing watching the battle that was playing out in the plains about a half mile from their city. As he had hoped the ground to the enemy soldiers was empty, not a soul within a few hundred yards. Now was the time to strike. He pulled his sword from its scabbard, taking a moment to look at the bumps which were lying around across the dip below him and towards the river. He pulled his shield towards him as he lay on his back and clashed the sword against the metal boss in the middle, the noise low but distinguishable. Men started to appear from the ground all around him, almost like the dead coming back to life. The soldiers began to crawl forwards, the two hundred paces of the dip suddenly filled with five rows of men all armed with short swords and a variety of mostly round and a few rectangular shields. Narcius nodded to Caelio, who pointed his sword to the left and his men jumped to their feet and slipped out of the low ground, five hundred pairs of arms and legs racing across the ground directly at the city of Napete.

An alarm bell sounded, the loud ringing turning the heads of the Etruscans in the rear line of soldiers, their leader Soticus turning at the sound.

"What is it?" he called as he played with the silver handled dagger from the back of his horse. Ahead of him the battle wasn't going well, the Romans seemed to have taken the initiative on the right wing, the Eques lost to a series of pits which gave free rein to their foot soldiers as they seemed to be marching forwards and Vitulus stretched his men across towards the river, thinning their ranks. *Not good*, he thought as he turned to see a multitude of Romans headed straight for the camp at the walls of the city behind him, the heavy wooden gates closing quickly as the people within shut out the new menace. *My gold and bronze* he said to himself, a sudden surge of anger rising in him as his eyes flicked to the small camp that the Etruscans had left by the walls to the city. The damned Romans were attacking their spoils. He flicked his eyes back at the fight in front of him. The lines of men were at a standstill, surely he would not be needed for hours yet, everyone knew that the phalanx could take a day to move a yard forwards. Yes, he would have to take some of the older men and stop these Roman scum from taking his precious belongings. "Marciciatus" he yelled "take three lines and teach those dogs a lesson" he grinned as a thick set man a head taller than any of the men around him saluted and yelled a string of orders. Within a minute nearly half of the Triarii, the Etruscan reserve line, had set off back towards the city. Narcius watched from the land by the river and smiled, *perfect* he said to himself.

****

"We cannot allow the people of Rome to continually be swayed by talk of treasures and spoils from campaigns; it maintains the status quo of the patricians leading the people to earn a crust in battle after battle. If we allow this to continue we will never see the plebeians rise above the status of half-slave" Apuleius said his disdain at the patricians clearly evident. "The state of affairs is simply ridiculous. Why do people simply ignore the arguments? Why can they not see that to jump when their *masters* call them just perpetuates the current situation, patricians tell us what to do and we jump and do it" he finished with a curl of his lip and a scowl.

The plebeian council sat in silence, the older men looking to one another unsure how to answer the question and the younger, power hungry, all nodding furiously, many vocalising their support of his statement with cheers. Apuleius raised his hand. "This *Dictator*" He said the word mockingly and shook his head dismissively "has the people in raptures. What is it about the people of Rome that makes them so fickle? I'll tell you what" he added as he leant forwards on the rostra "religion, money and food. That is it brothers. Religion that only the patricians have the *birth right* to control. How?" He looked around the room. "How can a god choose only a patrician? Look at our forefathers like Dentatus and great men of our time. Men such as Calvus. All great men, all beloved of the gods, but each was still only a half-man, not equal to the patricians because they cannot perform the religious rituals that only the patricians can do. And" he turned to stare at the faces of the men around the room "this Dictator calls himself *Camillus*. A mockery of the name and meant to remind us of our inferior status, we who have no power with the gods yet this man is so beloved he has chosen his true name to be that of *Camillus*, a religious servant. *And the people love it*" he threw his hands in the air in exasperation. "I tell you gentlemen it is a trick. I have heard of this prophecy of his, that his *Eagles* will lead Rome to great victories, and yes he has been lucky in warfare, using trickery and new machines that deny a man his right to die honourably in battle. Yes yes I know you are all unsure, but it is propaganda and nonsense I tell you. He is no more beloved of the gods than you or I Decius" he said with a long stare at the man sitting to his right. "But he is clever" he said as his voice became calmer and lower, the sudden change making the men sit forwards as he spoke. "Yes he is clever. He uses the name to evoke his patrician birth right and flaunt it in our faces. He uses the name and his constant focus on the absolute minutia of every ceremony to show us that we are not worthy of the love of the gods. Gentlemen if you do not believe me think on this" he said as a few heads shook at his words. "A Dictator has the one voice that none of us can deny. His word is law and he is the ultimate citizen of the Republic. But he is also the closest thing to a king that there is since the days of the tyrants" he snarled at the audience of faces. "A *king*, gentlemen. That is what this man wants to be. Remember the days when the kings were the only ones to complete the sacrifices, their word was law and our people" he looked slowly around the room "our people" he repeated. "They were the ones to suffer under the tyranny. This Camillus has brought himself to power through trickery and now he slams it in our faces. He reminds us that *he* is all powerful and it is *he* who the gods love. He tells us this by leaking stories of some great prophecy that we all grab like starving men at a food handout. He is clever, yes he is clever. He fights well and his *plebeian* Eagles win him glory. These men pledge allegiance to him and his Eagle. They even wear a charm, a *lucky* eagle on a chain around their necks as a sign of their loyalty. I tell you they are like the kings bodyguards from the old days, their silver talisman's meaning they could commit any evil and the king would allow it. You remember Amilictus?" he said pointing to an elderly man whose great great grandfather had been carried off in the night for plotting against the old kings. Amilictus nodded, his eyes wide in fear at the passion in Apuleius' words. "This man is trying to make himself our King" he said finally and sat down, his arms crossed and his eyes fixed at a point somewhere along the far wall of the building. A short silence fell before several men stood and applauded the words, Decius and others looking to each other and frowning but still showing appreciation for the strength of argument.

It took a moment before anyone else stood to speak. Decius had spent many years developing the plebeian council to be a debating stage from which the plebeians could work to improve their arguments for more political lea-way in Rome and whilst he didn't agree with Apuleius' words he felt he couldn't argue against them. He looked around the room at the stunned faces, many men appearing to be convinced by the words they had heard. "Does anyone have anything to say?" he asked as men shook their heads and looked away from him to avoid his eye.

"Well gentlemen" he said calmly. "I am not so sure that the very strong words used by our brother, here, are true, though he does give a very strong argument. One I am sure some of the older Greek statesmen would have been mightily impressed with. However" he continued "we must remember that it was Marcus Furius Camillus and his family who supported the law for soldiers pay. It was also at his behest that Calvus and the rest of the great men alluded to were appointed Tribunes in recent years. He argued strongly for more plebeian tribunes despite the Senate vetoing the motion. Without his support of the people the plebeians would not have gained some of the recent changes to laws and taxation in the city. As for the claim that he wishes to be King." As he said the word his face looked pained and he turned to the smiling face of Apuleius. "I cannot see the argument. The name was a simple choice after the saving of the Ancilia Shield from the temple those many years ago. The people called him Camillus wherever he went so it was a choice almost demanded by his own action. The prophecy" he shrugged "who knows? Yes there are rumours, but I have heard many rumours of prophecies over the years, men rising to power as they claim some god or other has given them divine support will often create such things to enhance their status. But most turn out to be trickery to steal bronze and silver from the people. He has not stolen anything that I know of and gives his clients more than any other patrician." Apuleius snorted at the remark and Decius smiled back at him. "He is a clever man. I agree." He paused for a moment in contemplation. "He cleverly changed the law to give soldiers pay so that their families would not starve. He has cleverly given the best armour from his vanquished enemies to his soldiers, but they fight in that armour for another the following year, not every Eagle soldier is a client of Camillus for *all* their years" he said with a smile. "The claim of kingly desires is a harsh one to throw at his feet. He is no more a tyrant than I am" Decius said calmly as he looked around the room "and he has no more a kingly desire than I do" he added. "I understand your anger at him Apuleius" he said as he looked at the man sat before him, his arms remaining crossed over his chest. "I know what it is like to have your strongest argument for cessation of war at Veii overturned because one patrician says 'no'. It has been the way for many many years my friend, and I know how it hurts. You must be careful that your personal feelings do not cloud your judgement and you should think strongly about your argument that he wishes to be King. This is a claim that you must prove with evidence. Hard facts" he said as he turned to the audience. "Such claims can be the death of the man who puts them forwards as well as the man he accuses" he said as he looked coldly to the younger man.

A silence fell as Decius moved across to the table and drank a small measure of the wine he had half finished earlier. "The council will not accept your argument and we will not back such talk with our votes" he added as the men in the room shuffled in their seats. "However" he said as he turned to the room "the argument was given with passion and energy, something that the patricians will struggle to deal with when you have the rostra with a series of facts and figures behind you." He slapped Apuleius on the shoulder and smiled at him. "Come on, let's get some more wine and talk though the discussions to increase the defences on the walls, that is something where we can deal with, facts and figures" he said as Apuleius nodded his head and stood to clasp hands with the older man, a determined look on his face despite losing the debate.

As he took the wine cup he seethed inside at the humiliation of losing the call for soldiers to leave Veii, the first debate he had ever lost. He smiled to the men who clustered around discussing issues of no interest to him and he vowed to see Camillus fall, somehow he would gain vengeance on the *patrician* for besting him just when his political career was rising.

*

Chapter 19

Marcus narrowed his eyes, his brow creasing as he stared into the fog of dust that was coming

from the rear of the enemy lines. Were they moving? He found himself rising on his horse

again to get a better view as the line of men to his left moved suddenly and caused him to

look back at them urgently. Scipio and his horsemen had disengaged, the remaining Etruscan

cavalry turning and fleeing. With a satisfied grin he saw only a handful of the few hundred

horses remained with a man on-board, the ground heavy with their dead. *Good* he thought as

he watched Scipio line his men up along the left flank and the foot soldiers rush to the dead to

retrieve their shorter javelins from the bodies of men and horse alike. On the right he scanned

the line and was pleased to see it was holding steady despite the attempt to overload that wing

by the Etruscan leaders.

A roar brought his focus back to the Etruscan centre as he saw the lines of tall spears begin to

march back to the city, *perfect* he thought as he raised a hand and dropped it, four loud blasts

coming from the trumpets as the signal carried across the field.

As the signal sounded across the field the Centurions screamed their order "push", "advance"

and "kill." The Romans heaved in the centre, pushing back the central defence of the

Etruscans as the centre line buckled under the sudden surge. Legionaries fell under the

sudden onslaught, their bodies stamped on by their own men as they were unceremoniously

pushed out of the way by the deep lines of men behind, each one screaming at the top of his

lungs as his shield pressed into the back of the man in front of him.

Marcus was holding his breath as he watched the centre of the attack move two or three paces

into the Etruscans before it came to a bloody standstill, the weight of the Etruscan rear lines

pressing back into the attack. As the power of the attack stalled Marcus peered to the left and

watched as Scipio and his horsemen attacked the left flank which was now vulnerable after the Etruscan horse defence had fled. His glance to the right told him that, as he had hoped, the leaders of the enemy were caught in indecision and the Eques to the far line stood impassively, still remaining as the support to their own left wing.

Scipio's men crashed into the defensive line, a horse skewered by a long spear as the men tried to wheel into the gap. Marcus watched as the Etruscans sent forward the remaining rear guard to support the flank, their leader charging forward with hate written all across his face. He grinned and waved to the trumpeter who casually licked his lips and blew one long note, the final blast which gave the officers their final instructions.

****

Narcius heard the note and stood, waving his men forward with a scream of "For Rome" and stepping over the rock strewn lip of the ridge he had been lying behind. Men jumped at his command and raced into the open ground. To their left the few hundred Romans who had left their hiding position moments earlier suddenly came to a halt and split into smaller groups of eight to ten men, turning back on the approaching phalanx of Etruscans. Narcius and his men raced at them, the faces of men in the rear line turning with fear in their eyes as they suddenly saw another threat.

Sentillius, bit his teeth together and ground them against each other with a grunt, almost in admiration, at the sudden turn of events as he twisted his head from left to right. The Roman had managed to split his rearguard troops at the same time as launching an assault in the centre of the line and from behind. *Damn he was good*, he spat on the ground cursing his poor leaders and shaking his head as faces turned to him for orders. Scanning the area quickly he saw his phalanx behind him were under attack from two areas, but men with shields were no match for a phalanx of men, so he turned back to the main battle in front of him. The centre was holding, the noise growing as men tired under the weight of pushing and shoving as they thrust their spears into the ranks of Romans ahead of them, but his right flank was weak. He had committed men to it, so he was happy enough with his position.

"Hold the line" he called to the faces around him. "The Romans cannot force us back and we have strength in numbers, we will win. Hold the line" he called loudly as worried faces twisted back to the fight in front of them. Sentillius moved his horse to the left slightly so that he could see above a sudden swirl of dust. The Romans had gained another yard in the centre, but still the men held as well as they could. *Hold* he thought, *hold and we will win*.

Marcus felt his fingers gripping the reins tightly, his eyes switching across the scene and his breathing shallow and rapid. The noise level had risen and the centre was a cacophony of screams, yells, curses and grunts. He wished he was there, fighting with his men, but he knew that these all-out battles required one leader, one man who could orchestrate the troops, and that man was him. He licked his lips as he felt his throat tighten at the thought. He glanced to the sky, almost wishing to see a sign, an eagle, but none came. The centre of the line had been halted by the Etruscans again, as he had expected, it was now up to the tactics he had drilled into Narcius and his Eagles to win the fight by destroying the rearguard of Etruscans that was marching at his men. He knew that his new maniples, the Gaulish style he had seen all those years ago, were lethal in such conditions, but he also knew that if the gods were against him they would be cut down in their hundreds and the battle lost. Had he been made Dictator too soon? Was he really able to control all of the might of Rome? He swallowed hard at the thought, involuntarily clutching the Eagle around his neck as he stared into the dust and death ahead of him.

****

Narcius called to his men as they ran across the ground, seven men closing ranks with him as other groups began to cluster together, the phalanx snarling at them as they approached. "Quickly and steadily" he shouted, the order repeated by the officers and maniple leaders as they jogged across the ground. He gritted his teeth, feeling the rush of air through them as his legs beat a steady pace. "Come on lads, this will be like plucking chickens, one feather at a time" he laughed as nervous eyes laughed back at him. He hefted his shield a little as he felt the man to his right step closer and press against him "Walk" he ordered as the first spear of the phalanx clattered into the shield of the man ahead of him, the spear slicing down and aiming for his shins as was often the first strike. The legionary crashed his foot onto the wood and pushed aside another long spear thrust to disable two attacks as Narcius grinned at the perfect training and stepped into the small gap with his sharp, short, sword and punched the blade into the arm of the spear holder, the only thing he could reach at this distance. The Etruscan screamed and the spear fell, his fellow soldiers pushing forwards at the attack as the man lowered his shield momentarily and Narcius whipped his sword back into the space and landed a slice across the man's face, the eyeball bursting into a red spray as he quickly retreated, the seven men around him leaning backwards in a tight ball as they cheered at the attack. Instantly the closest four spears thrust at them, all missing and causing the phalanx to stumble as the small group twisted to the sudden speed of movement of the small band of Romans. Along the line the same thing was happening. Narcius grinned as he saw Etruscans fall in unison as Roman groups stepped in and out, their tactics playing havoc with the formal lines of Etruscans who tried in vain to wheel against the smaller groups. To his right the bulk of his attack were attempting to get behind the phalanx as they were ordered and Narcius snatched a look to the main battle some two hundred yards ahead and to his right, exactly as Camillus had said, there were no horse coming to the defence, Scipio must have decimated them, he grinned and yelled "For Rome" the new energy coursing through his body as his men screamed with him and rushed at the phalanx in their tight unit.

****

Sentillius cursed again. A look behind showed him that the phalanx he expected to defeat the Romans was stalling, the *scum* seemed to be split into smaller attack groups and surrounding his men. *Damn.* He looked urgently to his left and waved to the Eques who were milling around on their horses unsure what to do. He lifted his spear and pointed towards the fight behind him, his eyes almost begging the officer to understand what he meant. As he waved the spear he heard another scream and the drumbeat of hooves as the left flank of the Roman heavy Eques, their leaders screaming, charged at his own men. Horses reared as the attack came, but the officers kicked their men into a stumbling charge. As he smiled, taking his eyes off that contest he saw the sky darken in front of him and he blinked, almost flinching at the sudden movement.

Marcus saw the Etruscan leader wave his spear to the horses on the flank and called his trumpeter to sound advance for his own to counter the relief force which might destroy the attack by Narcius. He swallowed hard again, this was a gamble. If the leader of the Etruscan cavalry turned to attack Narcius, even though it was a long way across the back of his own troops, then the Roman horses would be into them on the right. What would the leader do? Stay and protect the wing or turn and ride to their rear? He hoped they would stand and fight and he watched with bated breath as the spear waving leader screamed as the Roman cavalry charged away to the right and headed straight for the Etruscans. Marcus took a deep breath the moment the Etruscans turned and he waved his red cloak in the air to the line of Centurions at the rear of the thousands of Romans lined across the battlefield in front of him. The officers in the centre of the line all raised one arm and started to scream orders as Marcus' own rear guard of six hundred older men, all wealthier Triarii soldiers raced forwards with two of the javelins each and stepped behind their own pushing lines of soldiers. Marcus held his breath as the action happened, his last line of defence suddenly leaving all their long spears and rushing forwards shieldless.

Within a few moments the Centurions called the men into lines and the javelins were hefted into the air over their own soldiers, all of whom screamed more loudly at the sudden darkness that came over them as hundreds of iron-tipped spears crashed into the rear lines of the Etruscans who had no idea what hit them. The call for the second spear had already come as the first Etruscans panicked and raised their shields, releasing their press on the men in front of them in their efforts to catch the hail of death that was raining down on them.

The Triarii turned and raced back to their spears, turning with cheers as they lined up and started to march back at the Etruscans.

Marcus' eyes grew wide as the javelins smacked into the mass of men in the centre of the Etruscan line, the three back lines of the phalanxes buckling as the Roman line pushed harder as soon as the dark hail of javelins had appeared above them. A deep groan came from the Etruscans as the Romans stepped forwards three then four paces, the men at the sides of the advance slicing into the panicking Etruscan men around them. It was now or never Marcus thought as he licked his lips and glanced back up to Narcius, his men still harrying the solid mass of soldiers, thinning down the disorganised phalanx as he watched. Marcus raised his eyes to the heavens and thanked the gods for looking after him and his destiny.

*

*

Chapter 20

"Accept the surrender" Marcus said as he stepped into the city "but take every man, woman and child and bind them" he added as he clutched the sword he had been wielding in the final attack at the gates and slammed it into its scabbard. "Kill anyone who bears a sword against us" he shouted as the men ran screaming into the town, some already slicing into Etruscans who were too slow to defend themselves against the onslaught of the Romans.

He scanned the walls behind him, dead lying across the ramparts and on the floor. He winced at the fresh cut on his arm, a lucky blow as two men had come at him at once, the second attacker had caught him as he thrust at the first. The cut wasn't deep or long, but it would be a fine scar to show his son when he returned to Rome.

He moved into the centre of the square which led to the gates and scanned the scene. Men, women and children were being herded from houses, their wails and pleading rising as soldiers manhandled them into separate groups. Ignoring them he turned, "Messenger" he called as a man stepped over to him from the knot of officers and men behind him. He held out his hand for a tablet to write on and spoke as he wrote.

"Three messages, copy and send" he said as the officers stepped closer to listen. "One to Potitus at Veii. This will tell him of our great victory here" he said as he moved the stylus across the wax. "You must tell him" he looked into the eyes of the messenger "that he is to allow a small group of escaped men from here to enter the city of Veii. They must tell of our victory and how easily we have destroyed their allies" he grinned as the man nodded. He looked to the right as another messenger stepped forwards. "Go" he commanded to the first "but take three men with you, I don't want to lose this message to the enemy if you are caught by their fleeing lines" he added sharply. "Here" he said, holding out his hand as a scream came from a woman who was parted from her two children, the crying of mother and babes renting the air as Marcus shook his head. The messenger handed him a tablet. After a moment he looked up at the officers, Caelio looking at him with a blood spattered face, many of the others clean except for the dust on their clothes. "Rome" he said "for the Senate proclaiming our great victory and imminent march on Veii" he breathed out as he thought for a second, leaning the tablet back on his forearm to write additional lines. "return to Veii with any reply, we will meet your there" he said as the man saluted and turned, calling for two more men to join him as he rushed towards the horses.

The square was rapidly filling with screaming children and crying women, the older men defiantly cursing the Romans but receiving back handed swiped for their protestations. "Clear this lot outside" Marcus said as he looked around at the confusion. "I want this square clear and a command area set up here" he pointed to a well near the centre of the square and then turned back to the officers, scanning their faces.

"Caelio. Your men were magnificent" he said as the man stood stiffly to attention. "But I need them to search the city and the Etruscan camp and bring all the spoils here to the square, pile everything against that building" he said pointing to the wall of a three storey wooden townhouse which lay across the edge of the pavemented square casting a long shadow. Caelio saluted and turned, his shoulders sagging from tiredness as he left. "I want all the officers here in one hour" he called as he walked to the well and peered into its depths "we must complete the ceremony to thank the gods for our victory before we leave for Veii" he said coldly as he looked back across the square.

****

The hour passed with more skirmishes from within the walls of the city as families tried to defend themselves against the Romans as they went systematically through the houses within its walls, the dead filling the streets as crows dived onto unattended bodies to feast on soft entrails. Marcus had set out a couple of tables with a string of seats around them in the square and was receiving reports and sending messages as the final officer arrived at the briefing, his weary eyes telling of the death and destruction he had seen.

The officers waited as Marcus sent a messenger back out of the walls with another set of orders. He sighed and blew a long breath from puffed cheeks as he raised his eyebrows at the assembled men, their faces visibly relaxing at the show of exhaustion and relief on their Dictator's face.

"Gentleman" he said with a broad smile. "Half of our job is complete." He moved a goblet away from his hand and clenched his fist. "Veii awaits" he said as he looked up at the men and set his jaw. "The gods have spoken and shown their favour. If we stay here too long they will turn their attention elsewhere" he said with certainty as many heads nodded, all the men understanding his meaning. He looked to his right and nodded to the Optio who stiffened his back and started to read through a long list of lost men, some four hundred men had been killed or injured, the Etruscans losing countless thousands and their army smashed and fleeing across the countryside. As the words came to his ears Marcus put on his stoic face knowing that it could so easily have been his enemies sitting here recounting his dead. The Roman loss was minimal and he knew it would be seen as a great portent for Rome amongst all of the tribes of Italy, he silently thanked the goddess Juno for her support and made a mental note of the debts he owed her when the temple was completed back in Rome.

As the Optio finished Marcus nodded his thanks and stood to look at the soldiers around him. "A marvellous victory" he said with warmth in his eyes. "You all played your part exactly as ordered and I cannot praise you highly enough. That" he pointed to an enormous pile of gold, pottery, jars of oil, cloth, grain, spears and crates of bronze that was stacked against the side of the houses along the square "is your reward. Riches for you and your men. Riches for the treasury of Rome and glory for our gods" he said with passion. The men licked their lips at the treasures, some eying particular items they wished to gain for themselves. "And at Veii is a thousand times this treasure. A thousand times the glory and a thousand times the riches" he added as he saw the greed in many of the soldiers faces around him. "Within three hours I want the city stripped of everything of value it holds. The captured will be sold as slaves and the money placed in the treasury in Rome. These spoils will be split into the tribes you command, with one tenth delivered to Rome for the temples. Prepare your men, gentlemen, we march to Veii as soon as we are prepared and the slaves are sent to Rome."

****

The shouts grew, a great clamour of voices ringing through the air as Apuleius woke from his afternoon slumber, his eyes quickly adjusting to the light. He ruffled his hair and then straightened it before he stepped into the atrium and called to his door slave "What's happening Jixtur?" The slave bowed and spoke softly. "The word is that the army at Napete has beaten the Etruscans and as we speak they are now marching on Veii to ever greater glory" he smiled placidly, his tone measured and his eyes looking to the floor.

Apuleius turned on his heel and quickly strode to his bed chamber grabbing his toga and calling for his chamber slave to hurry up so that he could be one of the first men of rank to be at the forum when the Senate appeared to speak of the great victory.

So Camillus has won, he thought as he lifted his arms and the heavy cloth was draped across his body. He will certainly be the topic of conversation and now would be a good time to sow some seeds of doubt, small morsel which would help his cause later when the man inevitably made some mistake or other. His mouth curled at the edges as he thought about his options. Camillus embodied the patricians and all they stood for. His *so-called* prophecy and the love the gods had for him being yet another story conjured up the leading classes to hold men like himself in place, to keep them as the underclass. He scowled at the thought.

Leaving the house with a thick set ex-soldier named Macius he set off for the forum at a fast pace, Macius pushing some of the crowds out of his pay-masters path as they dropped down the steep slope to the east of the forum. Macius was broad shouldered but not much more than average height and Apuleius could see over his head as they approached the thronging mass of the forum, the people rushing into the space from every side street. *Damn* he said to himself, how had so many people heard the news before him? He resolved to pay for better spies and informants so that he could be one of the first to know of any news from Veii. As Macius pushed his way through the forum people pushed back angrily. Apuleius was barged from left and right and despite the burly ex-soldier in front of him he was making little

headway into the crowded forum. Ahead on the steps to the Comitium he saw Decius and two

other plebeian leaders, all looking serene, as if they had been there for hours. He cursed as a

man jostled him, the smell of sweat hitting his nostrils. Macius had almost come to a

standstill, his angry shouts disappearing amongst the ear-splitting noise around them as

people barged and pushed to get closer to the front. Apuleius gripped Macius' shoulder and

nodded to the row of shops on their right, his message clear. Both men pushed away to the

walls and then headed along the shop front towards the Comitium. As he arrived at the place

where his plebeian colleagues were standing he was just in time to hear Cicurinus call to the

crowd for silence as Senator Ahala stepped forwards with a scroll in his hands.

People hushed and called for silence as heads stretched to peer at the toga clad elite standing

at the head of the forum, the senate leaders dressed immaculately and all wearing the broad

smiles that told of good news and victory. As they pushed forwards into the backs of the

crowd he missed the first words of Ahala's speech, the crowd hushing those closest to them

who were intent on chatting about the weather or the poor sanitation in the streets.

"...will bring glory to our City and to our greatest gods" the words came to his ears as

Apuleius reached the end of the shops and was within a few yards of the plebeian leaders

who had gathered as close to the patricians as they could. Nodding to the men who glanced at

him he stifled his anger and set his eyes on the white clothed men as they stood and waved a

series of votive candles in the air and took oils and other instruments for the auspices before

nodding to each other and then turning back to the crowd. Every head was silent, the sea of

faces staring intently at the leaders of Rome.

Cicurinus and Ahala took a step forwards and Ahala waved a small wooden tablet in the air, a

broad grin appearing on his face as his eyes moved around the crowd. Apuleius felt the power

that the patricians held over the mob in front of them and despised it, the arrogance causing his mouth the move into a sneer and his eyes to narrow. The crowd seemed to be holding its breath awaiting his words, some exclaiming the love of the gods and begging for good news. Ahala was a master at picking the right moment and he began to lower the tablet and his face became darker, the noise of people taking a deep breath grew as he moved before he looked up to the gods and spoke.

"People of Rome" he said as he turned his body to the left and right and waved the tablet over their heads as if by doing so they would be imbued with some divine power from the words which were held within. "Our great Dictator Marcus Furius Camillus has given us a great victory..." Apuleius didn't hear the next words or see the faces of the patricians as a great shout rang out across the forum, thousands of voices cheering and men and women hugging each other as if saved from death. Apuleius gritted his teeth as he smiled, though inside his anger was rising again.

Ahala waved his hands for silence as Cicurinus moved forwards and, smiling from ear to ear, suggested that Ahala let the crowd show its appreciation, at which more cheers rang out across the wide space of the forum. Ahala laughed as he held the tablet even higher as if it was a sign of something stupendous that the crowd should all look at in awe. Apuleius shook his head at the way that the patricians could play the crowds and watched as men jumped up and down, some praying to their gods, other simply cheering. Power was everything, he thought as he was slapped hard on the back by a man behind him, to whom he turned and nodded warmly, though his eyes betrayed the anger he felt inside. As he scanned the crowds he noticed the way that the patricians were lapping up the applause, some actually waving to the crowds as if they had personally slain the enemy and been in the front line killing the Etruscans. He looked to Decius, who was also standing looking at the crowd in a more restrained manner and nodded at the older man. Decius nodded back and quickly turned his head back towards the group of patricians who were now starting to speak again as the noise quickly abated.

"The Etruscan threat at Napete has been wiped out. Jupiter and Mars have brought their wrath on the heads of our enemies. Enemies who bore no right to wage war against us and had no legal voice to challenge us. As is *our right* under the laws of the gods we have taken their city and property. Slaves" at this he held his head down as the majority of the crowd did the same, everyone obeying the custom of lowering your head when talk of freemen becoming slaves from war was mentioned. "Have been taken and will be sold to good Romans. All monies will be given to the treasury. Great treasures in abundance has Camillus, your Dictator, taken from the enemy and great treasures will Rome give to its people." Before he had finished speaking the crowd were cheering again as Apuleius considered the words and the way the crowd reacted. As usual the patricians had used the gods, the laws and the spoils from war to work the people into a frenzy of excitement, yet the people were too stupid to realise that it was this that held them down under the foot of the patricians. Apuleius started to form a plan in his mind. He had to prove to the people that the patrician class were not the favourites of the gods; it was the only way to control the minds of the population of Rome. He noticed Decius looking at him curiously and smiled back at him with a nod as the man turned his head back to the patricians.

"People of Rome" called Ahala, his voice slightly shaky. "Your Dictator marches on Veii to smite our enemy at their door. The auspices are good, the gods are with us and the wrath of Mars and Justitia are coming to Veii. Too long have they held us at bay. Too long have their taken our sons from their homes. Too long have they held back the might of our great City. But the time has come to right the laws of the laws they have broken. The time has come to destroy their arrogance and by the divine rights given to us, *your chosen leaders*, we will bring victory to every man and woman of Rome."

As the cheers rose in volume Apuleius noted the inherent use of the term *your chosen* and noted it, it would be one he could use in one of his own speeches the future. As the noise continued Apuleius was lost in his own thoughts of anger and hatred for the men standing in front of him.

****

It had taken less than twenty four hours for the Romans to strip the camp and city, taking everything that they could carry and loading baggage carts to breaking point. The Etruscan camp and city had been loaded with so much treasure than Marcus was in awe at the volumes, more than any campaign he had seen in many years. In fact there was so much that Caelio had suggested giving sacks to each of the new slaves to carry rather than leave the less precious items at Napete. Over four thousand slaves lined the roads as they set off to Rome, the women half naked as they were jostled into long lines tied together with ropes and chains. Many held children in their arms, their sad faces showing the horrors they had endured as the men of Rome ransacked their city and dishonoured their mothers. The older men had been killed, some standing and fighting as they knew their fate and others too frail to work and so useless to the conquering Romans. A small force had been sent with the new slaves as they marched back to Rome and its slave market and Marcus had turned his back on them as they had set off in the early mist, his mind on the task that lay ahead at Veii.

As he approached the Roman camp outside the great walls of Veii after a half a day's hard ride he was pleased to see the scouts and pickets were alert and the fortifications clean and war-ready; Potitus had done a good job whilst he had been away. The city of Veii loomed over the Roman earthworks which stretched towards the gates, the high ramparts were surrounded by men digging and lifting heavy stones into place to create the roadway on which the army would march over the walls. Arrows fell intermittently on the workers, but the wicker screens and thick shields of legionaries stationed as support to the working men held them at bay.

The gates of the fortifications were opened as cheering men waved at their approaching leader and his bodyguard, the noise growing as he entered the main fort and dismounted, his grinning face causing even more cheers from the men who came across and thronged around him before their officers called them back to their duties.

"Camillus" Potitus said from the doorway of the central building, its wooden frame scrubbed immaculately. Marcus waved to his friend and met him with a firm handshake and a final look back at the, still cheering, men in the fort.

"You must tell me about Napete, we received your report" Potitus said as he gripped Scipio's hand and they embraced warmly.

"We will have time later" Marcus replied as he stepped into the cool room from which Potitus had exited to greet them. The room was large and square with a series of wooden stools arranged along the left hand wall stacked one on top of another. Straight ahead was a long table around which several people could sit and Marcus headed across and looked at the map of Veii and his old wooden fort which was laid out as he had left it when he left for Rome.

"The army will arrive by nightfall" Marcus said as he looked at the scene on the table and the map of Veii with its ordered streets and various squares, ideal for fortifying and holding should the Roman march falter. His mind was already running through problems and issues and he looked up to see both of his friends standing silently watching him. He raised his eyebrows and frowned. "What?" he asked with a smirk. Both men looked to each other before shaking their heads and laughing.

"You are a driven man Marcus" Scipio smiled as he walked over and leant his hands on the table, his eyes wandering across the map and soldiers placed around the fort that depicted the city of Veii.

"Rome needs it" came the cold reply.

"Rome needs you to be rested and thinking clearly. When did you last sleep" Scipio said as he noticed Marcus' shoulders tense and his jaw stiffen.

"The enemy are not sleeping" he said as he stood and looked to both his old friends, their faces smiling but concern n their eyes.

"And neither are our soldiers Marcus" said Scipio slowly as he placed a hand on Marcus' shoulder and looked into his eyes. He noticed the tiredness on his face and the thin red lines within the whites of his eyes. He saw the young man he had known all those years ago, carefree and driven by the love of the gods with his focus on duty. Marcus started to protest but Scipio waved him into a seat and took the one next to him, Potitus bringing over a jug of wine and three wooden cups.

"Here" said Potitus. "The camp is secure since we moved the forts as you suggested. The work at the rampart continues but we have cleared the tunnels and they are ready to use. We have made four ladders for the final assault up the well and we have made several trips in the nights to check the city" at this Marcus' face lit up and his eyes moved quickly from face to face. "Yes, we have been busy and we are ready" continued Potitus. "But what we need now is our leader to be alert and prepared, giving the right orders at the right time. Without you *Dictator of Rome*" Potitus saw Marcus' face flush at the words "in the Triarii guiding the troops we would..."

Marcus shifted in his seat and stared back hard at Potitus "I will be leading the attack" he said forcefully. The two officers looked to each other momentarily, concern on their faces as Marcus looked to them defiantly.

"As you wish" said Scipio with a grin which went some way to placating Marcus. "Then you need to rest. A tired sword arm will be the death of you, and that would be bad for all of us." As he finished he handed Marcus a drink and sat across from him sipping his own watered wine as a short silence fell into the room.

"It has to be me" Marcus said after a moment. "The prophecy demands it" he said wearily as he looked into the half empty cup, his eyes feeling heavy. Another short silence fell into the room. Marcus looked up to his old friends, men who had grown up with him and knew how he thought and what his words would mean. He sighed and placed the cup down looking at Scipio and shaking his head. "I've been through it a thousand times" he said as he lifted the wooden eagle from the string around his neck. "The waters will shrink before him in his hour of need. The Eagle will lead Rome and the city must be purged" his heavy eyes flicked up to both faces as they looked to him. "It is all here. Veii is where the prophecy has led me" he said with certainty. "Fortuna and Mater Matuta serve his cause" he added. "Mater Matuta is within Veii. She has called to return to Rome in her Roman form of Juno. *I* must do this. *I* must defeat Veii" he said with a hungry look in his eyes. Both men stared at their commander, and neither spoke, as Marcus looked back to the map. "Here" he said "the water has shrunk and we have found these tunnels. Juno wants me to destroy this city *never to be a city again* the words say" he looked up as he said them "and so it must be done with my hand. *I* must be the one to lead the attack through the tunnels. Don't ask me why, but I know it *must* be me."

Scipio glanced to Potitus and then back to Marcus. "Then you must rest and formulate your plan" he said as he stood, his hands on his hips as he looked down on his commander and friend. "The army will be some hours yet so you have time to rest, sleep and eat before the officers arrive and we set out the orders" he placed a hand on Marcus' forearm. "The gods look over you Marcus, but your body is mortal and the flesh weak. Sleep, eat and prepare. If the gods don't demand it from you, *we do*" he smiled as Potitus, his eyes wide, agreed heartily.

****

Mella slumped onto the chair, his arms and legs ached terribly after the long march. Why had he decided to walk and not ride? He was getting too old for legionary marches. He winced at a blister on his right heel and decided he needed to heat a needle and burst it later. Narcius entered the small room and threw his sword belt and helmet onto the floor with a loud clatter. "Gods that was hard work" he added as he bent down and pulled a water pouch from the belt he had discarded and took several deep draughts before offering it to Mella, who was busy removing the thick leather chest-guard that he had worn for the march, dark patches of sweat under the arms and along the bottom edge.

"Don't let the men hear you say that" laughed Mella as he took the pouch. "Centurion Narcius. Nasty bastard, hard as nails, nothing stops him" he laughed as water dripped off his chin. Narcius grunted and half laughed before sitting heavily in a chair and unlacing his thick sandals, the heavy leather dusty and worn.

"What time's the briefing?" Mella asked after another deep drink.

"About four hours. I've got Maximus set to wake me in three" he said in a matter-of-fact manner.

"Good"

"I need to be up to get my *nasty* face on" he laughed as he edged past Mella and slumped on a low cot which lay across the edge of the room The door opened and Caelio walked in, his head shaking.

"Fifteen miles without a stop" he moaned as he threw his belt to the floor beside Narcius' and took the water pouch from Mella's outstretched hand with a curt nod. "I only lost two men, both left for the cart" he said as his lip curled "and the latrine ditches tonight" he finished.

"I lost six" Narcius said, his eyes remaining closed as he lay back with his arms behind his head.

"Twelve" Mella mumbled as Narcius sat bolt upright.

"Twelve?" he said incredulously. "Twelve" he said again with a glance to Caelio. "My father..." he started before Mella grabbed the water pouch from him and threw it in his direction. Narcius caught it deftly with a smirk, took a drink and lay back down laughing. "We know all about your father marching thirty miles in a day with a hundred men and all of them finishing without even a blister" he laughed as he shook his head and Caelio burst out laughing.

After a moment Narcius opened one eye "Truth be told I never believed that story. The old goat couldn't walk a hundred yards without moaning about his bad knee" he said affectionately.

"Well we will have some stories to tell our children after this" Caelio added quietly as he stripped to his tunic and simply flung the rest of his clothes to the floor. As he did so a small bag clinked off the inside of his belt and split, the noise of several heavy gold coins rolling across the floor bringing both Centurions to a sitting position as Caelio jumped up and started to gather the coins hurriedly.

Narcius eyed Caelio for a moment without speaking, the tension in the room growing palpably as the coins were gathered. Mella looked to Narcius and then back to Caelio, his eyes darting from man to man anxiously.

"You holding back on us, brother?" Narcius said as he sat forward, the muscles in his arms tensing and his eyes narrowing and flicking from the coins to Caelio's eyes. Mella placed a hand on the hilt of the dagger in his belt, the only one of the three men who had any sort of weapon on him.

Caelio swallowed hard as he looked nervously to Narcius. The man was a bull, solid muscle from endless training, arms like tree trunks and shoulders as wide as two men, there was no way he could win a fight with him. Mella was smaller and thinner but was a master with a sword and dagger, he had to think his way out of this one.

"Gods no" he said as he sat back and frowned, his face aggrieved at the words of the two men. He breathed out a long, slow breath and shook his head stretching his feet out in front of him trying to look relaxed though his heart was beating as fast as if he was on a run in full kit. He looked over his shoulder as if checking that nobody was listening despite the fact that there were only the three of them in the room.

"Look" he said as he lowered his head and held out the coins "Greek gold from my Uncle" he said as handed a coin to Mella, his voice placating and sounding almost embarrassed. "You know what he's like?" he said as his eyes looked at both faces as they bored into his. "He" he shook his head and pursed his lips tightly before continuing "he gave them to me in case I was captured. Said I could bargain my way out of any trouble" he looked to the floor to emphasise the embarrassment he was trying to show before looking back up at Narcius and shaking his head again at his disbelieving eyes. "Come on lads, where would I get this much gold? You don't think I stole it?" he looked even more exasperated as both the men in the room simply sat and glared at him for a moment as his words hung in the air. It was one of the rules of war that all spoils were listed and shared between officers and men with a percentage going to the state. Mella had fallen foul of just such a rule many years before at the hands of his, now, friend Fasculus and as such he looked long and hard at Caelio. He was a good officer and worked hard, his men respected him even if he was a little soft on them, but did he trust him? He had certainly spent many nights at Veii disappearing into the woods, but Mella just assumed he was seeing one of the women from the camp so had thought as little of it as any of the other officers who had seen him sneaking off and returning later flushed but smiling. He decided to give him the benefit of the doubt.

Mella broke the silence with a genuine smile as he lifted his belt and pulled a thick leather pouch from under his tunic, the bag of silver and bronze half the size of the gold that Caelio held. "My bargaining and betting has only earned me this, but my uncle isn't a Senator" he said as he glanced over to Narcius who eyed the haul suspiciously before shaking his head and putting his head down again.

"You could buy an army to protect you with that much, Caelio. I've never seen so much gold. Remind me to stay close to you tomorrow, I'd hate to see one of Mella's twelve men limp over to your dead body and find that stash" he said as he took a deep breath and strained with an arch of his back before a loud fart ripped the air and all three men burst into loud laughter.

****

The light had faded quickly as a roll of clouds fell into the sky, their grey mass suggesting rain despite the heat. In the shadows of the thin buildings along the road beyond the Pons Sublicius Apuleius jumped from his horse, handing the reins to a thick set young man with short cropped brown hair and a wispy beard. His eyes searched the trees and buildings nearby, but saw nothing suspicious, as he had hoped. The man lifted his leg and Apuleius cupped his hand to grip his shin and lift him onto the horses back; not his best horse but a good one nonetheless.

"Go now and you will be there by first light" Apuleius said as the face of the man he had chosen for the task looked down at him from his horse. "That fool Manlius left this morning, if you are quick you can find a place in his guard and seek out what I need" he said as he turned to the woman beside him, her deep blue shawl stretched over her head as she stood looking at her husband, his pock-marked face half visible under his hood. "Nobody will know that you didn't set off with them."

"The money?" the woman said, her face hard as she turned to Apuleius. Her brown eyes looked harshly at him as he lifted a heavy bag from his cloak and placed it in her outstretched palm.

"The rest when you bring me something I can use" he said as he looked to the woman and then the man.

"Go husband and come back safe" she said with an affectionate touch to his arm as he nodded grimly and kicked the horse into motion, the beast flicking its head as it stretched its legs and trotted away.

"And don't lose my damned horse" Apuleius said as he watched the man head off towards the salt road which led away from the Tiber and towards Veii, his shield and sword slung across his back. The woman turned back to Apuleius and tossed the coin bag up and down in her hands before she licked her lips slowly and raised her eyebrows seductively.

"Well I have an empty house and enough money to buy a large flask of wine" she said as she stepped closer to Apuleius, whose eyes held hers in a firm gaze as her head tilted to one side and she parted her lips. Apuleius glanced to her ample breasts and wide hips which were hidden under the thick stola and travelling cloak and nodded approvingly to himself.

"It would be a shame to drink alone" he said slowly as he pulled the hood of his cloak over his head and looked deeply into her alluring face. "Of course discretion is called for and I will be maybe a hundred steps behind you, so leave the door loose" he said as he touched her shoulder with his hand and drew his finger down onto her breasts before stepping aside to allow her to walk in front of him. His plan was coming together. The fool patrician would be brought down and *he* would be the man to do it. He watched the sway of the woman's hips as she wandered away and his heart beat a little faster at the thought of what they would do later that night, but he also felt it quicken at the thought of outdoing the great Camillus.

*

*

Chapter 21

Dawn had come with a slight drizzle, the cool air and breezy conditions not perfect for his

attack but also not bad enough to make him change any of his plans. The briefing the

previous night had been a long process as he drew out the attack plan, choosing officers for

each element and asking them to repeat the orders so that he knew they understood him. At

one point he had been surprised to hear that Marcus Manlius had arrived at the camp with

over a hundred armed men, all ready to fight for Rome and all of good fighting age, the last

straggler arriving an hour behind the others but clearly young and strong from working his

farmland. Marcus had been wary of Manlius at first. They had not been on speaking terms

since the discussion regarding the incident with Postumius and his brother Aulus, yet Manlius

pledged his loyalty to Rome and to the Dictator and asked to be in the leading men who

stormed the city.

It had taken some time to get Manlius up to speed with the attack, the news of the tunnels

bringing a wide eyed stare as he listened to the plan and nodded wisely, his mind running

through the plan as it unfolded. The meeting had stretched into the night and plans were

refined as Marcus made sure the officers drank only heavily watered wine and ate only bread,

olives and cheese under the flame of the candle to Mars. He had been fastidious in this ritual

for some years now after reading of the successes gained by Greek soldiers who ate and

drank only light meals on the night before a battle, their prayers to the gods acting as the food

they needed to smite their enemies.

In the light drizzle Marcus donned a thick cloak and stepped across from the square guard hut

to the wall, striding up the earth bank and onto the short ladder to the parapet. He listened to

the silence that the rain was bringing to the morning, the air heavy with slow falling sheets of

drizzle. Ahead lay the tall walls, unscalable and austere, the helmeted heads of soldiers standing guard were visible at set distances along the expanse of stone, the odd spear moved along from right to left as he watched the slow procession of the disembodied weapons. *Would today be the day?* He felt his heart quicken at the thought but he held himself in check as he watched the spears move back from left to right. The feint of an attack had to appear to be a full assault and the officers had discussed various ways in which this could be done without too much loss of life yet allow the men in the tunnels to embark on their attack without being noticed by the Etruscans. Marcus felt heartened by the words of his men, they were clear that the Etruscans had no idea how many men had arrived from Rome. Potitus had allowed a small band of escapees from Napete to get into the city, maybe twenty men at most and Marcus was thankful for the news, the Etruscans must know that their support had been wiped out to spread fear into the city and help the Roman cause.

As he stood and looked out at the walls Scipio appeared at his side and nodded, his unshaven face and tired eyes testament that he had only just risen from his bed. "Any changes?" he asked as he turned his face to the walls.

"None."

"They must know that our camp is bursting with men" Scipio said. It was true. The arrival of so many new soldiers at the Roman siege works had created an enormous logistical issue with new tents, new fires and latrine ditches creating a flurry of activity which the Etruscans could not help but notice.

"If the soldiers who escaped Napete are telling tales of woe as I hope they are then the city will be in turmoil. The King will be getting his advisers together and they will be working on a plan to hold us at the walls, assuming that they don't know about the tunnels." Marcus had woken from a dream in which he was running through an endless tunnel before the roof collapsed on him and his sword was knocked from his hand as thousands of screaming

Veientines charged at him. He knew it was just his fears finding a way to express themselves, but it still nagged at his mind. *Was it a sign from Juno to call off the attack?*

"They will man the walls as we expect and we will win this day" Scipio said with assurance as he placed his hands on the top of the wooden wall in front of him and leant over to look down into the space below him. "The ground isn't too soft, we will be able to march without a problem" he said. As he spoke the rain eased as a bright spot appeared in the heavens above them, the yellow-white spot of the sun attempting to break through the clouds.

Marcus grinned, *a sign*? He and Scipio both noted the change in weather and nodded as Marcus spoke. "We will set the men out as planned in two hours" he glanced to the sky "when the cloud breaks. The ceremonies will be observed and the screens taken to the rampart" at which he motioned towards the long ramp that stretched from the foot of the Roman camp to within ten paces of the walls of Veii, the engineers had worked hard to get as close as they could to the walls. Wooden planks and screens would be marched up the ramp and thrown over the walls under the covering fire of the scorpions as a part of the feint, men ready below to march when the planks were in place. It had to look like a real attack and Fuscus had volunteered to lead this part of the plan with Potitus leading the main army outside the city while Marcus entered through the well into the temple within.

Scipio was following the plan in his head. Potitus holding the central lines of men with Fuscus attacking along the ramp, Fasculus and Vulso holding the flanks and Scipio with the horse on the right. Marcus would lead the attack into the tunnels with Narcius, Caelio, Mella and Manlius. Quintus Fabius had also asked to join the attack in the tunnels but Marcus had refused his request.

Scipio looked at Marcus, his red cloak dank with rain, his face drawn at the cheeks behind his trimmed, dark, beard. The boy he had known was gone, the man standing next to him was so different from the person he had known; carefree; questioning; learning. The man standing beside him was driven by the passion to see Rome destroy every enemy before them and particularly to smash Veii. It was consuming his every waking hour and his pinched face and the gaunt look in his eyes told of the hardships war had brought to him. Scipio thought of the family members and children they had lost and the effect it had had on them both, their knowledge that life was short and the unexpected nature of sudden death bringing them closer together, yet somehow distant at the same time.

Marcus grunted and turned his head slightly as music floated over the walls, the unmistakable sound of flutes and drums. "A ceremony?" he said quietly as he frowned and turned his head to Scipio, who simply shook his head in response.

****

The King held his arms out as a slave draped the cloth around him, the elegant folds of the heavy cloth lying lightly across his shoulders.

"The bull is being prepared, your majesty and the oils are ready in the temple. It will be another half hour before the preparations are complete" his aide said, his voice dripping with servility.

Vanimus, the King of Veii stared at the wall, his anger still unabated despite the long discussion he had held with all his military advisers with regard to the sudden appearance of more Romans at his walls and the terrible stories that the men who had escaped from Napete brought to him. He shouldn't have drank so much either, he said to himself as he felt the acid in his stomach and the need to suddenly relieve himself.

"Wait" he commanded as he headed to the wooden structure at the corner of the room which held a hole in which he could do his ablutions. Momentarily he returned, his face wincing at the acid which remained in his stomach and throat. He sipped small amounts of water and held his eyes closed for a minute before he resumed the standing position and the slave continued to dress him.

"Any change in the Roman camp?" he asked.

"Not yet, Sire."

"Good. Send the priests to me I need to speak to them" he said. He had decided that the best way to reassure the people of Veii that their goddess still supported them was to hold a ceremony and get her to swear allegiance to the city. Since the damned Romans had held their ceremony at his walls and commanded Uni Teran, whom the Romans called Juno or Mater Matuta, to leave the city his people had been in uproar. How had the Romans managed to lower the water of the lake and spread even more of their diseased fears into his city? He shook his head angrily at the thought. This Camillus was clever. He had somehow stopped the flow of food and weapons into his city as well as caused his people to fear that the gods were losing the love of their city. Slavery, that was their biggest fear, not death at the hands of the Romans, slavery. The women filled the temples and begged their gods to keep them free and save them from slavery, to save their children from being made the puppets of the Romans. He cursed silently as the slave continued his work.

Since the news of the loss of their army at Napete, he cursed again at the thought of such loss, the cries for surrender and for proof that the gods still loved them above all others had risen. Every day some fool came to him decrying the Romans and asking the King to save his family. He dismissed them all. Yet now he had to prove to them that the city was still safe, and the only way to do that was to hold the ceremony and call on Uni Teran to confirm her love for them all. As he continued to consider the conversation of the previous evening he heard the door behind him and smelt the wood smoked air of the priests clothing come to his nostrils before he heard the words of the chief priest speak.

"Sire, we came as you bid" his annoyingly sing song voice said. Vanimus closed his eyes before he turned and looked at the leader of the priests of Uni Teran, his dark hair flowing beyond his shoulders and beard cut square three inches below his chin, as all the priests of the goddess did. Two other priests stood behind him, each with similar facial features behind their long hair and square trimmed beards, which made their eyes seem all the more prominently framed. One man had spots of blood on his left sleeve where he had been conducting sacrifices earlier that morning and Vanimus noted with satisfaction that the man looked immaculate apart from those small blemishes, as any priest should he said to himself. "Take a seat" he motioned to a low table to their right "and I will be with you momentarily" he added as the slave busily finished the final elements of his clothing and stood back and bowed deeply to the King.

As the king sat he looked at the priests, their calm faces looking straight ahead, none of their eyes looking directly to him. As he sat silently the door opened and in walked his chief adviser, the old soothsayer Galminius, his white beard held with the gold thread across the middle and his dark eyes firm and confident.

"About time" he chided as Galminius bowed and stood by his right shoulder. Taking a slow breath he turned to the chief priest. "What of the auguries say?" he asked, his eyes flicking to the spots of blood on the sleeve of the priest to the man's left.

The chief priest intoned steadily "the augurs show that the Romans will battle but the outcome is not yet decided. The bull..." As he spoke Galminius spoke over the priest. "The auguries were conducted with the correct procedures?" he asked forcefully.

Unperturbed the chief priest, his eyes steady as he gazed across the room, continued. "Having followed the correct procedures to the letter the reading is clear. The decision of the gods lies in the ceremony of the bull. its death alone will decide the fate of the coming war, whoever....."

Galminius spoke again, the voice of the chief priest falling silent, though a flicker of his eyes told Vanimus that he was angry at being interrupted for the second time. "The preparations of the bull? Has it been cleaned as the Disciplina requires, its tongue scrubbed?" he asked as the priest nodded and replied "yes."

"It has only eaten the sacred grain since being chosen?"

"Yes"

"And the oil rubbed into its skin?"

For the first time the priest sounded annoyed at the questioning. "Of course, as the letters of the Etrusca Disciplina demand." He fell silent again.

"Continue" the King said.

"The priests have communed with Uni Teran" at which all three men touched their hearts and bowed their heads in unison before the priest continued "and the readings are clear. The entrails of the sacrificial bull will tell us who will win this battle."

The king glanced to Galminius, who was gazing at the chief priest but seemed satisfied with his answers. "Good. Then you may go. The sacrifice will be completed at the time allotted. You have the knife?" he asked as the three priest made to move.

"The blade has been sharpened and the oils from the goddesses statue rubbed into the iron exactly as the Disciplina requires" his eyes flicked angrily to Galminius who simply stared into the distance as if he was not there.

"Good. I must prepare."

The priests stood, bowed and left. The king turned to Galminius. "I don't want any mistakes" he hissed.

"He has played his part well, the others do not know that he is following your orders, Sire" he stated. "The entrails of the bull will be given as the offering to goddess in front of all the leaders as you have planned. When they see that you hold the entrails as the symbol of the goddesses' love they will know that Uni Teran has no love of the Romans and covets this city and you as her king" he stated with a confidence which encouraged Vanimus.

"Good" he said quietly. "And the priest, is he happy to do this trickery?" He asked.

"All priests know what is good for them your majesty" bowed the soothsayer as the King nodded and placed a hand on the man's shoulder.

"Then I must prepare" Vanimus said with a grin. The Romans would not take his city today and the people would receive a message from the gods which would stop all this fear and complaining that was causing him endless sleepless nights. Life would return to normal and he felt a calmness coming over him as he stretched his back and felt the twinge of acid in his stomach once again.

****

The door burst open as Fabius launched himself into the room, his breathing hard and ragged as he stared at the officers sat around the table with Marcus. The optio barged in behind him and gripped his shoulder aggressively, his face a mask of anger that the man had managed to slip past him in the corridor outside.

"Dictator" he said, his face a mask of frustration. "Tell this man to unhand me, I have vital news of Veii" he said loudly as he bridled at the Optio, both men standing chest to chest and staring into each others' faces.

Marcus waved a hand to the Optio, who bit his lip before he closed the door leaving Fabius standing triumphantly within the room. "This had better be good" Marcus said as he sat back, the faces of several men turning to the younger man, his chest still rising and falling at the run he had taken to reach the officers briefing. He held up a palm and gritted his teeth as if what he might say would cause some anger amongst the officers. "I" he started, his eyes darting around the men and falling onto Marcus as they widened and he sucked in a breath. "I have been along the tunnel to the well" he said as several of the officers stood, the sudden noise of chairs scraping on wood and a few angry expletives causing Fabius to hold both hands out in front of him "wait, wait" he said as his eyes scanned the faces of the men. Only

Narcius, Mella and Caelio sat still, the rest of the officers angrily standing and staring at Fabius.

"Sir?" he said, his voice almost pleading. "They are preparing a sacrifice in the temple. A great white bull from what I hear" he said quickly as Marcus sat forwards at the words, his interest suddenly gained. "It will be slaughtered by the king himself. I heard two slaves talking about it as they drew water" he said, his voice trailing at the words. Marcus' eyes flashed with anger as Fabius took a small step backwards.

All eyes turned to Marcus as Fabius stood in the silence that fell into the room, his heavy breathing the only audible sound.

"Tell me exactly what you heard" Marcus asked slowly, his voice menacing and his eyes constricted into thin lines.

Fabius swallowed hard, his eyes roving the men as he took a step closer. "I crept into the tunnels last night" he said. "I was planning to join the attack by sneaking into the men as they went into the city" he shrugged as a few men shook their heads, Marcus along with them. "I slept at the bottom of the well, out of view" he added quickly to the sudden alarm in the faces of some of the men. "In the night a great noise came from the temple, the shutters were being drawn and hundreds of slaves were moving the furniture, dragging chairs across the floor and clearing the space where the throne sits. I heard two slaves coming to the well so I slid back and listened. They said that the king was performing the sacrifice to the goddess himself, a great white bull which would tell them of victory for Veii." he swallowed again. "So I got one of the ladders and crept..." at this Mella stood and waved a finger at him, but before he could say more than a few words Marcus had placed his hand across his forearm and motioned Fabius to continue. Mella sat with a thump and an icy glare at the younger man. Fabius continued.

"I crept up to the well and saw they were cleaning the throne and laying a sacrificial stone. I overheard another man, a priest" he raised his eyebrows as if this was really important "say that the sacrifice would be performed by the king and that everything had to be spotless" he finished with eyes wide as he stared at Marcus.

"Anything else?" Marcus asked. "The slightest detail might be important" he added as he scrutinised Fabius' face.

Fabius looked deep in thought. "The sacrifice will be made one hour before the sun reaches its zenith" he said "which is why I ran all the way back."

Marcus motioned all the men to sit and held a hand as Fabius started to move forwards as if to join the group. Fabius stopped, his face questioning as Marcus waited a moment before speaking.

"You, Quintus Fabius, could have given the Etruscans knowledge of our entrance to their city. Your stupid, impetuous actions could have caused disaster to Rome." Fabius' face fell as the words tumbled from Marcus' mouth. "Your stupidity and reckless behaviour could have seen every man here slain as they entered that tunnel, and worse still it could have given the damned Veientines a way into our camp. Mella go now and check the tunnel please, take a large force just in case we need it." Mella rose with a scowl at Fabius and saluted before dashing from the room.

"Nobody saw..." Fabius tried to say as Marcus spoke loudly over him.

"You are a hot headed bloody fool Fabius. How many times do we have to tell you to follow orders? How many times do you have to be told to hold yourself back from your reckless schemes? You have endangered every man in this camp with your stupid actions. If the Veientines had seen you we would have lost half the men in this camp, gods" he spat as he thumped the table with his palm, the slapping noise making several officers jump. Fabius' mouthed worked but no sound came out as his eyes widened with fear at the stern words from his commander. Marcus put his hands to his face and then looked to the officers around the table.

"We need to act now" he said urgently as the men nodded, some glancing with stony stares to Fabius. "Potitus, take the army and line it up for attack. Narcius, get the men ready to enter the tunnel within the half hour. Scipio" he nodded to his friend "You know what to do?" he asked as Scipio nodded firmly. Glancing to the candles on the table he held up his hands and closed his eyes. "Jupiter, Mars, Juno, we ask your blessing on our actions. Smite this enemy of Rome and we will give great thanks and blessings to you all." He held his breath before he opened his eyes and spoke again. "Then let's get ready gentlemen, the battle begins" he grinned as the men saluted and started to leave the room, Fabius moving to the side as many shook their heads at him.

****

"Sire, the Romans are lining up their troops to attack" came the urgent voice of one of the guards, his face unconcerned as he relayed the information. The officer wandered to the walls and watched the gates to the siege works creaked open and men started to stream from them. He smiled at the futility of the act, knowing that they could not breach the walls. "Tell the commander that they are lining up their men" came the bored tone of his reply as he leant on the stone and watched with interest as the men began to line up in deep rows along the front of the city. Within a few minutes the leader of the watch appeared and leant on the wall next to him.

"Looks like a full scale attack" he said, his voice calm and measured. "Not had one of them for a while" he laughed as the officer joined him.

"Do we tell the King?" asked the officer.

"What and disturb the ceremony? Gods no, more than my life's worth. I'll send a message to the general and we'll just have another game of dice before he replies and tells us to throw a few arrows at them" he shrugged as he turned and walked away.

The officer smiled as he continued to watch the troops lining up. This part of the attack usually took a good hour so he turned and set off back to the small room where he had been discussing the dowry he would get for marrying his daughter to Patricius the baker. Good fresh bread every day from now on he thought as he set off with a smile.

****

Mella had confirmed that despite the stupidity of Fabius the tunnel remained a secret and the noise within the temple suggested that it was rapidly filling with the nobles of the city as they awaited the ceremony that was to be performed. Marcus had quickly been around the officers and given them final instructions, his curt words showing his anxiety as the final moments of the attack on Veii edged closer.

Behind the long wooden walls which had been built to shield the entrance to the tunnel from the city he now stood with his helmet under his arm. It felt strange to be going into battle without a shield. The ladders were despatched along the tunnel and Marcus felt his heart beating quickly in his chest as he nodded to Manlius, Narcius, Caelio and Mella, each man nodding grimly as he turned to the tunnel and stepped into the darkness, more than a thousand men primed to follow him, another thousand ready once the first attack had started. The tunnel was dark and cold and the men shuffled along slowly with their arms touching one wall at their sides and holding the belt of the man in front, heads bowed. Potitus had been clear to all the officers and Centurions that they must progress slowly along the tunnel to avoid any loud noise which might alert the people in the city above them. Minutes of shuffling stretched as the men moved slowly along like some giant snake with thousands of legs, the slow trudge muffled by the darkness. At the front of the snake Narcius held the long rope which was attached to the wall and guided him to the entrance to the well. Several guards stood with small oil lamps at set intervals, the men nodding as the long, slow, line of men moved past them. Eventually Narcius reached the foot of the well, the light streaming from above despite the loose cover that had been placed over the stone aperture.

As Marcus approached he saw the feet of the ladders stretching up into the light and his heart quickened again as the anticipation started to build in him. The noise of drums and other musical instruments began to drift into the tunnel as he reached the foot of the first ladder and peered up to see a circular opening with three loose fitting planks set across it. Narcius beckoned to the ladder and both men started to climb, one to the left and one to the right. As they approached the top Marcus could hear words being spoken in the Etruscan language, the priests were intoning Uni Teran and various other gods to bring safety to the city. With his knowledge of the ceremony he guessed they had a full ten minutes until the bull was brought to the sacrificial stone, assuming they were following the Disciplina correctly. He put his eye to the gap between two of the planks, but could see nothing but the ceiling directly above and a little to the right. He looked to Narcius who motioned to move the planks a little to see if they could see anything and Marcus nodded taking his helmet off and passing it to Narcius carefully. Tilting his head he placed his forehead against the wood, angling as much as he could so that he could see as much as he could possibly see without lifting the wood too much. He pressed his hands against the wood and gently lifted the planks, slowly breathing out as he did so, his teeth clenched. The wood was light and moved easily, his pressure suddenly releasing as it moved too quickly. What he saw made him grin, Narcius frowning with questions in his eyes. Marcus pressed harder and the planks lifted, joined together by two long strips across their top. The entrance to the well was surrounded by a series of large screens, broken chairs and odd pieces of wood sat against the wall to his rear, but he could not see out into the temple and therefore they could not see in to see him. He wondered if he dare attempt to climb out and nodded to Narcius, using his eyes to suggest he lifted the planks at his end of the well, which he did slowly, allowing Marcus to take another step upwards, slowly lifting the wooden cover as Narcius did the same, his eyes showing relief as his head rose above the edge of the low wall. Silently Marcus took the weight of the cover and placed it along the edge of the well, sitting on the wall before lifting it to the floor and placing it on a sack which was thrown behind the dark screens. *They were in.*

****

Potitus called the scorpions forwards as men with heavy screens ran, in pairs, up the long slope towards the far end which was within arrow range of the walls. As they ran missiles fell all around them, most hitting the screens and standing proud as the men edged the screens forwards, more slowly as they got closer to the wall. More screens followed, this time with the scorpions which would line the edge of the ramp. Potitus knew it was futile, but they had to make is look like a full scale attack. The ramp was on his left, though he remained far enough back from the front edge to maintain a good view of the walls to his left and right. He looked over his shoulder and waved to Vulso who, on the command, sent archers forwards, their wicker screens held out in front of them as they scattered into the dead ground before the walls, their short steps bringing cheers from the Romans who stood in their thousands watching the start of the attack.

Potitus marvelled at the men who were giving their lives for their city. He watched as archers placed their screens and then bobbed up and down, searching targets before letting loose a series of arrows, none of which struck home despite the efforts being expended. The first distinctive thump of the scorpions brought his attention back to the ramp, the men on the wall diving for cover as the heavy shafted arrows crashed into the parapet or sailed over the top to inflict untold damage inside the city. The legionaries had been told to load slowly and not to waste too many of the precious missiles which took an age to build and were extremely expensive. Regardless of these facts he smiled at the effect they had, men diving for cover as the sound presaged each attack. The battle had started with the usual slow attacks, but to make things appear real Potitus knew that he must commit men to the walls, men who would undoubtedly die at his command. He watched the walls looking for the right moment to launch his first attack, the men with the long ladders already edging forwards through the ranks of Romans. He saw that the Etruscans had also seen them, men moving across the walls and spears clustering at the likely attack points.

On the far right Scipio and his horsemen were cantering along the outside of the walls to draw fire at them in a vain attempt to distract the attention of the defenders. As the ladders appeared Potitus noted the sudden surge of movement at the walls, helmets and spears appearing in their hundreds where moments before there had only be one or two. Good, he thought, they are preparing to man the walls. His mind went to Marcus and the tunnels and he wondered whether they had reached the end yet and whether they had started the attack. He raised a hand to the men with the ladders and their Centurion raised a hand in reply, calling his men forward into a silent trot before the screams of encouragement of the standing Romans split the air along with the sudden increase in arrow fall from the men behind their wicker screens. Potitus prayed to Mars war-bringer that they win this day.

****

Vanimus stepped from his gilded throne, the carved snakes painted in gold for the occasion and his red robes flecked with gold thread resplendent in the light of the temple. He felt the power of his position as the hundred richest and most powerful leaders in the city sat watching him. A surge of pride welled up inside him as he stepped up to the sacrificial stone and the great doors to the temple were opened, the intricate bronze carvings catching the light as they slowly opened to reveal the dancing priestesses and the white bull being led by a thick bronze nose ring. The animal raised its head slightly as it was paraded into the temple, he hoped that whatever it has been given to make it dozy was working, a bad display during sacrifice could put pay to all his schemes. As the bull entered the temple the doors closed slowly behind, the dull thud of their closing resounded around the temple as the animal moved forwards and the dancers remained outside.

The chief of priests raised his arms, speaking lowly so as not to alarm the animal as it was brought through the crowd of seated nobles to its inevitable death. As the words were spoken he heard a clatter from the corner of the room to his left, his eyes flicking towards the old well which was surrounded by screens as it was most of the year before the priests sudden calling to Uni Teran was repeated by all in the room and his attention was brought back to the bull. The animal eyed him suspiciously as he stepped down towards it and his kingly robe was removed and placed back on his throne by one of the junior priests, the white robe of his religious office was then draped across his shoulders. He noticed one of the priests giving the bull a handful of some foodstuff or other to keep it calm as it stood, the whites of its eyes showing periodically as it stared at the strange scene around it. The bull took the food and munched happily as the king approached slowly and was given the iron knife, its thick handle carved into a winding snake emblem, the symbol of his family. He turned to the nobles as he spoke.

"Uni Teran accept this gift and guide us with thy wisdom. Give your people the sure knowledge that your will is to destroy these men from Rome who stand at our gates and empty our sacred lake, destroying our farms and starving your children." As he spoke the last words he bent down and used the long knife to slice up and into the throat of the bull as two priests gripped its sides to stop it kicking out. Whatever sedative the priest had given the beast worked as the animal made no sound but simply collapsed slowly to its front knees momentarily before falling onto its side, the blood pooling in dark circles as its life bled from its veins. The priest acted immediately and pulled the carcass to the stone altar, the chief priest taking the long knife from the king and slicing the heart from the beast and placing it in a silver dish. He then cut a long and bloody series of entrails from the stomach and, covered in red gore, he placed them on the sacrificial stone before removing the liver and placing it next to them. The silence in the temple stretched as the priest intoned the mother goddess and worked his way through the reading of the liver, using specially prepared oils and candles as he did so. The king stood watching the audience, seeing their gullible faces as they stared in awe at the priest as he prepared to announce the reading, his assistant theatrically smiling and nodding as the priests sliced the heart and held it up to the light. The king knew what was coming next and prepared to step forward as the priest turned to the audience, a look of wonder on his face.

*

*

Chapter 22

The ladders slumped as the men fell from the wall, several not moving once they hit the floor as hundreds scurried back from the third attempt to scale the walls. Each attack had been cheered by the Romans and followed by deep groans as cheers rang out from the defenders as soon as the attackers turned and fled. Potitus saw two defenders fall from the walls with arrows in their necks and his lip curled as they fell to their deaths. Roman dead lay all along the wall front, men who had not known about the tunnels or the attack that Marcus was leading. Potitus felt no pity for them, just a sense of honour that their lives would help Rome to victory. The last attacker limped to the lines and was cheered through by the phalanx of men. The attack had been going for a full twenty minutes now and Potitus hoped that Marcus was inside the city, though no sign came from within that anything untoward had occurred. A sudden dread came over him, a cold shiver down his spine as he tapped his sword three times to avert the evil eye, an old soldier's tale but one that he reacted to unconsciously. He looked over to Scipio who raised his arm and waved, Potitus nodding to the trumpeter who blew a

long note and another attack of ladders set off towards the walls, the enthusiasm of the men

remarkable as they had seen all previous attempts fail.

****

Marcus cursed as the legionary dropped his helmet into the well, two men clambering to

catch it before it landed with a thump to the side of the flow of water below. He held his

breath as he stared in anger at the man, his eyes to the floor, who had lost his helmet. Narcius

gripped the man by the shoulder and gritted his teeth at him, the snarl more than enough to let

the man know that, should they live through this attack, his life would be a series of menial

tasks. Marcus simply shook his head and bent low to repel any attack which the noise had

caused, but none came, thankfully. Twenty men had now climbed over the wall and stood

silently behind the screens, the space nearly full. Marcus had whispered to Narcius that he

should take ten men and hold the doors whilst he took another ten and attacked the king, but

as he finished he heard something that held his attention and every man suddenly looked to

him, jaws agape before he launched himself at the screens screaming at the top of his voice.

****

The priest turned to the king and held up the sliced heart and liver portions which remained.

"The reading is clear" he said as he scanned the eyes of the men in the room. He raised his

voice loudly as he spoke his next words. He turned and pointed the sacrificial knife to the

entrails of the bull on the sacrificial stone. "Uni Teran offers her grace and service to

whomever cuts the intestines of the bull and offers them in sacrifice to her. Whomever that

shall be will be the *victor* of the coming battle" he said loudly, his face sincere despite the

words being rehearsed since two days ago when the king had offered him the bribe.

The king beamed, his face coming to life as he turned to step up the two steps to the stone

altar before a sudden scream from the screens next to the old well caused him to jump back in shock, several loud gasps coming from the audience as the wooden screens were thrown to the floor and banged furiously with a loud clatter. Men ran at him, he grabbed the knife from the priest and ran to the altar gripping the entrails as a sword slashed across his arm and he screamed, the blade dropping to the floor as he felt his arm break and he tumbled to the side, the entrails falling on top of him.

Marcus wasted no time in gripping the entrails that were still held in the useless fingers of the king as Narcius and his men sliced into the crowd, most of whom carried no weapons and were butchered as the sacrificial bull had been just moments before. The bloodletting was fast and furious as men streamed into the temple, the priests standing and staring at the scene with terror in their eyes. The king scrabbled across the floor and gripped the sacrificial knife in his left hand and tried to stand as Marcus kicked him in the face, his jaw cracking as his head thumped against the pillar behind him. Marcus held the entrails up to the faces of the few Etruscan leaders who remained alive surrounded by his men. He stepped over the king's prone body and placed the entrails at the foot of wooden statue that had been draped in garlands of flowers and fruit for the ceremony and turned quickly to the priests. "Give me the robe" he said as the priest jerked at his clear Etruscan and pulled the robe from the kings limp body.

"Holding the entrails at the foot of the statue Marcus took the iron knife and sliced them into sections as he said "Uni Teran, Juno, mother goddess. You have given us your blessing and agreed to follow your victorious soldiers to your new temple in Rome. I accept your words, victory is ours." The priest stepped forwards and knelt, Marcus simply glanced to Narcius and nodded, ignoring the priests' supplications. The temple was filling fast with Romans as thumps were heard on the door behind, the short lived commotion in the temple clearly causing anguish outside. Narcius nodded to the legionaries who held knives to the throats of the rich and each man was asked a simple question "slavery or death?", those choosing death dying a quick and honourable death as the floor ran with blood.

"You have your orders" Marcus said more loudly, breaking the silence as he noted the man who had dropped his helmet slice the throat of a noble who had chosen wisely. "We meet at the gate, go" he said as several men pulled at the doors and raced out at the wide-eyed guards who started to turn and run at the sight of Romans in their midst. "You" said Marcus as he pointed to the man who had dropped his helmet "name."

"Aebutius" the man said, his head lowering as he expected the worst.

"Aebutius, you are with me and Narcius. Earn yourself our favour" he growled as the man looked up with hope in his eyes and Narcius growled at him.

****

Marcus exited the temple to screams and the sound of running feet, his target was the south west wall from where he would attack the small group of soldiers who manned the left hand side of the gates before heading to the gates themselves. Mella and Caelio were heading directly to the square and then to hold the road to the gates as best they could and Manlius was taking the long route to the south east to come at the Etruscans from their left. Manlius had the trickiest attack as he needed to follow Mella into the square before disappearing across it and into the back streets before turning toward the gates.

The roads were wide, clean and well kept and Marcus raced along unhampered by a shield but feeling naked without it. The men had been told to strike quickly and find weapons and shields as they went, but so far there had been no resistance and Marcus ran straight through two Etruscans who appeared from a side road, their faces falling as they suddenly saw a hundred men racing towards them. The first man had barely called an alarm before Narcius slit his throat at a run, the body spinning and falling as the blade slid through his neck, the second man simply falling open mouthed as two legionaries fell on him quickly. Screams came from behind them as they ran, then to the left as sounds of fighting broke out within the city. Marcus wondered if Potitus had heard them as he pumped his arms and thrust himself into a man who stepped from his house with a long curved blade, the metal clashing against Marcus' own blade as he swung it at the approaching men. The curved blade was heavy and well struck but the momentum of the Roman forced the sword arm of the Etruscan back and Marcus thumped his elbow into the man's face, wishing it was a shield which would have knocked him senseless. Without stopping, there was no time, he picked himself up and raced on noting that Aebutius had driven his sword through the man's guts and was already two paces behind him.

The walls approached at an alarming speed as Narcius raced round a bend and saw the foot of the wall at the end of a short, straight, wide street. Soldiers were moving to the left as he ran towards them, faces turning towards them at the sudden appearance of running men, some unsure who they were before they spotted the look of hatred and death in the Roman faces. Thirty paces, then twenty as the soldiers, thick shields and long spears, attempted to turn towards the attack from their left as they were marching to the gate, caught unawares by the Romans within their own walls. Marcus glanced to Narcius and both men grinned as they screamed death to the Etruscans.

****

The legionary climbed out of the well and slipped on the blood soaked floor, his sword falling to the ground with a clatter as the soldiers coming from behind gave him a wide berth. Cursing he stood and looked around the temple, was there anything in here that could help Apuleius, his mind worked furiously as men streamed past him and ran off towards the doors, some slipping but no others falling as he had done. He ran away towards the carcass of a bull, the thick blood caught in the gutters of the floor where it had been slain, the sluice holes in the floor testament to its sacrificial usage. He glanced quickly around knowing he would only have seconds before someone called him into the attack, but it took only those seconds for his eyes to fall on the throne and on it lay a red cloak flecked with gold thread, the kings robe, and a long sceptre with an orb and an eagle on the top gilded in gold as they said the old sceptre of King Romulus had been decorated at the founding of Rome. He ran across and quickly stuffed the robe into his tunic his grin splitting his face as he looked at the sceptre but disregarded it, it would be too difficult to hide. He turned and ran outside noisily and prayed that he would survive long enough to get it back to the man who would set him and his wife up with a life of luxury for this.

****

Marcus was thrust forward by the press of men behind him, slipping on the flagstones as he narrowly avoided a lunge by an Etruscan who screamed curses at him before his face was thrown back by a stabbing spear from behind Marcus, the Roman who had thrust the spear letting it go as he switched to his sword and screamed death to the Etruscans. On his left Marcus saw the line of men splitting as the leading edge of the men carried on towards the gates and others turned to face the new threat from the Romans at their rear. Another spear thrust at him from the front and Marcus ducked and gripped the shield of the prone man who had a short thrusting spear sticking out of his face.

Aebutius suddenly gripped his shoulder and pushed him lower as a spear raked along his back and across the man's thigh before he stabbed his sword into the guts of the attacker, wrenching it clear as he hopped back and swore loudly. Marcus gripped the shield and pulled it clear, instantly feeling safer as he saw other men doing the same thing. Aebutius was next to him, his leg bleeding but clearly not causing any problems, Marcus muttered thanks as he thumped his shield into a spear that was jabbed at him, the clunk leading him to roll his left shoulder and lean to the right to open the man up to a quick stabbing movement. The Etruscan dived forwards at the strike and Marcus missed him entirely, his mind applauding the move despite the fact that he hadn't killed his man. He stepped back quickly as a shield clashed against his from the right, the shield wall staring to grow. Aebutius had disappeared but Marcus didn't have time to consider this as the attacker thrust again, his white teeth showing through his brown beard as he yelled for more men. *Their leader* Marcus thought that's why he was so good.

As Marcus stepped forwards the man disappeared into the background, more spears falling in front of him as he grinned at Marcus and winked, the movement causing Marcus to frown before he ducked another strike which was thrust at the shield wall. The men had come to a standstill, the road lined with shields from the Roman end and spears and shields from the Etruscans. Narcius called for the men to step back, the call instantly responded to by the trained soldiers as they all took one step backwards and the Etruscans, pressed from behind, stumbled against their shields allowing the shield wall to open and several faces to gasp as swords ran them through and the Romans pressed forwards again. Marcus stabbed down at the heart of a man who was still alive but had a gaping wound in his stomach, his bared teeth and whistling breath disappearing as he stepped over his dead body and pressed on.

Narcius called the beat and the men responded, press, release and stab. A few Romans fell as the quick learners in the Etruscan lines understood the movement and managed to catch a slow legionary. Inexorably the Roman line butchered its way along the street and the Etruscans began to thin out.

A scream from above made Marcus flinch as a man fell from the wall, an arrow in his chest as his body impaled on the spears of two Etruscans in the back line, the winking leader knocked to the floor by the suddenness of the action. "Charge" Marcus shouted as he heaved into the press of men in front of him to take full advantage of this gift from the gods. The Romans took moments to slice through the Etruscans, the rear line running and the middle falling over the prone bodies that lay across the street.

As the Etruscans raced away Marcus called to Narcius and the two men took a moment to look around them. Behind them were streets filled with the eight man groups of Romans he had set out into the city to kill any one and draw the defenders out of the city square. Men of the city were falling even as he watched, doors slamming shut as the Romans killed anyone who stood in their way. With him and Narcius were seventy or eighty men, all blooded and ready to charge into battle.

"We must get to the gate" Marcus said as he turned to the fleeing enemy. He knew the gate was little more than two hundred yards along the road and around the next corner, but he also knew that by the time they got to the gates the road would be awash with men. "We need more men" he said as Narcius nodded and turned to a man next to him. "Round up as many of the maniples as you can and send them along here" he said quickly as the man turned and ran into the street behind them.

"We go at a steady walk and we hold our line" Marcus said as they set their shields forwards, the rag tag of different shapes and sizes not creating the shield wall that they were used to but adequate under the circumstances. Another man fell from the walls ahead of them as Marcus raised his eyes upwards, Potitus was starting the real offensive, he had clearly heard the screams from within the city and knew that the walls were now vulnerable. The road was empty now, doors closed and windows barred along the wide street. It was unnerving. Screams, the sounds of fighting and the clatter of men running sounded all around them, yet ahead of them was silence. They approached the left turn which led at an angle to the main gates and Marcus stopped the line of men and bent low to peer around the corner, whipping his head back just in case a sword might strike at him, but what he saw made him return his head to the street without fear. Narcius appeared next to him.

The road in front of him was filled with people, citizens all screaming as they hurried towards the gates, the soldiers being jostled as they tried in vain to hold back the tide of women, young children and old men. Panic had hit Veii and Marcus turned to Narcius and grinned back at his smiling face. To his right the narrow road along the wall was empty, a dog barking from its chained position on the wall the only living thing he could see or hear. He breathed slowly and turned to Narcius. "If we charge into the rear of that lot they will turn and run up the roads to the left back towards the square" he said as he pictured the roads and streets on the map of the city.

"The soldiers will kill them all" Narcius replied "and save us a job" he shrugged.

Marcus noted several groups of men arriving behind him, the call for support clearly being responded to.

"Then we stick to our orders. We reach the gates through those people" he said "but we will need to make as much noise as possible to cause the maximum panic" he stated coldly as he looked at the men behind him and nodded to the closest faces. "Victory is there men" he said pointing his sword. "We must get to the gates. Riches and glory are in our grasp" he yelled as the men leered hungrily at him. "Let's go" he shouted as they rounded the corner and lined up before they clattered their swords on the shields they held, the noise reverberating off the walls of the buildings around them.

The people at the back of the crowd trying to get to the gates turned and screamed before they started a frenzied push at the soldiers blocking the road in front of them, blood spraying into the air as they tried in vain to escape the Romans as they approached the rear. Marcus grinned as the first men and women turned and fled down the alleyways to their left, the tide of people suddenly rushing turning into a stampede. As the final citizens disengaged from the soldiers Marcus lowered his body and glanced to Narcius, nodding as both men screamed the charge and the Romans picked up their pace to a run at the line of Etruscan spears across the road which led to the small piazza by the gate.

The press of men was lung busting, the squeeze of bodies getting tighter and tighter as both sets of soldiers leant into their shields. Marcus grinned at Narcius as both men took deep breathes and screamed '*release*', the men behind suddenly stepping backwards a moment before Marcus and Narcius, along with the front line of Romans, did the same, instantly pivoting and slicing their swords into the Etruscan front line as the men behind pushed them forwards.

Blood spattered into Marcus' eyes as his sword bit into the shoulder of the man in front of him, his body twisting at the energy behind the thrust. Dragging his arm back he managed a second thrust into the man's ribs, the familiar crunch of bones and jerk of his head telling Marcus that the man was dead before his body crumpled to the floor and another Etruscan was pushed over his dead body, a short sword instantly stabbing through his exposed back as he stumbled. Marcus put his foot on the dead man's back and leant into the gap that had appeared before him, a spear glancing across his helmet as the defender to his left tried to wield his weapon at him in the confined space. He managed to get the point of his sword into the thick soft muscle of a thigh before he stood back and felt his shield clatter against the soldier next to him as he rolled his shoulder, feeling the muscle ache but knowing that he was still far from tiring. He didn't have time to relax as a spear shaved the top of his shield, the eyes of the attacker filled with hate as he lunged at him. Marcus needed to know what was happening beyond this line of defence and his attention was distracted as the man lunged again, his shield lifting the spear attack up as he stepped forward, followed by all the men along the line. The attacker froze as his face came almost within a hands width of Marcus and his mouth gaped as Marcus thrust his short sword through the gap between their shields, his eyes already searching beyond the dying face of the Etruscan as his hand mechanically twisted the sword through his guts. A warm red pool fell to the floor but the man's body was trapped by the press from behind as Marcus continued to scour the scene, the curses from the Etruscan dying in his ears.

"We are nearly there" he called as a cheer came from behind him and the men pressed harder, Marcus struggling to release his sword as it was lodged in the guts of the dead Etruscan. He grunted and took short, sharp, breaths as he felt the heat of the bodies around him and tried to remove the sword, but he couldn't move his elbow due to the press of men. Fifty yards ahead was the gate, but the road was thick with people. Soldiers, citizens, Roman attackers and even a horse, its legs kicking wildly at anyone who got too close. The noise was horrendous and Marcus knew that they had come to a standstill. He needed to do something, and quick, or the attack would stall. He looked up and saw fighting on the walls and he cheered, his cheering causing others to look up at the Romans who were fighting for their lives against the Etruscan defenders above them.

"We have the walls" he screamed, knowing full well that this was not the case, but anything he could do to dampen the spirits of the defenders was worth a try. He called again. "We have the wall men, Rome will win" and he felt a sharp pain in his shoulder as he gasped at the point of a spear that had been thrust through the arm of the dead man who lay against him and into his shoulder. He screamed at the dead face, which seemed to mock him as the spear was thrust harder from behind. The spear had gone through Marcus' shoulder guard but was angled upwards so had missed the bone, tearing into the soft flesh on the outside of the muscle. He clenched his fingers and was relieved that he still had full control of his sword arm as he snarled back into the line of men in front of him. He looked to Narcius, who grunted as he pushed but his body didn't move.

"Back" screamed Marcus as he tried to look over his injured shoulder.

"Step back you bastards" he screamed. "We need room to use our swords." Urgent yells went up around them as the adrenaline coursed through his body and he felt a slight release from behind which allowed the body in front to slip slowly down towards the floor. The spear of the attacker was jammed in the body as it fell, the owner trying desperately to pull it back as it was yanked downwards. He stared disbelievingly as Marcus lunged over the top of his shield and plunged his sword into his cheek, the crack of bone causing all the soldiers along the line to look across as Marcus pulled his arm back and stabbed again, the sword bursting through the man's neck and spraying blood in every direction. Marcus screamed a guttural cry as men's eyes turned to fear and, with the press of bodies suddenly releasing he took his anger out on the man to his left, battering his shield into his spear and slicing the sinews at his elbow, the arm almost severed as Marcus thrust the short sword back and thrust it up into his arm pit, the sword bursting through his back and his body clattering into the man behind him, who stepped back at the ferocity of the attack. Marcus didn't have time to scream as a legionary stepped into the short gap that was created on his right and hacked his sword into the face of the man next to him, his hot blood splashing the faces of both men. The soldier moved into the gap quickly, twisting his shield left and right as he sliced at thighs and shins, catching two Etruscans who turned and screamed, their backs open to attacks which other legionaries quickly dealt with. The Etruscan line buckled and Marcus stood still as the Romans stepped ahead of him. He stretched his neck to look over the heads of the defenders and grinned as he saw Manlius and his soldiers slicing into the defence on the far side of the gate, not as advanced as his men, but moving slowly forwards with guttural screams as the Etruscans squeezed more men into the area in front of the gate.

He grinned as he saw Narcius stagger and slip as he thrust forwards with his sword, the blood on the flagstones causing men to struggle with their footing. Taking three deep breaths Marcus screamed "For Rome" and stepped back into the battle, the cry echoing around the walls as he slammed into the nearest Etruscan and took him off his feet.

*

*

Chapter 23

Potitus watched as the left wall was breached by the legionaries as they scampered across a plank which was laid flat from the ramp to the wall, enough men getting across for the Romans to throw several more long planks across the gap and men to race to their support, the defenders falling to the thick bolts of the scorpions. He had called the assault as soon as the tactic had worked. The screams from within the city meant that the plan at the tunnels must have worked and he had disengaged the rear three lines of men to enter the tunnels in support just as Marcus had planned. *It was working.*

He waved to Fasculus and Scipio and both men called their soldiers forwards, the heavily armed men of Fasculus moving directly towards the gate and Scipio's horse staying just out of reach of the arrows but ready to attack anything that came through the gate should an attack be launched at Fasculus' men.

Potitus sat and waited, the minutes stretched as he watched Fasculus move to the appointed position and set his men ready to charge into the city. The screams in the city grew louder and he wondered if he should commit more men to the tunnels, but he decided that the men he had already sent were probably still working through the tunnel and into the city. He held his breath as his lips tightened at the scene in front of him. He was desperate to know whether his friends were still alive within the walls and he tapped his sword three taps at the thought, shaking his head at how superstitious he had become. The men on the wall were spreading out and waving, he lifted his head, a sudden leap coming to his heart as he heard cheers and saw more Roman hands waving. Groans and screams came from within the city as the gates started to move slowly outwards, the cheering Romans on the walls turning and throwing stones and missiles back into the city as a crescendo of screams rose as the gates widened. Fasculus had already committed his men to the march at the opening gates, velites racing ahead with javelins and stones, as Potitus looked back to see them move, his heart skipping a beat as men ran through the gates and scampered left and right looking for escape. The last of the guards? He thought as riders from Scipio's horsemen charged into them and took them with their long spears.

Victory. He couldn't believe it. *Victory.*

His eyes fell on the trumpeter to his right who had turned and was staring at him wide eyed and questioning. Shaking himself to the present he nodded and waved a hand forwards as the trumpet sounded the advance.

****

Marcus fell against the gate, his shoulder screaming in agony but still usable. His face was covered in blood and he wiped it with the back of his hand, blinking away the remains of the gore that was stuck to his eyelids. The body of Aebutius lay at his feet, the man taking a sword in the guts just as the gates began to screech open. Marcus frowned at his bad luck and remembered the old saying that things came in threes, good and bad. The poor man had dropped his helmet, been stabbed in the leg and then killed right at the end of the fighting. He momentarily considered his own wound, but dismissed it. He didn't really believe that Aebutius was a victim of bad luck, just coincidence. The men guarding the gate screamed at the citizens as some tried to get out of the gates and others turned and fled back into the city as best they could, though the Romans now seemed to hold every road from the piazza to the square ahead of the gates.

"Gods" called Manlius as he slumped next to Marcus, his chest heaving at his exertions. He pulled his helmet from his head, a large dent in the side and threw it away as the Legions started to cram through the entrance at their side, cheering and screaming rising to a greater furore as they did. Marcus noted that Manlius was cut across his cheek and had another deeper wound along his forearm, a previous scar now criss-crossed with a new one.

"I'd forgotten how bloody hard it is to stand and fight" he rasped, his lungs clearly screaming for air as he laughed loudly. "Gods" he called again as he stood and looked straight into Marcus' eyes. "We're heroes now Camillus" he said with a manic glint in his eye. "There'll be a triumph" he said as soldiers cheered as they marched into the city. Marcus started at the words. *A triumph*. He hadn't even considered it. The greatest glory there was, a parade of the conquering heroes through the city of Rome with the Dictator, *him*, at the head. Manlius caught his look and grinned at him. He laughed aloud and turned to the remains of his party of men. "permission to find some loot" he called to Marcus as his men suddenly perked up and turned their faces to Marcus, who waved at him with a grin and then turned to watch the men marching into the city of Veii. He took a moment to compose himself and then turned to the skies and held his arms aloft as he saw Manlius running off into the city followed by several screaming men, their blood up in the hunt for gold and silver.

"Jupiter. Mars. Juno" he called as faces turned to him. "We thank you for your blessings and guidance and we will honour our prayers and devotions to you" he added as his voice faltered and the pain in his shoulder bit deeper. As he took a deep breath and winced he saw Aebutius move, his hand gripping the sand and a moan coming from his lungs as he drew his knees under his body and started to rise. Marcus looked to the skies and grinned. Veii was taken and miracles were happening.

****

Darkness had fallen and Marcus had spent some hours recuperating in his tent outside the walls of the city whilst behind him the Romans and Etruscans were still fighting running battles in the streets. Thousands of slaves had been taken, mostly women and children, though some men, injured and sick mostly were also being held captive in an enormous pen which was being continually added to by the Romans as more people were led from the city.

The soldiers had been merciless and the screams and death had carried on for hours as the Romans took out ten long years of frustration on the Veientines within their walls.

Marcus had started to pace the tent, the pain in his shoulder still bad but not enough to keep him in his bed. He'd read most of the reports but had called for the officers to give their reports face to face so that he could understand their losses and the issues he faced for the logistics of returning the spoils and the slaves to Rome. He moved his arm up and down feeling the skin pull on the wound and suddenly deciding that the pain that it gave him suggested it was probably a bad idea. He clenched his fingers and released them, happy that he felt he could still hold a sword. He gripped the wooden eagle motif around his neck and closed his eyes to utter a silent prayer to his patron goddesses.

Caelio arrived with a kick at the tent pole to announce his lumbering frame had entered. His face was heavily swollen and his left eye bruised so badly his eye was closed behind a wall of purple and red bruises.

"Gods that looks bad" Marcus said as the man winced at him and laughed. "You should see the Etruscan who gave it me" he laughed before wincing again, both men chuckling at the age old joke.

Mella strolled in, his eyes glancing to both men as he smiled and held the tent flap open for Fasculus, his left arm in a sling and a fresh wound across his temple. Narcius followed, his equipment already cleaned and his new wound stitched, Marcus raised his eyes at the efficiency of the Centurion and nodded to one of the few seats, which Narcius strode to and sat as Mella looked at him indignantly. "Surely your elders should sit first" he asked with a smile as Narcius grinned back at him crossing his arms and leaning back in the chair with a smile as Mella shook his head at the Centurion.

Scipio and Potitus entered together deep in conversation, which quickly abated as they looked at the faces of the men in the tent. Marcus waited a few moments before Manlius arrived, his face flushed as he saluted and looked for a seat, of which there was none. More men arrived, Marcus nodding to each one as they arrived, noting those with fresh cuts and those with pristine, shining, armour. Marcus stood and looked to Narcius.

"Vulso?" he asked as Narcius shook his head and looked to the floor. "Fuscus?"

"With the medics, he will probably lose his left arm" he added as Marcus shook his head. "So how many men did we lose?"

Faces turned to Narcius but it was Potitus who spoke and all eyes then moved to him. "We don't have the full details yet, Sir" he said as he pulled a wax tablet from a pile he was carrying "as fighting is still going on in the city." He cast his eyes along the list that was written in the wax for a moment. "Close to two thousand dead, maybe four hundred injured or wounded. No horses lost" he said with a smile as he looked up at Marcus who smiled to Scipio. "We haven't counted the Etruscan dead but so far we have at least four thousand bodies."

Marcus took a moment to take in the news. "Thank you" he said sombrely as the men all stood quietly. He looked at each of the men around him and nodded his head. "Manlius said to me that we are all heroes" he said as people looked to Manlius and then back at Marcus. "And he is right. We are heroes of the Republic. Our losses today were small compared to our enemies and this victory will send a strong message to all of the tribes that we are strong and will accept nobody as our equals. Rome will endure" he said firmly as heads nodded at his passionate words and the fire in his eyes.

"How are the men?" he asked as his eyes scanned the faces in the tent.

"They are mostly drunk and singing your name as loudly as they can" Mella said with a smile as a few men laughed, Marcus noticing that Manlius seemed nonplussed by the words.

"So they are in good spirits?" he asked as the officers nodded and stated that they were.

"Good, good" Marcus said as he looked at them all. "You men have done a great job today" he said, his eyes catching those of each man. "What *you* have done nobody could do for ten long years. *You* have defeated Veii." He smiled and shook his head with a glance to the floor before looking up at the officers again. "I doubted it would ever happen" he said as he looked at the back of his hands, his fingers clenching as he spoke and his voice dropping to a quiet whisper "but the gods willed it and it is so. Tomorrow we must plan our next tasks and what steps we must take to return to Rome. The city, must be purged and left to rot" he said forcefully. "I want the fields salted and the gates ripped from their hinges" he said as the officers stared at him, Manlius suddenly twitching as if a thought had come to his mind. "After the misery this city has caused us it cannot be left to be repopulated by anyone. The Etruscans have shown that with the right support this city can withstand a siege as long as Troy itself" he added as he strode along the back of the tent. "We don't have the time or the energy to destroy the walls, but we can destroy the capability of the city to grow again, poison the wells, salt the lands and fire the wooden houses" he said as the men stared at him, nobody speaking.

Mella looked to Potitus and caught the moment of hesitation that came to his face as he glanced to Scipio, all the men unsure what to say.

"Camillus" Manlius said as his face fell into a puzzled frown. "Surely we should consider opening the city to the citizens of Rome. There are many plebeians who would welcome the opportunity such a new start could bring to them and their families. Of course we would place a few of the older families as leading citizens to ensure the correct sacrifices and procedures were carried out to maintain the love of the gods" he said as he saw Marcus frown back at him.

"Manlius speaks wisely" Scipio said, his face serious as the tension in the tent began to grow. Marcus looked to both men, but his mind was set. The words of the prophecy were clear *'never to be a city again'* and he had to follow the words of the gods. Before he could respond Fasculus raised an arm and received a nod from Marcus to say his words.

"Many years ago it was Tribune Postumius who faced the same dilemma" he said warily as his eyes scanned both Marcus and Manlius, the history between them always causing men to worry if they would eventually come to blows. "The old soldiers wanted to populate a town not far from here to settle their families and start a new life, a life away from Rome but as a new member of the alliance of tribes" he said. "The Tribune simply said no. The men demanded reasons but he denied them even that knowledge. It was *reasons* that would have won over the plebeians and the soldiers and stopped some of the issues that came afterwards" he added as men glanced to each other. They all knew the issues he spoke of, the death of a Tribune at the hands of his own men in Rome.

"The issues are clear" Marcus said forcefully as he took a deep breath and glared at Manlius. "Veii has held out against Rome for too many years. What would stop another force, in a few years from now, doing the same? It is better to focus our energy and effort into building a stronger Rome, a more glorious city for our gods and goddesses. Haven't they shown that we should destroy this place and take all of its wealth back to Rome? Juno has certainly spoken and wishes to leave this place" he said dismissively. "The gods do not wish to honour this city any more, that should be enough for any man" he said with a shrug as he moved his eyes from man to man seeing the light of agreement in some faces but hesitation in the eyes of others.

Manlius didn't react, his face impassive as Marcus spoke but his eyes showing that he was calculating his response. A heavy silence fell into the tent, the sound of screaming and crying from outside permeating the silence as new slaves were dragged to the prison. Men shuffled nervously as the impasse seemed to grow and the silence stretched.

"Well" Narcius said as he stood, his movement catching everyone by surprise as his tall frame stood to attention and looked to Marcus. "What are your orders, Dictator, Sir?" He said, his words clear to all in the tent. Marcus' words were the law in the camp and also in Rome. As Dictator his decision was final and no debate was to be held on the matter. Marcus nodded with a nervous flash of his eyes to Manlius as he turned and moved to the table at the bank of the tent.

"Orders" he said as he handed a series of instructions to Narcius, who took them smartly and opened them, handing tablets to the officers as they started to breathe more easily under the familiar routine of taking orders from their superiors.

****

After two days the destruction of the majority of houses in the city and the fields outside was complete. Stones were piled across all the roads in the city where the houses had been pulled over, thick red spots of blood remained on the wide roads where bodies had been dragged from the city and burned in great pyres, the full religious ceremony presided over by Marcus himself as the thousands of women and children taken prisoner wailed and sobbed into the night. Everywhere Marcus looked was a picture of death and destruction, the smoky smell of death hung in the air and the half ploughed fields, filled with salt and ash were grey in the afternoon sunlight.

Thousands of carts and wagons piled high with treasures lined the dusty road which led back to Rome, the convoy having left over four hours earlier but still clearly visible on the flat road which headed across the Tiber and toward their own city. Behind them were the chained prisoners, all heading for Rome's slave markets, their lives now in the hands of the slave masters and whichever master bought them.

Marcus stood at the centre of the Roman army, the men lined up along the front of the destroyed city of Veii as they prepared to march back home, many for the first time in years.

The women of the Roman camp had swarmed all over the city as soon as the soldiers had taken anything that appeared of value, the camp followers hunting longer and more deeply amongst the rubble to find everyday items of unfound treasures. Marcus noted some of the women and camp followers were clothed in brightly coloured garments and wearing new headscarves which had clearly been brought from the city. He smiled at the thought, but a sadness came over him as he looked along the lines of men, most still bearing the signs of the battle they had fought in. He stepped forwards and moved towards the small wooden plinth that had been created as a Rostra from which he could speak to the men before they set off for Rome. As he moved a great cheer came from the ranks, the sound hitting him like a shock wave as he stepped up and looked out across the faces that cheered and yelled his name. *Camillus, Camillus* they cheered *Beloved of the gods* others cheered as he looked out over their faces, his cheeks flushing at the sudden burst of noise which had greeted him. He stood for a moment unable to speak as the crowd continued to cheer and shout, some crashing their swords into their shields. *Destroyer of Veii* came a call from a group of men to his right which was instantly taken up enthusiastically by all the soldiers, a new crescendo of noise assaulting his ears as the words rang out across the fields, a strange echo coming back from the walls of the city making the words almost indistinct as the noise finally began to decrease. Marcus looked to Scipio and Potitus who were cheering enthusiastically with the men and was momentarily lost for words. As he raised his hands and the noise disappeared into a few calls and then silence he felt the hair on the back of his neck rise as he considered the enormity of what he had done, what *they* had done and how he had fulfilled the legacy of the words spoken to him by Antonicus all those years before. Stepping forwards he took a deep breath.

"Men of Rome" he called. "Veii was once great. This city was once equal to Rome. But look at her now" he called as he swept his hand towards the walls, their grey blocks and whitewashed paint still covered in streaks of red where men had slid to their deaths. The walls remained, too difficult to break, but the gates were smashed and burned and all internal walls pulled down wherever the men could do so. In his mind Marcus heard the words *never to be a city again* as his eyes looked over the, once again, cheering and jeering men. "Our enemies have become our slaves" he held his head low as he heard a deep groan from many of the men, a hiss from others who were saying quick prayers that such fate never befall them. "It is now time for us to return to our beloved home and to enjoy the fruits of the harvest we have gained from Veii. It is time for you brave men who have given up your farms and families to return to your hearts" at this cheers rang out across the soldiers. "We, men of Rome should be proud that we have done the will of the gods, achieving the glory that we set out for them. I, Marcus Furius Camillus will honour my pledge to build a new Temple to the great goddess Juno in Rome. I will see her raised back to the glory she had in the days of our fathers as she watches over her new home" he said as more cheers rang out across the field. Marcus had heard stories that when the priests had come to take the old statue and return it to Rome one of the boys who were to carry the statue had jokingly asked the statue if she was happy to return to Rome, and the statue had, in fact, nodded. The movement was seen by several of the men who were to carry the statue from her sacred place in the temple and had gone some way to placating those who were still angry at the destruction of the city, the rumour raising even more men to Marcus' cause to destroy the city once and for all despite the continued discussions to the contrary which were being led by Manlius.

As silence fell Marcus lifted his face to all the men and held out his arms to them as his gaze wandered across the sea of soldiers. "You have earned the love of the gods and of the fathers of Rome" he said, his voice faltering. "Return to your homes and put away your swords until our enemies raise their spears again" he said as he waved the first section of men away, their

Centurions saluting smartly before the noise of men marching off into the distance filled the air, cheers still ringing out and echoing from the still walls of the city of Veii.

****

The alleyway was filled with grey and black shadows in the low light of the day's weakening sun, the returning men of Rome had long headed towards the forum for the start of the formal celebrations. There was to be a triumph for the glorious hero Camillus the next morning and this was the final link in the chain of events that Apuleius had been working on for over a week. He stood silently as the cool chill of the end of the day started to descend upon the city, noises of cheering and singing coming from all around the lower hills as he waited in the dark, his heart beating rapidly.

A noise to his rear startled him and he knelt and turned as a rat raced along the alley, stopping for a second as its twitching whiskers recognised his presence but ignoring him as it continued along towards the drain and disappeared.

Apuleius felt a flush of anger. Where was the idiot and his whore of a wife? Since bedding the stupid woman she had started to blackmail him into ever more expensive gifts saying she would tell her husband of their affair if he didn't continue to meet her and bring her more trinkets. Apuleius was angry at his own weakness but also resolved to his cause, Camillus must be brought to heel. He embodied the patricians and all they stood for, their over-bearing, god-given rights to rule Rome, their patronising and aloof conversations in their Senate and the continued belittlement of his people, the plebeians. He sneered at the thought of what his plans would do to the great Camillus. Even the name made him angry and he spat onto the wall in front of him as he heard another sound and turned back towards the road, the light just about illuminating the entrance through which he had entered half an hour ago.

"Is he there?" came the soft whisper of a woman's voice. Apuleius grinned at the sound, he knew it was her.

"I can't see" came the rough voice of her stupid husband, his thick arms reaching out to the walls as he stepped into the long alley, his back hunched as he slowly stepped forwards. Apuleius slipped the dagger from its scabbard slowly and deliberately as he moved forwards in a crouch.

"Stop" he whispered hoarsely as the man's face contorted and the woman let out a quick moan.

"Wait" said the man, his eyes trying to look into the darkness ahead of him.

"It's me. Come in further, away from the wall. Both of you" he added quickly as the woman seemed to stop at his voice.

After a moment the three figures were crouched half way along the alley in near total darkness, the low light from behind the newcomers allowing Apuleius a slightly better view of the two figures in front of him.

"Do you have it?" he asked.

"Where is our money?" said the woman, her voice grating on Apuleius as he considered simply launching at her with his dagger and ending her pointless life.

Apuleius let the bag of bronze and silver jingle as he saw the woman's hand reach out. "Show me the robe first" he whispered as the man fumbled and held out a bundle.

"And this is the kings robe from Veii?" he questioned. "How can I trust you?" he asked both questions quickly.

"There were many people who saw the king and knew of his robe. It has the golden silk and the snakes sewn into the hem. When you get it into the light you will not be disappointed" came the man's reply.

"And nobody knows you have it and nobody knows you are here now?" Apuleius asked quietly, his voice remaining low as the man's head moved slowly back and forth and the words "no" came back from the darkness.

"Good" said Apuleius as he started to shove the robe into the sack he had brought to hold the item and keep it clean and then he turned and placed it behind him quickly.

"Our money" hissed the woman's voice as Apuleius gripped the dagger more firmly and moved his left hand upwards before letting the bag drop heavily to the floor.

"Fool, you've dropped it" he said angrily as the woman hissed and her husband cursed before bending lower and waving his hands along the dark, cold floor.

Apuleius crept a yard forwards and checked the distance. He had one chance and one chance only and he stood slightly to bring the whole of his body weight onto the blade, stabbing it down and into the spine of the man as he leant forward scrabbling for the bag of coins. Two strikes, then three and the man's legs had stopped kicking, the woman started to scream and grabbed at the blade. Apuleius sliced the blade back and caught her hand silencing the screams to a whimper, warm blood spraying onto his own hand as he thrust it down and felt it bite into her throat, her cry disappearing to be replaced by a deep sigh of air as she moaned her last gasp and slumped forwards onto the body of her husband. He stabbed into her back again to make sure she was dead, feeling the power he had over them coursing through his veins as he gnashed his teeth. He leant against the wall and stared into the alleyway, watching the entrance to see if anyone came to see what the scream was, but nobody appeared. Feeling for the woman he ripped the chain from her neck and rings from her fingers and placed them in the sack with the robe before shaking his head at their lifeless bodies and stepping back out towards the city, the music and singing loud in the night sky. Apuleius smiled to himself as he stalked off towards his own home, the instrument he needed to undermine the patrician fool Camillus now firmly held in his grip.

*

*

Chapter 24

"You are as close to a god as any man has ever been, Camillus" fawned the priest as he bowed to Marcus and supplicated himself on his knees.

Marcus shook his head and replied coldly "no man is a god, we are but mortal instruments of their divine will."

"But the gods love some more than others" the man said again, his sing-song voice grating on Marcus' nerves. He stepped forwards and placed the purple cap on Marcus' head, the thin band of gold around the lip of the cap marking it out as one that was used for Apollo. Marcus set his jaw and considered how he had reached this point. Upon returning to Rome he had been astounded by the gathering of the people, flocking the roads and bridges and cheering the soldiers for hours as they trudged past with their heavy loads of spoils from Veii. The women of Rome had cheered loudest at the return of their sons from ten years of war. After presenting the war trophies to the senate he had found himself carried around the forum, people arriving in their thousands to cheer and wave, others presenting their sons and daughters to him for him to touch his *divine* hand on their foreheads. He had baulked at the requests but the throng of people had grown and he was thrust forwards by his own soldiers to placate the crowds. His friends had disappeared into the mass of people as he was carried off around the City, given treasures by rich families and offered the best slaves by others. All of which he could do nothing but accept, vowing to return them as soon as he could. The crowds and soldiers had feasted and partied long into the night and as a few small fires had created panic in the streets it had taken a group of ex-soldiers to bring calm and order back to the people of Rome, their shields and voices enough to frighten most rowdy citizens into returning to their homes.

Snatching a few hours sleep he had been called to the forum at dawn and given the details of the parade, his triumph through the streets with the statue of Juno at its head, prisoners chained in long lines and the greater treasures of Veii piled high on carts and wagons to show the people what enormous spoils they had won from their long-time enemy. As he felt the cap fitted to his head he took a moment to reflect. The purple cap was used on statues of the gods, especially those of Jupiter and Apollo to show that they were divine. He looked back at the priest.

"I'm not wearing this" he said firmly as he scrunched the cap in his hand and held it out to the face of the priest.

"But, sir, it is what the people want. They cheer you as divine, as the saviour of their sons, the greatest warrior of Rome, the man who has single-handedly beaten our enemies" the priest said with large round eyes, the three priest helpers behind him all nodding as Marcus shook his head.

"I will not" he said again. "It isn't right. No man should mock the gods. The army beat Veii, not one man"

As he spoke three men entered the room, Fidenas, his old, lined, face grinning as he entered first followed by Atratinus and Mugillanus.

"Ah Camillus" said Fidenas as he stepped slowly across. "The plebeian tribune is here with some words for you" he said as he considered the cap in Marcus' hand curiously. Marcus was dressed in a long blue tunic with gold flecked edges. Over his shoulder was the red cloak of Dictator with a thick golden clasp at each shoulder. His shining breastplate of bronze was tight across his chest and his sword hung from his right hip. His hair and beard was neatly set and lightly oiled, almost shimmering in the light. Fidenas looked at Marcus and nodded his head slowly.

"You are, indeed, like a statue of the gods Camillus, as the people say. I have never seen such a man" he said as his face broke into a smile "it is no wonder our enemies fall before you" he said as Atratinus narrowed his eyes.

A knock at the door signalled the arrival of Apuleius, his smiling face entering with several escorts, all carrying gifts for the conquering hero. As the gifts were laid on the floor and the finer elements pointed out to Marcus he began to feel uncomfortable, as if the speeches he was hearing from Apuleius and the plebeians were too much, almost too lofty and too full of praise. He held his tongue as the man continued to talk of the success of the soldiers at Veii, the clever use of the tunnels and the fact that Juno herself had agreed to come to Rome with the Romans, and how the statue herself had nodded in plain sight of several of the soldiers. All of this, he said, pointed to Camillus's *divine* nature.

Marcus protested, but was held in check by the Senators. The plebeians had demanded a show of force from their heroes as a way of showing the people that Rome was divine, that the gods favoured their City and that the people of Rome were special to their gods. Marcus had argued against it, but every voice, even that of his friends Scipio and Potitus had argued that it would do Rome good to celebrate something after ten years of constant hardships because of the war with Veii and the other tribes. It had been Scipio who had argued that Marcus had, in fact, said that the people needed something to celebrate and that the message such celebrations would send to Rome's enemies could not be underestimated. The most astonishing thing was how the plebeians Apuleius and Decius had agreed, rallying the cheers for the divine Camillus to parade in a Quadriga, the four white horses and chariot of Jupiter. This, Apuleius had said, would show the people that Rome was the greatest City on Earth and was beloved of the gods. After fruitless debates Marcus had reluctantly agreed but he still felt uncomfortable. As he looked at the gifts and shook his head he handed the cap back to the priest, who smartened it up and replaced it on his head.

"Your chariot awaits" Apuleius said with a twinkle in his eyes as he moved aside.

Mugillanus and Atratinus moved to the side as he swept past them, his Dictators robe flowing behind him. He didn't notice how Apuleius stepped up behind him and followed him out of the room and into the corridor which led to the courtyard. As he entered the courtyard a wall of cheers came from people standing all around the edges, flowers rained down on him as one of the horses skittered and whinnied. The statue of Juno was being carried by four white-robed priests, the vestal virgins ahead of them, sombre and calm as they always were; the lights of candles held within wooden frames to show that the divine candles had been lit for the occasion.

Ahead of them, and directly behind Narcius and his troop of immaculately dressed soldiers, was the heavily muscled white bull that was to be sacrificed at the end of the parade, its entrails and viscera to be offered to the gods in return for their love. He took in the scene momentarily before the priest edged him forwards towards the chariot. He suddenly felt over-awed by the enormity of the cheering crowds, the faces staring at him, the statues of the gods all paraded in lines in front and behind the chariot. His people wanted this he said to himself as he stepped up to the chariot and looked back at the three Senators as they nodded to him. Water and oil were sprinkled onto the floor around the chariot, spots of red showing the sacrificial blood that was within. He held the reins and looked up to see Narcius smiling at him awkwardly; so at least one of the people close to him was finding this as difficult as he was himself.

The Quadriga was edged with gold, garlands of flowers were attached to the body and the spectacle was a powerful image of the glory of Rome. Marcus nodded to the Senators as Apuleius stepped up and draped another red robe over his Dictator's robe. Marcus frowned momentarily as Apuleius whispered "the robe of the last Dictator, for luck" and stepped back down as the heralds held their trumpets to the sky and three long blasts set the wheels in motion, the chariot's iron bound wheels screeching on the flagstones as they set off into the streets and the noise grew to a deafening crescendo.

****

"That didn't go too well" Scipio said with a frown as Marcus entered the room, his face red with anger. Marcus rounded on him, his jaw clenched, but he held his breath and turned back, taking out his anger on Scipio would do little more than alienate another friend.

"The tenth was dedicated to the temples, the soldiers knew that. It was not a tenth of *my* trophies, but a tenth of *everyone's* trophies" he said wearily, the words of the argument he had presented over and over again at the meeting still ringing through his ears. "The goddess looked out over every soldier at Veii and helped us to a great victory. She demands her rights as I, as Dictator, agreed them. They know that" he said, his anger rising again. "Every man should give a tenth of his spoils back for the temples and the golden crown, they know it and so does Apuleius."

Scipio remained silent, not wanting to raise Marcus' anger again as Apuleius had done at the meeting. "The truth of the matter is that you did proclaim the temple and you did proclaim it in the name of Rome, so the soldiers should return their tenth and give it to the temples" Scipio replied. "But that snake Apuleius is clever; damn he is clever" he added as he sat in the chair across the desk from Marcus and placed his elbows on his knees as he lowered his head and let out a long breath.

It was two days since the triumph and Marcus had set out the plans to build the new temple to Juno, resurrecting an old temple that sat on the Capitoline with a new facade and some terracotta statues like the ones he had seen in Veii, gilded in bright colours and garlands of flowers as the goddess deserved. Yet Apuleius had rallied the plebeians and claimed that the people had understood that Marcus Furius Camillus had dedicated the new temple from his own wealth, not that of the people who had suffered ten years of hardship because, as he had argued, of the patricians desire to hold them from their families and enslave them at their enemies walls. Marcus had committed the cardinal sin of losing his temper with the man as his argument went on to include an accusation that Marcus saw himself as a god, wearing the cap of Apollo as if he were a god, driving the chariot of the gods and even wearing the robe of the dead king of Veii as a sign of his *kingly* stature. The final claim had caused uproar and the meeting had been quickly adjourned, but Marcus knew at once that he had been duped and had railed at the plebeian before he was dragged from the rostra, his voice one of hundreds which were shouting and screaming at each other as the meeting ended.

"That son of a dog Apuleius has played me well" Marcus spat as he clenched his fists and sat forward, his face stern and angry as he was clearly grappling with the accusations that had been raised against him. Was Apuleius the friend of the people who was not their friend that the prophecy spoke of? Marcus winced at the memory of the words, knowing that once again he had not understood them until it was too late.

Scipio simply sat and watched his friend. Since the triumph the rumours had been spread by the plebeians that Camillus saw himself as a god and wanted to be treated as such. The issue of the giving of one tenth of the spoils of Veii as a tribute to the temples and for the building of the new temple to Juno had added oil to the fire, with heated debates declining into angry shouting matches across the city. Marcus knew he had been taken for a fool by the plebeians, but so had many of the Senate, their faces full of anger as they turned their backs on Marcus and his popularity suddenly lurched. Even some his own soldiers had complained that they believed Marcus was dedicating the temple from his own funds and the angry rebukes from his loyal supporters had turned to angry scenes of jostling fisticuffs in the forum.

Manlius had stepped into the breach, taking the claims of the plebeians and trying to act as peacemaker. His voice stood out alongside that of Marcus among the patricians as he claimed that the tenth should be returned to the treasury and a golden crown created for Apollo to appease the anger of the god which was, as he said, turning men's minds to greed. Marcus had baulked at the accusation that even Apollo was angry at his triumph but had bit back his anger as he saw the faces of his friends begin to turn away from him.

"You have done nothing wrong Marcus" Scipio said quietly, making Marcus open his eyes and look to his friend. "You were clear with your message and you followed every legal procedure to dedicate the temple. It is easy for men like Apuleius to twist words and find holes in every argument. When did that snake ever hold a sword against an enemy or stand next to his fellows as they died" he sat, his teeth clenched. Marcus looked at the spite in Scipio's eyes and smiled, the old anger was coming back to his friend and he thanked him for it, his mind also adding a thank-you prayer to Juno for the sign that he was not totally forsaken. A thought came to his mind.

"I am still Dictator and I still have the right to be heard" he said as he stood, Scipio looking to him with sudden interest. "I will call an official debate and I will make the final decision. We have several issues to resolve" he said as a curl came to his lip. "Veii will never be a city again whatever Apuleius and Manlius argue" he said as his head nodded slowly "I will make sure of that in the name of the goddess" he added. "I will dismiss this nonsense of kingly ideals and upon doing so I will resign the Dictatorship as a sign that I wish to return to being a happy citizen of the Republic." Scipio smiled at the words. "And I will ensure that the Temple is agreed and dedicated as *we* the soldiers agreed at Veii" he said as he slapped the table and grinned.

****

"Move them here" came the quiet voice as several men shifted the great weight across the wagon and then moved around to hold the sides. The two men on the wagons strained to lift the heavy object as the men underneath grunted at the weight.

"Hold it there" came the urgent call from the foreman as he raced forwards and held the left edge as the tall structure, at least eight feet high, was lifted and shuffled across to lean against the wall the wooden frame bolted over the top as protection crunching as it hit the stone.

"Good" said the leader, "now the other one" he pointed to the second large structure which was also covered by a layer of thin wood to prevent damage. The men moved across and began the same manoeuvre again, lifting the end and sliding it across to be picked up by the straining men underneath before laying the structure against the wall.

The foreman went to the doorway and kicked the bottom of the door three times as he shifted his hair across his face, a bead of sweat dripping from the exertion of carrying the heavy objects. The door slave opened the door warily and looked at the man, clearly unused to such visitors.

"Yes?" he asked haughtily, the foreman snarling at the slaves manners.

"Delivery for your master. Set of doors from Veii" he said coldly as the slave leant forwards and peered at the two large wood-covered objects to his left.

****

The debate in the Curiate Assembly had raged for several hours, the main protagonists arguing for the repatriation of men to Veii to alleviate the overcrowding in Rome and for the patricians to give more powers to the plebeians within the state. Marcus had sat impassively as every argument was listened to. He watched as those who had tried to better him turned purple with rage as he stood and vetoed every motion, his powers as Dictator allowing him the ultimate say. The plebeians had been outraged by his show of absolute power and were rounding on him at every opportunity to bring up any claim they could to discredit him personally, their arguments becoming more and more wild as the day had progressed.

As Apuleius took to the rostra again to make another claim that Marcus embodied all that was against the morals of the Republic Marcus smiled to himself, the time had come to strike the final blow and to resign the Dictatorship, the City did not need him to act as protector now that he had dismissed all of the changes that the plebeians wished to put in place.

As Apuleius prepared his next barrage, his tongue licking his lips like a snake about to strike, the doors to the Temple burst open and two men fell into the chamber, one man half dragging the other as two guards tried to lift them and bring them forward. Apuleius looked to the right and, huffing, he stepped down from the rostra, his anger showing in his eyes.

Marcus stood, looking to the guards and the two mud-covered men and asked "What is it?" One of the men tried to stand, his left leg buckling before a guard caught him and held him upright.

"Sir" he saluted. "The Falerians have launched an attack. They have defeated our soldiers at Caminitia Longina and taken a great many of the men hostage." He stared wildly around the room as a series of gasps came from the assembled crowd, low mutterings spreading across the Assembly.

Marcus narrowed his eyes. The gods were telling him something. They did not want him to resign his place as Dictator, he was needed again. Turning to Ahala and Cicurinus he nodded as the two men stepped forwards, Apuleius grunting audibly as he stepped back and sat heavily in his chair, his eyes raking Marcus with utter hatred.

"We must avenge this defeat and send our glorious armies to Faleria" Ahala said loudly as cheers rang around the room alongside angry shouts. His voice was drowned as he called for Marcus Furius Camillus to avenge Rome and to take his army to Faleria at once and return with the heads of those who had dared to attack their soldiers.

Within minutes men were scurrying from the Temple, messages being relayed to every part of the city and Marcus was heading home to contemplate what message the gods were giving him now. Clearly Rome had to defeat all of its enemies, and his time as Dictator was not done. He grinned as he strode along, people once again cheering him as he followed the twelve lictors that cleared a path for him. Juno and Fortuna were still gracing him, helping

him to make the right decisions and he nodded his head as he walked, his mind running

through what would be needed at Faleria. He knew the city, he knew it had strong walls, he

almost laughed at the thought of *strong walls*, nothing was comparable to Veii. As he strode

along he caught sight of a group of mourners heading away towards the Pons Sublicius with a

small body wrapped in cloth, another victim of the continuing plague that had never yet left

the city. As he walked his mind ran through thoughts of how to clean up the streets. Death

came easily when filth and dirt were commonplace. The streets of Veii had been so clean, so

wide and water was plentiful. Rome had a lot to learn from the Etruscans, but today his

energy would be focused on force marching his army to Faleria. He grinned, he was going

back to war.

*

*

Chapter 25

The Falerians had retreated back to their city, its low walls surrounded by intricate ditches

which were stalling the Roman attacks. Marcus had requested the return of the prisoners the

Falerians had taken, but they had refused, as he had expected. With brutal force he had

destroyed the farmlands surrounding the city, burning every house within two miles and

laying waste to the farmsteads, the thick smoke drifting into the sky for days. His advisers

agreed that until the prisoners were released it would be better not to attack the city in a full

scale attack, a few weeks of starvation might change the attitude of the Falerian leaders, they

said, and he, reluctantly agreed.

As he stood watching a party of men working on the defensive ditch around their own camp

he heard a shout from the watchtower and turned his face towards the approaching rider. His

brow creased as he recognised Fasculus racing across the ground to the gates, his legs kicking hard at his horse as the animal sweated rings of white foam as it charged towards him. He hurried urgently towards the gate, surely this must be some terrible news if Fasculus had brought the message himself. Fasculus reined in, a thick cloud of dust rising into the air as many face appeared, all looking nervously to the rider as Fasculus saluted and spoke lowly to Marcus, both men turning and marching directly to the command tent near the centre of the camp, their voices low as Fasculus muttered words which turned Marcus' face red with anger.

Inside the tent Marcus pointed to a chair and handed Fasculus a cup as he took the wax tablet and cut the seal with his dagger as his jaw tightened. His eyes scanned the words as they flicked up and down, his mouth opening as he read the words.

"What?" he said as Fasculus took another long drink, his eyes never leaving his commander.

"Doors? What doors?" he asked as he stopped reading the words and snarled at Fasculus who simply shrugged and took another mouthful from the cup.

"I don't understand. How can this be? Who is bringing this charge?" he asked incredulously.

"Apuleius has raised the claim" came the cold reply as Marcus thumped the table.

"Him.? What does that man have against me to make such accusations?" he said loudly as Fasculus waved his free arm slowly and nodded his head towards the tent flap to suggest Marcus calmed down a little.

Taking heed he took a deep breath, his eyes narrowed as he scanned the words again. "Tell me what is behind these words and what people are saying" he asked in a calm, but agitated voice.

Fasculus licked his lips slowly as a small trail of water dripped down his chin. He placed the cup down and started to speak, his voice hushed but firm. "Since you and the army left a few days ago the plebeian leaders have continued to challenge the issue of the tenth of the spoils to be returned, despite the fact that most of the soldiers have already done this voluntarily" he said with a shake of his head. "Apuleius asked for the documented evidence of the spoils and had his men scour them for any errors. It seems that he came across that" he pointed to the tablet "and raised it with the Senate. You know what he's like, the man spat venom and fire at you, claimed you had taken more than your share of the spoils from Veii and then affronted the gods and the people of Rome by claiming that they should give back their share of the spoils when you have cheated them yourself." Fasculus took a deep breath and held up his hand at the angry face that stared at him. "That is what he said" Fasculus replied to the stony glare.

Marcus seethed. How could this be? "I know nothing of the bronze doors of which he speaks" he added coldly as he looked at the words of the legal summons and then back to Fasculus. "And how can I return to Rome to fight this case when I am needed here? The man is a fool" he added with an angry sigh.

"I've been to your house and discussed it with your wife" Fasculus said. "The slaves say that these very doors were delivered to your back gate on the day that the riders arrived to tell of the attack by Faleria. The men who delivered it have disappeared, nobody knows who they were or who sent the doors" he added, his eyes wide as he spoke. "The doors are solid bronze, thick with details of the war at Troy and scenes of battles, they must be worth a fortune."

"Bastards" spat Marcus in a low grumble as he stood and paced the tent. "I remember Lucius telling me of just such doors" he added quietly as he returned to the desk, his eyes darting across the words on the tablet once again. "I cannot return to the trial, we have work to be done here. I will reply to the lawyers and tell them that my work here is too important." He looked at Fasculus as he spoke, the man nodding at his words "and they will have to wait until this war is concluded" he finished.

****

The morning had reached the point where men were tiring of their duties and wished to eat and relax when a sudden series of shouts split the air, a trumpet calling men to arms. Marcus jumped from his chair and raced to the tent entrance as he heard more shouts from the gateway. Glancing to his right he saw the Centurion of the watch running across towards him, his hand holding his sword in place as he jogged meaningfully directly to him.

"Sir" the man saluted as soldiers appeared from their tents and began to form loose lines facing the gate as they had been trained to do. Cheers and calls came from the gateway as the Centurion raised his voice so that Marcus could hear him. "There is a" his lip twitched as a puzzled look came over his face "*deputation* coming towards the gate" he added as he stood smartly to attention and stood as if to allow Marcus to pass him.

"A deputation?" Marcus said as he started to walk forwards. "Call the officers" he ordered as he walked toward the centre of the ground where the men were forming lines, long spears and thick shields now set in ranks as the junior officers called men into their formations.

As Marcus looked towards the gate he saw several men stomping into the gateway, their shields locked as if penning whatever, or whoever, was being escorted into the camp within their square barrier. The leading soldier caught Marcus' eye and instantly called the square forwards towards him as a strange noise came to his ears, was it *crying*?

As the soldiers arrived and the leading edge of the square split Marcus' jaw fell open. Within were several children, some as young as five or six years, others in their early teens, all male. A dark robed, long bearded figure stepped out from the square, his light eyes beaming as his eyes darted around the soldiers and fixed themselves on Marcus. The children wailed even more loudly as the man turned and shouted at them to be quiet, some of the younger children looking at his with frightened eyes as he rounded on them.

"What is this?" Marcus demanded as the man turned and looked back to him, his arms coming up to his sides as if in supplication. He fell to his knees and closed his eyes as he put his head back and spoke.

"Great Camillus" he said, his voice loud as the children continued to cry and sob. "I am Fertivus, teacher of the children of the leaders of the Falerians" he said as his eyes fixed Marcus with a frightened stare. "I bring you a gift" he said hurriedly as he half turned and nodded to the children, his right arm waving slowly in their direction. "I beg of you Camillus that you will spare my life as I have brought these hostages to you from the city and that you use them to gain surrender from your enemies" his eyes pleaded as they widened. Marcus remained silent as he simply stared at the prostrate man and then to the children.

"Yes, mighty Camillus. I have seen it in a dream" he said. "You will fire the city and destroy everyone in it, killing your enemies" he added as his eyes flicked to the soldiers. "But I do not deserve to die in this city with masters who abuse me and give little thought to my skills. These children are yours, Camillus, a gift so that I can go free and you can bargain with the leaders to take the city" he added quickly.

Marcus stared at the man, his eyes growing more fearful as the silence stretched, the only noise anyone could hear was the continued sobs from the children. Marcus looked with loathing at the man before he turned to the Centurion. "Bring chains" he said as he turned back to the smiling face of the teacher.

"Yes, chain them up, good, good" he said quickly, his eyes watching the Centurion as he set off into the camp.

"No, stay kneeling" Marcus said as he stepped forwards and looked at the boys, the oldest staring defiantly back at him.

"You, young man. What is your name?" he asked as the boy raised his chin, his jaw trembling slightly as he put on the stoic face his training had started to teach him. The teacher went to speak before Marcus grunted at him and the man cowered, the smile disappearing from his face.

"Maximus" the boy said as a smaller boy gripped his hand, the older boy's eyes not leaving Marcus' face as the hands wrapped together.

"Maximus, a strong name" Marcus said as he looked back at the returning Centurion who had brought two soldiers with clasps and chains from the tents beyond his vision. "And this is your brother?" Marcus said more softly as the younger child, his red rimmed eyes looking up at his older brother, took a deep breath and a small line of tears fell from his eyes. Maximus nodded curtly and his eyes too filled with tears. Marcus heard the Centurion arrive.

"Chain *him* up" he said as he pointed to the teacher.

"No" cried the man, as he tried to rise.

Marcus kicked him in the chest and he fell to the floor, instantly set upon by the two legionaries with the chains. "You have committed a despicable act Fertivus of Faleria. Bringing these children to the camp of an enemy at time of war" he shook his head as the soldiers watched him, many grinning as the teacher now sobbed more loudly than the children had done.

"We are Romans, not some barbarian scum who would treat with fools to enslave children. We follow the rules of war to the letter, following the laws of the gods and acting with piety in all our ways. What disasters did you try to bring on us for this despicable act? What gods did you think we would anger and call down their wrath for taking mere babes into our prison?" He turned angrily to the teacher and spat at him. "I curse you, you dog, for putting your own life ahead of these noble children. I curse you for bringing the name of Rome in your plans and I curse you for being the coward who would hide behind these children to save your own skin." The soldiers fell into a cold silence as the teacher, his eyes bulging from his head, stared up at Marcus.

"No. *Please*" screamed the man as his head was cracked by the butt of a spear from one of the soldiers, the dull snap causing the teacher to curl up into a ball and whimper like a dog.

"Maximus" Marcus said as the boy stepped back, another cry starting from his brother's lips. "Rome will do no harm to children" he said softly. "Know that we will only do harm to those who oppose us in war and stand against the rules laid out by the gods" he added as he knelt on one knee in front of the boy. His eyes scanned the group of children, all staring at him as if they were unsure what was going to happen next.

"Centurion" Marcus said as he stood. "Detail three men to take these boys and this *creature*" he said with a nod to the whimpering teacher "back to the city." At this Maximus took a small step forwards and spat at the teacher, the small gesture causing a few angry shouts from the boys behind him as they started to curse the man who had led them to the Roman camp. "And give these boys some sticks with which to beat some sense into this dog as they go" Marcus smiled as Maximus held his gaze and returned it with a beaming smile.

*

*

Chapter 25

Apuleius sat and took in the information, his eyes fixed on the table in front of him as he listened. The story of the teacher trying to buy his own life with the children of the leaders at Faleria had reached Rome two days earlier, the people praising Camillus as a true *father* of Rome and singing his name in the streets for hours as they praised his noble words and consideration for the ethics of war. But within another day the leaders of Faleria had sued for peace, their anger at Rome abated by the gesture of kindness from Camillus. The acceptance of the surrender had angered many of the Roman leaders, some saying that it denied their soldiers their right to spoils and payment for their days of warfare against the city. Yet others had proclaimed it a great victory, one with hardly any loss of life and another city annexed into the Roman alliance. Rome was, once again, full of talk of Marcus Furius Camillus and Apuleius had become more and more angry as the fickle Romans began to support him once again. Without hesitating he had raised his claims against Camillus for with-holding spoils from Veii and had paid a large fee to two patricians to get the case brought forward to the day after Marcus arrived back in Rome from Faleria.

"Dead?" he asked.

"As close to death as the slave could see" came the reply.

Apuleius wasn't sure if smiling was the right thing to do, but his lip curled as he thought about the news. "And he won't attend?"

"No"

Apuleius sat and placed a silver coin on the table, the elderly slave woman slipping it quickly into her wrinkled hand as she eyed him cautiously.

"Who will defend him?" he asked in a low whisper as he closed his eyes and began to consider his argument and how best to play this new information.

"His friend, the military man Scipio" came the tight lipped reply as the woman glanced around the room. Nodding, Apuleius gave no reply and she nervously clenched her fingers as she watched his face, his eyes closed and breathing very slow.

"Good" came the reply as his eyes slowly opened and the pupils dilated to fix her in a cool stare. "Here" he said, taking another silver coin and sliding it across the table with a single finger.

The old woman took if gratefully and her eyes flicked to the door. "Yes you may leave" came the reply which sent her scuttling cross the floor and out of the room.

So, Camillus had fallen to another family tragedy, another infant who would not make it to his Toga Virilis. Surely this was a sign from the gods that the man had fallen from their grace. Apuleius picked up a stylus and began to write his speech, it would be humble but it would be as sharp as a blade in a dark alley. If the gods had decided that Camillus was unworthy then it would be he, Apuleius, that would be the light of the people and destroy the myth that only the patricians could be close to the gods. Thoughts of the challenges to the five Tribunes ran through his head as he contemplated how he could work such words into his speech. As he wrote the door opened slowly with a knock and a small man peered around the door, his grin splitting his face and showing two missing teeth from his lower jaw.

"Master" said the man with twinkling eyes. "There is more news" he said as Apuleius put down the stylus and looked at him quizzically. "Camillus has been to the new temple to Juno and was challenged about the doors by one of your men" he said with a leer as his head nodded enthusiastically. "It is said that he claimed loudly that he knew nothing of the doors and that some treachery was afoot, but master" the man said as he wrung his hands and his tongue ran along his lower lip. "As he stepped from the temple he stumbled, master, just as he was claiming the goddess's protection. It's a sign" the man said with a long stare at Apuleius.

Apuleius picked up the stylus and placed it on the wax, the grin spreading across his face.

"Get me the best wine Memux" he said as the slave nodded happily and made to leave.

"Wait" came voice of his master. "Get some of the cheap wine for yourself and pick any of the new slave girls, you deserve it" said Apuleius as the slave's eyes widened and he left muttering thanks to his master.

****

"I will not waste my time Scipio" Marcus said in a low voice, his eyes still red from lack of sleep.

"But Camillus, *Marcus*" he replied. "If you do not appear at today's trial they will impeach you. You will be found guilty and ordered to pay an enormous fine. It will bankrupt you" Scipio argued.

"I will not go. The gods know that I am not to blame for this trick from the plebeians. I won't lower myself to their schemes" he replied as he turned back from the door and moved into the dark room.

"This is madness" Scipio called.

"Then who will stand by me?" Marcus called over his shoulder. "All my so called friends have disappeared, all forsaken me and left me at the hands of lawyers who use trickery and words to do what no man can do with a sword. I will not lower myself to it. If they find me guilty I will choose to leave Rome for good – see how they fare without me" he added with venom.

Scipio stood and watched as his friend disappeared around a corner, the door slave looking anxiously to Scipio and then back into the gloomy interior as the silence of the interior was suddenly cut by the singing of the mourning song. It had been days since the death of Marcus' youngest son but the house was still shrouded in darkness, the oils and candles were spread around the Atrium and into the house in the old style and the slaves all wore a dark headband as befitted the occasion. Scipio shook his head angrily but turned on his heel and left. If Marcus wouldn't fight for himself then there was nothing he could do, he would have to stand up and claim that the accusations were lies with no proof that they were not. He shook his head again and grunted in frustration as a sense of foreboding came over him. Had the goddess forsaken him as quickly as his friends had done? What was it that Marcus had done to deserve such losses and such enemies when he had done everything that the goddess had requested from him?

Quietly he loped along towards the forum and the waiting crowds who had turned up to listen to the trial of Marcus Furius Camillus.

****

The long trail of wagons slid silently through the gates of Rome, the ex-soldiers hired as guards walking slowly and deliberately alongside the goods they had to protect. Crowds had gathered and lined the roads, women crying, children shouting and some of the older men of Rome standing with long Reeds which they waved at the wagons as they trundled past as a sign of sorrow at their leaving.

Scipio walked silently beside Marcus. As they crossed the bridge towards the gate he turned to look over his shoulder at the crowd who followed them along the road. The plebeian leaders walked with folded arms, a sign of their anger at Marcus' decision to leave Rome, the old sign of banishment plain to see for all despite the fact that Marcus had made it clear that *he* had chosen exile and had not accepted any of the arguments against him.

As the men reached the gate the lines of patricians grew thicker, those who were happy to see Marcus leave standing silently with arms folded and cold, hard, looks on their faces. Marcus didn't look at the faces of men he knew, but he saw who they were, some of them he had called friend when he celebrated his triumph, others he had been wary of and now knew why. The anger of the people had turned into riots following the decision of the court, the fine of ten thousand Denarii was beyond belief to most people. Some of his closest friends had offered to pay the fine for him, including Narcius who appeared at his door with two trunks of treasures from his own personal belongings. But Marcus had refused. His anger was hidden under the pain he felt for the loss of his third child and the near loss of his beloved Livia. To him a self imposed exile was the honourable thing to do, paying the fine would be seen as admission of guilt and he simply would not allow it.

At the Porta Trigemina he turned, the faces of the people behind him hard as they stood and watched the wagons rolling away into the distance. Marcus looked up at the walls of Rome and then down at the faces of the men standing closest to him. Scipio shook his hand and some of his soldiers cheered his name, Narcius, Fasculus and Mella cheering the loudest, as a chorus of booing appeared from the back of the crowd.

Marcus raised his hands as if in prayer and turned to the crowd scanning their faces before he turned his face towards the Capitolium, the final location at the end of his triumph only weeks before.

"City of Rome I love thee" he said loudly. "I have been thy servant and true to your laws and customs" he said as people in the crowd jeered him whilst others hushed them with long hissing. "Gods of Rome" he said as his eyes moved up to the heavens. "I have been your faithful and true servant" he added as he cowed his head. "But your people have grown and in that growth they have bad blood. Bad blood which would see your favourites cast aside to pursue their own greed." Catcalls and boo's continued to be interspersed with the calls for silence as people strained to hear what Marcus had to say.

"Greed it is that has forced me to leave my beloved city. Greed from men who do not understand what it is to love a City more than they love themselves. Greed for the death of the laws and rules set down by our founder Romulus and his brother Remus. Greed that has driven them to accuse men of honour of deception and theft. Well I call on you Jupiter, greatest of the gods, and you divine Juno and Fortuna who has looked over my family and friends to look at these people of Rome" he said as he moved his body to face back into Rome as he closed his eyes. As he opened his eyes he spoke even more loudly. "I call on the gods of Rome and our founding fathers to teach these ungrateful people that they need Marcus Furius Camillus more than they know."

He finished to a chorus of noise as he turned slowly and set off, pulling the cord from around his neck on which hung the carved figure of the Eagle. Ahead of him his only surviving son, Lucius, stood waiting for him and Marcus stopped and placed the cord over the boys head with a smile. "The goddess will look after us son" he smiled as the boy gripped his hand and they turned their backs on Rome.

*

THE END

*

*

*

*

Historical notes

In this story I had an enormous amount of 'history' to fit into a few pages, and as such I have shortened and changed a few timelines to make the story work more seamlessly. In doing so I hope to have created a good background to the times in which Marcus lived, especially the plotting and scheming of both patricians and plebeians alike. The siege at Veii took some ten years and evidence of what Marcus did for that time is almost non-existent, so I brought elements of the timelines closer together to fit with the story in The Fall of Veii, part one. As stated the siege lasted ten years and during this time the plebeians argued against maintaining the siege in the same terms as I have outlined – the main protagonists are real people from the period. I changed the years of the Tribunes slightly to fit my story, with a few of the battles prior to the fall of Veii changing too. As an example Sergius and Virginius' story is a real event, but this happened four or five years into the siege at Veii and so it didn't fit with my desire to use it as a part of Apuleius' anger against the patricians and plot to impeach Marcus. By changing the dates slightly I was also able to add more background to the siege and move Marcus into a position where his continued successes as a soldier outshone many of his peers. In fact it was the losses suffered by Titinius and Genucius which led to Marcus being made Dictator so I changed the order slightly to make my story and characters meet the needs of the story.

As I wrote of the siege I wondered how Veii could hold out for so long with a wall of Romans surrounding them and it made sense to consider that somebody was allowing food and weapons to enter the city. Linking this to Javenoli was always my plan, and adding his nephew Caelio into the inner circle of Marcus allowed me to build more mystery with regard to if, and how, Javenoli must meet his comeuppance. The stories of the two-headed calf and the waters of the Alban Lake are both true. Livy tells us of the calf, but doesn't explain what the Romans made of it – the description in the story is my own. It struck me that as the early Romans were so superstitious it would make sense for Marcus to use the lowering of the waters and the link to the statue of Juno in the City as ways to strike fear into the hearts of the people in Veii. The prophecy of the water in the Lake is also given to us by Livy, though there is no description of how the waters were removed or who had uttered the prophecy, again I developed that as a backdrop to the more important story of the tunnel through which the Romans entered Veii. The story of the soothsayer at Veii is also described in various accounts; some say he was a 'plant' by the Senate or a man who had been planted by Marcus himself to support the story of entering through the tunnels. I chose to describe it differently to link to the clever way that Marcus had used religion to create fear in Veii by using the ceremony to Juno and calling for her to leave the city along with the water spirits from the lake. Seeing the gods leave the city through the falling of the water in the lake would certainly have had quite an effect on the people within the city.

The ongoing dispute between plebeians and patricians plays out as I have written, with constant arguing for more rights for the plebeians from their tribunes. As also stated, the patricians used every trick they could to hold on to power, calling on plagues and bad winters as signs that the gods were not happy that plebeians had been given the consulship in 399 BC. Evidence suggests that Calvus, as the first plebeian consular tribune did such a good job that the following year five of the six tribunes were plebeian. In an effort to regain power patricians used a reading of the Sibylline books and a delegation to Delphi to create a story in which the gods were confused about who led Rome and demanded a return to patrician only Tribunes. I chose to touch on this as a bone of contention for men like Apuleius, for whom the window of opportunity given to Rufus, Calvus and his fellow plebeians had seemed to close three years later when he came to prominence. The tensions in Rome must have been extremely taught at the period and I chose to make Apuleius have a deep 'hatred' of the patrician clans and at the same time a personal, and passionate, dislike for Marcus because of the love that the people seemed to show towards him.

There *were* battles at Faleria and Capena, though they were probably in 401 BC and 398 BC, not 396 BC as I have portrayed them to fit into a tighter storyline. Marcus did defeat both, and it seems he defeated Capena twice, ruthlessly destroying the town for a second time in 398 BC for their continued support to Veii. It was clear that he used clever tactics to defeat Capena and his military status was high and growing at the time.

There are different versions of the story of the tunnels at Veii, and I chose one in which Marcus was compelled to enter the city himself and to take the entrails of the bull in his own hands within the temple. In my mind Marcus is driven by the prophecy to destroy Veii and so he must lead the attack himself to fulfil his destiny. The Romans slaughtered the entire male population of Veii and sold the women and children as slaves, with so many slaves being captured that slave prices fell to an all time low and many of the remaining captives were actually given Roman citizenship rather than be sent back to Veii.

Marcus held a triumph and did, indeed, parade in a Quadriga and wear a purple cap, which angered many of the Roman population who felt he was mocking the gods. I've tried to link the use of the chariot, the cap and the link to the dead king's robe as a way to portray the political intrigue and back-stabbing of the time (the king's robe is my invention and not mentioned in history). It also links to the later story following the sack of Rome in which Marcus is again accused of 'kingly desire.'

Marcus did veto the suggestion that the Romans move to Veii, though Livy tells us that it was actually the majority of the patrician population that wished to move to the city, not the plebeian's per-se. Whatever the arguments were Marcus was forceful in his decision to veto any move to Veii and as such I made it an element of his prophecy such that he had reason to state that Veii would never be a city again.

The battle at Napete was also a real battle. The Etruscan council met and agreed a plan to support Veii with a strong force of allied troops. History tells us that Marcus beat them in a set-piece battle but doesn't explain how. I used the story to enhance the development of Marcus' changing fighting tactics and how he has used the fighting style of the maniples he learned from the Gaul's along with the fighting style of the day. All of this will be needed if he is to defeat Brennus in a coming story.

The battle at Faleria is also well documented, as is the teacher who brought the children to Camillus at his camp. As portrayed, the teacher was tied up and whipped back to the city by the very boys he had tried to use as bargaining tools. I hate to think what the leaders of Faleria did to the man, but soon afterwards they surrendered to Rome, stating that they were deeply touched by the humanity of the Romans and so surrendered without condition. This angered many of the Roman nobility who felt that the lack of spoils from Faleria was an offence to the public purse and that Marcus had 'sided with the enemy' in accepting their surrender.

The battle of Faleria is actually in 395 BC so approximately a year after the fall of Veii. As such I changed the timelines to keep the story tighter and to avoid long stretches of political debates which, whilst interesting, don't add to the glory of the military might of Camillus. I hope that the shortening hasn't underplayed the political scenes and background which led to Marcus' impeachment.

The story of the doors is mentioned in one of the various stories of how Marcus Furius Camillus came to leave Rome, though it is only mentioned in passing. It is clear that a long series of legal and political challenges were faced by Marcus at the time and that he grew more and more frustrated with the people of Rome and the courts of law. The story of his words as he left Rome and looked back to the Capitolium is true and taken directly from history. He felt aggrieved that his friends had deserted him and he left Rome in self imposed exile, though even this story is challenged by historians who feel that his leaving Rome at this time was simply a good excuse to have him return as a conquering hero at a later date.

Quintus Fabius, Caelio and Javenoli will play a part in the next story, though Marcus Manlius will play a central part in the fall of Rome as he becomes the hero of the people that we know today.

Marcus will return as Rome faces its greatest enemy before Hannibal and the men who turned against him and led to his exile will call for him to become the saviour of the greatest city on Earth.

Printed in Great Britain
by Amazon

78921202R00182